Catherine Bennetto worked as an Assistant Director in the film and television industry, working on shows such as *The Bill*, *Coronation Street* and *Death in Paradise*. She can generally be found travelling the world and spends her time reading healthy cookbooks (not necessarily cooking from them) or at the beach. *How Not to Fall in Love, Actually* is her first novel.

How **NOT** TO FALL IN **LOVE,** *actually*

Catherine Bennetto

**SIMON &
SCHUSTER**

London · New York · Sydney · Toronto · New Delhi

A CBS COMPANY

First published in Great Britain by Simon & Schuster UK Ltd, 2016
A CBS COMPANY

This paperback edition, 2017

1 3 5 7 9 10 8 6 4 2

Simon & Schuster UK Ltd
1st Floor
222 Gray's Inn Road
London WC1X 8HB

www.simonandschuster.co.uk

Simon & Schuster Australia, Sydney
Simon & Schuster India, New Delhi

A CIP catalogue record for this book
is available from the British Library

Paperback ISBN: 978-1-4711-6000-4
Trade Paperback ISBN: 978-1-4711-6289-3
eBook ISBN: 978-1-4711-6001-1
Australian eBook ISBN: 978-1-4711-6245-9
Audio ISBN: 978-1-4711-6349-4

This book is a work of fiction. Names, characters, places and
incidents are either a product of the author's imagination or are
used fictitiously. Any resemblance to actual people living or
dead, events or locales is entirely coincidental.

Typeset in Bembo by M Rules
Printed and bound by CPI Group (UK) Ltd, Croydon, CR0 4YY

MIX
Paper from
responsible sources
FSC® C020471

Simon & Schuster UK Ltd are committed to sourcing paper
that is made from wood grown in sustainable forests and support the Forest
Stewardship Council, the leading international forest certification organisation.
Our books displaying the FSC logo are printed on FSC certified paper.

To my grandmother,
Helen

CHAPTER ONE

'CUT! WHERE IS FIGHTING PROSTITUTE NUM
BER THREE?'

I shot out of my slouch and grabbed the radio off my desk,
finger hovering over the transmit button.

*Fighting Prostitute Number Three? Fighting Prostitute Number
Three? Is today Prostitute Day? I thought it was Car Accident Day?*

'Quentin to Emma,' the radio crackled again. 'Bring
Fighting Prostitute Number Three to set, please.'

Ignoring the plea, I flipped through a chaotic folder and
scanned my extras booking sheet. Injured Pimp Number
One, Injured Pimp Number Two, Boy with Broken Leg,
three Nurses, two Doctors, one Porter and a partridge in
a pear tree. OK, not the partridge. But also not Fighting
Prostitute Number Three.

'Oh no.'

I looked at the two people I shared the office with: Sophie,
a pixie-haired, 26-year-old from Somerset whose parents

made cheese, and Douglas, who, twenty-seven and balding, with steel-framed glasses, looked every bit a misplaced accountant. How he'd found his way into the shitty world of low-grade medical soap opera production was beyond me.

Sophie looked back with bloodshot eyes. 'You forgot to book her?'

I nodded.

If Fighting Prostitute Number Three did not start crying in A&E our female lead (a 22-year-old former child show jumper who, despite being four foot two, looked down her nose at absolutely everybody) could not soothe Fighting Prostitute Number Three and quell her harrowing sobs. And if the lead male character (an overly tanned git with only two brain cells, one of which he left at home each day) did not witness Fighting Prostitute Number Three being given solace, he could not fall in love with Shorty Pants Horse Lover and we could not shoot the scene.

'QUENTIN TO EMMA, ARE YOU HEARING ME?'

'Shi-it.' With an imploring look at Sophie, I raised my radio and pressed the transmit button. 'Yes, sorry Quentin. Ah . . . we need five more minutes on Prostitute. Over.'

Sophie shook her head, her tiny diamond nose stud catching the light from the overhead fluorescent tubes.

'Please, Soph, I'm *begging* you!' I stood in front of her folder-laden desk.

'Uh-uh, Em. No way!' She picked up a wad of messy schedules. 'I've got new scripts, a schedule that is never going to work and my First AD has changed the entire day for

2

tomorrow *again*. I have to rebook forty amputees and I can't find enough wheelchair-friendly Ubers! I've asked them to share, but the armless can't push the wheelchairs, can they? And—'

'Oh, come on . . .' I clasped my hands together. 'I was Self Harmer for you last week.'

'Does the prostitute have to be a woman?' Douglas, pushing up his spectacles, offered his services.

Our friendship had been cemented the day we both started on the show six years ago and found there was no real coffee. He'd brought me in a Costa every morning since.

'Because I could do it. Most of my work is done, and I—'

'Thanks, Douglas, but it's definitely a woman. A small *vulnerable* woman.' I looked pointedly at Sophie, who held up some papers and answered her phone.

'Sophie speaking . . . OK, are you legless or armless?'

'Quentin to Emma,' contempt dripped from the radio. 'Bring the girl in immediately.'

'Arse.' I pushed the transmit button. 'She's on her way.'

It was past nine thirty that evening when I opened the door to my dark flat in Tooting. My job in television was supposed to have provided me with exotic locations, inspiring scripts and a large enough wage to warrant buying my salami from Waitrose. I was to have been an integral cog at the forefront of the British drama machine. I was meant to come home to a Jo Malone-scented flat where a Persian cat worthy of its own jelly meat commercial would be waiting, licking its poofy paws. But instead I was just a regular cog. A regular cog working in a 1970s squat brick building designed by somebody who believed in the return of the window tax. And my flat smelt of drains, dirty fridge and tomato sauce. I stepped over some stinky skate shoes and plonked my bag on the hall table among the many glossy leaflets advertising two-for-one pizzas and cheap calls to Poland. Damp of wall and noisy of radiator, our flat was a ground-floor box that Ned, my boyfriend, had found and at my look of despair had exclaimed, 'But it's got carpet in the kitchen!' like it was a good thing. Next door was a busy brothel, and on the other side was a couple who liked to spank each other during sex – loudly. The working girls seemed nice, if a little jaded, but the spankers were constantly nailing things to the other side of our bedroom wall at odd times of the night. Possibly each other.

'Ned?' I called.

'In here,' came his muffled reply from the bedroom.

Ned sat in the corner hunched over his computer screen. Scrawled notes littered the unmade bed.

'Hey, babe!' He sprang out of his chair and seized me in a bear hug, his sparse three-day-old stubble grazing my cheek. 'How was your day?'

'Oh, you know. The usual.' I looked at his computer screen, which seemed to display an unoriginal collection of motivational quotes geared towards starting a hugely success-ful yet unspecified business, then at a pile of washing on the floor. 'Get much done today?'

'Research,' Ned said. His phone trilled. He bounded across the room, grinned at the message then got busy with a reply.

I traipsed to the kitchen and found it foodless, drinkless and sticky of floor. I abandoned the idea of sustenance and collasped on the sofa, flicking the TV to an old *Friends* episode. After a few minutes Ned came into the living room, his jeans hanging off his thin frame and a hole in one of his mismatched socks. Closer inspection proved it to be my sock.

'Did you get anything for dinner?' He flopped onto the sofa and threw an arm round my shoulder.

I couldn't believe we were going to have this conversation. Again. I felt as though I only entered his thoughts as I entered the front door at night.

'Did *I* get any food?' I bulged my eyes.

'Ah ... well ...' He blinked. 'You pass the shop on your way home, so I just thought, you know ...'

'Did *I* get any dinner?'

Ned eyed me sideways. 'Um ...'

'Me? Who left at five thirty this morning while you lay in bed till god knows when, then probably spent the rest of the day scratching your arse?'

Ned quickly stopped doing just that.

'Me? Who had to dress as a beat-up prostitute *all afternoon* because one actor got stuck in traffic, one had "hair continuity issues" and one demanded a gluten-free pizza with rennet-free cheese before he'd go on set, and there was no time to change?'

'I could heat up some beans?'

'Me, who walked out of work *forgetting* about the fucked-up hooker *make-up* –' I circled my finger wildly in front of my face '– and had to go back to the studios when a woman on the street asked me if I was OK and offered to call the police? Me? ME? Did *I* get any food?!' My left eye twitched as Ross and Rachel kissed on the TV.

'There's some ...' Ned pointed a tentative finger at my nasal area. 'You still have a little bit ...'

I ran a bath by the light of a bare low-wattage bulb. In the kitchen a pot crashed to the floor and Ned yelped. If he was attempting to make dinner, he was going to have to get pretty creative with out-of-date chicken stock and a very questionable tomato. Or it might have been an apple ...

I slipped into the bath and shut my eyes. Ned and I had been together since my twenty-second birthday, when I'd turned a corner while moving from bar to bar, lost all my friends, tripped over my own feet and landed in a heap beside a guy sitting in a doorway eating a bag of crisps. Ned Dixie. He'd shared his crisps and bought me a birthday kebab, which I'd found in my handbag the next morning and had eaten for breakfast. Ned had come back to my flat that night, and I'd stayed up laughing at his impressions of Basil Fawlty at an all-night rave. His ginger hair stuck straight up from his head at different angles and a smattering of freckles ran across his nose. How I loved a ginger man. Kenneth Branagh; Eric Stoltz circa 1985; the one from *Homeland*; Tim Minchin.

Chucky. No? That one just me? Anyway, Ned had ginger hair, expressive eyebrows and a wicked grin and I thought he was sexy. He was an 'ideas man'. He saw the potential for improvement in everything. Esca-Wipes: Escalator handrails that sanitised your hands on your commute; Loven the Lunch Oven: a lunchbox that baked pies; Fartfume: air pouches in your back pocket that, if you accidentally farted in a public place, you'd activate via a discreet button in your front pocket and perfumed air would waft out, masking your odour. Oh yes, he had ideas.

Within weeks we'd commenced smitten coupledom and were looking for our own flat. He was an eternally chipper, overeager, unrealistic, hilarious bundle of disorganised clumsy affection. And I was hooked. Once, I was at work with a paralysing hangover (the kind where, if you move your eyes too fast, a cold sweat sweeps down your neck and you kind of half-faint) and I'd got a message saying Ned was in hospital with a badly broken leg. I'd raced out of the studios cursing Ned for telling the little old man from three doors down he could fix his satellite dish. I'd rounded the corner of the tube station, fighting the urge to vomit up pure tequila and there, leaning against the station wall with a big smile, a massive bacon and egg bap and two fully functioning legs, was Ned.

'Thought you might need a Duvet Day,' he'd said, putting out his free arm.

I'd crumpled gratefully into his embrace. We'd caught the tube home and Ned spent the rest of the day being my hangover nurse. He stroked my hair, made a bed on the sofa and watched *The Princess Bride* with me for the 1,217th time. I thought I could see my future. Curled up on the sofa, tucked under the arm of a guy who was happy to repeat 'My name is Inigo Montoya. You kill my fadda. Prepare to die' in a Spanish accent that sounded more Chinese takeaway lady till his girlfriend had giggled her hangover away. It hadn't worked out so well when we'd googled a broken tibia and fibula (what he'd told the receptionist at work) and realised Ned would need to wear a fake cast to my work party two weeks later. We'd had to buy a 'medical walking boot' from eBay, and Ned created an elaborate story involving an unattended scaffolding platform, a stranded baby bird and one of the better-looking prostitutes from next door.

He started an online business course and declared he'd make the big time in New York as an entrepreneurial something-or-other. We'd researched Brooklyn flats, investigated breeds of apartment-appropriate dogs and dreamt about me working on a Weinstein film. I'd gradually worked my way up the ranks from tea-maker/rubbish collector to Second Assistant Director and had started putting a little away each week. But Ned hadn't finished his course. And no invention got past the scrawled-notes-on-the-back-of-the-water-bill stage. My New York dreams floated away and I'd yet to replace them with anything.

'Babe?' Ned tapped at the door. 'Babe, are you coming out? I've got something for you.'

Last time he'd said that I'd opened the door to see he had

his foreskin pulled over the waistband of his jeans, was calling it his dried apricot and was guffawing like a schoolboy. I wrapped a radiator-heated towel round myself and opened the door to Ned's smiling face.

'Follow me, my lady,' he held out an arm and guided me to the living room.

Spread on a blanket on the floor, in mismatched pots and on chipped plates, was a carpet picnic. Sainsbury's Basics candles dripped wax onto the coffee table.

'Madam, tonight we have . . .' Ned raised the lid on an old beige pot '. . . minted baby peas.' He lifted a napkin off a small tin. 'Tuna à la spring water – dolphin friendly for the lady, of course – served with a side of Huntley and Palmers Cream Crackers.' He took a cracker and bent it without it breaking. 'Slightly stale.' He pointed to the apple/tomato drooping on a brown plate. 'And I don't know what that is.' He gave a hopeful grin and I felt myself un-bristling.

He inched forward and pulled me into a kiss. Ned may have left his debit card on the tube (complete with pin number written on the back) twice in the past year; he may have driven to the supermarket, done the shopping then bussed home more times than is strictly reasonable and he may be a little too freckly for polite society, but damn he was a good kisser. I dropped my towel. My stomach did twirly flips of pleasure as he kissed me from my mouth, over my breasts, down past my belly button and then . . .

After a few minutes I raised my head.

'Do you need—'

'No.'

Despite his kissing proficiencies, the exact location of the clitoris tended to evade Ned. He'd find it eventually, so to pass the time I thought about the coming weekend. I was meeting my friend Helen for brunch. She was an events coordinator for a media investment company in Russell Square which specialised in promoting only the zeitgeist-iest of musicians, scriptwriters and executive producers, so she always had stories that finished with 'and then we ended up at 5 a.m. in a disused slipper factory watching a private screening of this Dutch director's new film shot entirely in black and white, on an iPhone, in Alaska with Russian-speaking puppets'. We'd talk about Helen's latest shag (generally someone she'd met through her work who was skinny, socially unusual and on the brink of stardom) then we'd order. Eggs, bacon, sausages and—

Mushrooms!

He'd found it!

Sprawled on the sofa an hour and a half later (once he'd located it, it was all stations go) he leant over and kissed my ear.

'I'll buy some food tomorrow, babe.' Then he got up, grabbed his beer and left the room to trawl eBay while I curled up and watched *Would I Lie to You?*.

'Hmmmm.' I stretched, my eyes still closed.

I'd not had a glorious sleep like that since those peaceful nine months in the womb. I opened my eyes. I was still on the sofa.

'Oh my god!!' I leapt up and ran to the bedroom.

Ned lay fully clothed on top of the bed, a can of corn emptied onto my pillow. I snatched my phone from the nightstand. Eighteen missed calls!

'Ned, I'm late!'

Ned shot up like Dracula from a coffin, his hair vertical on one side and corn stuck to his cheek.

'No! You can't be!' He looked horrified.

'Well I bloody am!' I rifled through the mess on the floor. 'Work has rung eighteen times. The phone was right next to you. I'm going to get fired, and I'm the only one that earns any money!'

I launched myself into some jeans.

Ned's face relaxed to being just hung over. 'Oh, that kind of late.' He lay back in his bed of corn. 'I thought you meant women's stuff late.'

I stopped wrestling with my fly and did some menstrual maths.

'Oh, no . . .'

I looked at Ned. He was unconscious again, safe in the thought I would only be fired, not pregnant.

'I can't think about that now.' I kicked my feet into some trainers and flew out the door.

I dashed into the office unwinding my scarf, getting my arms stuck in a handbag/scarf/parka sleeve bind and nearly toppling the Christmas tree over with its lone bit of tinsel and Rod Stewart angels I'd made one slow afternoon.

'Has Quentin been asking for me?' I panted, dumping

the handbag/scarf/parka knot on my chair and retrieving my radio from Douglas's neat desk. 'Anything gone wrong?'

Sophie and Douglas looked at each other.

'What?'

'We-ell,' Douglas started. 'It probably wasn't your fault—'

'You forgot to book Dead Homeless Man in Swamp.' Sophie interrupted.

She picked up her cigarettes and walked round her desk towards me. 'And unfortunately, or fortunately, depending on how you look at it, Quentin happened to fit the costume.'

'Noooooo,' I groaned.

'He had to lie face down on the edge of the Wandle for about an hour this morning,' Douglas said.

Forgetting to book featured extras two days in a row was bad enough, but the First Assistant Director – and my boss – having to step up and lie face down in a swampy bit of river in December was ... was ... I felt sick thinking about it.

'He ... he's not happy,' Douglas said, shunting his spectacles.

'It was so cold the make-up girls had to defrost his face with a hairdryer before he could talk properly,' Sophie added.

'Oh *god*.' I slapped my hand to my forehead.

'Come on.' Sophie held out her cigarettes. 'Everything's fine now. They're in the studio, Quentin's got all the feeling back in his lips and you look like you need one of these.'

I nodded.

'Douglas? Cover for us,' Sophie said, walking out.

We sat outside in the designated smokers' area, a metal

cage flanked by the catering skip and a noisy air-conditioning unit.

'You're quiet,' Sophie said, watching me stare at a mound of something mushy beside the skip while trying to do more detailed period calculations.

'Just thinking how quickly time goes when you work here, that's all,' I replied.

'Tell me about it.' Sophie launched into a soliloquy of how she woke up last Friday and realised it was December again. Then she realised that instead of being twenty-five she was twenty-six, and hadn't she ought to be getting grown-up things like a long-term boyfriend, life insurance, bras without holes, sofas you're not allowed to sit on, cars you're not allowed to eat in?

I became aware of the cigarette in my hand. I threw it on the ground and stamped it out.

'. . . And when is the official time to stop having soft toys on your bed? Nobody actually tells you these things. I mean, I've never even *seen* a French film. I was in France once and went to a film and it was in English but the subtitles were in French . . . Does that count?'

'Arse,' I mumbled.

CHAPTER TWO

'Go straight through,' the cheerless receptionist said as I arrived in the doctor's waiting area early the next morning.

I'd called in sick to work, and when Ned had asked why I'd stated women's problems. He'd paled and found some socks that needed balling. I walked down the tatty hall and let myself into the doctor's office.

'Ah, Emma.' My uncle got up from his tiny NHS desk and planted a welcoming kiss on my forehead. 'What a lovely surprise! But shouldn't you be at work? Are you poorly?'

I shook my head and, not knowing what to say, burst into tears.

'Hey, hey.' Uncle Mike stooped to look into my face. 'What's this all about?' He led me to the fraying chair next to his desk and sat down opposite. 'Something happen at work? Ned? It's your mother, isn't it? What's she done now?'

He passed me a tissue and watched me blubber it into a pulpy mess. 'Oh, sweetheart, what's the matter?'

The pregnancy test came back positive, and I dissolved into body-shuddering sobs. Uncle Mike gave the rest of his appointments to the junior locum and took me to the greasy spoon round the corner.

'So.' He considered me with his hazel eyes.

'I don't even know where to begin.' I picked at the skin around my nails. 'What to think about first. Does that make sense?' I took a sip of my tea and pushed the mug away in disgust.

'Perfect sense.' He took a gulp of his coffee and placed it to the side, grimacing. 'Until you decide, we'll take each day as it comes. Your scan is in two weeks, but Emma, you're ten weeks gone. You and Ned need to make a decision.'

'I know.' I gave a weak smile.

Uncle Mike squeezed my hand. His slender fingers were always a bit cold. He'd been the father I'd never had. Well, I did have a father but he'd run off with a woman who was older, shorter and duller than my mother when I was five and my sister Alex was only three. We'd had nothing except a dwindling number of birthday cards ever since. Mum said she could never recover from a blow like that. Had the woman been a Cindy Crawford replica she could at least have understood. But the woman's name was Ruth and she worked as a receptionist for Merton Council.

I gazed beyond Uncle Mike to the street outside. I didn't want to leave the café with its plastic seats and nasty tea. It would mean stepping out into a different life. One I didn't feel even the slenderest bit of control over. A builder eating a bacon and egg roll caught my eye. His rotund stomach pressed against the Formica table and egg yolk pooled at the corner of his mouth. My stomach lurched. I leapt up and raced to the bathroom.

Fifteen minutes later, I gingerly took my seat again opposite Uncle Mike. The road worker was gone, our table had been cleared; Uncle Mike had paid the bill and was folding the receipt into a swan.

He smiled. 'Come back to the house.' He gestured at the empty table. 'Have a decent breakfast.'

I nodded. 'Yeah, OK.'

I hoped my little cousin Archie would not be at crèche and I could play with his Play-Doh and pretend none of this was really happening.

As we left the greasy spoon, Uncle Mike opened his briefcase and handed me some NHS pamphlets.

'Just in case.'

I read the covers. 'Healthy Pregnancy'. 'You and Your Foetus'. 'Choosing the Right Birth'. 'Coping with Morning Sickness'.

'Thanks,' I said, quickly stuffing them in my bag.

'The last one will be particularly relevant at the moment. Might help you with those sudden rushes to toilets, rubbish bins, side of the road.'

I looked at my feet as we crossed the street.

'You know, when your mother was pregnant with you she threw up right outside a busy café in Chelsea. She leant on a postbox and retched into the gutter.'

I looked up, interested to hear more.

'She had terrible morning sickness,' he said with a fond sparkle in his eye. 'It lasted the whole pregnancy.'

'No kidding?' I mused, my own recent vomiting session still fresh in my mind ... and the back of my throat.

'When one of the café staff came rushing out with a chair and a glass of water, your mother scolded them for the water being too warm. She sent them back inside for ice and demanded a piece of carrot cake too.' Uncle Mike smiled and shook his head. 'She sat there on the footpath in the middle of Chelsea with her big pregnant stomach, eating cake while the waiter held her iced water.'

I snorted with laughter. My mother was not known for her subtlety. Or for worrying about what other people thought of her.

Archie and I played at the kitchen table while my aunt Sinead sat at the other end feeding Millie, their chubby-armed nine-month-old. Mum had been nine when Uncle Mike was born (a wonderful accident, Grandma had called him) so my cousins were much, much younger than Alex and me. Millie was spitting her mashed vegetable crap out over her chin and onto the table, blowing raspberries and giggling. It was a messy affair. One I was careful to keep away from.

I may not be the most fashion-conscious girl around but I at least liked to keep my unfashionable clothes clean. Uncle Mike was at the Aga cooking up a feast. A cup of tea wafted its bergamot aroma under my nose. No more strong black coffee; not good for unwanted foetuses, apparently. Sinead was telling Uncle Mike about a charity dinner they were required to attend.

'Another one? Really?' He got eggs out of their retro blue Smeg fridge and stepped over one of Archie's toys.

Their huge house was always in chaos, in spite of the housekeeper's efforts.

'Can't we just give them money and not go?' He cracked the eggs with the ease of someone at home in the kitchen.

Sinead didn't cook, or work. Sinead had babies. Alice was eight, Jess was six, Archie was four and Millie was last.

'Dad's expecting us to make an appearance. You know how he gets.'

'Yes, I do. But just one weekend I'd like to stay in with my wife, cook up some spicy chicken wings and watch a little television.'

Sinead scooped food off Millie's chin and spooned it back into her mouth. Millie spat it back out again. I secretly applauded her. Second-hand, chin-dribble food was disgusting.

'Should've moved to Yorkshire and started my own practice in the country,' Uncle Mike mumbled as he distributed bacon among waiting plates. 'None of this charity nonsense and balls and kisses in the air. Why kiss the air anyway?'

'Darling, you're mumbling to yourself again.' Sinead mopped at Millie's grubby face.

I was enjoying the distraction. 'To go or not to go to a charity ball' was a much simpler problem than my own 'to have or not to have an accidental baby' dilemma.

'You're doing it wrong, Emma,' Archie pointed out.

He was quite right. We were supposed to be playing Fairy Lions with the Play-Doh, and as I had no idea what Fairy Lions looked like I'd made a rather pathetic-looking purple cat.

'Oh, sorry.' I allowed him to tear apart my cat and commence serious Fairy Lion construction, glancing up now and then to make sure I was paying attention.

'Breakfast's up,' Uncle Mike said, bringing food-laden plates to the table.

A hunger like no other came over me. I shoved the Play-Doh to the side, slicked butter on a piece of toast, took huge bites and swallowed it down after only three chews. I needed to feel some weight at the bottom of my nauseous stomach.

After a few minutes of comfortable silence Sinead lifted her coffee and spoke. 'So, Emma, are you going to get rid of it?'

With her neat brown hair pulled into a low slide clip at the nape of her neck and her almost uniform-like choice of clothing, white linen shirt and black or brown ironed trousers, she looked innocuous enough. But her conventional attire concealed a punishing frankness and blasé attitude to suitable conduct.

'Bloody hell, Sinead,' Uncle Mike said.

Archie looked up from his breakfast.

'Sorry, Archie, I didn't mean to say that. Eat your toast, darling.' He shook his head. 'Honestly.'

Sinead shrugged.

'Daddy?' Archie said, looking thoughtful. 'Why did you say sorry?'

'I said a rude word and I didn't mean to, OK? Eat your toast.'

Archie went back to his breakfast.

'I don't see why we shouldn't talk about it. She's nearly a third of the way through.' Sinead turned to me. 'You have to make some pretty quick decisions.'

I started feeling sick again. 'Well . . .'

'What wude word did you say, Daddy?' Archie said.

'It doesn't matter, darling. Eat your toast.' He turned back to Sinead. 'Emma needs to think about this in her own time—'

Sinead ignored her husband. 'You hear all this crap about "giving life", but let's be real, it's more like having it taken away from you.'

'Was it "shit", Daddy?'

We looked at Archie innocently waiting for an answer.

'No, Archie. Sinead, would you *please* let Emma be.'

'It's OK. I guess I do need to think about what to do,' I offered, trying to avoid a heated conversation about my situation.

'See,' Sinead said. 'She's fine talking about it. We're all family—'

'Was it "fuck", Daddy?'

Uncle Mike's eyes widened. Sinead looked a trifle amused. I sniggered behind my teacup.

'No, Archie. Shush now. And eat your toast.' Uncle Mike glared at Sinead then turned to me. 'You do whatever you feel is right. We're here for you, no matter—'

'Was it "wanker"?'

'Archie!' Uncle Mike shook his head. 'Where's he picking up this language?'

'From me, dear,' Sinead said matter-of-factly.

'I feel sick,' I muttered.

'It will pass soon.' Sinead patted my arm. 'You're a bit skinny. Get your hands on some Krispy Kremes.'

'Daddy?'

'Yes, Archie?' Uncle Mike said warily.

'"Bitch" is not a bad word if you're driving when you say it.'

Uncle Mike shot his wife a beaten look. She sipped her coffee. I put my knife and fork together, excused myself and retired to the music room. Sloping sunlight from double-height French doors warmed the Persian rugs and a ten-foot real Christmas tree, decorated in evenly spaced red and gold bows and baubles, wafted the welcoming scent of pine. I flicked through the iPod, picked out an album and lay on the sofa.

So.

I was pregnant.

Did I want a baby?

I was twenty-seven, I didn't own my own home, I had a few thousand quid in the bank – not much, but not terrible – and although I'd been clawing my way up the illustrious film and TV ladder for the past few years, one foot was still on the bottom rung. And, despite his enthusiasm for entrepreneurial conferences and 'Money: Master the Game' Tony Robbins apps, my boyfriend hadn't earned a penny in two years.

No one my age was having kids. Life was too expensive to settle in your mid-twenties (twenty-seven is *so* still your mid-twenties!), buy a house and think about life insurance. And too much fun. People my age were still going on gap years, spending their Christmas Eves having lines of coke off the back of a toilet cistern in clubs and figuring out what they wanted to do 'when they grew up'. Which I guess we all thought happened sometime in your thirties.

Later that evening, Uncle Mike's Porsche turned into my dark Tooting street and pulled up outside my flat, disturbing a scruffy drunk taking a leak on our brick wall. Uncle Mike watched the man zip up his jeans and trip over his own feet, a familiar look of concern on his face. We'd travelled the short distance from his warm, pine-scented house in Wimbledon to my scuzzy flat in Tooting in silence. In two weeks I had a scan at St George's Hospital. And by then I'd have to have made a decision. I was pretty sure I knew what I had to do. I was in no position to be caring for a baby.

I opened the car door. 'Can you say thanks to Sinead for putting up with me today?'

Uncle Mike waved away my request with a smile. I gave him a peck on the cheek, shut the door and looked away from his tail-lights as my phone rang. The caller ID said 'Alex'.

'Hey.'

'I just called to tell you I hate my job today,' my little sister said in a chipper voice.

Alex worked for the UN in Dhaka on a water sanitation project. She lived in a concrete apartment with bars on the windows and an outdoor toilet. She sat in a flimsy-walled office in forty-degree heat and typed reports, analysed spreadsheets and printed budget initiatives that no one ever read. And for the privilege she paid for her own flights, accommodation and food. She was allowed to hate her job.

'You loved it last week.'

'Yes, but last week I was allowed out in the field. Last week I watched a three-year-old boy drink clean water for the first time in his life. His mother cried. I cried. *Last* week was great.' She sighed. 'I've just had enough of the wooden crate. I want to sit on a real toilet.'

'Doesn't your placement end in a few weeks?'

'Yeah, but I don't even know where my next posting is. It could be here again. I know I'm supposed to love what I do because I'm helping to change people's lives, blah blah blah, but some days I just want to wash my hair in water that doesn't smell like poo.'

'We all do.'

Alex laughed. 'I'll be fine. I do actually like my job. I get

23

to see some pretty weird stuff. There's an eleven-year-old boy outside my building who has a stall selling guns and honey.'

I was silent. Alex would know there was something up. Usually we wouldn't let each other finish a sentence, so keen were we to regale each other with the contents of our lives.

'What's wrong?'

'Nothing.' I pulled my coat round me.

'Liar.'

'Not.'

'Are too.'

'Not.'

'Something's wrong.'

'Isn't.'

'You're one-wording me.'

'Am *not*.'

Alex groaned. 'Well, can I guess?'

'If you want.'

'You broke up with Ned?'

'No.'

'Mum did something?'

'That's just a given.'

'You're pregnant?'

'Yes,' I said in a little voice. 'But I also think I might get fired.' I pressed my lips together.

Alex was quiet but only for a second.

'You're kidding, right?'

'No.' I wiped my nose on my sleeve.

'Are you sure? I mean, *really* sure? Why don't you go to Uncle Mike and get a proper—'

'Already did. Definitely am.'

'Well . . . are you happy about it? You don't sound happy. What did Ned say? Oh my god, does Mum know?'

I could picture Alex pacing her office, her mind working overtime to find the most sensible solution. Sometimes I thought it was Alex who was the elder sister.

'I don't know what I want. I only just got back from Uncle Mike's. I haven't told anyone. Not even Ned.'

'I thought you were on the pill?'

'I was.'

'Well, how did it happen then?'

'I dunno . . .' I said unconvincingly.

'How did it happen,' Alex pressed, her voice taking on the tone of a reprimanding headmistress.

'Well, there was this one week . . .'

'Oh *Emma.*'

'I was just so busy at work and I couldn't make a doctor's appointment, then I forgot but I figured it would be fine because I heard all these women at work who talked about how it took them a year to get pregnant after being on the pill. It was only one week!' My head hurt. 'Can we talk about something else?'

'We really should keep talking about this.'

'Please?'

'OK. Ah . . . Cal got a promotion.'

'That's good. What's he do now?'

'It's still investment . . .'

Alex let forth a torrent of words that individually I understood – stock, floating, finance, sector, margin, exchange, hedge – but all together were as decipherable as Stallone speaking Klingon. Alex had been with Cal since university. He did something with money. All I knew was that he was relocated to a different major banking city every year or so. Alex could never be the typical banker's girlfriend, sitting in plush apartments and shopping with bankers' wives, so she'd followed her dream of working for the UN and had spent the past couple of years being posted from New Delhi to East Timor and finally Bangladesh. They survived on trust, skype and a few weeks together a year.

Eventually Alex ended with, 'You understood none of that, did you.'

'Is he rich?'

'He makes other people rich.'

'He's doing it wrong, then.'

Alex snorted a laugh.

'Want me to come home?' she said after a brief moment of quiet.

Affection bloomed across my chest. It wasn't an empty offer. If I said yes, my fiercely loyal little sister really would be on the next barely welded–together Bangladeshi plane out of there. But Dhaka needed her and her unread audit reports.

After saying goodbye it was time to talk to Ned. I checked my face in a compact mirror and turned towards the flat.

'What the . . .' Whorls of smoke coiled out from under the doorframe. 'Shit!'

I shoved my key in the lock and flung open the door. Thick smoke billowed out.

'NED!' I screamed. I covered my mouth with my jacket and stumbled inside, feeling my way down the hall to the bedroom. I pushed open the door but the room was empty; the computer still on. 'NED! WHERE THE HELL ARE YOU?'

I lurched towards the kitchen from where plumes of smoke were swelling out, cursing Ned for taking the batteries out of the smoke alarm to use on his latest invention (a remote-controlled remote control). Smoke pitched from the stovetop. My eyes stung. I took a breath of the marginally clearer air in the hall and staggered across the kitchen using my jacket to lift a billowing pot off the stove. I dumped it in the sink and turned on the tap, ducking away from the hissing, spitting water. On the kitchen bench sat an open can of baked beans, sauce dribbling down the side. I inspected the pot in the sink. A hard, black substance was scorched to the bottom. Stone-cold toast sat in the toaster. When the house was clear of smoke and I'd thrown the ruined pot in the bin, I grabbed my phone and saw a text from Ned.

GN TO GERRYS. WRKNG ON BUSINESS
IDEA. NT HM 4 DINA. LV U. X

I dialled his number. My fingers went to the groove forming between my brows.

'Babe!'

'You're an idiot,' I said, my voice steely calm.

'Wha'? What've I done now?' Ned's whine made me feel like his mother, not his girlfriend.

'You nearly burned down the house – that's what!' I heard the unmistakable sound of a beer can cracking open. 'Are you drinking?'

'Babe, it's a Saturday night.'

'It's Wednesday!'

CHAPTER THREE

Sunday morning arrived at last, and I hustled through chilly Borough Market, meaty aromas wafting from the various mobile cooking devices. My best friend Helen was already in the café and had commandeered the pick of the tables.

'Hi.' She gave me a breast-mashing hug, a fragrant kiss on the cheek and stepped back to examine me from under her dark fringe. 'You've put on weight.'

Both Helen and my mother had an uncanny ability to detect a fluctuation in weight to the ounce. And were only too keen to point it out.

'Most girls would find that comment insulting,' I said, shrugging off my parka and pulling out a chair.

'Yes, but most girls are fat cows. You were getting too skinny.' She sat down opposite me and gained the attention of a waiter with a mere tilt of her chin.

Despite her job 'requiring' her to be up all hours with burgeoning indie rock stars or political graffiti poets, she never had a mascara-coated eyelash out of place. She'd encased her voluptuous form in a snug scoop-neck sweater, body-hugging jeans and knee-high boots. Her half-exposed bosoms rested in their cashmere nest like two globes of rising pizza dough. She was the sexy side of plump. Even I was attracted to her. I, on the other hand, had on my customary jeans and hoodie with my wet hair piled in a bun on top of my head.

'Dad is obsessed with Japanese game shows,' she said to my enquiry about her parents. 'He streams them on the internet all day long. I wish you'd never shown him how.'

'It was Ned,' I said, remembering Helen's parents' twenty-fifth wedding anniversary barbecue, and how Ned had spent the entire afternoon inside teaching Helen's father the wonders of the internet. I was pretty sure they still emailed each other.

'He showed Mum an episode where a lady drank fermented squid guts. Mum vomited.'

'Ew!'

'Then the dog ate it.'

I gagged.

'Then the dog vomited.'

'Oh my *god*!'

We dissolved into laughter.

A young waiter delivered our order and was barely able to remove his eyes from Helen's semi exposed breasts. I wasn't above using my boobs to advance my opportunities, but no one was interested in my grapefruits when Helen's gala melons were around. She leant back and flung an arm over her chair, maximising the waiter's view. The boy blushed a shade darker than plum and shuffled off. A man at the next table got a sharp look from his lady friend.

Later, with a sense of contentment only bacon can offer, I pushed my plate away and looked out of the window.

'You're thinking about Ned, aren't you?' Helen clattered her cutlery on the plate. 'You've got that woe is me, sad little deer face.'

I sighed. 'He treats me like his mother.'

'That's truly wrong.'

'Not in that way.' I winced. 'I tell him when to shower. I buy his undies. I give him lists of things he needs to do around the house and scold him when he doesn't do them.' I sagged in my chair. 'I'm one pair of dirty socks in the bottom of the bed away from grounding him.'

Helen gave a pitying shake of her head.

'Emma ...' She spoke in a way that let me know some serious counsel was about to be dispensed. 'Know that what I'm about to say comes from a place of love and from having had it up to my tits with you and Ned and his goddamned muthafucking Jesus Christ socks.'

'Go ahead,' I said through grim lips.

'You need to break up with him. I know he's sweet and we all love his Lohan As A Llama routine, but sweet and funny only go so far.'

I felt her scrutiny from across the table. I kept my eyes on my hands.

'He's been to every fucking business course on offer,'

she continued. 'And I see no business. You work your arse off, and I know he may "make the big time one day", but I honestly don't think that day will come before you hit the menopause and his pathetic amount of chest hair turns grey.'

Helen stared me down while I folded the edges of my place mat. When Ned and I had first started dating I'd found his foibles endearing. I guess I'd enjoyed having someone to mother and fuss over. He was so affectionate, and he truly meant well. I'd been able to overlook his inability to cope with the more mundane aspects of being a functioning adult, like bill-paying and clothes-washing. But as the years ticked by and I'd had to assume all the responsibility in the relationship I'd found his unrealistic nature tiresome. I was a naggy cow, and I didn't like who I'd become around him. I felt older than my years.

'I don't know what to do,' I said in a feeble voice.

'You need to break up with him,' she declared. 'Then you need to sleep with a lot of men. And women, if you want.'

'But—'

'No buts. You've already wasted most of your acceptable slut years with that noodle-armed dreamer. Dump him, and do it *now* – it's frowned upon to slut around in your thirties.' She gave me a pointed look, signalling it was her final word on the matter, and made a bill-summoning motion to a distant waiter.

'Some people frown upon it in their twenties,' I mumbled.

'Some people are effing nuns.'

*

Two weeks later I squeaked across the lino floors of St George's antenatal unit, approached the counter and gave my name.

'Take a seat, love. I'm afraid it's quite a wait. People with problems get seen first so you may get bumped.' The woman scanned her notes. 'You don't have any problems do you, love?'

Barrel-loads. But instead I said, 'No, not today,' and sat down on a plastic seat beneath a wonky swathe of green tinsel. It was the day of my scan, and I was nervous. I still hadn't decided what I wanted to do. My head had been firmly in the sand for the past two weeks. I'd gone about business as usual while Ned tried to make up for his baked bean incident. He'd cooked a special dinner, which contained both chicken and fish but tasted of neither. He'd done a load of washing and shrunk my favourite woolly jumper. He'd gone out, left the keys inside and the shower running, flooding the hallway. My frequent nauseous rushes to the bathroom heightened Ned's guilt. He thought I was in the bathroom crying. I still hadn't told him about the pregnancy because I didn't know what I wanted from him. Until I did I was keeping it to myself, processing my thoughts at night as he lay snoring beside me. Uncle Mike had pointed out that I was on the skinny side and I'd need to up my calorie intake if I wanted a healthy pregnancy. I told him I wanted no pregnancy but ate extra carbonara anyway. My stomach rounded accordingly so I'd taken to wearing loose-fitting tops and strategically draped scarves. I hadn't told my mother, but that was easy. I wasn't *hiding* the truth – I just hadn't seen her. She was in Tuscany turning the inside of a fifteenth-century villa into a homage to 1980s neon Miami for an Italian fashion designer. At work I'd barely been holding it together. I'd had to race off set to vomit during a take and was then accused of being drunk in the workplace (not my fault – the baby's); I hadn't booked enough extras for a hospital riot scene for the director's ambitious plan (not my fault – the production manager gave me a minuscule budget); I'd been screamed at by a nasty actress for neglecting to read out her lines to her answer machine the night before (definitely was my fault – I just thought she could read her own friggin' script for once) and had consequently received a formal warning. Alex had called, skyped or texted every day. Sometimes from her sweaty office, sometimes from her sweaty apartment, sometimes giggly from a sweaty Bangladeshi bar. But always supportive. And sweaty.

'Miss George?' A nurse in a creased uniform stood in an open doorway, a file in her hands. She led me to a small room where a friendly-faced female sonographer sat waiting for me.

'Just lie back and unbutton your jeans for me,' the sonographer said after checking my file.

Her gentle voice put me at ease. I wriggled my jeans down and lay on the semi-reclined bed. She snapped on some rubber gloves and pulled a trolley with a screen and keyboard towards her.

'Had a good day?'

'Yes, thanks.'

I'd spent the afternoon in Uncle Mike and Sinead's kitchen eating Fortnum & Mason gingerbread people (Archie informing me that it wasn't right to call them men as women were important too; Sinead informing me that Archie's nursery teacher was a little 'politically annoying' and 'lesbian-ish') and watching my aunt and uncle bicker about my situation and what I ought to be doing. Archie had come home from nursery at lunchtime and when I'd asked him how his day was, he'd said, 'Oh, I've had a vagina of a day,' in an American accent, then asked for a peanut butter and jelly sandwich. Uncle Mike had glowered at Sinead when she explained he'd picked it up from her visiting American stock-broker friend. I'd spent the next hour with Uncle Mike as he tried to get the personal mobile number for Supernanny.

'Feeling OK? Any nausea?' The sonographer picked up a bottle with a nozzle on the end and shook the contents.

'Oh, a bit sick, but all right. Really tired.' I *was* tired. By two in the afternoon I was nearly face down in my hot chocolate.

'Yes, that should start to ease in the next few weeks. Drink plenty of water and get plenty of sleep. And eat your vege-tables.' She smiled again.

I didn't want to tell her that this baby might not be here to stay.

'I will. Thank you.'

'OK then. Ready to see your baby?'

I didn't answer.

'This will feel a bit cold.' She held the bottle above my stomach and flicked the nozzle open. Cool blue gel landed on my skin. 'OK . . .' she brandished some apparatus like a barcode scanner at me '. . . there'll be a slight pressure but it won't hurt.'

She lowered the scanner onto my stomach and moved it over the blue gel. A computerised heartbeat sounded through the room and the monitor by the bed sprang to life. I quickly turned my head away. If I didn't see it, it wasn't real and I could make a logical, emotionless decision. The right decision.

The sonographer slid the scanner over my belly muttering positive expletives, 'good, OK, yes, there we are' and so on. She clicked at the keyboard and wrote in my notes while I concentrated on a poster of a cross-sectioned woman's torso in various states of pregnancy. It looked to me as if the baby got bigger and bigger with no thought to the vital organs it was crushing. The size of a fully grown baby and the size of the canal it had to travel out of were wildly unsuited.

'The nuchal measurement is good; the placenta is healthy and in the right place,' she said, writing in my notes. She clicked her pen, placed it in her coat pocket and smiled. 'You seem all set for a healthy pregnancy, Miss George.'

I looked at her, willing my eyes not to move a foot to the left and view the screen.

'Shall we see if we can get some photos of your baby to take home with you?'

'Uh . . . oh, um . . .'

Without waiting for my reply she slid the scanner across my lower abdomen with determination.

'I think that's a good one, just there.'

I stared at the cross-section again.

Big baby, small canal.

'Let's see if we can get this wee one to move. I want to get a nice profile shot.' She dug the scanner in and clicked a few buttons.

Really big baby. *Really* small canal.

'There we go. That's what we want. Stay there, little one.'

Click. Click.

Fucking big baby. Where's that canal again?

'Ah look, she's waving!'

Before I'd thought about what I was doing my head swung round and I was face to screen with my baby.

'See that?' She tapped a fingernail on the screen. 'She's got her hand up.'

There it was. A tiny, bean-shaped baby. Its miniature upturned nose in profile, with one hand raised in a wave. Tiny fingers were visible and the beginnings of tiny toes. My throat constricted.

'She's almost fully formed now. All she has to do is get bigger.'

'She? You know it's a she?' I strained to see the absence of male items but the tiny legs were too close together.

The sonographer's eyes creased as she smiled. She handed me a tissue.

'No, dear, I call all babies "she" at this stage. We can't determine the sex until around twenty weeks.'

I tried to swallow but there was a dry brick blocking my throat.

'Shall I give you a moment?'

I nodded without taking my eyes from the screen.

'I'll get you some water.' She left and pulled the door to after her.

A baby . . .

My baby.

Two legs, two arms, a head and a butt. Perfectly formed without my instruction or permission.

I reached up and put my fingertip to its little waving hand.

I swallowed down my dry brick.

I loved it.

The front door slammed. I heard Ned kicking off his smelly trainers and hitting the same spot on the wall they always did. There was a permanent dirty smudge no amount of scrubbing would get off.

'Babe?'

'In here.' I sat in the living room, warming my hands on a third cup of tea. I'd been waiting for Ned to get home from Gerry's for two hours.

'Gerry and I have come up with a new business idea,' his voice travelled up the hall.

I rolled my eyes.

'You know Ben and Jerry's?' He rounded the door, his face flushed with excitement.

I nodded.

'Well, what do you think of Ned and Gerry's?'

'Ned and Gerry's what?'

He looked at me like I was slow.

'Ice cream? Duh.' He flopped next to me, an expectant expression on his freckled face.

I paused, my mouth opening and closing trying to find the right words.

'I think it's a stupid idea.'

'What?! It's brilliant!' He stood and paced the floor. 'Think about it. You see Ben and Jerry's on the shelf with its chocolate dunky-monkey or whatever and right next to it, Ned and Gerry's.' He stopped pacing. 'Now which one are you going to go for? The same boring one you've always had or the exciting new one sitting right there in front of you?' He raised his palms in a question.

I kneaded my temple.

'We'll start with ice cream vans, hit the summer festivals.' He commenced pacing again, his arms waving about, infused with zeal. 'We'll invent our own flavours. Gerry wants a Bloody Mary one. I'd triple our savings—'

'No!' I said. 'You are not touching that money again. I've worked too hard to build it back up.'

Ned paused at the end of the sofa.

'Emma, this is a no-brainer. By the end of summer we could have enough for a deposit on a flat! Or a trip to

New York.' He extended his palms towards me, fingers splayed.

His pale ginger eyebrows were elevated convincingly. I'd adored those enthusiastic eyebrows once.

'I'm pregnant.'

Ned blinked at me. I blinked at him.

'Twelve weeks.'

He stood motionless, hands still extended.

I took a deep breath, got off the sofa and faced him. 'I'm keeping the baby.'

Fear shot across Ned's face.

'I won't stop you being part of our life but I think ... I think we should break up.'

Ned's hands dropped to his sides. He arranged his mouth as if to speak but nothing came out. His eyes darted round the room as if searching for the origin of my words.

'I ... I don't think I love you any more and ...' My eyes filled with tears and I faltered. 'I ... I don't think you love me.'

His eyes stopped zipping around and settled on me, a probing look on his face.

'Em ...' He took a step towards me and reached for my hand but stopped at my involuntary flinch.

We stood, Ned with his hand outstretched and me with my arms folded across my chest, looking at my toes. After a moment Ned pulled his hand back. I could hear the neighbours banging away at the adjoining wall.

I sniffed back a tear.

'Babe?' Ned reached for me again.

'Please don't.' I stepped back, keeping my eyes on my fluffy socks. 'I know what I want and it's to give this baby the best life that I can.'

'And I'm not part of that?' Ned's voice cracked.

'No,' I said to my feet. 'A baby needs stability.'

Ned's eyes watered. He twisted his mouth, a sign he was trying not to cry.

'I don't want to be a father.'

'I know.' I swallowed thickly.

'Not yet, I mean.'

'I know.'

'Are you sure you can't just get rid—'

'Stop. Don't say it.' I wanted to forget the similar thoughts I'd been entertaining only a few hours ago.

Ned stepped forward and grabbed my hand in both of his, squeezing urgently. 'I don't want to break up.' His eyes searched mine.

'But I do.'

CHAPTER FOUR

'So he's all moved out then?'

The omnipresent sound of 1970s fans flick-flicked in the background. I'd rung Alex as soon as the front door closed behind Ned.

'He has to come back tomorrow while I'm at work and get his computer. He doesn't have much stuff. Most of it's mine.'

'Was it awful?'

'Not really. He doesn't want to be a father. Too much responsibility, doesn't have a job, blah blah blah.'

'Mmmm.'

'There was no fight or anything, and after a while he kind of agreed we'd ... outgrown each other.'

'I guess that's good?'

'Not good for the ego. I wouldn't have minded a touch of "I can't live without you" or some irrational pot-throwing. I feel a bit of a loser.'

'It had to be done.' Alex was pragmatic.

'It had to be done,' I agreed.

'I'll miss him, though. Do you mind if I still email him? He's really interested in the work we do out here and—'

I coughed my irritation.

'Sorry,' Alex said, contrite. 'Well, you know what you have to do now?'

'No.' I did know, but I really didn't want to do it.

How do you tell your mother that, at age twenty-seven, you didn't notice your missing periods for two months? That you'd had a scan, decided to keep the baby and broken up with the father? And were in danger of losing your job?

'Tell her you're a responsible adult and you know what you're doing.' Even Alex didn't sound convinced.

'I could tell her it was peer pressure.'

'You could tell her it's not Ned's. Then she wouldn't mind so much.'

'Oh, yes! Whose could it be?'

'I was kidding.'

'There is a really gorgeous instructor at my gym. Maybe it's his?'

Alex snorted. 'You don't go to the gym!'

'Yes I do, they have a Starbucks.'

We sniggered together. Twelve thousand miles away and I felt like she was right beside me.

'What's the time where you are?' I said through a yawn. I was exhausted. It was past 11 p.m. and I had to be back at work early the next morning. I'd told them I'd been having a family emergency. It wasn't far from the truth. I was going to be personally adding to my family and it was throwing me into a state of emergency.

'It's about five in the morning.'

'Oh, sorry.'

'No, you didn't wake me. The guy who crashed his rickshaw into the night stalls at the bottom of my building did.'

'Is he OK?'

'He is. His rickshaw's not. The stall isn't. And now everyone is shouting at each other. Here, listen.'

She held up the phone and I heard shouting, sirens, horns and traffic. Just like in Tooting. After saying goodbye, I switched off all the lights except the hall light, which I instinctively left on for Ned, and went to bed. When I realised what I'd done I went back into the hall and turned the light off. Then I got depressed at how life had changed so quickly and turned it back on. And off. And on again. After a good few minutes of lighting deliberation, I paused. Weary from the emotional past few weeks I decided to leave it on before the neighbours thought I was hosting a private midweek disco. I climbed into bed, pulled the covers up and looked at Ned's empty side briefly before turning over and dropping off to sleep immediately.

'Morning!' I drifted into the office after the first seven hours of good sleep I'd had in a long time.

Sophie jumped up to greet me. 'Hey! Where were you yesterday? Is everything all right?'

'Hi, Emma.' Douglas smiled from behind his computer.

'Hey, Douglas. Yes, everything's fine.' I walked round to my desk, Sophie at my elbow. 'Just a few problems at home.'

'Did someone die?'

'Sophie!' Douglas scolded.

'No, someone didn't *die*.' I turned on my computer and sat down, making sure my scarf pooled in my lap and covered my stomach.

'Oh.' Sophie almost looked disappointed.

Douglas frowned at her. 'Well, you missed something very funny yesterday.' He leant round his computer with a grin.

Sophie looked enquiringly at Douglas, then remembered. 'Oh, yes!' She pealed into giggles.

'Yeah?' I started scrolling through my emails.

One day off, and 157 unread messages. I opened the first one, a request from the producer that we try not to schedule any of the upcoming elderly lady scenes at night, as the actress they'd cast was really quite old and frail. A fair enough request, but maybe he should have thought about that when he approved the script about an elderly Alzheimer's patient being found in a disused quarry in the middle of winter, in the middle of the night. I was going to enjoy passing that information on to Quentin. I clicked to the next email and realised Sophie and Douglas hadn't answered me. I looked up to see Douglas, shoulders heaving and Sophie, bending over, silently cackling in the middle of the room.

'What?' I said.

'Quentin . . .' Sophie clutched her sides.

'Flasher.' Douglas removed his glasses and wiped at his eyes.

'What?'

The pair of them writhed with restrained hysterics.

'Worried about his friends seeing him!' Sophie hiccuped.

'Will you just tell me what happened!'

Sophie leant against her desk and waved at Douglas. 'You tell, you tell.'

Douglas replaced his glasses and gathered himself. 'They were shooting the scene where they find out the hospital flasher is the janitor,' he said, his voice still a little squeaky.

I nodded. I'd booked the janitor the week before, spending ages choosing the perfect guy from the extras agencies' websites.

'Well, the extra you booked to be the hospital janitor was too young, or something. The director didn't like him.'

I groaned. Typical of that anally retentive, lentil-eating, yoga-posing director. Bring on my final warning, then.

'The director stomped around for a bit, apparently, then looked Quentin up and down.' Douglas's voice wobbled. 'Quentin got quite mad, I'm told.'

Sophie ran her wrist under her running nose.

'No way.' I knew I was going to be in trouble but it was too dreadful not to enjoy.

'One of the actors ran around telling everyone what was happening and the entire building went down to set.' Douglas began to lose his recently regained self-control. Tears trickled down his flushed face.

'The whole building was there,' Sophie said, her voice squeaky.

'Everyone had their phones out taking pictures.' Douglas removed his glasses again.

'Quentin had to run through the hospital corridors in tighty-whities with the nurses shouting "Flasher! Flasher!" and throwing rubber gloves at him!'

We erupted into convulsions.

'They had to do fifteen takes because Quentin kept tripping on the rubber gloves!' Sophie squealed. 'One of the actors put it on YouTube!'

When we'd recovered some self-possession, Sophie and I asked Douglas to cover for us while we went outside, Sophie to smoke and me to pretend I was on a detox.

'How come you're detoxing then?' Sophie took a deep drag of her Camel Light.

I pulled my jacket tighter round me. 'Dunno, really.' I looked at her cigarette. I didn't even feel like one. 'I'm kind of detoxing my entire life. I broke up with Ned.'

Sophie raised her triangular eyebrows. She looked like Tinkerbell. Tinkerbell with a fag hanging out the side of her mouth.

'*Really?*'

'Yup.' I nodded, surprised by how at ease I felt.

'Oh man, that's so sad,' she said, her eyebrows sloping. 'I like Ned.' At my look, she reddened. 'But . . . ah . . . remember . . . remember when he found those orphaned baby foxes and brought them home and you guys both caught mange?'

'I do,' I said, giving her a 'what-the-fuck-are-you-doing' look.

'Or what about that time he tried to make home-cured prosciutto and hung that pig leg in your wardrobe and everything smelt like rotting bodies and you had to buy new clothes? Remember *that*?!'

'Yes.'

Ned had read the list of preservatives on the back of my favourite prosciutto with disgust. He decided he could do it with far fewer chemicals (and experience) but was proved incorrect by the putrid ooze that dripped onto all my shoes and permeated every item of clothing we owned with a stench so bad we'd contemplated moving flats.

'And remember that pigeon he brought home with the club foot that shat everywhere then died in your bathtub?'

'Uh-huh.'

'Or what about the time—'

'I remember them *all*, Sophie.'

'Sorry,' she said, sheepish.

'It's OK.' I looked at my watch. We began shooting in fifteen minutes; Sophie and I really ought to be sat at our desks, radios at the ready. 'Let's go inside and look up Quentin on YouTube.'

'Oh god, yes!' Sophie threw her cigarette on the ground and stubbed it out with her pink Converse.

We rounded the corner of our office and saw Quentin drumming his tobacco-stained fingers on top of my computer screen.

'Oh, no,' I whispered to Sophie, but she was already scuttling past me to her desk.

'Hello, Emma.' Quentin stood by my desk, his mouth curled into a sneer. 'Decided to come to work today, I see.'

Bitchy sarcasm looks ugly on a grown man.

'Uh, hi Quentin.' I rushed to my desk. 'I am *so* sorry about yesterday – I promise it will never happen again. I am totally one hundred per cent not going to make any more mistakes. It's just that I've been—'

'I feel the need to check you've actually booked everything for after the Christmas break.'

His patronising tone made me want to shove a stapler up his flaring nostrils.

'Right.' I grabbed my file. 'Really, I can assure you—'

'And *I* can assure *you* that the next mistake you make will be your last.' His eyes narrowed.

I was opening my mouth to defend myself when an actress so vile we'd called her 'Devil's Armpit On A Hot Day In Hell' ('bitch' just didn't seem enough) stormed round the corner clutching a script, her jowly face contorted with fury.

'Where is that nitwit Emily?'

Philomena (her real name) was a masculine-looking woman of around sixty with saggy pouches under her eyes like a couple of well-used leather satchels and an expression that showed it pained her to be surrounded by us non-famous people. So much so, she never bothered to learn anyone's name. Therefore I was sometimes Emily, sometimes Eleanor, sometimes Emma and sometimes Rebecca.

She threw the script on my desk sending schedules, pens, scripts and my desktop light-up Christmas tree flying. The production coordinator and her secretary arrived in the doorway clutching paper cups of coffee and chatting, but on seeing Philomena swivelled on their heels and scuttled away. I scrambled to clear up the mess, a fierce heat rising to my cheeks.

'What can I do for you, Philomena?'

I didn't dare look her in the eyes lest I be turned to stone.

'Are you such an idiot that you cannot do your job?'

Well, how does one answer that? Ah, no, I'm just a minor idiot, thank you. It doesn't get in the way of my job at all.

Two young runners appeared, each carrying a stack of colourful script amendments. They headed towards Douglas's desk, giving Philomena a wide berth.

'Sorry, Philomena, I'm not sure what the problem is,' I said with as much confidence as I could muster.

'Nobody phoned my answer machine last night and read out the changes to today's script. Am I expected to go on set not knowing my lines?' She rotated her hefty bosom towards Quentin. 'It's not a hard job, is it? All they have to do is ring us each day with the changes. A monkey could do it.'

Quentin shook his head, the corners of his mouth curling.

Not a hard job? Philomena got a driver to and from work each day; her script was read out to her over the phone and the publicity department diarised her entire life. I'd even had to organise her grandchildren's Christmas presents. I wanted to shove something up her nostril too.

'Let me just check the original script,' I said, getting my folder.

Philomena folded her arms across her chest. 'If you could.'

My cheeks burned and a light sweat settled behind my ears. Sophie and Douglas peeped out from behind their computer screens and the runners looked as if they wanted to dissolve into the carpet. I flicked through the pages of my original script till I'd found the scene she'd thrown at me, then ran a finger down each line of dialogue checking it against Philomena's script. When I got to the end I looked up.

'It's – it's only one word, Philomena.'

She raised her eyebrows. '*Excuse* me? Are you trying to tell me how to do my job?'

'Well, it's only one word. Instead of "It's malignant, sir", you say "It's benign, sir". Also I wasn't actually here yesterday—'

'Enough!' She placed her liver-spotted hands on my desk and leant close to my face, the sharp tang of her cigarette-and-coffee breath making my oesophagus contract. 'The whole tone of the scene is different! You can let the director know that I have to go to my room and *relearn* my lines.' She pushed her huge frame off my desk, snatching her script pages.

As she stalked off I looked at the official 'shooting clock' on the wall.

'OK, but you're due on set in four minutes,' I said.

She turned back, her expression warped and nasty.

'That's *your* problem. I will need at least twenty minutes to relearn this scene, and if anyone knocks on my door I will not come to set at all!' She turned on her heel and marched towards the doorway.

'It's only one word. Jeez, a *monkey* could do it.' I muttered as I tidied my files and willed my face to stop blushing.

'What did you say?' Philomena spun round. Her eyes glinted like Chinese meat cleavers.

'Yes, Emma, what did you just say?' Quentin smirked.

I felt a gear change occur deep in my body. Like that scene in *Titanic* where they see the iceberg and have to throw the forward-moving ship into a grinding reverse. I looked at Quentin and Philomena and they were already in my past.

I stood, took a step towards Philomena and met her challenging gaze. 'I SAID, IT'S ONLY ONE FUCKING WORD! A MONKEY COULD DO IT!'

Sophie clamped her hand over her mouth. Douglas adjusted his glasses. The runners' lower jaws dropped.

Philomena's eyes turned to little slits. She spoke through bloodless, stiffened lips. 'How dare you. How *dare* you!'

'And before you worry about "having my job", or telling me I'll "never work in this industry again", you can shut that wrinkled old pie-hole because I would rather clean the sewers at Wandsworth Prison – naked – after Curry Night – than have to work with people like you ever again!' I jabbed my finger at a dumbstruck Quentin and a horrified Philomena. I unclipped my radio from my jeans waistband and shoved it at Quentin's chest. 'Hopefully the only time I ever see you again is on YouTube in your pants.'

Quentin paled. Sophie grabbed my coat for me and gave the tiniest of thumbs ups before returning to the safety of her desk. Douglas gave a brief nod of solidarity.

'Well then,' I said, grabbing my handbag and looking cheerily from Sophie to Douglas. 'See you guys later!' I turned and floated towards the door, raising a silent middle finger to Philomena on the way out.

I trotted down the long halls past producers and editors, writers and assistants saying 'hey', 'hi', 'morning', 'all right?', 'yes thanks', and bounced out of the studios into the chilly early morning. I looked at my watch. Only 8.17 a.m. I did a quick mental calculation of the time in Dhaka; 2.17 p.m. Alex would probably be sitting in her stinking office fanning herself with an audit report. I dialled.

'Mmm?'

'What's wrong?' She sounded sick.

My mind filled with horror images of her dying alone, drenched in sweat from diphtheria or malaria or another third world disease ending in 'ria'.

'Nothing. You rang me; I answered.'

'Yes I know, but you sounded sick when you answered – are you sick? Do they have a hospital there?'

'Emma, I'm fine. Sweaty and covered in mosquito bites the size of buttons, but fine. What's wrong with *you*?'

'Nothing. But you're all right? You're not sick?'

'Emma! I'm *fine*, for god's sake.'

'Oh. All right then. Guess what!'

'What?' She yawned to show her extreme interest.

'I quit my job!'

Silence.

'Alex?'

'I'm here.'

'Well, what do you think?'

She didn't sound nearly as excited for me as I had hoped, and my adrenaline was seeping away. I needed encouragement or I'd curl up on the footpath and fall into a deep denial-shaped sleep.

'That is the best news I have heard from you in ages. Apart from you having a baby, of course. How come?'

I beamed into the phone, happy to have my little sister's approval.

'Remember that horrible actor I've told you about?'

'Horse Lover?'

'No . . .'

'One Brain Cell Guy?'

'No, the—'

'The one who you have to speak to through his PA? Oh! The one who leaves porn on in his dressing room?'

'No! Remember the one who got that runner fired for spilling tea on her laptop, even though it was actually her who'd spilt the tea? And the runner wasn't even in the room at the time?'

'Ah, yes. She sounded delightful.'

I regaled her with the Philomena/Quentin exchange. 'I don't know what came over me but I just got so . . . so *mad*!'

'Hormones.'

'Guess so.'

'So what are you going to do for money? You need a job; you're having a baby.'

Trust Alex to bring reality so quickly into the conversation.

'That's true. I hadn't really thought about it.' I had a brief panic but decided to do a Scarlett O'Hara and think about my problems tomorrow. 'I'll get something. Anyway I have my savings, so I'll be fine for a while.'

'OK; good. Well, I'm really happy for you.' Alex yawned again.

'You sound exhausted. Can't you go home for a bit?'

'It's no better at home. At least here I have people to talk to. And no bed lice.'

'I can't wait till you get posted somewhere else.'

'Me neither.'

'OK. I'm going Christmas shopping. So exciting! I can't remember the last time I saw daylight during the week!'

'Don't buy from anywhere that uses child labour. Love you!'

'I won't. Love you too!'

I hung up and was just rounding the corner of the tube station when my phone rang. I looked at the caller ID. Uncle Mike.

'Hi!'

'Hello dear, how are you?'

'Great, actually. Guess what!'

'Ah ... Emma, sweetheart? I have to tell you something.' Uncle Mike's voice was low.

My stomach dropped. Had something happened to my mother? Sinead? Archie?

'What?'

'It's Grandma. She – she's passed away.'

CHAPTER FIVE

At home, I packed a bag. Mum was flying back from Italy and the family were congregating at her place. It was Christmas in four days, so I was packing enough stuff to last. I couldn't believe Grandma wouldn't be with us, sipping her tea, watching her son and daughter bickering with a look of contentment on her lightly powdered face.

Our family Christmases were as routine as the rest of England's, but I loved them nonetheless. Presents doled out before breakfast; under-slept, overexcited children squealing; Mum and Sinead swapping gifts as soon as the wrapping was off; a hot drink spilt on a designer homeware item, Uncle Mike with the baking soda; a broken toy five minutes after unwrapping; the inevitable discussion about how much alcohol before lunch was too much; endless eating and eventually afternoon naps for all the adults while the kids ransacked the house, wired with sugar and acquisition. Grandma Ivy would sit in the corner and titter into her Earl Grey while she knitted. I still wore the chunky pink sock-booties she'd made me three Christmases ago.

I stopped shoving an extra five pairs of knickers in my bag (is it only me who, when going away, packs knickers like they've only recently embarked on toilet training and will be requiring at least three changes of pants a day?) and rested on the edge of my bed, thinking about Grandma. Sure she'd been old and had become increasingly delicate; she got pneumonia and bronchitis and every chest-orientated illness going, but it never stopped her knocking up a fresh batch of scones then patting the space next to her on the sofa and asking about work, or Ned. Or if I'd read the latest Jodi Picoult.

Later that day, after a stuffy tube ride across London, I arrived at my mother's home in Belsize Park. It was one of eight tiny houses down a cobbled lane. Uncle Mike's Porsche was parked badly across the front door. Sloped rectangles of light shone across the wet cobblestones and the aroma of fires and roasting meat wafted through the air. Mum had bought the house, then a musty, run-down old place, after the divorce and gone about a complete transformation. Both of the new house and herself.

Dad and Mum had been childhood sweethearts who'd married when they were both just twenty-one. Dad had read English at university and wanted to be a poet, but when Mum fell pregnant with me at twenty-two he'd put aside his literary aspirations and got a 'proper' job at BT. Then, apparently, became a bitter miser. He regulated every penny, gave Mum a meagre grocery allowance and refused to pay for childcare so that Mum could attend fashion college – if he couldn't follow his dream, neither could she. He organised her a job at BT and Mum said she'd felt her life force draining away. The divorce had been an unshackling event for her. She now got up early to grab the day by the nuts. She drank, ate, exercised, shopped, travelled, danced, loved and nurtured a previously unexhibited addiction to McQueen scarves, obscure photographic art and anything neon.

I let myself in and was hit by a wave of warm air and girlish squeals.

'Emma! Emma! Watch this!'

Alice and Jess, Uncle Mike and Sinead's eldest two, were standing at the top of the narrow staircase. Jess swung her leg over the banister, slid all the way to the bottom and landed in a heap of Roberto Cavalli cushions.

'Very good!' I said as Jess bounced up, pushed her wayward hair behind a sticky-out ear and gave me a hug round my thighs.

'Now me!' Alice hurtled down the banister towards us.

I pulled Jess out of the way and before I knew it I had two messy blond-haired girls wrapped round my waist and was dragging myself down the leopard-print-carpeted hall.

'Where's Ned?' Jess asked.

'He's not coming.'

'Why not?' Jess, the tomboy and younger of the two, had always liked Ned. He'd taught her how to make blow darts with wet toilet paper that Sinead's housekeeper had spent hours cleaning off the ceiling.

'Shh, Jess.' Alice glared at her sister and spoke in an exaggerated stage whisper. 'Remember what Daddy said?'

'What did your dad say?' I stopped and looked at the girls.

Jess wrinkled her nose.

'*Remember*?!' Alice attempted a stern look far beyond her years.

'Oh, yeah!' Jess suddenly remembered and grinned at me. 'Mummy said that you'd got rid of that potato-brained . . . potato-brained . . .?' She frowned enquiringly at Alice.

'Bastard,' Alice offered from my left hip.

'Yes, that potato-brained bastard and that you also . . .?' She looked at her sister for further assistance.

'Got fired,' Alice said.

'Yes. You are fire red,' Jess confirmed.

'Daddy told Mummy off for talking about your personal eclairs, and also for swearing, then Daddy sat in the music room with the Supernanny book,' Alice said, tucking her chin towards her chest and trying to emulate a knowing look.

'I didn't get fired,' I said in a small voice.

I was suitably dismayed that my eight- and six-year-old cousins knew about my troubling 'personal eclairs'.

'Alice! Jess!' Sinead came into the hall. 'Ahh, Emma.' She pulled me into a bony hug, all elbows and shoulder blades. 'Girls, off your cousin. Your father's made biscuits.'

Alice and Jess scooted to the kitchen shrieking and pushing each other into walls.

In the living room, flames cavorted in the marble fireplace.

Fairy lights hung down the side of the mantel. The nostalgic aroma of winter spice candles hung in the air. The latest Pixar movie played on the flatscreen in the corner, mesmerising Millie and Archie, who rested in an armchair with a copy of my mother's Madonna *Sex* book on his lap. Uncle Mike sat in a black chesterfield swirling whisky in a crystal tumbler and Mum was leaning against an oversized gold Moroccan pouf in front of the fire. She too was swirling her whisky, looking pensive. And a little drunk.

'Hi Mum.'

She turned away from the hypnotic flames.

'Darling!' She stood with a swiftness and grace that belied her years, shoved her whisky at Uncle Mike, who'd nearly nodded off, and flew across the room, pulling me into a tight embrace. She was wearing her 'go to' outfit of tight black jeans, a white shirt open to the top of her cleavage with gold chains and pendants dangling in between her tanned breasts.

'I've missed you so much, my baby.'

'I've missed you too,' I said, tears leaking. 'I'm so sad about Grandma.'

'I know, I know.'

After a quiet minute being clutched to my mother's golden bosom she released me from her grasp.

'Your boobs look bigger,' she said, dabbing at the corners of her eyes and scanning my attire instinctively. 'Are you wearing that push-up bra I sent you? Didn't I tell you a little discomfort was worth it? You're a bit bigger round the hips too, my darling. Have you been . . .' Mum became aware of everyone looking at her. 'Why – why are you all staring at me?'

I looked at Uncle Mike, Uncle Mike looked at Sinead and Sinead looked at me. I gazed at my feet. Just as Sinead opened her mouth to blurt out what I was not ready to, Uncle Mike jumped up and saved me.

'I think we are all just a bit emotional.' He led me to the purple velvet sofa. 'Emma dear, take a seat. I'll get dinner started. Sinead, a little help?'

I gathered Millie onto my lap and Mum and I caught up by the fireplace while Uncle Mike and Sinead cooked dinner and gave me some space in order to tell Mum my news. But no time seemed appropriate to say 'yes, I agree – Grandma had been getting ill more often, I too was worried about her living alone at her age; oh hey, I'm pregnant, jobless and single'.

After dinner Mum and I watched the circus involved getting Alice, Jess, Archie and Millie bathed and into bed with their various favourite toys, blankies and bedtime stories, then we collapsed in the living room, the lights down low and the fire cranked high. I sat in my favourite position in the corner of the sofa stroking Grandma's cat, a mottled tabby called Tabby.

'Has anyone rung Alex?' I asked, giving Tabby a scratch under her chin.

Mum looked questioningly at Uncle Mike. He shook his head and turned to Sinead.

'Don't look at me, I never know what country that girl

is in!' she said, flicking through the pages of the Madonna book, turning it upside down on occasion.

Mum stood. 'I'll call her.'

She left the room, dialling.

'Well?' Sinead demanded.

'Well what?' I picked at the skin around my fingernails.

'When are you going to tell her?' Sinead held the book close, examining something.

I turned to Uncle Mike for reassurance.

'I'm sorry, sweetheart, but you do need to get on with it.'

I slumped further into the sofa. 'Guess so.'

'Her phone's off.' Mum came back into the room and took her seat on the sofa next to me. 'I'll try again soon.' She turned to me, curling her legs under her. 'So, my darling, where's Ned?' she said, forcing a smile.

I accepted Mum's dislike of Ned. It came from the right place. According to Mum, Ned was a dreamer who would end up travelling the same path my father had. The unachieved, frustrated, bitter, spiteful one. (In that order.) It was her fear for my future that had had her purse-lipped and icy-natured around my generally affable boyfriend for the past five years.

'We broke up.'

'Oh, that's ...' Mum broke into an involuntary smile then forced the corners of her lips down, '... awful, darling, just ...' Her body betrayed her and she grinned again. 'Really, really ... terrible.' She frowned, and tried to set her mouth into some semblance of concern. 'Tell me what happened.'

'Nothing happened,' I said. 'I just realised I needed somebody more . . .'

'Motivated,' Mum said, elation itching on her skin.

'Ned *is* motivated. He just lacks—'

'Skills? Intellect?'

I scowled. 'Follow-through. I'm still upset, you know.'

'Yes, of course.' Mum's eyes flitted guiltily to Uncle Mike. Sinead observed the scene, the Madonna book discarded at her feet. I looked at Uncle Mike who nodded in encouragement, the light from the fairy lights dancing across his frameless oval specs.

'Well, now you can focus on your career,' Mum said. 'Go after the big jobs overseas. I met a producer in Malta—'

'I quit.'

'What?!' Mum looked confused. 'Why?'

'Well, if I didn't quit then another formal warning would be on its way and I'd be fired.'

'Oh. Right.' She leant back in the sofa. 'What happened?'

'I said some stuff . . . and gave the finger to someone.'

'I see.' Mum dragged a hand over her brow.

'There's more.'

'What?' Mum eyed me through red fingernails.

Sinead stared. Uncle Mike fidgeted.

'I'm sort of . . . kinda pregnant?'

Mum sat up, eyes wide.

'Thirteen weeks.'

'Oh, Jesus.' She fell back into the sofa again.

'And I've decided to keep it.'

'What?' She shot up again. 'Who's the father? Please tell me it's not — it isn't?'

'It's Ned.'

'Oh, *Jesus*.' She slumped back and threw her arm over her face. 'I need a whisky. And a towel. A hot towel. No. A cold towel. Oh, Jesus.'

Uncle Mike slipped out of the room. Sinead passed Mum her whisky glass and sat at our feet, spellbound.

'Couldn't it be some gym instructor's? One with fewer freckles?' Mum's voice was pleading.

I rolled my eyes, remembering my conversation with Alex. God, how I wished she were here with her younger-sister authority, telling Mum to behave.

'Or maybe . . .?'

'It's undoubtedly Ned's.'

'Oh, Jesus.'

Uncle Mike came rushing in with a towel, which Mum snatched and threw over her face.

'Mum, you keep saying "Oh, Jesus".'

'I know, darling, but he's not listening to me,' she muttered from under the towel. 'He never does.' She lifted her towel and her whisky glass disappeared under it.

The only sounds in the room were the cubes of ice tinkling in her glass. Sinead gave me the double thumbs up.

'OK?' I mouthed to Uncle Mike.

He nodded and mouthed, 'Well done.'

'Sinead? Mike? You're awfully quiet. What do you think of this?' Mum's voice was muffled under the towel.

Sinead and Uncle Mike froze.

'We're shocked!' Sinead started. 'Shocked to our very—'

'We already knew, Diana,' Uncle Mike said.

The towel flew to the ground.

'You *what*?!'

'Sorry Mum, I—'

'Sinead?'

'She needed advice.' Sinead shrugged.

'Advice?' Mum turned to me. 'Who better to give you advice than your own *mother*?'

'You were overseas . . .' I tried to make my eyes wide and wet and pitiful like a vulnerable little rodent in a Disney movie, but Mum's face remained hard.

'Diana, dear—' Uncle Mike began.

'Oh, don't you "Diana dear" me!'

'Mum—'

'No! Don't bother, darling.' She stood, clutching her whisky to her breast. 'I know when I'm not needed.'

Sinead, Uncle Mike and I watched as she picked up the phone, pressed speed dial, threw a woeful look my way and headed into the hall. 'Hello, darling,' we heard her sniff. 'Not good. My mother's passed away, my firstborn is unemployed, knocked up and single and my Terence Conran console hasn't arrived yet . . . Not sure, delayed shipment, I think . . .' Her voice faded as she headed for the kitchen.

It was most likely Charlie Mum had phoned, her long-term partner. He'd been in our lives since I was eight and Alex was five and although they had never married, he was as much a part of our family as anyone. Apart from the fact that he still kept his own place in Fulham and would quite often spend a few nights a week there, he was like any regular stepdad. He was an eco-architect and had been pioneering eco-building since the 1970s. The only bone of contention between Mum and Charlie happened when Charlie would point out that fourteen zebras were on the verge of malnutrition, an iceberg had melted and a tiny Pacific island had disappeared into the ocean so Mum could have her designer carpet.

'Well . . .' I started.

'Hmmm . . .' Sinead mused, picking up the Madonna book again, the drama now over.

'It went well.' Uncle Mike grimaced.

I looked at my watch.

'I'm tired.' I stood, feeling the weight of the past few weeks in my body. 'Can you tell Mum . . .' I faltered. 'Just . . . can you tell her?'

Uncle Mike got up, put an arm over my shoulder and guided me to the door. 'Off you go. She'll be fine.' He smiled. 'And if not, we'll get her good and drunk.'

About an hour later Mum wobbled into my bedroom 'whisky-fied', as she called it. Most people would say sloshed.

'Darling? Are you awake?' she whispered.

'Mum, my light is on, I am sitting up and I am reading. I think I might just be awake.'

'Oh.' She giggled softly and wobbled towards the bed. 'May I?'

I shuffled over and she plonked herself down.

'I spoke to Alex,' Mum said.

'I know. She texted me.'

'I told her not to fly back for the funeral.' She looked fragile. 'Was that the right thing?'

I'd been too consumed with my problems to properly comprehend that Mum had just lost her own mother. It was a tragedy at any age.

'Yes, Mum. Don't worry.'

She didn't look convinced.

'It would take Alex about four days to get back. Probably involving a ride on a cow-drawn cart and a very near miss of an arranged marriage.'

A small smile flickered at the corners of her mouth.

'She really is in the middle of nowhere. And Uncle Mike said the funeral was going to happen soon. It was the right thing to do. Definitely.'

'OK,' she sniffed.

We sat mushed up against each other on my single bed in silence, each mulling over our thoughts.

'Darling?' Mum put her whisky glass down on my bedside table.

'Yeah?'

'I'm sorry about the way I acted. I was ... I was just shocked.' She looked at me with genuine regret.

'It's OK.' I fingered the corners of the magazine.

'Are you sure you want to keep it?' Mum said, her voice soft. 'Are you sure that's a good ...?'

'I'm keeping it,' I said, putting both hands on the magazine, covering Gwyneth's freakishly white smile.

I'd run over this speech so many times in my head and had it down perfectly, but now that I was here, sitting in my childhood bed with Reuben, the toy rabbit I'd slept with until I was thirteen staring at me with his big plastic eyes, I felt incredibly young and my speech came out in fragmented, teenage-like bursts.

'There's just no way I could ... not after I'd seen it. It's just ... I just can't ... I'm having this baby and – and you'll just have to get over the fact that it's Ned's, OK? And yes, there is a very good chance it will be freckly, but I want you to love it anyway. It's my body and, well, *you* were a single mum for a while, and look how we turned out. Actually I'm fine, just pregnant and jobless, but apart from that, well. Alex turned out OK, she works with poor people. Anyway, you never even liked Ned. I just—'

'OK,' Mum said, putting a placating hand on my flapping one. 'It's OK. I'm your mother, and I just have to make sure you know what you're doing.'

I stared at Gwyneth. This shit never happened to her.

'If you want to keep the baby,' Mum took a deep breath. 'Well then, we'll be here to help every step of the way.'

I looked up at her. She squeezed my hand tight.

'And we will *love* that baby. Oh my gosh, how we will love it.'

I smiled and rested my head on her shoulder. She picked up her whisky glass, took a dainty sip and returned it to the bedside table.

'Mum?'

'Hmm?' She stroked my hand, checking my cuticles for signs of biting.

'I'm scared.'

'You're going to be fine,' she said, patting my hunched-up knees.

'Really?'

'Yes. And I'm very sorry about before. I'm proud of you, no matter what you do.'

'But Mum, you don't think I'll forget to feed the baby, or accidentally wash it with bleach, or leave it at the shops in the pushchair like you did with me?'

She shrugged. 'Probably.'

'What if I am so crazy with sleep deprivation I put it in the washing machine? You know you can't open those things for, like, a minute after it's turned on?' I tossed my magazine aside and faced Mum. 'What if I forget I have a baby and go out and leave it at home? What if I drop it down the stairs? What if I fall asleep while it's in the bath?'

'Because you are normal. Ish. And you just won't.' Mum considered me thoughtfully. 'Lie down, darling.'

I snuggled under the covers. Mum adjusted her position and her hand stroked the hair from my forehead.

'When you were born I loved you *so* much I couldn't bear it when I had to put you in your cot.' She smiled, the lines round her eyes crinkling. 'I would come into your room and kiss those gorgeous cheeks over and over and over and tell you how much I loved you and how beautiful I thought you were.' I closed my eyes, yielding to the sense of comfort the sound of my mother's (slightly slurred) voice gave me.

'I would go and sit with your father on the sofa, but five minutes later I was back in your room, staring, watching your little chest rise and fall and your long, long eyelashes resting on your cheeks. I'd lean over the cot and breathe in your beautiful baby smell then kiss you again and again and again until your father came in and told me to leave you be.'

'Then I'd sing you a song.' Mum began to sing in a soft whisper. 'Hush little baby, don't say a word, Mama's gonna buy you an exotic rare bird . . .'

I giggled softly and felt myself inch towards sleep.

'. . . and if that bird gets eaten by the cat, Mama's gonna buy you a Marc Jacobs hat . . .'

CHAPTER SIX

The next morning, I entered the kitchen wearing my pink flannel pyjamas, my ponytail in a sleep-fashioned tumble on the side of my head.

'Morning,' I yawned to the room in general.

Mum raised her coffee mug at me. She paced the kitchen, her phone to her ear, her black peep-toe heels click-clicking across the marble floor. A fitted white silk shirt and navy leather pencil skirt showed off the results of thrice-weekly 'Viking Method' sessions. Being 'whisky-fied' the night before never stopped my mother owning the day. Uncle Mike made trips from stove to dining table serving up a breakfast banquet and the kids sat at the table industriously stuffing their faces. The delicious but forbidden smell of coffee filled the air. I looked at the coffee pot as one would an old lover, then sat down next to Archie.

'So what's the plan for today?' I asked, reaching for the juice.

'I guess I'm going shopping for *purple* outfits for the children and myself,' Sinead grumbled. 'I can't believe you two have organised the funeral for tomorrow. It isn't enough time.'

Uncle Mike let out an irritated puff of air.

'Tomorrow? Purple?' I looked at Mum, who was still on the phone. 'Tomorrow and *purple*?!'

She frowned and made a motion with her hand for me to be quiet. If we put aside the fact that one day couldn't possibly be enough time to organise an entire (purple) funeral, tomorrow was also Christmas Eve. Could you even have a funeral on Christmas Eve? Would Jesus mind?

'Yes, tomorrow, and, as per my mother's final wish, yes – purple.' Uncle Mike poured himself a coffee. 'Diana is making the last arrangements now. If we don't do it tomorrow we'll have to wait until the New Year and, well, we're all just a bit busy then.'

'It's far too—' Sinead started.

'*And*,' Uncle Mike continued, 'I do not want Mother sitting alone in a fridge on Christmas Day.' He gave Sinead a single nod indicating the discussion was over, turned to me and softened his face. 'Now, I have to pop to the surgery for a couple of hours and you, my dear, have nothing to do except relax and maybe get yourself something purple to wear that doesn't make your blossoming shape look like an aubergine.'

'See!' Sinead exclaimed. 'It is ridiculous! Emma will look like an aubergine, I will look like a corpse – please excuse the bad taste but I *will* – and Archie has already asked if he can go as Barney.'

It took until lunchtime for Sinead to get all the kids showered, dressed and for us to make our way to Oxford Circus to attempt the mad task of finding a purple funeral outfit two days before Christmas.

'Let's split up.' Sinead gathered the children to her on the crowded street. We agreed to meet later and she bustled off, absorbed into the Christmas crowds in seconds.

Oxford Street had a coating of icing-sugar frost. Twinkly lights glowed and reflected in shop windows and a low layer of stone-coloured cloud created a cosseting effect.

I quickly became disillusioned with clothes shopping. I was three months pregnant and had only a slight tummy, but everything I tried on made me look like a beer-swigging, football-watching chav who ate too many pies, not the blooming yummy-mummy-to-be I was aiming for. It was getting dark outside. I checked my watch and dashed into Topshop, determined to leave with something. I finally settled on a dusky lilac (that just about passed as purple) woollen shift dress. With a cleverly draped pashmina it would look quite cute – and, I hoped, disguise my 'beer belly' baby pouch. I'd not yet told anyone outside of Ned and my family. I didn't think I was ready to come out of the pregnant, single and jobless closet just yet. And I especially didn't want to come out of that closet at my grandmother's purple funeral.

I texted Sinead while I waited in the long queue, looking

forward to getting home and having a hot chocolate by the fire.

'Next!' said the girl behind the counter.

I hurried forward. The salesgirl glowered from under heavily painted eyelids.

'Hello.' I handed over my dress.

The salesgirl rang up the item and flung it unceremoniously into a bag, all the while talking about how much she hated working during the Christmas period to her workmate at the next till. I smiled. There was a certain comfort in having a surly teenage sales assistant wearing too much make-up and tight jeans that bared more hip flesh than appropriate make you feel insignificant and annoying at Christmas.

'Fifty-seven fifty,' the girl said in my general direction.

I punched in my pin. The salesgirl watched the card machine.

'Denied,' she said, rather too loudly for my liking.

'What?'

'Denied? Your card?' She looked at her spiky-haired teen colleague with inflated exasperation.

'Uh, it can't be. Could ... could you try again please, I must have entered the wrong pin.'

'Then it would have said "incorrect pin", not "denied" and it says "denied", yeah? See?' She brandished the card terminal at me.

I could feel the long line of irate Christmas shoppers behind me communally clench. I hesitated, my cheeks heating. I didn't understand why the card would be denied. I'd hardly touched my accounts since leaving my job.

'Can't you just pay cash, yeah?' She drummed her fake nails on the counter, eyebrows raised. The nail had fallen off her ring finger and the real nail was bitten down to the skin.

'Uh, I don't have enough,' I said, looking in my wallet and weighing up my options.

I could leave the dress behind the counter, try and get cash out of the machine that would probably be empty this close to Christmas and then line up in this hideous queue again, or head home without an outfit and suffer the funeral in Mum's choice of purple torture. I didn't like either alternative.

'You ready?' Sinead appeared at my side, kids and shopping bags trailing behind her.

'My card is denied and—'

'Kids! Stay close!' she said as her motherly sixth sense registered her three children with the ability to walk begin to disperse in different directions. Millie slept in her pushchair, laden with shopping bags. 'OK, well . . .'

She was distracted. I was just about to abandon the dress when the salesgirl spoke to Sinead.

'Can't you pay for your daughter's stuff?'

Sinead snapped her head in the direction of the salesgirl. '*Daughter*?'

Oh shit. Sinead was only forty-one.

'Let's just go,' I said.

The salesgirl gave a huge sigh and a theatrical roll of her eyes. 'So I'm pressing void, yeah?'

'Yes, that's fine.' I motioned to Sinead to go, wary of the fidgety customers behind us.

'No. You are getting that dress. I'm not having Diana dress you as a purple snow leopard.' She opened her wallet. 'Archie, darling? Come here, will you?' She narrowed her eyes at the unwitting sales assistant.

Back at home, Sinead perched on the sofa, shopping bags at her feet, and recalled how Archie had helped bring down the salesgirl a peg or two by pointing out her muffin top, slapper nails and 'hooker' make-up. Uncle Mike was slumped next to her, sipping his tea, a harried look on his face. The kids played upstairs while Millie slept on in her pushchair; Mum was at Charlie's, so, apart from Uncle Mike's hand-wringing, the living room was peaceful. I sat in an armchair by the fire, checking my bank accounts.

'Then Archie started pointing out other slappers, which was quite funny, wasn't it, Em?' Sinead said as she sorted through her purchases, holding the odd item up to Uncle Mike, who nodded distractedly.

'It's *not* funny. Honestly, what happens when—'

'FUCKER!' I yelled.

Uncle Mike spilt his tea; Sinead blinked. 'What?' they said together.

'That *fucker*!' I stared at my laptop.

'*What*?' they said with more urgency.

'My money's gone . . .'

I'd forgotten Ned had access to my accounts. We'd set up

a joint account that only I'd contributed to. In fact, I didn't just contribute, my entire wages went into it and it held all my savings.

It was empty.

Before anger could properly take hold, a sick feeling gurgled up in my throat as I realised the gravity of the situation. I was pregnant and single with no job. I'd always been fairly good with money. I didn't spend loads on fashionable clothes, preferring instead to live in a uniform of jeans, slogan t-shirts and coloured Converse. I'd debated for hours with Mum over nature versus nurture during the occasions she would insist I go 'boho' to school and I just wanted to wear my trainers and merge into the crowd. I was only eleven at the time.

'Are you sure?' Sinead said, dropping an item of clothing into a shopping bag.

'Well my account says zero where it previously said a few thousand, and I don't seem to have a few thousand in my wallet, so yes, I'm sure,' I said, then immediately regretted it.

Sinead had bailed me out of a very embarrassing situation not two hours before. She leant back in the sofa and looked at me, concerned.

'Sorry,' I said quietly.

She shrugged, over it already.

'Oh my god.' I buried my face in my hands. 'I have to call him.'

I grabbed my phone and dialled his number. Straight to answer machine. I didn't trust myself to leave a message without crying and/or flinging stuttered abuse, so I tossed my phone on the coffee table and fell back into the armchair, mentally numb. Not a thought went through my head for a full minute. The room was still.

'Shit,' I said.

'Shit,' Sinead repeated.

'Shit,' Uncle Mike muttered.

Sinead and I looked at him.

'Well, you're right.' He shook his head. 'He *is* a little fucker.'

We sat in the room gazing at the fire as if it held a solution. Our silence was broken by the sound of the door slamming and Mum's heels clacking down the floorboards. She floated into the living room carrying bags of wrapped presents.

'Hello, my lovelies, I've picked up some—' She stopped by the sofa, detecting our sombre faces. 'God, *now* what?' She looked from me to Uncle Mike, to Sinead and back to me again.

I covered my face with my hands, too embarrassed to reveal the news.

'Ned has emptied Emma's bank account,' Uncle Mike said in a grave voice.

'What?' Mum dropped her bags. 'Are you sure?' She strode round the sofa and perched on the edge of the coffee table.

I removed my hands from my face and gave my Mum a 'don't go there' look.

'That little *fucker*!' she spat.

I smiled weakly. It was unanimous, then. Ned was a little fucker.

CHAPTER SEVEN

I stood in front of the mirror, a shapely aubergine ready for my grandmother's funeral. I'd spent most of the previous night drafting what I was going to say to Ned. I'd left a message early that morning when his phone, again, went straight to voicemail. I remained calm when I told him my mother was going to hunt him down and de-male him. I did not cry when I told him his child was going to be left starving and naked, and I did not wail when I asked his messaging service why he was so selfish and such a goddamned wanker. Then I'd cried and wailed in a high-pitched voice telling the message service I had to go to my grandma's funeral and that he had better call me later and explain himself; and that's when Mum grabbed the phone from my shaking hands and said she was going to rip his ginger whiskers out and make him eat them and Sinead stood in the background and called him a fuck-knuckle.

I pulled my hair back into a loose ponytail.

'Can I kill it in Africa?' Mum stomped up the stairs, barking into her phone. 'When I requested *animal print* samples I meant leopard, zebra, cheetah. You know – the *usual*. I did NOT mean grim, greige Welsh fucking field mouse.' She stopped in my doorway. 'I do trust you . . . Fix it for me. *Please*, I said please, didn't I?' Mum tossed her phone on my dresser. 'Lovely,' she said, scanning my outfit and smiling her approval.

Mum's smile could lift a room. She was charm personified, even on the day of her own mother's funeral.

'You think?' I twisted, scrutinising my bum in the mirror.

I was definitely plumper now that I was three months pregnant and I couldn't have cared less. My cellulite looked like the top of a crumpet.

'You have such lovely hair. I wish you'd wear it out sometimes,' she said, looking at my standard scraped-up bun.

'Yeah, yeah, you're going to have to get over it. This is me. Hair up, no eyeshadow. And my underwear doesn't match.'

Mum gasped and her hand flew to her chest. 'Have I *hurt* you?' she said, feigning shock. 'Why you feel you need to say such things . . .' She shook her head and her smile returned. Her hands rested on my shoulders. She was a good foot taller than me, helped by the lofty heels she lived in. We looked at each other in the mirror. Her face dropped its bright facade.

'I'm going to miss her.'

'Me too.'

'Even though this purple funeral has given me exactly fourteen new grey hairs, I will still miss her.'

I gave an understanding nod.

'Now I'm an orphan.' Her eyes dampened. 'And I am stuck with that bloody cat of hers that does not go with my décor *at all.*'

She glanced at my rounded belly. 'We've lost one life, but we're gaining another.' She checked her mascara in the mirror. 'I feel too young to be a grandmother.'

'I feel too young to be a mother.'

'I had two children by the time I was your age.'

'You were married. And that was the olden days.'

Mum's lips tightened and she gave me a stern look.

'I'll wash my mouth out,' I said.

Mum checked her watch. 'You'll think about my offer, won't you?'

In light of my recent monetary discovery Mum had offered to lend me the exact amount Ned had taken and had asked me to move in with her till I got back on my feet. I was hesitant. If I took money from my mother it would be an admission of my failure as an adult. It would be the beginning of a downward spiral, culminating with Mum and I at home wearing matching slippers and knitting scarves for characters on *Corrie* because 'they looked like they might catch a chill last night on the telly'.

I smiled, not willing to commit to anything. 'I'll think about it.'

It took only five minutes to drive round the corner to the local crematorium. The car park was crammed with zippy little elderly-people cars and I wondered how my mother had managed to contact this many people and get them to attend a funeral on Christmas Eve at such short notice. To say she was a capable woman was like saying Gandhi once went on a diet.

The family waited silently in the foyer. The double doors to the car park opened and Uncle Mike, Charlie and the other pallbearers, each wearing a purple rose in their lapel and a purple handkerchief in their breast pocket, appeared with the coffin. I waved at Charlie. He was deeply tanned, having spent the past few months on a research trip in Africa, and cut a suave figure in his dark suit with his chocolate-brown eyes. He smiled then; catching sight of the children (Alice and Jess as purple princesses, Archie as Barney and a blueberry-esque Millie), he threw Uncle Mike a grin. Uncle Mike reddened. He'd really been very against the costumes. He'd even said he was 'putting his foot down', but I don't think Sinead was worried one jot where he placed his foot. She was 'absolutely not going purple clothes shopping with the children two fucking days before Christmas again'. Quite right.

We fell into place behind the coffin. A burly young guy with ginger hair (phwoar) and sturdy knees poking out of a kilt emerged from somewhere and began a mournful drone on a set of bagpipes. His calf muscles were like a couple of Vienna loaves under his hairy skin. He looked like a young version of the raffish Scottish groundskeeper in *The Simpsons*.

We followed the hot guy with his tartan bag of record-ers into the main room. I looked at the mourners absorbed with the vision of the coffin and watched as they clocked the collection of purple Nickelodeon outcasts wandering behind like they'd walked off the stage of a school concert and got horribly lost.

'Everyone's looking at us, Mummy,' Jess whispered loudly.

An old couple smiled. I held Archie's dinosaur paw. His purple tail whacked the knees of the people in the aisle seats and he had to keep shoving his dinosaur head up so he could see where he was placing his oversized feet. Mum followed behind. She appeared reserved in her purple cashmere belted dress. An understated (for her) collection of gold bangles jangled on her wrist as she took her slow steps. I neared the middle of the room and caught sight of Helen, Sophie and Douglas sitting together. Sophie giggled into her fists, her eyes on Archie. Douglas was making unsuccessful attempts to get her to quieten down. He pushed his glasses up his nose and threw me an apologetic look. When I'd phoned Helen last night to give her the funeral details I'd told her about Ned emptying my bank account and, like any good friend, she'd offered to get her chavvy cousins from Peckham to 'rough him up a little'. She gave me a nod of support, then, ever observant, her steely-grey eyes shot to my faintly swollen belly. I pulled my pashmina together and quickly looked away so as not to meet her querying glare, and saw someone totally unexpected.

Ned.

His red-rimmed eyes followed the coffin up the aisle. He blew his nose into a hanky. Ned had been close to my grandmother, their having had a mutual fondness for orphaned animals and the perfect cheese toastie, and despite my anger I was touched by his obvious sorrow. But the shock at seeing him threw me and I faltered in my step.

'Darling, you OK?' Mum followed my gaze. 'Little *fucker*,' she muttered, then made a slitting motion across her neck and pointed a manicured finger at Ned.

His face drained of colour.

'*Mum*,' I whispered. '*Stop it.*'

Mortified, Douglas, standing two rows in front of Ned, mistook the deathly gesture for himself and pointed a shaking finger at his chest, eyebrows raised.

'Not *you*.' I mouthed with tight lips. I made subtle head movements to indicate Ned behind him but Douglas's eyes were wide and glued on Mum.

Sophie, having noticed the throat-slitting actions, swivelled in her seat and saw Ned behind her, trembling, searching for a way out of the packed room. She turned back to Douglas and began to shudder with restrained laughter.

'*Shit*,' I said under my breath as we continued our glacial move forward.

The hot bagpiper reached the front as the rest of us took our seats. I shot Ned one last look and tried to convey to him, with entirely undecipherable eye movements, to wait for me at the end of the service but his anxious gaze remained on Mum.

For the next forty minutes I forgot about the filler of my womb, the emptier of my bank account behind me and instead focused on remembering a lady I'd known only as old and furry-cheeked with a bathroom full of cosmetic products the modern world didn't use any more – like talc and Yardley fragrance. Mum wept; Uncle Mike was glassy-eyed throughout. We sang, we cried, Millie filled her nappy and then Mum took to the microphone one last time and recited a poem of mine.

> *When you die*
> *You just go*
> *Not to above*
> *Not to below*

I was twelve when I'd written it. I'd been following Grandma round her garden munching on the various beans, parsley and cherry tomatoes she picked and it had dawned on me that she would die one day. No more popping peas from their shells while I talked endlessly about my friends, my teachers and my friends' teachers. I'd wandered inside and written the poem, giving it to her over afternoon date loaf. She'd loved it so much she'd cross-stitched it onto cream linen and it hung on her bedroom wall.

> *Why do people like to pretend*
> *That your time as 'someone' doesn't end*
> *It does*
> *It stops*
> *You're not around*
> *But traces of you can always be found*

You're in the smell of a certain flower
You're in the scratch of a particular sock
You're in the taste of a lemon so sour
You're in the placement of a garden rock

An apricot, warm from the sun
Extra raisins in a sticky bun
A scarf, a joke, a grey cat's tail
EastEnders, *chicken tenders, a pink fingernail*

Grandma's coffin began its descent into the bowels of the funeral parlour. I sobbed. For my cheerful grandmother. For my mother, whose heart was breaking. For my baby, who was coming into such an uncertain life. For Ned, and the damage in the wake of our relationship. And for my sister, who I missed terribly.

But you'll stay right here, Grandma, always here
In my heart, in my mind, in my life, my dear

The coffin disappeared. As the congregation began to rise and file into the foyer I craned my neck and saw the tips of Ned's messy hair bobbing in the middle of the room.

'Take this.' I handed Archie's paw to his mother and pushed my way, as politely as one can in a room full of wobbly, teary geriatrics, to the foyer, hearing snippets of warbled conversation.

'Ah, she'll be having a wee sherry in the sky.'

'Never worn purple to a funeral before.'

'Fascinating, that wee dinosaur.'

'Did you see Ivy's daughter slit her neck in the middle of the procession?'

I squeezed through the double doors into the foyer and stopped to scan the mass of purple folk. Sophie's hand shot through the crowd.

'Hey!' Her pixie face appeared. She'd changed her diamond nose stud to a tiny purple amethyst. 'Quick, he's over here.' She disappeared into the throng, dragging my sleeve with her.

I shuffled apologetically past people I knew and people I didn't.

'Found her!' Sophie said, pushing me forward.

I emerged from the crowd and saw Ned up against a wall, detained by Helen. All five foot one of her was braced threateningly a foot from his anxious face. Sophie shoved me towards Ned and scuttled back next to Douglas, who was hovering nearby.

'Hey,' I said.

'H–hi ...'

'I think you might have a bit more to say than that, don't you, you maggot–kissing shite?' Helen moved her nose closer to Ned.

He shrank into the wall. Sophie chewed on her fingernail.

'Guys, I'm OK. Do you think you could ...' I motioned for them to leave us alone '... you know, give us a sec?'

Douglas nodded and started to move. Sophie followed. Helen stayed put.

'Helen?' I tapped her on the shoulder.

'I'll be watching you,' she growled, 'from right over there.'
She pointed to a spot not too far away.

Ned gulped. She backed off and I stepped nearer. We
looked at each other for a moment. The last time we were
face to face I'd been telling him he was going to be a
father.

'Ah . . . it was a nice service,' he offered.

'Hmm.'

'I like the purple.'

'Yeah.'

'Doesn't go with my colouring, though.' He pointed to
his ginger hair.

'You fucker,' I said, my eyes watering.

'Please don't cry,' he said, looking round him.

'Why not? Don't you want people to know what you've
done?'

Disgrace shot across his face.

'How am I going to pay for stuff? I don't have a job.' I
lowered my voice. 'I'm having a baby. *Your* baby.' I dug my
nails into my palms.

'I know. I know. I–I'm sorry. I'll pay it back, I promise.
I—'

'Did you spend it all?'

Ned nodded.

'On what?'

'An ice cream van. Gerry and I—'

'Gerry and you are total idiots!' I cried.

Helen took a step towards us. Douglas held her back. Sophie chewed her nails.

'I'll pay it all back.'

'How? Do you have a job?'

Ned looked at his feet. 'No. But Gerry and I have a business plan and—'

'Just . . .' I blinked away hot, angry tears. 'Just shut up.'

I looked over at the crowd of people. Some were leaving, heading to my mother's house for the wake.

'Why don't *you* have a job?'

'What?' I said, distracted.

'Your job. What happened?' Ned looked genuinely concerned.

'I said some things to Quentin. And gave Philomena the finger.'

'Awesome.' Ned grinned. 'They totally had it coming.'

'Yeah,' I said, the corners of my mouth turning up, encouraged by Ned's approval. 'And then I quit.'

My face fell again when I realised it was actually my own fault I had no job. I'd quit. At really a most inappropriate time. If only I'd bottled up all my frustration and just got myself stress-related alopecia instead.

Ned grabbed my hand. 'Em, I . . . I miss you.'

'And I just want you to give me my money back.'

Hurt spread across Ned's face.

'Em, please? Can't we—' He suddenly dropped my hand like a detained subject drops his gun. 'Oh, no.'

I followed his panicked gaze and saw Mum striding

towards us through the crowd, eyes ablaze. I turned back but Ned was gone. I caught a glimpse of the back of his head hurrying through the car park.

'Yes, you run, Freckle Boy!' Mum shouted across the foyer. 'I'll find you! And when I do ...' She threw her fist into her palm with a loud slap.

'*Mum!*'

Ned turned back to us, safe on the other side of the car park. He gave me one last penitent look and was off. I turned back to Mum and my friends.

'So?' Helen said.

'So,' I sighed.

'No. I mean – *so*?' She glared pointedly at my stomach.

'Oh, yeah.'

CHAPTER EIGHT

'I'll kill him!' Helen spat.

'I will too.' Sophie shoved a canapé in her mouth and grabbed two more from the passing waiter.

'What the hell was he doing at the funeral?' Helen slammed her empty champagne glass on the coffee table.

'He got on really well with Grandma. I guess he just wanted to pay his respects.'

Helen raised a dubious eyebrow.

'She used to read him the classics, you know; *Treasure Island*, *Black Beauty*, *Huckleberry Finn*, while he digitised her knitting patterns on the iPad.' I shrugged. 'Ned's really good with the oldies. Particularly grandmothers.'

'Gross,' Sophie said, getting the wrong idea.

I looked away from the concerned faces and glanced round my mother's bustling living room. Mourners gobbled canapés and quaffed champagne cocktails. Mum knew how to throw a party, even if it was a granny-packed wake.

'Em?' Sophie shifted in her seat. 'I just wondered, um, how come you're keeping the baby?'

Douglas nearly choked on his blini. Helen's unyielding gaze settled on me. I knew there would be a grilling. Friends wouldn't be friends if they didn't tell you your skinny jeans made your arse and legs look like an upside-down bulb of garlic, your boyfriend was a maggot-kissing shite or keeping a mistake baby was, well, a mistake. Three sets of eyes regarded me intently.

'You don't know what it's like,' I sighed. 'Have you ever looked at something and just knew it had to be?'

'Yes,' Helen said. 'That perfect sand-coloured Hugo Boss trench. The one that makes my waist look like a ballet dancer's and emphasises my boobs in that "I-could-be-naked-under-here-and-you'd-never-know" porno-but-classy kind of way. I knew *that* had to be.'

I rolled my eyes. 'OK.'

'But Em.' Helen leant forward. 'It's a fucking coat. I don't have to get my boob out in public for my coat. I don't have to get up fifteen times in the middle of the night for my coat. My coat will never be sick on me, and when I want to wear my coat I do not have to get it out of my vagina.'

Douglas's eyes shot to a couple of elderly gentlemen seated to his right.

'Yeah, and if she gets bored of it, she can always put it on eBay,' Sophie added. 'You can't do that with a baby.'

'Exactly,' Helen said.

'Nit shampoo!' Sophie said, her eyebrows shooting up.

'Kids get nits.' She nodded, serious. 'And the shampoo is *sooo* expensive. If you want the good stuff, that is. And you really *should* get the good stuff. It smells, but you . . .' She trailed off at Helen's slow shake of the head.

'Fucking *nit* shampoo?' Helen said. 'There's going to be vaginal stitching and you're talking about—'

'*Helen*,' Douglas said, trying to shield the little old men with a shift of his back.

I slumped in my chair. My friends were concerned, that was all. We were roughly the same age and still felt incredibly young. A feeling of isolation crept over me. With no partner to share this with I was really counting on the support of my friends. For about the millionth time I wished for my sister's presence. I felt bolstered just being near her. How very *dare* she be helping the poor when I needed a dash of bolstering? We sat in silence. Sophie twisted her glass round and round on the table. Douglas studied me with a look of concern that brought an uncomfortable tightness to my throat.

'Emma, you've got to—' Helen said.

Douglas put his hand up. 'If I may?' He turned to me, his pale hands closing gently round mine. 'What did you see when you looked and knew it "had to be"?'

'A fuzzy grey bean shape.'

'Yes. But what did you *see*?' he said, gesturing into the ether.

Helen made a face at Sophie.

'I saw – I saw myself holding the baby at the hospital?' I ventured.

Douglas nodded.

What had I seen?

'I saw little fingers curling round mine. I saw tiny nappies and tiny socks.'

Sophie bit her fingernail and leant in.

'I saw . . .' Warmth blossomed in my chest. 'I saw wispy hair and midnight bottles and tears and exhaustion. I saw pushchairs and parks and older mothers looking at me, judging me.'

Helen bobbed her head with a rueful smile.

'I saw my mother buying tiny Burberry jumpsuits and animal-print bibs. I saw bathtime and bedtime. I saw Disney films and school plays, first smiles, first tantrums, buckets and spades on the beach, terrible artwork I'd have to hang on the fridge, chubby-armed cuddles, gobby kisses, first steps and first words.' I looked at Douglas, grateful. 'And that's when I realised I could handle all of it because . . . because it was mine already.'

Douglas smiled and shot Helen a triumphant look.

'That is so . . . so . . .' Sophie said, wiping her nose on her sleeve.

'Oh, pull yourself together, you daft pixie tart.' Helen elbowed Sophie and dabbed at the corner of her eyes.

'Emma, my girl!' Charlie's deep voice boomed clear across the room.

He wormed his way over and grabbed me in a bear hug, lifting me off the ground. Helen and Sophie checked themselves quickly. Charlie was in his late fifties but none of his appeal had left him. Or so I was told frequently by my blushing girlfriends. To me he was just Charlie, my mother's partner who'd been around since I was eight years old. The man who taught my sister and me how to do dive bombs one year in Greece, how to do skids on our bikes and how to kick a guy in the goolies and make off with his wallet.

'Sweetheart! You look lovely. Blooming, as they say.' He released me and placed me gently on the ground. 'Your mother has told me all your news, and my goodness, there's a lot of it. You take one little trip to Algeria looking for sustainable cork . . .' He grinned.

'Yeah, well, I'm living the dream,' I said, detangling myself and adjusting my hemline. 'Although most of the time it feels like a nightmare. One of those ones where you find you're naked in the school playground and everyone's laughing at you, or you're driving a jeep off a cliff and your foot can't find the brake pedal.'

'Are you naked when you're driving?' Sophie asked.

'No, Soph. I'm wearing clothes. The scary part is flying off the cliff.'

'Oh. Right.' She smiled at Charlie. 'Hi, I'm Sophie. I work, well *worked*, with Emma before she went and abused everybody and walked out, but we're friends, we still see each other, we—'

'Sophie, *breathe*.' Helen rolled her eyes. 'Idiot.'

'Oh yes,' Sophie huffed.

'Pleasure to meet you, Sophie, previous-colleague-but-now-just-good-friend-of-Emma's.' Charlie winked at Sophie and kissed her on the cheek.

Sophie sat back down next to a bemused Douglas, putting a hand up to her blushing cheek.

The bagpiper walked across the room and Helen's attention was snared.

'I'm going to enjoy unpleating his kilt,' she purred. 'I'm going to fix my make-up.'

'Me too.' Sophie stood, brushing canapé crumbs from her lap.

'You don't wear make-up.' Douglas looked at Sophie as though seeing a different person.

'Well, I'm going to start. It's a woman's prerogative to change.' She pointed to the floor by Douglas's foot. 'Hand me my purse.'

'You don't *have* a purse.'

'Then –' Sophie glanced self-consciously at Charlie and lowered her voice '– just hand me the plastic bag with all my stuff.' She jabbed at the floor. 'Right *there*.'

Frowning, Douglas picked up the bag and handed it to Sophie.

'Thank you.' She spun on her purple Converse and disappeared into the throng of cheery mourners.

'FERDINAND!' Mum stood at the other side of the room gesturing wildly in our direction. A captivated group of white-haired ladies surrounded her.

'I'm being summoned. Her Royal High-heel-ness looks like she's about to be granny-bashed. Sweetheart, we'll talk properly later.' Charlie kissed my forehead then wove his way back through the crowd.

'Ferdinand?' Douglas said. 'I thought you said his name was Charlie?'

'It is.'

'Right.' Douglas scratched his chin. 'But your mother just called him Ferdinand.'

'Charlie proposed to Mum years ago and Mum declined, saying she could never be "Charles and Diana". It was bad luck, and too weird.'

'Because of Prince Charles and Princess Diana?'

'Exactly.'

'I see . . .' Douglas didn't really see.

'Mum said she'd only consider marrying him if he changed his name – knowing he was never going to do that.'

'Right.' Douglas furrowed his brows.

'Anyway, now she calls him every name in the Biggest Book in the History of all Names Ever except Charlie. Charlie keeps proposing, Mum asks him his name, he says Charlie, and she turns him down again.'

'That's . . . weird,' Douglas said, gazing over at my mother with her arms round Charlie's waist.

'I'm so used to it now I don't even think about it. He's Charlie to me and he's Hans, Reginald, Moses or whatever to Mum.'

'He doesn't mind?'

'Nah. He knows the real reason. After all the crap with my dad, Mum will probably never marry again. It's become rather mundane, really.'

'I think it's romantic,' Douglas said.

We looked over at Mum and Charlie. Charlie's arm was wrapped round my mother's waist. She was grinning at him as he entertained the gathered grannies.

'I just realised something!' Sophie plopped down on the sofa next to Douglas. 'I can be your birth partner!' She fizzed with expectancy.

Douglas clamped his lips together and shot me a wide-eyed look of amusement tinged with alarm.

'Oh, I don't know . . .' I recoiled at the thought of Sophie chittering, singing and bounding round the room, dropping stuff and getting tangled in my gas and air pipe.

'I can totally do it. I helped out with calving as soon as I was tall enough to reach in.' She stood and made a rummaging motion with an outstretched arm.

CHAPTER NINE

The next morning the children launched themselves out of bed to discover 'Santa' had filled their stockings incorrectly. Alice's doll accessories were in Jess's stocking, Jess's popgun and mini basketball hoop were in Alice's stocking, Archie's tugboat was in Millie's stocking and Archie's stocking was lost. But, to my credit, they all got a clementine. Original Santa had had too much champagne at the wake and crashed out on top of the bedclothes in her loafers at 9 p.m. Santa Standby had collapsed next to her at approximately 9:04 p.m., and Santa Last Resort was still on the whisky lamenting how the mottled Tabby threw out the colour equilibrium of her living room.

A quick explanation that St Nick had probably left his glasses at home therefore couldn't read the names on the stockings satisfied the youngsters, and the hung-over adults (except me) found solace in a strong coffee on the sofa.

After an hour of staring into our mugs, Mum clapped her

hands together and insisted we start Christmas Day over with a better attitude. Grandma would not have wanted us moping in her honour. (I personally was moping in honour of a few additional details: pregnant, jobless, skint and single, but kept it to myself.) Mum made the executive decision that 'hair of the dog' was the only way forward and made the next round of coffees Irish (except mine). We put 'Snoopy's Christmas' on repeat, Sinead put dark glasses on and we handed out gifts in a much cheerier mood.

'You need to make more of an effort, Emma,' Mum said in response to my look of alarm at my Christmas present, a turtlenecked poncho thing that was undoubtedly enormously fashionable but had buckle-y things round the neck, a complicated drapey front bit, tie-up sides and was something I was sure would take at least five minutes to get into. 'You should not merely look in the mirror before you leave the house and think "all essential bits are covered – I'm ready to go". I do not accept your fashion mantra "at least I'm not naked".' She smiled and began unwrapping my gift to her: a scarf knitted by Sophie's great-aunt.

'I don't have a fashion mantra,' I said, dodging Jess's mini-basketball.

Mum looked up sharply.

'And I don't always look in the mirror before I leave the house.'

She narrowed her eyes. 'You actively try to wound me. It's just plain cruel.'

Jess clambered over the sofa, knocking Tabby to the floor and spilling Sinead's coffee.

'Jesus, Jess!' Sinead said, righting her mug. 'Calm the feck down!' She stomped out of the room.

I put the poncho thing to the side. 'It's beautiful, Mum. Thank you.' I gave it a stroke of reverence for her benefit. 'And it will be quite practical as I get bigger. Once I figure out how it works.'

'Well, obviously I didn't buy it with pregnancy in mind, seeing as it's *unplanned* and all,' she said, throwing me a look of disapproval. She pulled her gift free of the wrapping and examined it for labels.

'Daddy.' Archie walked across the room with Sinead's giant hamper of Montezuma chocolates. 'Can I please have a chocolate?'

'I'm not sure, actually,' Uncle Mike said, leaning forward in the chesterfield to be level with Archie's face. 'You see, I'm still a little unhappy when I think about how you broke Alice's new toy.'

Alice glanced up from her neatly sorted new toys with a downcast expression.

'Well,' Archie placed a hand on his father's wrist, 'why don't you think about something I haven't bwoken so you can be happy?'

Sinead came back into the room with a cloth, grabbed the chocolates and declared them 'adults only'. Mum attempted to help herself to one and Sinead backtracked, announcing that seeing as she shared everything else in her life she wasn't going to share the fucking chocolates. She stepped back and trampled Alice's recently repaired toy. Alice burst into tears, Uncle Mike and Sinead dropped to the floor to calm her, Jess's ball flew past again and Archie and Mum took the opportunity to swipe a chocolate from the unattended hamper. In the melee I received a text.

I'm outside.

Ned.

'I'm just going to ...' I stood, took in the chaos and realised none of them would notice my absence, so I pulled on my coat and slipped out the front door.

Ned's mother's Volvo estate was at the end of the lane. He drove forward and pulled up at the kerb. The passenger window lowered and I bent down.

'Hi,' Ned said with a tentative smile. 'Merry Christmas.'

'What are you doing here?' I said, the edge in my voice making his smile falter.

Ned was mad about Christmas and had always made a huge fuss. Decorations were up on the first of December; cookies and beer were left out for Santa Claus on Christmas Eve; I'd wake to an overstuffed stocking and a huge mound of thoughtful presents under the tree (bought with money borrowed from his mother – Ned was adamant I was not to fund my own Christmas presents). He'd play carols all day, roast chestnuts and make sure everyone tried the mulled wine he'd been perfecting the whole of December. Some years we'd have our Christmas Days apart from each other, but I always knew I'd be going back to a toasty flat, a pile of festive-themed DVDs and one last 'surprise' gift at the very end of the day. Despite my fury at him clearing my bank account, I'd been missing his infectious excitement.

'Sorry, I just – I wanted to bring you your presents,' Ned said, reaching to the back seat. 'I had them yesterday at the funeral but, well, your mum scared the shit out of me.'

He passed a supermarket bag full of wrapped presents through the open window.

'You didn't have to,' I said, feeling awkward.

'I know.' He shrugged. 'But I wanted to.'

'I left yours at the flat,' I said, trying to remain emotionless even though a sadness was creeping in. 'You can let yourself in and get them if you like. They're at the back of the wardrobe.'

'OK, cool,' Ned said. 'Thanks.'

We looked at each other, cautious and unsure how to behave.

'Well, I'd better go back in . . .'

'Oh, hang on.' Ned reached into the back seat again, then passed a small box through the window. 'That's . . . that's for the baby.'

'The baby?'

I looked from the small box to his sincere face. Yes, he was an irresponsible man-boy who'd spent every penny I had on yet another pipe dream when we'd only just found out we were going to be having a baby, but he was also one of the

104

sweetest people I knew. Had I made a mistake breaking up with him? Was I depriving my unborn child of a constantly present, kind-hearted, indulgent father, or was I protecting it from a life of instability? Ned reddened under my gaze.

I indicated the box. 'Can I . . .?'

Ned smiled. 'Of course.'

I opened the lid. Inside lay a tiny silver tankard with patterns etched around the side. I pulled it out and twisted it round, examining the delicate engravings. It was no bigger than a plum and was just about the loveliest thing I had ever seen.

'Ned, it's beautiful.'

'I got it on eBay,' he said shyly. 'So the baby and I can have our first beer together.'

I smiled and bobbed my head, biting back tears. 'Sounds like a good plan.'

Ned beamed.

Just then the front door flew open and Mum marched out followed by Tabby.

'Oh, shit!' Ned said. 'Bye!' He threw the Volvo into gear, squealed the tyres and screeched down the road.

'DON'T THINK I WON'T GET YOU, YOU ROBBING GINGER BASTARD!' Mum yelled at the fleeing vehicle.

'Mum, shut *up*!' I said, checking the neighbours' windows for curtain twitches.

The car screeched to a halt and suddenly it was reversing back towards us in an uncontrolled wobbly line.

'THAT'S IT, YOU SPINELESS SHITHEAD, COME BACK HERE AND FACE UP TO WHAT YOU'VE DONE!'

'Mum!'

Ned bounced the large car over the kerb and came to an abrupt halt at our feet. A handful of gifts came flying through the open passenger window and tumbled to the ground as Mum made a grabbing motion for his wing mirror.

'For Archie and the girls!' Ned shouted, and he threw the car into gear, jolted off the kerb, hurtled down the tiny street and almost drove on two tyres as he disappeared round the bend.

'I'LL GET YOU!' Mum hollered after him. 'AND WHEN I DO—'

'Oh, no,' I said, looking at the spot on the kerb where Ned's tyres had been.

Mum turned to where I was looking and gasped. 'Tabby!'

'So what did you do with the body?' Alex asked, her pixilated hand popping a bhaji into her mouth.

'Buried her in one of Mum's giant pot plants.' I shifted on my bed and got under the covers. 'She cried a lot, even though she'd been complaining that Tabby doesn't match her wallpaper.'

'Poor Mum,' Alex said with genuine sympathy.

'Alice made a cross out of branches. The kids hung baubles on it and sang "Hail, Holy Queen", the *Sister Act* version.'

'Aw, sweet.'

'The soil was pretty frozen, though. We couldn't dig deep enough, so after the kids went inside Uncle Mike dug her up again and put her in the freezer. He's going to take her home and bury her in the garden.'

'What a weird Christmas,' Alex said with a snort.

'Yeah, and then Sinead got drunk again and gave me a detailed speech on life after childbirth and motherhood.'

'And?'

'Apparently my nipples are going to be so enlarged after breast-feeding that a casual nipple tweak will be more like turning a doorknob.'

'Nice.'

'I will pee myself if I try running, sneezing, trampolining, laughing – basically anything more energetic than sleeping.'

Alex chortled and jammed in another bhaji.

'And apparently if I have sex while I'm still breast-feeding my nipples may spurt milk when I orgasm.'

'So no sex for you for a while.'

'Not ever, probably. But you know, I quite like the songs from *Sister Act*, so maybe I'll forget sex and men and become a singing nun.'

'Glad to see you have realistic plans afoot. I'll stop worrying about you.'

'Oh yes. Definitely stop worrying. Here, I'll give you a little preview: "Triumph all ye Cherubim, *CHERUUUUBIIIIM* ... Sing with us sweet Seraphim, *SERAPHIIIIIM ...*"'

'*HEAVEN AND EARTH RESOUND OUR HYMN!*' Alex bellowed.

Fifteen minutes later I switched off the light and lay down with the tune in my head and a smile in my heart.

CHAPTER TEN

'Darling.' Mum and Charlie arrived in front of me wearing white sporting attire, racket bags slung over their shoulders. 'Aloysius and I are going to play badminton.'

Charlie kissed me on the forehead. I smiled up at him from my prone position on the sofa.

''K.'

'Why don't you come and be line ref? You'll have to stand on Elmer's side' – Mum threw a thumb in Charlie's direction – 'he tends to cheat.'

'I'm not the one who needs to take two rackets.'

'It happened once and you were cheating.' Mum turned back to me, taking in the slovenly clutter on her coffee table. 'Well? Interested, darling? You haven't been out of the house for a week.'

'Nah.' I tossed my magazine to the floor. 'I'm gonna watch a movie.'

Charlie tried to lead Mum away. She didn't budge.

'How do you intend to lose the baby weight?'

'Via some kind of montage.'

'Montage?' Mum said, her tone suspicious.

A smile twitched at the corners of Charlie's mouth.

'Yeah, you know, I start off overweight and miserable in a dirty tracksuit with a crying, snot-encrusted baby. My hair will be greasy, my skin spotty. There'll be shots of me doing laundry and a couple of me bickering with my nagging mother.' I shot Mum a glance. She was not impressed.

'Then I'll see a picture in a magazine of a hot young mother and her cute baby standing next to a guy with organised stubble and white teeth. A few bars of a ballad by Kenny Loggins ring out and determination will set in. As the music gathers pace, I'll struggle a sit-up or two, then all of a sudden I'm swathed in Lycra, running in slow motion through Hyde Park, teeth whitened, hair highlighted, boobs so perky they're almost a shelf, pushing my baby in an ergonomic, kinetically engineered, completely compostable three-wheeler. Men turn their heads away from their pouting model girlfriends to appreciate the loveliness that is me.'

Charlie laughed but stopped at Mum's sharp look.

'Very funny,' she said.

'I thought so.'

'Come on, our court booking's in fifteen minutes.' Charlie winked as he herded Mum away by her arm. 'I'll let you win. And you can save that spare racket for next time.' The front door opened.

'Let me win ... Honestly Marvin, you've never won in your life.' Mum's voice carried from outside.

'I'm a winner every day because I have you, my princess.'

'Yech.'

The door slammed.

What was it about moving back into your parent's house that made you regress to an obnoxious teenager-like state? After realising that financially I had no other option, I'd given up my flat, packed up my stuff and moved into my childhood bedroom. I'd spent the past few weeks moving from room to room in my pyjamas, drinking cups of tea or calling/texting/skyping Alex in Dhaka. Mum had put money into my account with the strict condition that I was to get every last penny back from that thieving impregnator (her words, not mine). After putting in a few calls where Ned had spluttered excuses or talked zealously about vast and unrealistic profit margins for a Moscow Mule-flavoured ice cream, I'd lost the willpower to argue. And I flatly refused to call the police on him as Mum had suggested. I'd have to find another way of paying her back.

New Year's Eve had been a particularly sobering event. Sophie, Helen and I had gone out for dinner with some of Helen's workmates then club-hopped round Shoreditch and Hoxton. I'd watched, sober and with increasing exhaustion, as Helen and Sophie threw back cocktails and danced while Helen's workmates stood around in their angular clothing, adjusting their clear glass specs, looking wearied and unaffected. I'd gone home with the realisation that my life was changing and that I had to get on and find my new place in the world. For lack of a better offer, that new place turned out to be in front of daytime TV in my pyjamas at my mother's house.

I lifted my pyjama top and ran my fingers over my belly. At sixteen weeks it was now a pleasing taut-skinned little bump. I hadn't felt the baby move yet but the pregnancy books assured me it could be any day. There'd been a couple of occasions when I thought I'd felt something. I'd even gathered family round, getting them to place their hands on the tiny rise, but those gurgly ripples always preceded a large and rushed posterior offload (and disgusted looks from the dispersing family), so I was still waiting for my baby to make itself physically known.

After watching four episodes of *Friends* back to back, I looked away from the TV, bored. That's not to say I could ever be bored of watching *Friends*. It was a tonic, an elixir of happiness as accessible as pressing buttons on a remote. I picked up my phone. Eleven thirty in London, which meant it would be about five thirty in the evening in Dhaka. Alex answered after three rings.

'Hel-looo,' she trilled.

'I'm blue,' I said in the saddest voice I could muster.

'Really? I'm a golden-brown colour.'

'Ha ha.' I moved positions on the couch, getting comfortable so I could have a long and distracting conversation with my sister. She sounded rather more chipper than when I'd spoken to her the day before and she'd found a family of rats (and by family she was talking distant cousins and six degrees of the rat version of Kevin Bacon) behind the sagging ceiling panels above her bed. 'Are you drunk?'

'Noooo,' she said seriously. 'Just alcoholically enhanced.' She giggled. 'So what's up? Why are you blue?'

'I've watched every episode of *Friends* from the beginning to the very end when they all move out and Jennifer Aniston cries way more than necessary for the content of the scene.'

'Right. And that has made you blue?'

'No, not the fact that it's ended; I can just press play from the beginning, of course. But it's just, well, the crying isn't realistic, you know? No one would ever cry that much over their friends moving house in the same city. I think they allowed Jennifer to get a little carried away with her own emotions over the series ending and not being true to "Rachel's" emotions. Don't you think?' There was silence at the end of the phone. 'Are you there?'

'You have issues,' Alex said. 'Are you really talking about that Jennifer Aniston over-cry again?'

I was worried Alex might curtail our conversation, so I scrabbled to come up with something else to keep her on the line.

'OK, OK, we can talk about something else . . . Hey, you know Dr Phil?'

'I gotta go,' Alex sighed. 'Seriously, Em, you have a freaky obsession with Dr Phil.'

'He has such a great relationship with his wife, and—'

'I'm going!'

My shoulders slumped in defeat. 'OK.'

'Love you.'

'Yadda yadda, whatever. Love you too.' I hung up.

I scrolled through the phone a bit before deciding to call Helen. She was always up for a lament on Dr Phil and the merits of dating a mega-rich psychologist with his own TV show. Helen's phone went straight to answer machine. Of course it would. It was Saturday morning. She was probably still in bed, a doting and naked man at her side. Sophie! I dialled her number.

'Hi Em!' she puffed. I heard a muffled voice in the background. 'What's up? How are you? It's so nice of you to ring—'

'Soph. Chill.'

'Oh yeah.' She exhaled. 'Um, so how are you?'

I heard the voice again. A male voice. Sophie covered the mouthpiece and shushed someone.

'Do you have a guy there?' I tried to hide my annoyance, as it was completely unreasonable.

'Ah ... no?' Sophie had all the cunning of a 2-year-old with chocolate over their face, trying to blame the empty packet of biscuits on their stuffed Elmo toy.

'Who is he?'

'He's ah, he is, ah ... there's no one here. It's ...' I could almost hear the cogs in her head making their slow rotation. 'It's ... my cat. He has a cold.'

I rolled my eyes. 'Well I was just ringing to see if you wanted to go and get some lunch, but you probably have to look after your "cat", I guess.'

'Yeah.'

After we said goodbye, I was left with a nasty taste in my mouth and a feeling in the pit of my stomach I couldn't explain. I felt betrayed by my friends and couldn't understand why. Dr Phil would have some insight, but his show didn't start for another few hours so I decided to go into the kitchen and see if anything inspired me in there. I stood at the kitchen table looking out of the French doors to the diminutive back terrace soaked from a constant drizzle. I pulled out a chair, sat down and slumped, my head in my hands. An unoccupied mind and an occupied uterus.

An insistent rapping at the door woke me. I lifted my head and realised I'd fallen asleep on my folded arms at the kitchen table. Wiping a dried bit of dribble off my cheek, I opened the front door. Alice and Jess flew in, attached themselves to my thighs and squealed 'Hi Emma!' in unison.

'Hi girls.' I prised them off. 'Where's Mum?'

'In the car. Millie pulled Archie's hair,' Alice said disapprovingly.

'Archie called Millie a little bitch,' Jess added.

'And Mum is on the phone to the movies.' Alice summed up.

I sent Alice and Jess to the kitchen and went outside. I found Sinead sitting in the front of her four-by-four on the phone, Millie in the back crying and Archie studying what looked to be a storyboard, a list of pictures put together by a director of the shots required for a day of filming.

'Where'd you get that, Archie?' I said, unbuckling him from his booster seat, rain trickling down my back.

Sinead waved at me while 'uh-huh'-ing on the phone.

'The fat lady gave it to me.' He pointed to a picture of a small cartoon boy next to a tent. 'That's me.'

'OK,' I said, putting Archie down on the cobblestones and wondering what the hell he was talking about.

He trotted inside, shielding his storyboard from the rain. On seeing me, Millie stopped crying and extended her chubby arms. I pulled her from her car seat. She gave me a wide-mouthed grin and a river of shiny saliva escaped. Sinead stepped out of the car and followed us in, holding her bag over her head, still on the phone.

'Well, can I appoint my own?' she said, stalking inside and shutting the front door against the elements. 'No, I can't do it . . . because I have a life, that's why . . .'

I plonked down on the sofa with Millie on my lap. She lunged forward and began playing with my necklace. Sinead paced the floor.

'He wasn't trying to be offensive . . . she *is* fat . . . OK, fine, thick-boned . . . she needs thicker skin if you ask me . . . Fine. I'll get one myself. Thank you.'

Sinead threw her phone in her bag. 'Shite. Got any baking?'

While I made tea, Sinead sat at the kitchen table buttering cheese muffins for her ever-hungry children and explaining the reason for the storyboard.

'Archie got a job in a movie.' She got up, poured glasses of milk and handed them out.

'A movie?' I said, looking at Archie.

He turned the page of his storyboard and studied it with his elbows on the table and his cheeks resting on his fists. His muffin sat untouched next to him. In stark contrast Millie had muffin in her hair and ears and Alice and Jess had milk moustaches and were unsuccessfully seeing who could be the first to fit a whole muffin into their mouth.

'Yep. He plays a ghost. Or he sees ghosts. Or something.' She sat down and nibbled on a muffin.

'A proper acting part? With lines and everything? On a proper movie set?' I stopped mid-tea-strain.

Sinead nodded, her mouth full.

'Great.' I got back to the tea with a little more force than necessary. 'I've spent the last six years of my life making shit TV with third-rate actors and my 4-year-old cousin gets a part in a movie. Please tell me it doesn't have Emily Blunt in it.'

'It doesn't have Emily Blunt in it.'

'Good. Who's in it?'

'I don't bloody know,' Sinead said, pulling the plate of muffins away from Jess and Alice. 'They all look the same to me. Teeth, hair, boobs.' She gesticulated wildly to show abundance. 'Anyway, Archie's chaperone just quit, so now I have to find one or go in myself.'

'Quit? Why?' I sat next to Millie and leant away as her sticky fingers reached for my hair.

'She offends easily, apparently,' Sinead said, shuffling primly.

I raised my eyebrows but Sinead ignored the appeal for

elaboration. She watched Archie affectionately, then her eyes widened.

'You could do it!'

'What?!'

'It makes perfect sense!'

'I can't. I've got—'

'Got what, exactly?' Sinead said, frowning. 'A date with daytime TV and more cellulite to cultivate?'

I opened my mouth wide, offended to the core. How dare she? Sinead, with her busy schedule of squeezing out kids between lunches with her friends. Although I did have to concede that there was a rather large amount of cellulite gathering in the gluteus maximus region. If ever I were lucky enough to have a close encounter with a man again, an amorous butt fondle would feel more like caressing a flaccid old cauliflower through a plastic bag.

'I've never been a chaperone. I wouldn't know what to do.'

It was a lie. I was fully capable of doing it. It was just . . . I didn't know, exactly.

'Bollocks,' Sinead said.

'I'm not CRB checked.'

'We can get that done on Monday.'

'I'd have to do a course.'

'It's a one-day seminar.'

'It can take ages to get a chaperone licence. All the paperwork . . .'

'Dad has contacts; we'll get it pushed through in a day.'

'But . . .' I searched for another excuse.

'But nothing,' Sinead said, triumphant. 'It's a perfect way for you to get off your arse and back into the real world.'

I picked up my muffin. 'Irish bloody princess. What do you know about the real world?'

Alice and Jess had been following our exchange like spectators at a ping-pong tournament. With the banter over, Jess picked up her milk and gulped, most unladylike.

'Mummy,' Alice said. 'Archie's storyboard has a bloody head on it.'

CHAPTER ELEVEN

Archie's storyboard did indeed have a bloody head on it. Because Archie was starring in a B-grade zombie movie that, if my predictions were correct, would go straight to the DVD bargain bins. Archie was playing a young boy, Billy, whose father, while on a camping trip, gets bitten by a zombie virus-ridden cat and becomes 'infected'. From what I could deduce with my brief skimming of the entire script (a skill I had picked up after years of having to read the most mundane scripts known to the world of celluloid), Billy and his twin sister Bella had to find their way out of the woods, taking care to avoid the zombie cat pack, some zombie campers (including Daddy) and get back to Mummy in London and convince her to return to the woods and kiss her zombiefied husband. Because Daddy was only a 'beating heart' zombie, not a full undead, with his wife's love he could become human again. Apparently. (I wasn't sure how the specifics would go down with zombie fanatics. I'd have to ask Douglas, a Comic-Con-attending, *Lord of the Rings* costume-owning, *Game of Thrones* forum-debating weirdo.) As the twins moved through the woods they'd encounter other campers fleeing the zombies (both the cat and people variety). It was a tongue-in-cheek slasher/zombie/romance/family film. If that is even a thing.

I put down the script and looked at Sinead. We'd moved to the living room where the girls were building a cushion fort and Archie sat studying his storyboard.

'Did you even read it?' I said after explaining the basic storyline.

'Er . . . no,' she said with a guilty smile.

'Well, he has quite a big part, you know. And it's zombies, not ghosts. *Zombies*.' I looked over at my cousin. Mature for his age, but nevertheless he was only four. 'There are scenes with girls running around in bras too. And one where a zombie gets chopped up in a deli salami slicer. The script actually says "guts fly across the room".' I turned back to Sinead and gave her a good hard stare. '*Guts*, Sinead. Guts and bra.'

'Hmmm,' she said, noncommittal.

'How'd he get the job?'

'He was spotted in Regent's Park a couple of weeks ago,' she said. 'This lady came up to us and said she was scouting for a replacement because the original "Billy" had broken his leg two days before the movie started. All the other children were running around screeching and Archie was sitting on a bench watching a lame pigeon trying to eat another lame pigeon.' She looked over at Archie with his storyboard. 'What do you call that? Life imitating art?'

'I don't know what you call it,' I said. 'What did Mike say?'

'Oh, you can't tell him,' Sinead said, her green eyes wide. 'You can't. I forbid it.'

'You can't forbid me!'

'Yes I can, I'm your aunt. And as your aunt, I forbid you from telling my husband that his son is starring in a zombie guts–and–bras movie.'

'Are you listening to yourself?'

We looked at Archie, so innocently perceptive.

I exhaled. 'Well, the least I can do is be his chaperone.'

Sinead's head shot up. 'Seriously?' Her eyebrows were in excited little points. 'You're going to do it?'

'Someone needs to make sure he isn't comprehensively corrupted by the time he's five.' I smiled.

I was actually quietly thrilled. I'd been out of work for only five weeks, but when you were used to working twelve- to fourteen-hour days, five weeks was a lifetime. On a Monday, Friday night would seem an unreachable eternity away. And I did have to admit, eating doughnuts and watching *Oprah* reruns was losing its appeal. Mum would return home, and I'd follow her round the house chittering and chattering about Dr Phil and Oprah and Jeremy Kyle like they were my chums. And although I felt Dr Phil really did care, I missed having 3D friends.

An hour or so later, after Sinead had organised the fast-forwarding of my chaperone licence, Mum and Charlie walked in followed by Uncle Mike and a few minutes later Grandma's lawyer arrived with his briefcase, his three-piece suit and his big words and we sat round the fireplace with cups of tea. The lawyer opened his briefcase, rustled papers and said things I didn't understand. There were specifics about certain paintings and jewellery. And other things with no real monetary value: Uncle Mike got recipe books, Mum a scarf collection, Sinead got a fur coat she'd always coveted. Certain first edition books went to the kids and Charlie was given her gardening books with handwritten notes in the margins. After what felt like forty days and forty nights of legal speak, the lawyer turned his austere gaze to me.

'Emma.'

I straightened in my seat. My body was used to having an afternoon nap and the man's dreary voice was just the right tone to lull me to sleep.

'Yes,' I said, my voice croaky.

'Your grandmother left you something.'

'Uh-huh.'

'To you and your sister, Alexandra.'

'Uh-huh,' I said, trying to sound interested.

'A three-bedroom cottage in Wimbledon.'

'Uh-huh – what the *fuck*?!'

The lawyer straightened his glasses. Mum, nestled against Charlie, grinned.

'You knew?' I said.

She nodded. 'Mum had it written into her will after your father left.'

123

'Does Alex know?'

'No, I thought you'd like to tell her.'

Charlie kissed her forehead. I sat quietly, processing the news. Just this morning I didn't have a penny to my name. Now I had a job and had become a London property owner. The cottage was round the corner from Sinead and Uncle Mike's house. Uncle Mike had decided to move close to Grandma when it became apparent Sinead was not going to stop chucking out kids. It sat in the middle of a lovely row of five other cottages on the edge of the common. Grandma had her one painted a soft lavender about twenty years ago and the neighbours had followed suit, painting theirs in various sherbet shades. Roses lined the front garden and wisteria grew over the archway at the front gate. Rhubarb grew in clumps in the back garden and ended up in a crumble served with home-made custard. And now the tiny cottage with the mosaicked sundial I didn't know how to read was mine. And Alex's, of course, whenever she chose to leave her philanthropic lifestyle.

'So,' Sinead said, clapping her hands together. 'Looks like we have a new babysitter round the corner.'

The next morning we stood shoulder to boobs (Mum in her snakeskin Louboutins, towering above me in my Converse) on the footpath outside Grandma's cottage. It was freezing but the sky was clear and the low-slung January sun reflected off the cottage windows. Young families wrapped in puffa coats like sleeping bags headed onto the common taking the opportunity to get some vitamin D while it was on offer.

'You open it,' Mum said, putting her own set of keys in her Chanel handbag. 'It's yours now.'

It hadn't taken much for the property to be handed over to Alex and me. We signed a few things, Alex doing it digitally from afar, and I was ceremoniously given the keys. Mum and I were there to check what needed to be done before I moved in. Which couldn't happen soon enough. Mum had banned anything high-carb from her house, and I'd started hiding pastries in my knicker drawer. I'd ended up with an ant problem and crumby smalls.

'It's going to be weird, her not here,' I said, walking under the bare knotted branches of the dormant wisteria.

'Hmm,' Mum said.

I slid the key in the lock and opened the leaded-light door. Sun flooded down the hall from the French doors at the back of the house. It was as if she had just popped to the shops. Her purple wellies sat next to the front door and her winter coat hung on the coat stand. On the half-circle table sat a small pile of unopened mail. Mum squared her shoulders, shook her hair into position and stepped inside. The stillness was unnerving. Grandma's talcum-y perfume still hung faintly in the air. The cottage was a simple square with a central hallway. Two bedrooms, a bathroom and a narrow staircase led off the hall, which then opened out to the kitchen/living room at the rear.

After a brief, grim-faced glance into Grandma's faded floral bedroom Mum headed down the hall, her heels sounding out slow taps on the wooden floor. I followed, my

Converse making squeaky noises. I stopped by some photos on the wall. There was one I loved of the family gathered round Uncle Mike asleep in a wicker pushchair. My grandparents beamed at the camera and Mum, nine years old and sporting a home-made smocked pinafore, looked contemptuously down on her new brother. It was the same look she'd used the other day when I'd shown her a pair of second-hand maternity jeans I'd bought on eBay.

I arrived in the kitchen/living room and approached Mum, who stood motionless by the sofa. The kitchen was to the left, with terracotta tile flooring and a round pine table in the centre, the wooden edges softened with age. To the right was the living area, with a beige patterned sofa and two matching armchairs drawn up round the fireplace. Grandma's knitting bag sat beside her favourite armchair. Double French doors led from the living room to the bricked terrace and the flat grassy garden beyond. I looked at the kitchen, cosy and comfortable. Recipe books sat in busy piles in the window above the sink. Mum made a whimpering noise and clasped her hands to her chest, her handbag dangling in the crook of her elbow.

'Mum?' I put my hand on her shoulder. 'Are you OK?'

She nodded. 'I look at this place,' she fanned her arm round the room, 'and I just think, why didn't she let me decorate?'

'What?'

'Those beige sofas. That ugly red carpet.' She spun on her heel towards the kitchen, grimacing. 'Varnished wood panelling. Why?'

'Mum?'

'I'm all right, darling. I really can't understand bad décor, I just . . .' She picked up a hand-crocheted cushion of browns, yellows, magenta and turquoise and tossed it back down in disgust. 'Can't understand.'

'OK . . .' I stepped away as she ran a condemnatory fingertip over the back of the sofa.

I walked towards the French doors and looked out at the cold garden. The trees were bare, the branches spiky and cruel-looking. In spring the garden was a riot of clashing colours. Fuchsia bougainvillea would tumble down the left-hand side of the pergola and honeysuckle would wind up the other side to greet it. Multiple pots with multiple patterns would be clustered together spilling over with multiple-hued flora. I was gazing at the side wall of the garden, where runner beans grew over the bricks in summer, when a wrinkled face appeared at the top of the wall. Untamed wisps of Antarctic-white hair had broken free from a low bun and hovered round the inquisitive face like tufts torn from a knot of candyfloss. Her eyes darted across the garden like the crazy tracks of a bee on a hot summer's day. When her gaze landed on me, her eyes widened, her neck elongated and she ducked out of sight. Before I'd had a chance to blink she was back again with a loud-hailer in one hand and what looked to be a handycam in the other.

'INTRUDER!' her warbling voice and a shrill blast of feedback screeched through the megaphone. 'INTRUDER, BE WARNED – I HAVE YOU UNDER

SURVEILLANCE! YOU CAN TAKE YOUR CRACK PIPES AND PROSTITUTION ELSEWHERE!'

Mum rushed to my side.

'Who the hell is that?' I said as Mum fiddled with the locks.

The little old lady thrust her head round the side of the raised loud-hailer and scrunched up her face menacingly.

'WHO'S THERE? THE POLICE HAVE BEEN ALERTED! SHOW YOURSELF!'

Mum flung open the French doors. 'Harriet!' She took long strides towards the tenacious old lady. 'Put that away! It's me, Diana!'

The lady lowered the loud-hailer and squinted.

'Oh Diana, dear! I didn't recognise you. How *are* you?' Her face crinkled into a sweet smile as she took in Mum's attire. Tight black jeans, impossibly high snakeskin heels and a Burberry trench. 'That's a lovely parka, dear. And who is this delightful young lady?' The old lady looked down from the top of the seven-foot wall and her mouth curved into an expectant smile. The apples of her cheeks rose, arranging the wrinkles into numerous soft furrows. Her skin was lightly tanned, like a farmer's wife or someone vaguely Spanish. She looked like a friendly walnut.

'This is my daughter, Emma,' Mum said, putting an arm round my shoulder. 'Emma, this is Harriet Spencer. She moved in next door a couple of weeks before . . . before your grandmother died.' She squeezed my shoulder.

'Ah, very sad, that,' Harriet said, pursing her lips and

shaking her head. 'Such a nice lady. We were looking forward to being her neighbours. Made us feel very welcome, she did. Made us some scones the day we moved in. I've kept my eyes on her cottage, I have. An empty place like this, you have to be careful of squatters.'

'Harriet, what on earth are you doing with that?' Mum said, pointing a painted fingernail at the loud-hailer.

Harriet's gnarled hands flew protectively to it. She reminded me of a squirrel.

'For safety.' She peered down at us, eyes narrowed. 'A woman of my age cannot rely on her physical ability to protect herself from the murderers and the muggers and the sexual opportunists. I take it everywhere now that I live in the city.' She finished with a brusque nod. 'And!' She perked up. 'I find it quite useful around the house.' She raised the loud-hailer again and faced it towards her own property. 'ARTHUR DEAR, PUT THE KETTLE ON! WE HAVE GUESTS!'

She lowered it and smiled, sweet as a choirgirl.

CHAPTER TWELVE

'Daddy tried to eat my bwains—'

'Try to say "brains",' I said. 'With an "R". Brrrrains.'

'Bwai- Bwai … Bwains … shit.' Archie frowned. 'Brrrrains.'

'Well done.' I returned Sinead's mirthful look with a dis-approving one.

'What do I say in this picture?'

Because Archie couldn't yet read properly he'd learn his lines by studying the storyboard and memorising what to say in each picture. He remembered entire scenes better than some actors I'd worked with. But I guessed Archie's brain wasn't addled with cocaine or consumed by calorie-consumption maths. I twisted from the front seat of Sinead's four-by-four to see the picture Archie was pointing to. It showed a lady running from a zombie, her dressing gown opening to reveal a gratuitous amount of cleavage, and 'Billy' holding a fire poker.

'You say, "*Run, Mummy, run!*".'

Archie repeated the line a few times to himself, committing it to his astounding little memory, while Sinead pulled the four-by-four up at a line of orange cones, one with a sign saying UNIT BASE. A man wearing a padded parka with the hood pulled tight around his face and a rollie hanging out of the corner of his mouth directed us to a car park at the foot of a glass block of apartments. Sinead kissed Archie goodbye and squealed her tyres towards relative freedom for the next few hours.

I guided Archie into the lift, bustling with anxious energy. I'd not worked for weeks, and when I had it had been with the same show for six years. I knew the actors; I knew the crew. I'd become safe in my little soap opera hell. I was nervous about being on a proper movie set. I'd read in Archie's cast list that Scott Vander, a multi ab-ed actor who did a lot of undie and whisky commercials, was the main star. When I'd excitedly mentioned it to Sinead she'd had neither a clue nor a care. Helen demanded I take her to the wrap party as soon as I told her, then set about planning her 'get sex' outfit.

I yawned one of those gaping yawns where the back of your head touches your shoulder blades. It was a shock to be up, clothed and out of the house by 7 a.m. Getting dressed had been most problematic. Parting with my pink leopard-print flannelette pyjamas had been upsetting. There'd been a moment where I thought I wasn't quite ready for out-of-doors attire.

The lift doors opened on to an enormous room in endless

shades of cream and white thronging with busy bodies. Out on the balcony lighting assistants were hanging large swathes of black fabric, inventively called 'blacks', over the windows. Grips with muscled arms and overloaded tool belts laid track across the living room floor. A member of the art department walked past carrying a box labelled 'blood pouches'. People stood in clusters jabbing at scripts, discussing shots or jamming food into their mouths while sorting through equipment.

'Hi Archie!' A skinny blonde girl with early-twenties flawless skin jumped in front of us with far too much energy for such an unsociable hour. 'How are you, sweetie?'

She crouched, hands on her denim-covered knees. Ugg boots covered her slim calves and rather than looking frumpy and unkempt as I felt I looked in mine, she looked casually hip and off-duty model-ish. Her jeans were impossibly tight (how did *she* avoid camel toe? Was there some kind of insert on the market for camel-toe avoidance I'd yet to discover?). Her off-the-shoulder black t-shirt showed the strap of her hot-pink bra, which matched her nail polish. Mum would love her.

'Hi Amy,' Archie said with a small smile.

I thought I could see the beginnings of his first crush.

'You must be Emma? Archie's new chaperone?' She stood and put her hand out. 'I'm Amy, the Third AD.'

I shook her hand. I knew the Third Assistant Director job well. In my not-too-long-ago life they would have reported to me. Now I couldn't go to the bathroom without first checking with Amy if there was time.

Amy rushed us into Wardrobe (back down the lift to a heated trailer in the car park), where Archie was greeted by a host of voguishly dressed males and females. I couldn't understand it. When I'd been a Second AD the wardrobe department was at work at the same hour as me (ungodly) yet they found the time, and the inclination, to put together an outfit that contained non-essential decorative items. Like waistcoats or knotted scarves that were worn at non-neck-warming places like the left hip belt notch or round the wrist. Given the opportunity to look awesome or have an extra four minutes' sleep and just wear a t-shirt and jeans from the washing pile and look like a reject from a Louis Walsh 90s band, I'd go for Louis Walsh every time.

Once dressed, we were escorted through the apartment to Make-up, passing crew who were doing the name/job drop ('Oh, I just came off blah with blah'), while members of the art department rushed around with harried looks on their faces adjusting paintings, taping down carpet edges and giving stern looks to anyone who was in the way. People were perched on sofa arms, kitchen stools or wooden camera boxes making notes in folders and having intense conversations with each other. Everyone held, or was in close proximity to, a paper cup of coffee.

'That's the children's greenroom.' Amy pointed to a closed door.

She swished her slim hips down the hall past some mus-cled grips in snug vests and industrial-looking tool belts who flexed and made noises like 'cor', 'orright?' and 'hey babes'.

Her radio sprang to life, a bossy female voice – probably the First AD – asking for a time estimation on Melody. Amy unclipped the radio from her waistband, gave an efficient 'checking now' and opened a door to a gleaming marble bathroom. A console ran the length of the room, and it was here that two make-up artists had set up their stations.

'Hi ladies!' Amy said in a singsong voice.

'Hey, Ames,' said a friendly-looking make-up girl.

She was tending to the tresses of a dazzling blonde woman who I definitely recognised. I had the feeling I'd seen her in a suit with a gun. *CSI*, maybe? *Criminal Minds*?

'Guys, this is Emma,' Amy said. 'Archie's chaperone.'

'Oh, hi there, I'm Melody,' the actress said in a Californian accent. 'I play Natalie, the mother.'

'Nice to meet you,' I said, taking in her smooth skin and aquamarine eyes.

'And this is Claire and Caroline,' Amy said, indicating the make-up girls, who raised their bangle-laden hands respectively. 'Claire does Archie's make-up.'

Claire would have been very much at home in a Sex Pistols music video. Her platinum hair sat in a teased quiff, blood-red lipstick emphasised her pout and rips in her grey jeans showed off a lot of pale but firm thigh. Archie trotted over to her and she helped him into the make-up chair. Bangles and studded leather straps took up the majority of her forearms, and I wondered if they doubled as some kind of resistance training.

Amy turned back to me. 'We usually do make-up in the

vans, but it's like two degrees down there today and the costumes don't exactly provide much warmth.'

'I'm already in my costume!' Melody trilled, opening up her robe to expose her naked torso.

Her suntanned breasts bounced gently as she did a little jiggle.

'Melody!' Caroline said, tapping her on the shoulder with the hairbrush and giggling.

Claire smiled like it was nothing she hadn't seen before. Melody tinkled a laugh and wrapped her robe back round her tiny waist.

'Caroline, can I get a time check?' Amy said, the impromptu flashing barely registering.

I watched Archie chat comfortably with Claire, while Caroline and Melody discussed hair-parting options and Amy listened like she gave a fuck when she probably just wanted the actress out of the chair and on set because she knew any hair parting that happened now would be ruffled in minutes, on account of the actress being about to leap out of bed and run away from a zombie. Claire said she'd bring Archie back to the greenroom, so I stepped through the door and into the path of a gasp-inducing man.

'Sorry.' I moved round his well-proportioned frame as Amy bustled out of the make-up room.

'Oh, hi Andrew,' she said, adjusting her facial muscles so her cheeks hollowed and her lips pouted. 'What's up?'

'Do you have a room I can put these lenses in?' He held an industrial-looking black case. 'I don't want them knocked.'

'Yeah, sure,' Amy said, eyelashes aflutter.

Andrew was quite a sight. His strong shoulders were apparent even beneath his fleece. At least six foot two, he stood as straight as a Corinthian column. His dark hair was dishevelled in a practised way. A day or two's stubble grazed his jaw and tanned skin set off his blue eyes.

'You can put them in the master bedroom,' she cooed. 'No one's allowed in there. Just don't tell anyone I let you, OK?' She grinned and walked off, forgetting I even existed.

'Thanks.' Andrew followed Amy's lithe figure down the hall without so much as a glance in my direction.

'How was your weekend?' she asked, disappearing round a corner.

'Great. Went to the Cotswolds. Yours?'

And they were gone. I stood, incredulous, then trudged along the hall looking for the door to the greenroom.

'This is Emma. Oh, hi Emma, how are you, what do you do here?' I mimicked Amy and Andrew childishly. *'Oh, me? I'm a chaperone. You know, nothing important. You can totally ignore me if you want. Oh OK, Emma, we'll do just that. Oh my, Andrew, what big muscles you have, oh, and Amy, you have such small hips, do you mind if I grab them tightly while I shag you from behind? Of course, I will be looking at myself in the mirror while I do you, is that OK? How does my jaw look? Strong and manly?'* I opened the door to the kids' greenroom, still muttering to myself, and was greeted by a man in glasses, a woollen vest and tighty-whities, jogging floppy-limbed from one side of the room to the other.

'Aghhh, a zombie,' he read in a toneless voice from a script in his hands, his sagging white bottom jiggling with each footfall. 'Aaaah. Aaaah.'

'Oh, sorry.' I coughed back a snigger. 'I was just . . . I have the wrong room. Sorry.' I shut the door and scuttled away.

'I've also chaperoned on *Harry Potter*. That was really hard work. But the absolute best was a movie I did with Clive Owen. He's sex on a stick, don't you think? What other jobs have you chaperoned on? Any I'd know?' The verbally and physically well-endowed other chaperone, Martha, sloshed another spoonful of chicken curry onto her avalanche of rice.

I stood beside her abundant frame waiting for my turn at the steaming bain-marie. We'd spent the morning shooting 'Billy', 'Bella', 'Natalie' and 'Neighbour' (the guy in his pants) running around the apartment trying to get away from a zombie (who was an extra named Peter I'd once booked to be an overdose victim). We'd broken for lunch just before 'Natalie' harpoons the zombie with a fire poker. So while the majority of the cast and crew ate lunch, the art department, SPFX and Costume were rigging Peter's chest with squibs – small remote-controlled exploding devices filled with fake blood – and testing the retractable poker.

'This is my first chaperone job, but I—'

'O-M-G. *Really*?' Martha stopped, mid-spoon. 'Well, I can teach you *everything*.' She turned back to the food and resumed fervent ladling. 'I'll lend you my revised *Filming with Children* handbook; I've made additional notes. Always, *always* have it with you. You can*not* let the ADs push you around.'

'Actually I'm a—'

'They have absolutely no regard for the child. Oh look, poppadoms.'

The serving spoon was relinquished, with a nauseatingly sweaty handle, and Martha progressed down the line stacking her plate and preaching about never going over the legal child hours and how to read a call sheet, her deep-set eyes flicking in my direction, assessing my rapture.

'Hey. Going OK?' Amy arrived in the lunch line and grabbed a plate.

'Yes thanks,' I said, glancing in the direction of the crew eating their lunch. Andrew was sitting with the director having a deep, hand-gesturing discussion. He'd turned out to be the DOP/Camera Operator.

'It's a big crew. I haven't been on a shoot with this many people before.'

'Really?' she said, walking past the rice and spooning the tiniest amount of curry onto her plate. 'Do you mostly chaperone for TV?'

'No, this is my first chaperone job.' I looked over at Archie and Tilly, the girl playing his sister, 'Bella'. They sat side by side eating mini-burgers and fries and looked just like a real brother and sister. Martha was fussing with Tilly's burger, trying to cut it into toddler-sized bites.

'I'm actually a Second AD.'

'No way!' Amy said, perking up. 'Why are you doing this?'

'I'm doing my aunt a favour. Archie's my cousin.' I decided against telling her about the quitting/near firing of my last job.

'Cool!' she said with new interest.

Martha waved at me from across the room. 'Emma! Emma, over here!' She patted a seat next to her.

After I'd eaten and listened to Martha list the stars she'd worked with, all told with a gleam in her eye and a bit of broccoli in her teeth, I took Archie for a walk outside. I wanted to get him away from Martha, who was busy grilling Tilly about learning her lines. She was only five, for god's sake.

'Do you like acting?' I asked Archie as we strolled hand in hand.

He seemed so unfazed about being on set; he delivered his lines, remembered his moves and chatted with the director like he'd been doing it for years.

'Yip,' he said.

'And you're sure you understand that poker didn't really go into Peter's chest? It was just a trick poker, wasn't it?'

'Yip.' Archie said. 'It's wetwactable.'

'Retractable. Exactly.'

We walked around the car park looking into the backs of the film vehicles. The wardrobe trailer held a harried lady on a sewing machine. Two assistants prepared an afternoon tea platter in the catering bus. Claire, the Sex Pistols-esque make-up artist, leant against the make-up trailer swathed in a fur-trimmed parka, talking on her mobile and puffing on a Marlboro. Sitting on the back of one of the lighting trucks were two guys from the sound department. A distinct marijuana-y smell wafted from their direction. They waved at Archie.

'Emma?' Archie stopped and looked up at me. 'What's a ore chasm?'

'Um . . .'

'Now there's a question,' a voice said behind me.

I spun round and saw Andrew jabbing at his phone. He pressed a final button and slid the phone into his jacket pocket.

'Hi, I'm Andrew,' he said, extending his hand.

'Emma.' I felt my cheeks burn through the cold. Andrew was the opposite of Ned. Burly, manly, deep-voiced and probably in possession of a strapping penis. 'I'm Archie's chaperone.'

'Do you know what a ore chasm is?' Archie said. 'Emma doesn't.'

I tried to laugh a response, which came out as a strangled snort, and then coughed as I choked on my own saliva.

Andrew chuckled. 'I think Steve and Damo might know.' He pointed over to the sound guys. 'Why don't you go and ask them?'

'OK.' Archie took confident steps across the car park towards the back of the lighting truck.

'Let's see what they come up with,' Andrew said with a mischievous grin.

I smiled while trying to undertake what everyone else seems able to do: talk and breathe and control their own saliva without asphyxiating themselves.

'I haven't seen you before,' he said. 'What happened to Fran?'

'Quit, I think,' I said. 'Archie's my cousin. I'm not really a proper chaperone, I'm just helping out.'

'Cool.' He bobbed his head. 'Archie's a great kid, real little professional.'

We watched Archie ask the sound guys his question. They looked at each other, slapped their knees and threw their heads back, laughing. Archie waited patiently at the foot of the truck for an answer. The lanky, dreadlocked sound guy, Steve, raised his gangly arms above his head and flailed them around while the other one, stocky and short with a shaved head, sat grinning and nodding. I could feel the warmth from Andrew's body even through my coat. I stole a glance at him. His profile was Bond-like. Strong nose, pinkish lips that had the faintest pout about them and an angular jaw. A faint ski mask shape was apparent in his tan and a taut tendon in his neck let me know there was a strong body under his parka.

'Andrew!' Amy appeared round the side of a trailer, clutching her arms round her thin waist against the cold. 'They want you inside to talk about the next scene.'

'OK.' Andrew turned to me. 'Nice to meet you.'

'You too,' I said, smiling, wishing I'd bothered to wear

some concealer. Well, wishing I bothered to own some, at least.

Andrew joined Amy and rested an arm casually across her shoulders.

'Emma,' Archie said, tugging at my coat. 'It's a bomb.'

'What is?' I watched Andrew hold the door to the apartment block open for Amy.

'A ore chasm. It's a bomb.'

'Oh, right,' I said, refocusing my attention on him. 'Is it?'

'Yes. And girls and boys fight over who gets to let off the bomb first. Because when it explodes there's a party.'

'Hmmm,' I said, looking over at the two sound guys.

They gave the thumbs up.

'I want a ore chasm at my five-year-old birthday.'

'Do you?' I said, ushering him back inside for the next instalment of 'guts and bras' for preschoolers.

CHAPTER THIRTEEN

I tucked the last of my clean washing in my suitcase as the doorbell ding-donged through the house.

'I'll get it!' I hollered, clomping down the stairs.

It was Sophie, Helen and Douglas arriving to help me move into the cottage. Charlie was in Manchester giving a lecture about sustainable insulation, and I hadn't asked for Mum's help in case she was tempted to redecorate the cottage with, say, the vintage model skeleton she'd had flocked in neon fuchsia last week. Archie and I had survived our first day together on the film set and he wasn't called again until the next Monday. There hadn't been *that* many guts, and he'd not really noticed Melody's half-exposed bosom, so I didn't yet feel guilty about 'not-saying-a-word-to-your-uncle-or-I'll-tell-your-mother-you-got-up-the-duff-on-purpose' as Sinead had so sweetly instructed.

Mum and I had cleared Grandma's cottage with the help of Sinead and the kids. We'd had five broken ornaments, honey spilt in the knitting box, a tumble down the stairs (Alice), a sprained wrist from jumping on the beds (Jess) and Archie had somehow managed to get BBC *News* stuck on Mandarin voice-overs. Despite Mum's protestations I'd decided to keep most of the furnishings. Like the old beige sofa she detested. I remembered cuddling next to Grandma on the sofa while she peeled and sliced an apple for Alex and I with a paring knife. One slice for me, one for Alex, one for herself. Then she'd start again. Those apples doled out by the fire were the best I'd ever tasted.

I opened the front door to a freezing blast of air and three beaming faces.

'Hi!' Sophie said, throwing her arms round my neck a little too enthusiastically. 'I'm so excited!'

I prised her stripy-gloved hands from around my neck. 'That's ... great, Soph,' I said, looking at her tiny frame. It seemed all the cells in her body were jostling with joyfulness.

'Pixie Twit is a little high on life at the moment,' Helen said. 'Now move it, Tinkerbell, it's freezing out here.' She gave Sophie a friendly shove over the threshold, planted a perfumed kiss on my cheek and walked through the door, peeling off her coat.

Douglas, a grey woollen coat buttoned to his chin, came in rubbing his leather-gloved hands together.

'Good morning, Emma. Chilly day for a move.' He gave me a cold-lipped peck on the cheek and joined Helen and Sophie in the unloading of coats, scarves, gloves and hats.

'So, this hot guy at your new job.' Helen unwound a ruby

knitted scarf from her neck. 'Should I be meeting him? And by meeting, I mean—'

'I know what you mean,' I laughed, happy to have my friends around me again. I'd been missing my daily office banter with Sophie and Douglas and the fifty or so emails Helen and I would exchange in the average workday. 'But you can forget it. I don't want to look at him and know you've had your lips wrapped round his whatever a few hours before.' I smiled but pointed my index finger to show I meant business.

'OK, OK, bossy.' She flicked my outstretched finger and walked past me to the living room. 'But if he wants it, who am I to deny him?'

'Who indeed!' Douglas shook his head and gave me a smile. 'You know, it really does surprise me that *you* are the one with the accidental pregnancy.'

'I heard that, my bespectacled friend. You're on my list, you know!' Helen called from the living room.

'What list?' Douglas looked worried.

'It's either her Shit List or her Sex List,' Sophie offered as she took off the last of her many coloured layers. 'I'm on the Shit List.' She grinned, showing her lack of concern.

I linked arms with Sophie and Douglas and led them to the living room, where Helen was on the sofa flicking through a copy of *Vogue*.

'Tea?' I said, feeling content.

After delaying the inevitable over numerous cups of tea, some recent baking, a tête-à-tête with a highly vexed Douglas about the flaws within the zombie storyline and many discussions on the appropriateness of sex with co-workers, we headed upstairs to grab my stuff. I didn't have much. Ned and I hadn't owned any furniture, unless you count a drinks trolley with a missing wheel Ned found on the street one night. Douglas loaded Helen's car with my bags while Sophie, Helen and I went up to Mum's office to say goodbye. We climbed the last of the narrow stairs and knocked on the door.

'Come in!'

I opened the door and was greeted by the Lycra-clad back end of my mother, mid-downward dog.

'Hello, darling!' she said from between her legs. Her iPad lay on her yoga mat, a runway report playing.

'Hi Diana,' Helen said.

'Oh, hello girls.' She pressed pause on the iPad.

'Mu-um,' I whined. 'Get up. It's embarrassing.'

'I think it's great! I hope I can do that when I'm old,' Sophie said cheerily.

Mum dropped out of her pose. 'Old?' She narrowed her eyes.

'Diana, do you mind if we look at your scarf collection?' Helen deftly changed the subject. 'Did you get the latest Katrantzou one?'

Mum, eyes on Sophie, waved her approval.

Helen grabbed Sophie by the elbow. 'God, you really are a total and utter imbecile. I bet you were dropped as a baby.'

The door closed behind them and Mum's frown evaporated. She stood and put her hands on my shoulders.

'You're leaving?'

'Yep.' I returned Mum's sad smile.

'I have something for you.' She leant behind her glass-topped desk and pulled out a selection of glossy shopping bags, tissue paper frothing from the tops like cream on a pavlova. 'Just a few things for your new place,' she said as I bent down to rummage through the bags.

'What kind of things?' I said, fighting with the tissue paper and giving up.

'A few items to make you feel at home. Not your kind of home, of course, my kind of home.'

'I don't want that bloody skeleton!'

'Oh I wouldn't dream of giving you that! That is Advanced Decorating. You're not ready for that. It's just some Ungaro towels, a Missoni throw for the back of the sofa – soft furnishings, darling. I'll get you on to the hard stuff later.'

'Oh, OK. Thanks, then.' I smiled. 'Well, I'd better get going.'

Mum clasped me to her bosom. 'I'm flying to Rome on Tuesday. Just for a day or two. But I'll come and see you as soon as I get back. You'll be all right?'

I told Mum I was going to be OK, hugged her, said yes, I would avoid carbs and wash the Ungaro towels separately on a gentle wash, hugged her again, told her to stop her snivelling – I was literally only a forty-five-minute tube ride away – grabbed the shopping bags, dodged another hug and took off down the stairs yelling out goodbye and yes, I would call if I needed an up-and-coming photographer's first edition print of 'Hands Under Public Toilet Hand-Drier' for my living room, and if the current throw pillows were not to standard.

By 3 p.m. I was sitting on Grandma's old sofa, sipping peppermint tea and absorbing the feel of my new home. The walls in the living room were bare. With my mother's intervention they wouldn't be that way for long. I put my tea on the coffee table, adjusted a crocheted cushion and lay back, resting the palms of my hands round my baby bump. The night before I'd felt the baby move for the first time. And it was not, as all the books had said, like a butterfly in your abdomen. That seemed a ridiculously flowery description now I'd experienced it. It was more of a dense, watery sensation. Like the fluid vibrations a swimming goldfish makes through the plastic bag you take it home in. It was a private little feeling. So deeply interior. I felt as if I had a wonderful secret that couldn't ever be shared. Those watery movements were mine alone to know and relish.

'Looks like it's just you and me, my parasitic little friend,' I said, patting my stomach.

Helen, Sophie and Douglas had unloaded my stuff and made swift exits to prepare for their individual Saturday nights. Helen was going to a club you had to access through a phone box at the back of a diner, a speakeasy for those bored with the common freedom of legalised drinking. Sophie was 'doing something', apparently, 'with someone'. It was all we could get out of her. But whatever it was, it had her bustling with anticipation. I wondered if the male voice I'd heard over the phone at her place weeks ago was the elusive 'someone'. And Douglas was taking a new lady friend to the theatre. I'd been quite relieved when they'd left. I missed the bubbling expectancy getting ready for a night out held. Often I'd found it had been my favourite part of the evening. My friends were radiating that Saturday-night expectancy and I wanted rid of them and their mid-twenties freedom so I could eat my way through an M&S box of eclairs and browse Netflix.

My MC Hammer 'You Can't Touch This' ringtone blasted the quiet. I answered it without checking the caller ID.

'Hello?'

'Emma?' the voice replied. 'It's me.'

Ned.

'Oh. What do you want? Going to pay back my money?'

'Ah, no,' Ned said. 'I'm ringing to see how you are. How ... ah ... how's the baby thing going?'

'The *baby* thing?'

'Ah, yeah. Is it ... going OK? Are you, you know, taking your vitamins?'

'Taking my *vitamins*? What the fuck, Ned?'

Ned sighed. 'I'm trying, Emma.'

'Yes, I agree. You are very trying.'

'*You* broke up with *me*. *You* decided to keep the baby.'

He was right. I'd done all of the above. But then he'd emptied my bank account, leaving me with nothing.

'What's your point?'

'I don't have a point, just ...' he said, his tone defeated. 'I wanted to check up on you and, I dunno ...'

I felt a minor pinch of guilt. He was the father; he had a right to ask about the baby. I'd be devastated if he didn't care at all.

He cleared his throat. 'Well, I do need to talk to you about—'

'I have a scan on Friday,' I said. 'I suppose, well, you don't have to – I don't need you there or anything, but you could come if you want.' If Ned was trying, then so could I.

I waited to hear his answer, expecting him to make excuses about Gerry needing help with his *Where's Wally* jigsaw or his Mum saying he wasn't allowed out until he'd matched up all his socks.

'Really?' he said, a note of disbelief in his voice. 'I could come?'

'You're the father, aren't you? I can't stop you,' I said, but there was warmth to my voice. Ned actually sounded interested. Keen, even.

'I won't have to, you know ... see your ... I mean, they won't make me look into your—'

'My what, Ned? Spit it out.'

'Your ... fagina?'

Not for our entire relationship could Ned bring himself to say that word. But when he did it was with an F instead of a V. I started to laugh.

'Yes, Ned,' I said. 'If you want to see the baby you will, in fact, have to peer into my vagina.'

'Shuddup!' he said with a smile in his voice.

He waited for me to stop tittering.

'I'm gonna wear a snorkel,' he added, which set me off again.

Ned made more inappropriate vagina-rummaging jokes and did an impression of a man lost in a uterus asking directions to the blastocyst and I laughed till I cried and the motion caused potential bladder issues. It felt good (the laughing – not the bladder concerns).

'It's Saturday night,' I said, wiping at my eyes. 'Are you going out?'

'Yeah, I have a date,' Ned said, still laughing, and then stopped, realising what he had said. 'Oh, um . . . yeah, I am going out, later on . . .'

There was no more laughter.

'Who's your date?' I said, trying to sound normal.

'Um, just a girl I met.'

We were back to being uncomfortable again.

'Right,' I said. 'Well, have fun then.'

'Yeah.'

We sat in silence.

'Emma?'

'Yep?'

'I'll see you at the scan?'

'Yeah, yeah, of course.'

We said an awkward goodbye. I hung up, tossed the phone on the sofa and stared into the fire.

Ned was dating?

*

'ARCHIE AND TILLY ON SET PLEASE,' the First AD shrieked down the radio. Amy, having found out I was a Second AD, was taking full advantage and had given me my own radio. Martha was more than miffed at the perceived privilege.

I pressed the transmit button. 'Archie and Tilly travelling.' I opened the door and motioned to Martha and the kids that it was time to go.

Martha put down her supersized bag of Twiglets and pushed past me.

'Scene Forty-seven, guys,' I said. 'The one with—'

'We know which one it is.' Martha shuffled on her heavy legs, gripping Tilly's delicate hand. 'I *have* been doing this for years, you know.'

'OK,' I said, making a face at Archie.

Archie and Tilly delivered their lines again and again while hiding from two zombies, one with blood spurting from where his left arm ought to have been and the other with an exposed ribcage. I should have been concerned that Archie was seeing too much gore for a 4-year-old, but he seemed fine – he'd been playing happily with a severed head during a lighting set-up – and anyway, I just couldn't get Ned and his date out of my mind. Did he take her to our favourite cheap pizza place in Balham? Did they kiss? Did they shag? Was she skinnier, prettier, cleverer or nicer than me? Would it become serious, or was he just playing the field? My heart sank. Ned was afraid of the field. Any date he was on would be with a girl he genuinely liked.

'CUT!' the director yelled. 'Where's the frigging blood?'

Blood was supposed to be spurting from a bunch of slippery, rubbery prosthetic veins coming out of the zombie with the severed arm. A tube in the prosthetic was attached to what was essentially a keg of blood and a standby art girl was to pump it through manually – she was pumping but we saw no spurting.

'I think it's blocked,' she said, pumping faster and faster. She had fake blood all over herself and had begun to sweat.

The man playing the zombie dropped his frightening charade and watched his shoulder of veins with a look of curiosity completely at odds with the decomposing nature of his make-up.

'Five minutes' break, people, while we sort this out!' the First AD called.

Crew and cast dispersed, placing scripts on chairs, booms on tables, cameras in lock-off mode.

'When's the baby due?' Caroline asked, while instinctively tidying and fussing with Archie's hair.

'The sixteenth of July.' I peeled the wrapper from a cupcake.

The crew were taking the opportunity to snack and smoke outside the studio while the art department rushed around with bits of tubing, worried faces and fake blood on their hands/trousers/sides of their faces. It got everywhere. I'd trod in it at some point, and the bottoms of my Converse looked like I'd walked through a crime scene.

Caroline and Claire had joined Archie and me at a picnic table. Claire was sitting opposite, her back to us, blowing smoke upward and chatting on her phone.

'Wow. Exciting! Do you know what it is yet?' She released Archie and looked at me the way make-up artists do: eyes moving over your face, assessing your collagen levels, the size of your pores and whether you need some eyebrow reshaping or upper-lip waxing.

'No, the scan is on Friday.' I crammed the cupcake into my mouth.

Caroline *uh-huh*ed and got out a sleek case of neutral-coloured powders. She dabbed a brush over a colour.

'Are you going to find out what you're having?' Her powder-loaded brush headed towards my face. 'Or do you and your partner want to keep it a surprise?'

Without any question as to whether the pallid skin, deep purple under-eye bags, wet hair pulled into a bun and way-ward eyebrows was actually a carefully considered look I was going for, Caroline commenced powdering.

'I don't have a partner,' I said, flinching and blinking. 'I'm just ... having a baby.'

'Oh.' Caroline nodded. She flicked open another black case and waved a large bristle brush over the glistening skin-coloured powder. 'Insemination,' she said, dusting my nose and cheekbones.

'No.' I coughed, inhaling the powder. 'My boyfriend and I broke up. But he's still, well ... he's coming to the scan.'

I went back to thinking about Ned and his date and

wondered if the girl was now his girlfriend. I hoped not. I would rather he date a variety of vacuous girls than embark on a new and meaningful relationship with some cool, tolerant girl who wanted lots of freckly kids.

'Wow. That's tough. Are you OK doing it on your own? Shut your eyes.'

Being a make-up artist required you to spend your working day inches from someone else's face. This created some sort of false intimacy that saw make-up artists asking probing questions and actors unloading their souls. Actors treated make-up artists like therapists. Therapists with glitter. I shut my eyes to receive the unasked-for makeover and proceeded to do what many before me had done. Unleash my inner emotions to a near stranger because they had the ability to make me look pretty.

'Wow,' Caroline said again, after I'd told her the whole Ned story even down to the sexual position I thought I'd been in when I'd got pregnant and the size, the exact size, of Ned's penis. 'You're so brave. Good for you,' she said, brandishing a mirror.

Now it was my turn. 'Wow!'

Without so much as a slick of pink lipstick or a slash of green eyeshadow, Caroline had made me look quite lovely. Clever covering-up and colouring-in (not professional terms, of course) had transformed me from 'Pasty Pregnant Whore on Crack' to 'Glowing Woman in Charge of Own Destiny, Fit to be in a Plug-in Air Freshener Commercial'. I was impressed.

'I look like me. But pretty!' I said, turning this way and that, trying to find where the real me ended and Air Freshener Girl began.

'You are pretty. You just need to bring out your best features.' Caroline flicked open a powder case. 'All I did was use this one here, that down there, highlighted this with a bit of that one, mixed these two to match this area here and made small strokes with this one under here. Simple.'

'Uh-huh,' I said, unsure. It seemed as simple as painting a Monet with an eyelash. 'Maybe I will just use the stuff for under my eyes.'

Caroline shrugged.

A few minutes later the crew were called back to set.

I quickly checked that Archie remembered his lines. 'And you know that zombie on the floor isn't real, don't you?' I said.

'Yes. It's wubber.'

'*Rubber*. And the person chasing you is just Peter with fake eyeballs and teeth. You remember Peter? We met him in the—'

'*Yes*,' Archie said, getting impatient.

'OK, OK,' I said, glancing round the set and realising how bloody (literally) hellish it looked. 'And the blood is fake too, isn't it?'

'Yes. It tastes like chocolate.'

'Right. Maybe don't eat the fake blood, though.'

Archie nodded and trotted to his 'first positions' mark and I headed back to my hard plastic seat behind the monitors, passing Andrew on the way.

'You look very pretty today,' he said, looking down at me from his great height of godlike good looks. 'Have you done something different?'

'Yes, I've been renovated by Caroline.' I grinned beneath the nude contouring.

Andrew chuckled.

'OK, GOING FOR A TAKE!' screeched the First AD. 'EVERYBODY OFF SET!' She gave me a curt glare.

I felt Andrew watching me as I continued past him. When I turned and sat down he was still looking. He winked and turned back to his camera.

CHAPTER FOURTEEN

The morning of the scan I'd woken at 4.31 a.m. with a fear
the baby would be born with no brain or cartilage. Just an
empty head attached to rubbery arms and legs. I'd got out
of bed, turned the lights on and sat watching the last of the
dawn infomercials. I'd become very enamoured with a hair
curler that was also a hairbrush and a hairdryer and something else I'd missed when I went to the bathroom – maybe a
can opener. I'd then called Alex in Bangladesh and she'd told
me, with the screech of rickshaw horns drowning out every
second word, not to worry, my baby was going to be peachy
of cheek and wispy of hair with all essential brains, cartilage,
toenails and so on, and I'd ceased my shallow breathing. Alex
was good like that. Pragmatic to my preposterous. Rational
to my ridiculous. Working in squalor for the good of poorer
people while I ate Green & Black's for breakfast and hoped
my ex-boyfriend would get the clap from his date.

Later that day I walked out of the cottage and down to the

corner of the street, where Ned had agreed to pick me up in his mother's Volvo. Then stood around in the dimming light while my toes turned to toesicles for the next seventeen minutes. A car tooted at the end of the road. Not Ned. I pulled my feather-filled parka tighter round me. Very soon I wouldn't be able to fit my pregnant belly into the coat, but for now the zip could be coaxed over the bump with obvious strain. My phone rang and I immediately predicted the conversation.

'Em, it's me,' Ned would say breathlessly.

'Yes,' I would say tightly.

'I'm running late, can I meet you there?'

I'd hear Gerry in the background moaning about how my pregnant neediness was getting in the way of their alcohol flavour testing. Hic.

'I guess,' I would say even more tightly.

'Great. You're the best. Chelsea Hospital, right?'

'St George's,' I would spit.

'Yeah, that's what I meant. See you there,' he'd say.

And acid would rise in my throat and I would mentally castrate him. And Gerry. But when I pulled my phone from my coat pocket, it wasn't him.

'Hi.'

'Hello, darling!' Mum said with her customary enthusiasm.

It was never there when she was married to Dad. She'd worn navy blouses, sensible shoes, made our school lunches (Marmite sandwiches every day) and driven us to school in silence. She'd emerged from the divorce an exuberant butterfly complete with Prada wings, a Lanvin purse and more energy than a Pussycat Doll on speed.

'Are you at the hospital yet?'

'No. Just waiting for ...' I decided against mentioning Ned. 'A cab.'

'I want you to ring me the minute you're out. I need to make sure it has my nose and not your father's. You girls are very lucky you didn't get his nose, my goodness; it's like an aircraft hangar. I've put some money aside for surgery just in case.' I could hear a noise in the background like coat hangers sliding along rails and imagined my mother stalking round a boutique on the phone, bowling sales assistants and shoppers left and right. 'Do you have matching underwear on?'

'Yes.'

'You're lying, aren't you?'

'Yes. And the elastic's gone in my knickers.'

'Hmmm,' Mum grumbled. 'Now listen, I read an article about single motherhood in teens—'

'I'm twenty-seven!'

'Yes but darling, you're very immature.'

'Thanks.'

'Anyway, the article was talking about getting into the dating pool when you're young and have a baby and it said "If at first you don't succeed—"'

'Mum, I don't want to date.'

'Just listen.'

'No, thank you.'

'It said, "If at first you don't succeed, ask yourself—"'

'*Do you be-LIEVE in life after LOVE,*' I sang in a below-average Cher voice.

Mum was quiet for a second.

'Do you want my advice or not?'

'I do not.'

'It's no wonder you get yourself into these messes.'

'Well, everything happens for a reason, I guess.'

'Yes, but sometimes that reason is because you're an idiot.'

'Cheers.'

'I meant about forgetting to take the pill.' She made a half-sighing, half-laughing noise. 'I just worry, my darling.'

'I know.'

Mum was tactless and bossy, but her heart was in the right place. Perfectly positioned behind a tanned bosom and covered in an Yves Saint Laurent shirt with a generous spray of bespoke perfume.

'Now, one more thing.' Mum was back to being officious. 'Have you got your money back yet?'

'No, but I will. I just have to—'

'You just have to strap on a pair, Emma! I won't have you in the same situation I was in at your age. I refuse to fund his ridiculous ideas and your lack of balls.'

'I've got . . . balls, I'm just—' I paced the footpath. Why hadn't I been more forceful with Ned? I'd asked; he'd said he needed another couple of weeks and, well, that's where I'd left it. 'His phone . . . it's . . . he's off-grid. He's gone underground. He's—'

'Don't give me *gone underground*. He's not Jason Bourne,

and you're not in an episode of *CSI: New York* with that sexy man from *Forrest Gump*.'

'Huh?'

'Get the money. You have two weeks. Or I'll call the police on him myself.'

'He's the father of my unborn child! You can't call the police.'

'Darling, I love you, but I have to be cruel to be ... What's the saying?'

'Kind. You have to be cruel to be kind.'

'No, that's not it. It's something to do with revenge ...' She sounded preoccupied. 'Well, anyway, I just want you to stand on your own two feet. Even if they are in those tatty sneakers you insist on wearing. I was a single mother – now that's *lovely* ...'

'What?'

'Do you have this in a grey? A Spanish dove grey, not that horrible Argos polyester tracksuit grey you have your skirts over there in.'

I'd lost her. Lost her to a Bond Street boutique and a quivering sales assistant.

'Bye, Mum.'

'Bye, dear,' she said. 'No, that won't do. Get me—'

And she was gone.

I checked the time. I waited a few more minutes with a familiar feeling in the pit of my stomach. Ned had forgotten. I wasn't the last thing on his mind – I wasn't there at all. I dialled his number, said 'I hate you' childishly to his answer phone, then called a cab. While the taxi made the short journey through the backstreets of Wimbledon, Ned returned my call.

'Yes,' I said, feeling like I'd dropped my self-respect out of the cab window for it to be run over by a passing bus.

'I totally forgot!'

'I figured.'

'I'm coming to get you. I just have to wait for Mum to get back from the chiropractor.'

'Forget it. I'm in a cab,' I huffed. 'Look, if you don't want to come, then don't. I only asked you—'

'I want to come!' he whined.

God, how I hated him at that moment. My feelings towards Ned changed so often I was getting motion sickness. On Christmas Day, when he'd given me the little beer tankard (before he killed Grandma's cat), I'd wondered if it had been a mistake to break up with him. And only a few days previously I'd been jealous of the date he was on. Remembering how in the early days we used to go out for beer and cheap pizza, then go home and watch *QI*, Ned recreating the experiments with an impeccable Stephen Fry impression. We'd usually end up running from poorly measured, rapidly frothing concoctions, breathless with drunken hysterics. And yet a few weeks before, when I'd looked at my bank account and realised I couldn't afford the ergonomic baby carrier endorsed by all sorts of celebrity mums, that I'd have to tie the baby to my back with a piece of batik fabric like a rice paddy worker, and swing the naked babe round to my knee-length bosom for its feed while I continued to hoe the earth with my gnarled fingers, I'd wanted to turn him over to the wrath of Helen and my mother and cheer as he emerged a eunuch with bald patches and a dislocated nostril.

'Emma? Please?'

'I'm here now,' I said as the cab pulled up at the hospital. 'I don't care if you come or not.'

'I'll be there! I promise.'

I hung up and headed inside.

'Miss George?' A jolly-looking Caribbean lady peered round the door of one of the patient rooms holding a chart.

A few minutes later my maternity jeans were down low, my top was up high and Janice, the Caribbean midwife, was swinging the barcode thingy across my stomach, the cold blue gel slowly warming up.

'Hello, little one,' Janice said as a picture of the baby appeared on the screen. I looked up and saw what was now, so clearly, a tiny person.

'It's having a rest!' she chuckled. 'Look at its little hands!'

The baby was lying in the foetal position. Face down, bum up in the air with tiny legs tucked underneath. A foetus. Lying in the foetal position. I was undoubtedly constructing a genius child. There was a knock at the door.

'Come in,' Janice said, turning in her seat.

A young nurse popped her head round the door. 'Sorry to disturb you. The father's here. Can I show him in?' She looked from me to Janice.

I nodded, a small black cloud gathering above my head. The lady disappeared and a second later Ned's flushed face appeared at the door.

'Hi,' he said sheepishly. 'Sorry I'm late. I just ... Can I?'

'Grab that chair, young man,' Janice said, then turned back to the screen.

Ned dragged a chair over and stared at the screen, not noticing his chair leg was caught on my handbag and the contents were spilling.

'Is that ... our baby?' he said, captivated.

'No, that's a live feed to a woman's uterus in Brazil.'

Ned narrowed his eyes at me.

'Yes, that is your baby. From in there.' Janice pointed to my stomach and looked at me like I was unstable. She turned back to Ned. 'See how it lying? So sweet.'

Ned studied the screen. Janice continued with her duties, clicking and scanning, making notes and providing facts. The placenta was lying low, which was not a problem at this stage, apparently (although I'd already commenced fretting) but meant I'd need another scan in a few weeks' time to make sure it had moved. Ned asked Janice many, many questions and she answered them all patiently like she didn't have another fifty-five wombs to scan right after mine. She chuckled away while making notes, pausing now and then to clutch a hand to her bosom and emit a wheezy laugh at one of Ned's anecdotes. The two of them acted like I wasn't even in the room.

'It's amazing,' Ned said, staring at the screen where our baby had turned its head to face us and from what I could see, did not have the large beaky nose of my father. 'Isn't it?' He looked from me to Janice. 'We made a baby. It's just so amazing . . .'

Janice nodded and patted Ned's hand. I grimaced at the touchy-feely crap.

'Christ, it's just reproduction. Bacteria reproduce at a rate of, like, one billion per second.'

Janice and Ned chose to ignore me.

'Now, do you want to know what sex the baby is?' Janice asked with a broad grin.

'Yes,' I said.

'No,' said Ned at the same time.

'What?' My head snapped in his direction. 'Why not?'

'It'll be a nice surprise on the day.'

'The fact I am even having a baby with you is surprise enough,' I said sourly. I turned to Janice. 'I want to know.'

'Well I don't,' Ned said, folding his arms across his chest. I glared at him.

'Ah, it no good,' Janice said, turning away from the screen. 'I cannot get good picture. It got important bits facing down. Sorry.'

Ned looked smug.

If I was a particularly bitter and mistrustful person I might have thought Janice was choosing not to look properly just to side with Ned. But luckily I was fair-minded and rational.

'Yeah *right*,' I said as sarcastically as I could.

'But you can take some pictures home if you want?' Janice ignored my comment.

'Can we?' Ned said, overly enthused.

Janice clicked and chortled and took far more than the NHS-allowed number of photos while Ned chatted about his future as an ice cream magnate and I sulked on the bed, disappointed in myself for liking his idea of vodka-lime-flavoured ice cream being sold from a van at the summer music festivals but doubting he'd actually pull it off.

Icy air hit me as the hospital sliding doors opened to the bleak early evening. Ned trailed behind, enthralled by the grainy photos of my womb.

'Can you drop me home?' I said as we stopped near all the sickly smokers leaning on their drips.

Ned looked up from the photos, a frown on his freckled face.

'Oh, ah. No, I can't. I, ah, got dropped off by someone.' He fussed with his errant hair. 'I'm getting the bus.'

'Fine. I'll get a cab,' I said, looking in the direction of the empty cab rank. 'See you later.'

'OK. Sure.'

We looked at each other, both seemingly thinking the same thing. How had we got to this point? Standing outside a hospital, a baby we would have to look after for the rest of our lives arriving in four and a half months, too awkward or resentful to talk to each other? Talking was what we had done. Emma and Ned, laughing in the corner of the bar, ignoring our friends' calls to join them on the dance floor. Or staying at home with a few bottles of economy wine, telling stories we'd told many times, insular but complete. Then, without our really noticing, cheap wine and conversation got replaced by cups of tea and evenings on the couch, one eye on the TV the other on our individual laptops. The stories had been told, the jokes laughed at, the wine was gross. And now this; baby on the way, him living at his mother's dating nameless sluts and the only date I had was with the dent in the sofa shaped like my arse.

'Em, I've got something I need to—' he said at the same time I said, 'Look, Ned, I—'

We did the usual self-conscious 'you go', 'no, you were first', 'it's fine, you go' tussle back and forth before settling on me.

'I really need you to pay back that money.'

Ned's face dropped. 'But I—'

'I've got to start buying things for the baby. And Mum's threatening to call the police.'

'What?' His head shot up. 'No! I just need more time!' he said, his arms flapping. 'I'm about to crack this new recipe. *Please*? We are seriously on the verge of something here. I know it this time! And Gerry knows this dude who knows this other dude who has, like, the best whipping machines and . . .' His passion waned in the face of my silent cynicism. 'I just need more time, that's all. Please give me a chance?' His voice was quieter, defeated. 'Trust me this one more time? Please?'

'Jesus, Ned,' I sighed, glancing at the smokers, aware of them watching our exchange.

Ned looked close to tears. He really was passionate about this bloody ice cream. Why could he still get to me?

'Fine,' I said. 'You've got another few weeks, but that's it.'

Ned's face lit up. He nodded like one of those toy dogs in the back of a car. 'Yes, definitely. You'll see, Em; this is going to be massive. Thank you, thank you so much.'

'OK,' I sighed.

Ned thanked me again and again, then lolloped towards a bus stop on Blackshaw Road. I fumbled around in my bag looking for my phone just as a cab pulled up. The rear door flew open and out jumped a pregnant lady in her nightgown and a harried-looking man. They rushed inside, panic furrowing their faces, leaving the cab door still open.

'Are you free?' I asked, leaning through the open door.

'Never free, love. But I can take you where you want to go,' the taxi driver said. I jumped in, gave him my address and then slipped the scan photos out of my bag. I congratulated myself on how well I'd done forming a whole baby. Everything was accounted for: two hands, two feet, one head and a brain (phew), two ears, two eyes, one non-beaky nose. It was perfect, and it was mine. And a little bit Ned's. But mainly mine. I wished I'd found out the sex, but I had another scan. I could wait. I looked up as the cab stopped at the hospital exit and waited for a gap in the traffic to pull out onto Blackshaw Road. The meter clicked over £4.20 while we waited. I strained to see how far back the traffic went.

And that's when I saw it.

Ned in the front passenger seat of a parked car. A

familiar turquoise Ford Fiesta with ridiculous eyelashes on the headlights.

Showing the NHS photos to . . .

Sophie?

Why was Ned in Sophie's Ford Fiesta with the ridiculous eyelashes on the headlights? She was *my* friend. Why was he showing her the photos of our baby? *My* baby? I felt light-headed. Ned pointed at a photo and grinned. Sophie grinned back and, with a cold sweat shooting down my spine and dizziness threatening, I watched them kiss.

CHAPTER FIFTEEN

I slammed my front door, kicked off my boots, tossed my coat on the floor, stormed into the kitchen and sat at the table tearing a *Heat* magazine into angry little shreds. Had I been a cartoon, steam would have come out of my ears. The *betrayal*! What was Sophie thinking? It wasn't the injustice of her kissing someone I wanted to be with – no thank you. It was the kissing of someone who was part of *my* life. Not hers. He was my former boyfriend, yes, but he was my current money-stealing, impregnating, *ex*-boyfriend. Therefore he belonged, in a certain sense, to me. Where was the loyalty? As a friend surely she should be furious with him, not kissing him. And Ned? How dare he steal away my dippy, elfin friend who, no matter what life threw at her, was always cheerful? She too was mine. Now they were each other's. It wasn't right! And it wasn't fair. I felt extremely lonely. When all the vacuous faces from the magazine were torn and jumbled together like some big paper salad of life's desperadoes,

I scooped the *Heat* confetti into the empty fruit bowl and took it out the front door to the recycling.

'Hello, Emma dear.' Harriet stood on the footpath holding a black studded leash with a large Doberman attached to the end of it.

'Hi Harriet,' I said, peering over my gate at the huge dog sitting on its haunches. 'Who's that?'

'This is Brutus,' she said, stroking his head. 'Say hello, Brutus.' Brutus remained motionless. Harriet smiled sweetly.

'Is he yours?'

'Yes, I got him from the RSPCA yesterday, didn't I, my boy?' She tickled him under his rather menacing-looking muzzle.

'To keep?'

'Yes, dear.' She looked at me like I was on day release.

'But he's so . . . big.' I leant closer and put my hand out to pat his head. He growled a deep warning and I took a quick step back. 'And a bit scary.'

'That's the whole point!' she said, looking around her at the middle to upper-class mothers with their Bugaboos full of Gap-clad babies taking strolls on the common with a latte in one hand and diamonds on the other. 'It's dangerous here in the city! What about the rapists and the bludgeoners and the sexual sadists? People will leave an old lady like me bleeding on the streets. Bleeding! I have to take my own protection seriously. Brutus is a trained guard dog, you know.'

'Right.'

'I've been meaning to ask you, dear, are you a lesbian?'

'What?'

'A les-bi-an.' She stretched her mouth with each syllable.

I hesitated in my pink socks.

'You're pregnant and not married; I see no young fellow visiting you, and I just thought you might be a nice lesbian lady.'

I hadn't thought my day could get much worse, but I was wrong.

'Well, I'm not.'

'Oh, I don't mind if you are. My taekwondo teacher is a lesbian.' She raised a knobbly finger to her bottom lip. 'Well at least, I think she is; she wears trousers an awful lot.'

'OK, I have to go inside now,' I said, feeling a headache coming on.

'All right dear, lovely to see you. Say hello to your mother, will you? She's such a treat, isn't she?'

'She is,' I said, taking in Harriet in her cream pleated skirt, thick cream stockings and cream lace-up shoes next to Brutus with his studded leash and ability to maim and kill.

'And come over for cake later. I'll show you how Brutus kills a rabbit on command.' She waved goodbye and turned towards the village, her loud-hailer slung over her curved back on a leather strap. 'Come on then, Brutus dear, let's go and see Marjorie at the bookshop.'

A few hours later I was curled on Mum's sofa, a hot chocolate in a gold and black tiger-striped mug warming my hands and Mum at my side looking damp-eyed at the scan photos. I'd told her all about Ned not wanting to find out the sex of the baby and seeing him kissing Sophie in her Ford Fiesta with the ridiculous eyelashes on the headlights (Mum had said many, many unrepeatable words), then, with tears welling, I regaled her with the conversation with Harriet. Everybody thinks I'm a lesbian, I'd wailed. Well, stop wearing those god-awful Ugg boots, she'd said. But my feet will get cold, I'd wailed louder. Fashion is pain, she'd said, slipping off a Jimmy Choo to show how her toes remained in a permanent pointy court-shoe shape.

'And you might want to wax this,' she said, touching a blood-red nail to my upper lip. 'Big eyebrows are back, darling, but it's pushing the envelope to try to single-handedly introduce a moustache as fashion for women.'

Horrified, I fled to the bathroom and yes, there, faintly on my top lip, was a line of downy blond hair. I looked like a 13-year-old boy. My balls would be dropping soon. I returned to the sofa.

'I wanna trade lives with someone.' I flopped next to Mum, glancing at a copy of *Vogue* with Giselle on the cover. 'Preferably her.'

'It's nothing a little trip to the Balance Clinic won't fix. I can book you in with Amanda if you like.'

'Sure,' I moped.

Mum studied the photos again. 'So beautiful.' Then she appeared to be struck by a sudden thought. 'Did you tell Ned to pay you back? Did you tell him I'd call the police? Because I *will* do it, darling.'

'Ah, yeah, I did.' I got busy with my cuticles. 'He's, um, he's going to do it . . .'

Mum frowned.

'He has to do it in instalments, because of the repayment structure of . . . of the . . .' I cleared my throat. I didn't want to tell an outright lie, so was attempting to lay a vague haziness across the subject. 'It's fine. It's all sorted, and yeah, the instalments will be starting very soon.' I quickly pointed to the photos. 'Do you see its little nose?'

Mum was immediately re-enthralled. 'I think it's a girl.' She traced the photo with her finger. 'Maybe fashion sense skips a generation.' She glanced at my Mothercare leggings sagging at the knees and the Gap tunic top that I wore no fewer than four times a week.

My chin trembled. I was a cellulity single pregnant girl with a moustache, nipples the size of soup bowls and the silvery beginnings of so many stretch marks I looked like I'd previously dated Edward Scissorhands. And, as my mother pointed out, I also lacked any fashion acumen. I was destined for spinsterhood. I would sell the cottage, move in with Mum and collect teapots.

Mum stroked my face. 'You are who you are and I just love you, my darling.' She smiled and wiped a tear from my cheek. 'But I'm taking you shopping.'

Later that evening I sat in my cottage at my dressing table, looking in the mirror and running a finger over my velvety moustache, contemplating Sophie and Ned and a single life filled with teapot collector magazines when my phone rang.

'Hi.'

'Whatcha doin'?' Alex asked in a chirpy voice.

'Oh, you know. Stuff. Nothing.' I turned away from the mirror.

'Interesting. Do you want to know what I am doing?' She was perky.

'All right, what are you doing?'

'I'm ... PACKING!'

'What? Where for?'

'Vanuatu!'

'But I thought you still had a few weeks in Dhaka?' I said, disorientated. My body was expanding – was time contracting?

'So did I!' Her excitement was palpable. 'But I got a call from this guy who'd been over here as a consultant last year, we'd got on really well and he said he'd heard my contract was nearly up and he wanted me on his next project! It was an absolute last-minute assignment. He had to get his crew together quickly or they lost funding so I signed the contract, got released from my current position and I leave in three hours!'

'That's great!'

'And the best bit is, it's a promotion! I'm a project manager now, and I have a proper title: Water Sanitation and Hygiene Manager. I'll have two staff and my own accommodation. Apparently it's right by the beach! And I actually get paid this time.'

'Oh, man,' I said, hefting myself to the kitchen for some

necessary biscuitry. '*I* was supposed to have the exotic locations working in films and *you* were supposed to work in a
government building getting paid shit.'

'Yes, but you're working on a big film with Scott Vander,
and they're all going to love you and probably end up taking
you and the baby to Hollywood to work on more movies.'

My sister, the eternal encouraging optimist. I missed her
so much I could feel it in my back teeth.

'So what will you actually do as a water hygiene whatsit?'
I plopped on the sofa with a floral biscuit tin.

'Pretty much the same sort of project as the one in Dhaka,
but this time I'm really doing it, not writing reports about
doing it. I go round the island to all the local schools – they
have very poor water hygiene there, so I'll be teaching the
kids about washing their hands, not putting dirty water into
their rivers, the effects of disposable nappies, etcetera. Then
I help the village leaders construct a basic water treatment
plant.'

'You're a regular Mother Teresa.'

'I try. So,' she said, 'what's news with you?'

'Well ...' I took a bite of shortbread and swallowed it
down thickly. 'I'm a lesbian.'

'Great!' Alex cheered. 'It's always good to be open to
change. When did you decide that?'

I filled her in on Harriet, teapots, the scan and the moustache, but left out the bit about Sophie and Ned, and after
making a skype date for when she landed in Vanuatu, we
hung up.

For the rest of the weekend I skulked around the cottage ignoring calls and texts from my friends. Sophie left a message about a flyer she'd seen on a noticeboard at the Kennington Community Centre for a person who films your labour, and wondered if I'd like the number. Helen sent a text picture of a guy asleep in her bed. And then another with his measurements and endurance time.

I came up with a handful of unbalanced ideas on how to make enough money to start paying Mum back her 'instalments' which included selling things, i.e. my body, my baby, my half of the cottage; and/or renting things, i.e. my body, my baby, my half of the cottage. I considered putting an ad on Gumtree for a lodger, but worried I'd end up with a psycho who'd kill me in my sleep in the name of Napoleon or global consumerism or something. Then I contemplated putting some of my old poetry on Amazon. At around 2 a.m. on Sunday morning I'd formed a sonnet in my head, sure it was going to propel me to superstardom.

> *Ah the betrayal*
> *I like Rik Mayall*

It needed work.

On set on the Monday I was still in a delicate mood. I'd told no one except Mum about Sophie and Ned, and the trapped emotions were curdling my insides. Now when Sophie and Ned broke up I wouldn't be the only one with the story about Ned's thoughts on the 'movable clitoris'. But what if they didn't break up? What if they got married? Then my baby would call Sophie 'Stepmum', and maybe it would like her better than me. And wouldn't want to be picked up after spending the weekend at Sophie's parents' farm with all the free cheese.

Archie only had a few talking/hiding scenes on the 'Family Home' set with Tilly and Melody, which were pretty boring. From my seat behind the director's monitor I looked at Amy chatting with the sound guys. I hated her. I looked at the First AD busy rummaging in her AD's tool belt fishing out a particular flavour of sugar-free mint for Melody. I hated her. I hated Melody. And I hated sugar-free mints. Martha made an attempt to point out I was looking at the wrong scene and I told her to bite me. Which I wished I hadn't as Martha looked like she'd be keen to have a chew on almost anything.

Caroline sat beside me at lunchtime. 'How was the scan? It was last week, right? Did you find out what you're having?'

'No, the baby was in a funny position. I can try again next time,' I said, pushing a roast potato round my plate.

'Oh, that's a shame,' she said, looking much more disappointed than I was. 'Do you have the photos with you?'

I fished them out of my bag. Caroline pored over the pictures, studying each one and making little murmuring noises.

'They're beautiful,' she said, handing them back to me a few minutes later, her eyes glassy.

'Ah, thanks,' I said, thinking she was a little overemotional, but then again she was a make-up girl, and they were prone to ridiculous girlishness. (Except Claire, who was like a seasoned wrestler with red lipstick and studded ankle boots.)

'I get a bit emotional when I see pictures,' Caroline said, checking under her eyes in a compact mirror. She clicked it shut and leant towards me with a brave face. 'My husband and I have been doing IVF and it ... it hasn't been going too well.'

'Oh. I'm so sorry,' I said, thinking back to all the times I'd jokingly called the baby a parasite, a mistake or had bleated on about how it was not the right time and mentally gave my past self a kick in the shins. 'How long have you been on IVF? I hear it can take a couple of times.'

'Six years,' Caroline said with a sad smile.

'Oh.' I didn't know what to say. 'That's ... a while, I guess.'

Caroline nodded. 'I lost twins last year.' Two tears trickled down her cheek. 'I'd managed to get to fourteen weeks that time.'

'That's terrible.' My throat tensed as I fought back tears of sympathy. 'I'm so sorry.'

Caroline shrugged a single shoulder. 'My husband gets me a piece of jewellery each time we're unsuccessful.' She twisted a delicate diamond bracelet round her wrist. 'All it does is remind me how I've failed.'

I glanced at Caroline's jewellery: diamond studs, a Tiffany

necklace, a couple of bangles and bracelets on each wrist and felt very sad.

'I'm thirty-eight,' she said, dropping her hands to her lap. 'It's almost too late now.'

'But thirty-eight isn't that old?'

'Not really,' she sniffed. 'But my eggs are down forty per cent, so the chances are getting less and less.' She patted the corners of her eyes with a tissue then stood up with her barely finished roast meal. 'You're very lucky, Emma. Don't be too hard on that little bundle in there. Some people would love to be in your position.' She gave me a watery smile and moved through the busy film set.

Melody grabbed her arm and pointed to her hair, making a frowny face. Caroline nodded and smiled. She threw another look in my direction and headed into the make-up trailer with Melody while I quickly swiped away a tear. I'm sure she hadn't meant to, but Caroline had made me feel spoilt and ungrateful. Sure, it was not ideal to have an unplanned pregnancy and then break up with the father, and even less ideal to be doing it without money or a proper job. And it really wasn't nice that my ex was kissing one of my best friends (in a Ford Fiesta with ridiculous eyelashes on the headlights), but I had a healthy little person growing inside me. And my grandma, bless her twice-darned little socks, had given me a home. I thought of Caroline's jewellery, every piece a mark of loss. I'd coveted her jewels, but to her they were a far inferior consolation prize.

'Emma?' Archie said, resting his hand on my knee.

Catherine Bennetto

'Yes?' I grabbed him into a cuddle and kissed his head, avoiding the clumps of fake blood in his artfully dirtied hair.

'Can Tilly come for a playdate? She's going to be my best girlfriend.'

'Best girlfwiend?' I said, unable to hide a laugh. 'How many do you have?'

'Thwee. Tilly first, then Megan from Mummy's exercise class, then you.'

And even though Archie was only four, and was my cousin, and it was wrong on many, many levels, I felt happy that somebody loved me enough to make me their third-best girlfriend.

CHAPTER SIXTEEN

I lay in bed listening to the noises of the night. The baby, now twenty-three weeks, had discovered its legs and since eleven o'clock had been practising the *Fame* routine across my uterus. Trying to sleep was futile, and my thoughts wandered to my day out with Mum the week before. We'd arrived at the Balance Clinic, where Mum announced across the waiting room that her daughter was unintentionally making a 'transition' and needed a moustache removed immediately and she'd like someone to have a look at my bikini line, as she'd bet her Balenciagas I'd never had a wax and would probably be sporting home-made hairy bike shorts. It was true: when I took off my knickers it looked like a well-established hipster beard down there. I was still flaming with humiliation an hour and a half later when I was released from the calm sanctuary of the Balance Clinic hair free everywhere except for my head. And I mean *everywhere*. But I'd endured it all in the name of not collecting teapots. After removing all unsightly hair, and some hair that would never be sighted but got removed anyway, we'd gone shopping. Mum threw clothes at sales assistants barking that we needed it in grey, red, less mumsy, more busty. She'd thrown my eBay-purchased maternity jeans and favourite Gap tunic top in the bin and I'd left Oxford Street looking far less Pregnant Gypsy and much more up-and-coming Yummy Mummy, fit to be in the Richmond branch of Carluccio's discussing controlled crying and biodegradable nappy inserts.

At work, Andrew had said I looked hot. Hot. Yes, I was pregnant and the least likely choice for a man like Andrew, but I was allowed to dream and dream I did. Ones that involved nakedness, large willies and normal-sized erect nipples.

My mind flicked to Sophie and Ned, as it so frequently did in the dark, lonely hours. Were they a proper couple? Were they in bed together right now? Did she fall asleep giggling to his made-up jokes about an Englishman, an Irishman and a Scotch egg? Was Sophie able to direct him more clearly towards the clitoris? Was my clitoris just abnormally small? Or maybe Ned was right; it did retreat like a frightened tortoise. I'd ignored another couple of calls and texts from Sophie in the last couple of days. She was probably starting to suspect something – but then again, it was Sophie. She'd just as likely assume I'd been abducted by aliens. Or centaurs.

My thoughts were interrupted by a knock at the cottage door. My clock said 12.05 a.m. Only murderers knocked on people's doors at that hour! My heart hammered and I looked around for something sharp yet easy to wield. A pair of rusty nail clippers from a Christmas cracker was my only option but I paused while flicking open the bendable nail file and got myself a grip. Since when did murderers knock? Harriet's paranoia was contagious. I wished I'd installed the panic button she'd given me, though. The knocking got louder. I jumped out of bed, threw my dressing gown on and hurried down the dark hall.

'Who is it?' I said through the door.

'Hamisshh!' A male voice slurred from the other side. 'Open up. It's going to rain on your – hic – pie.'

Friday-night drinkers. The high street was frequently embellished with vomit of a Saturday morning.

'You've got the wrong house,' I called out. 'There's no Hamish here.' I waited to hear the sound of the man leaving. Instead I heard the shuffling of unsteady feet and hiccups.

'Hamish, I've finissshhhed your businessh cards. I'm shorry they took so long. But what kind of lawyer has a horse on their businessh card anyway, shouldn't you have that . . . you know . . . that hammer thing? Or a jail!' He giggled and hiccuped again. 'Hamish, I brought you pie!'

'There is no Hamish here!' I said as loud as I dared for the time of night. 'Please go away!'

There was a sudden and singular thump on the door. My heart skipped several beats.

'Look, Hamish,' the slurred voice took on a more consolatory tone. It was inches above my head and it sounded like he was leaning against the door. 'I know I've been out of touch

recently but I have, what do you lawyers call it? Extenuat-
extenu- exterminating circumcisions. But look!' he said,
suddenly cheery. 'I bought you pie! Look through your peephole and look at the – Heeeeyyyy . . . where's your peephole?'

'There is no peephole because it is NOT. HAMISH'S.
HOUSE.' I gave each word enough space for a drunk to
decipher. 'PLEASE. LEAVE.'

I did not want to be opening the door to a drunken
stranger in the middle of a cold Friday night. Even if he
did have pie. I contemplated my options. I could call Uncle
Mike. Or the police. Or a taxi, and hope he got in it.

Two sharp barks shattered the noiseless night followed by
a deep, hostile growl. Hamish's buddy with the pie yelped
girlishly.

'ON GUARD, BRUTUS!' Harriet's voice warbled.

'IT'S A HOUND OF HELL!' the man screamed. 'IT'S
CERBERUS!' Brutus barked and bayed.

'Just go away!' I yelled. 'He won't hurt you if you leave!'

'HAMISH!' The man banged on the door. 'HAMISH,
PLEASE!' Brutus's snaps and snarls reached frightening levels
of menace, reverberating in the otherwise quiet street.

'It's Fluffy from *Harry Potter*! Hamish, *please* let me in. It's
going to eat me! It's going to eat *your pie*!'

'Emma! Stay inside, my girl!' Harriet hollered in her
quivery old-lady voice. 'I'll call the police! Brutus will hold
him down!'

The man screamed and chanted, 'I'm going to die, I'm
going to die, I'm going to die,' to a background track of

growls and fierce barks. Cursing my security-conscious neighbour, the random drunk man and my general luck in life, I flung open the door. The sickly-sweet smell of beer and sweat wafted into the house. The man was backed against the doorway clutching a paper bag to his chest with both hands. He turned to me, his eyes glassy and wild.

'Oh, thank god! I thought you'd never—' He blinked. 'Hey . . . you're not Hamish.'

'No,' I said, my hands on my hips in what I hoped was a formidable stance. 'How very perceptive.'

The man looked me up and down, taking in my pale blue pyjama bottoms covered in flying pigs, my fluffy dressing gown and my pink sock-covered feet; my hair in its erupting volcano shape.

'This isn't Hamish's house?' He leant backwards on unsteady feet and looked down the lane. 'Am I in Catford?'

'You're in Wimbledon,' I snapped. 'And if you don't leave now my neighbour will call the police. She really will. So can you please just go.'

'Wimbledon?' he said, surveying the surrounding houses with a bewildered expression. 'Are you sure?'

I bundled past him and stopped at the sight of Brutus on his wiry hind legs, his front paws on the low brick wall that divided our front gardens straining in an alarmingly keen manner at the end of his studded leash. His black, jagged lips curled back revealing slippery pink gums and teeth designed to impart ruinous, ragged wounds. Frothy dog spit foamed as he emitted a continuous subterranean growl.

'Harriet!' I said, steering clear of Brutus's range of movement. 'What are you doing?'

'Hello, Emma dear,' Harriet said with a sweet smile not befitting the current circumstances. How she had the strength to hold Brutus back and film us I'll never know. Maybe she ate her Weetabix.

'You call the police. If he escapes I've got it all on camera.' She waggled her handycam.

At the mention of the word 'camera' the man snapped his attention towards the lens. He turned his head to the side and gave a wobbly-lipped attempt at a movie star grin, his eyes half shut.

'Why don't you pop back inside and leave this to me?' Harriet said. 'He might be a rapist.'

'Not a rapisht.' The man held out his hand to me. I ignored it.

'Me Joe. You Tarzan.' He convulsed into giggles, which turned into an attack of the drunken, swaying hiccups.

I leant away from him and Brutus made snapping, snarling endeavours towards me. I took a step back and bumped into the man. Joe, apparently. We struggled to balance, grappling with each other's elbows.

'Jesus!' I spat, flicking his hands away. 'Get off!'

'Ever so sorry.' He swayed towards my open front door. 'Is Hamish in?'

'For god's sake! There *is* no Hamish! This is not Catford! And we do not want your pie!'

'And we're going to call the police!' Harriet added.

'Hey, scary old lady, why'd you want to call the police?' the man said, his chin dimpling and his voice cracking. 'I was only bringing some pie to my friend. It's like that saying, "A pie with a friend is a dish best kept".' He sat heavily on the other low wall opposite Brutus, who was being tussled into submission by Harriet.

'Brutus, SIT!' she commanded. Brutus sat.

I turned to Joe. 'There is no saying like that. At all. Nothing. Never heard of it.'

'You're mean.' The man looked up and snivelled. 'Hamish was never *mean*.'

'Stop it with the Hamish thing, will you? There is no Hamish!'

'There is! We went to school together.' Joe lifted his chin. 'What a ridiculous thing to say.'

'OK,' I said in a cajoling manner. 'There is a Hamish. But he isn't here. Only me. So why don't I call you a taxi and you go home to sleep? You can call Hamish in the morning.'

'Could I possibly have a glass of water?' Joe said, looking past me down the hall. 'Maybe just a little lie-down? I'm terribly tired.'

'No!' I shouted.

'She has a panic button, you know!' Harriet, Brutus now sitting calmly at her side, waggled her finger. 'If she presses it a security team with assault rifles will be here in less than two minutes. You won't know what's hit you till you wake up in jail with your scrotum in your shirt pocket!'

'Harriet!'

Joe peered at Harriet as if assessing whether she were real or not.

Harriet glowered back then flicked her excited eyes to me. 'Press it! Go on!'

I stared at Harriet. She returned my gaze, eyes glistening. 'Well, dear?'

Joe smiled the indifferent smile of a non-comprehending inebriate. I leant inside to the hall table, grabbed the panic button, still in its packaging, and held it up. Harriet pressed her lips together and gave me a disappointed tut.

'I would just like to point out,' Joe said, 'that your panic button is not actually installed.'

'That's not the point!' Harriet interjected. 'The point is . . . the point is . . .'

'Tell you what,' Joe turned to Harriet. 'You go call the police—'

'Righto.' Harriet shot inside, Brutus trailing submissively behind.

Joe turned back to me. 'And while we wait, I'll install it for you. I'm good at DIY. Katy was always –' Joe stopped, lifted his chin and blinked at the night sky '– asking me to . . .' his voice faltered '. . . hang a new light in the hall, or . . .' he let out a sob and a tear trickled down his cheek. 'Knock up a couple of . . . bookshelves.' He dropped his head to his hands and commenced messy blubbering.

I looked up and down the street wondering why, of all houses, did he choose to knock on my little lavender one?

Why me? Did I not have enough to deal with? Was life testing me? I was going to fail.

Joe heaved a great sigh and let out another barrage of sobs.

'Excellent,' I muttered.

All I'd wanted was a nice quiet Friday night. To wake up on Saturday morning and potter around while I waited for Helen's hangover to subside. None of my neighbours would be offering to call the police. I would not be consoling a drunken man in possession of a greasy piece of pie. And I would not be standing in my courtyard at half past midnight with unsupported breasts. I looked at Joe. He had sandyish curly hair and about a five-day-old beard. He wore an old brown leather jacket, some kind of black band t-shirt with faded lettering, jeans and scuffed leather boots. And he sat on the wall hunched over, his face in his hands, blubbing like a little girl.

Harriet emerged from her house. 'The police are on their way – oh.' She stopped at the sight of Joe blubbering. 'Did you hit him, dear?'

'No I didn't *hit* him. He just ...' I glanced at Joe. 'Won't stop crying.'

'I'm sorry,' Joe moaned from behind his hands. 'I'm not usually like this.' I considered him, then with great doubtfulness placed a hand on his shuddering shoulder.

'It's OK,' I said, thinking the exact opposite.

'I've had a bit of a – hic – rough time of late.'

'Right.'

'Had to move out of my flat.'

'Mmm.'

Harriet motioned for my attention and handed a floral handkerchief across the wall.

'Had a fight with my – hic – fiancée.'

'That's terrible.' I shoved the handkerchief into Joe's fists.

'Thanks,' he sniffed. 'Was 'bout the wedding.'

'It'll blow over.'

'Came home from work.'

'Uh-huh.'

'Found her . . . she was . . .' He sobbed and snivelled something unintelligible.

'What was that, dear?' Harriet said, angling forward and cupping a hand to her ear.

'I . . . found her . . .' Joe mumbled another garbled sentence from behind his hands. I looked at Harriet and shrugged.

'I think he said he found her paddling a kayak in Berkshire,' Harriet mused, wrinkling her nose. She turned back to Joe and spoke sharply. 'That's a preposterous reason to be blubbering. Pull yourself together, young man.'

Joe sat up and lowered his hands.

'You're as deaf as a dead badger,' he grumbled. 'I said I found her STRADDLING A GUY THAT SHE WORKS WITH.'

His voice echoed round the empty street.

'Oh,' Harriet said rather plaintively. 'Well, that's a bit different, dear.'

Flashing blue lights suddenly lit up our unusual little gathering and a panda car pulled up. Two policemen got out. Joe stared at the cops. His nose ran and he blew it loudly on the floral handkerchief.

'You called in a disturbance?' the younger of the two said as they reached my gate. He was tall, handsome and severe. Harriet looked to me. I looked to Joe and he gazed back, a lost expression on his wretched face.

'Yes, Officer—' Harriet began.

'Sorry, it was a mistake,' I interrupted. What was I *doing*?

'A mistake,' the young policeman said, a long-suffering air about him.

'Yes. I thought I didn't know this man but I do … ah …' I looked at Joe, the crumpled paper bag now almost translucent with grease sitting on his lap. 'He's, ah, my, ah … my cousin.'

'Your cousin.' The policeman did not believe me.

'Yes. My cousin. I just haven't seen him in a while, that's all.'

'I didn't know I had a cousin in Catford.' Joe looked up. 'Are you on my mother's or my father's side?'

'Ha! He's just a bit drunk,' I said weakly. I put my arm round his shoulder. 'Aren't you, cuz?'

Joe grinned and encircled my thighs in his arms, making me stumble. I steadied myself and smiled at the policemen. The shorter, older cop studied me down the length of his hooked nose.

'I don't think you're telling the truth,' he said, his voice soft, almost curious. He turned to his partner. 'She's not telling the truth, guv.'

'No, she's not,' the taller, sterner one said, keeping his eyes on me. I opened my mouth to protest but the cop continued.

'But I'm afraid I don't care.' He glanced at his watch. 'Look, I don't know what's going on here, but it's the end of our shift. I'm going home to my wife. We're trying for our third baby and it's right in the middle of her ovulation and Reg here,' he indicated the smaller cop, 'is going home to read his caravan magazines and probably have a wank.'

Reg nodded.

'And you.' He rounded on Harriet, pointing an accusing finger. She straightened to attention.

'I don't know how you got my personal number but you're to stop calling it or I'll arrest you. Again.'

At the word 'again', Harriet threw a sheepish glance my way then nodded ingratiatingly.

'Of course. It won't happen again. Sorry, Dale,' she said, her voice syrupy.

'And don't call me that,' he said in a low voice, a flicker of embarrassment visible in his stern demeanour. 'It's Smith. Sergeant Smith.'

After seeing the irate coppers off, I turned to Joe.

'I'll call you a cab,' I said, turning to go inside.

'Got nowhere to go.' He blinked and looked through my open front door. 'Hydrangea!' he blurted, making me stop in the doorway. 'Ivy!'

'You know, I think he's a bit mad,' Harriet said. 'Shall we get Dale back?' She pulled an iPhone from her dressing gown pocket.

'Not mad. Hydrangea for Ivy. She in?'

'My grandma?' I said, puzzled.

'Yes. Ivy. Helped her choose a climbing hydrangea. Could I come in and see how it's going?'

'I don't think so, young man.' Harriet pursed her lips.

'How do you know my grandma?'

'Met her at the garden centre. Go to browse. And talk. Old ladies like to talk.'

'You go to garden centres to pick up old ladies?'

Harriet let out a horrified gasp. 'I knew it! I knew as soon as I saw him. He has a fetish!'

'Interesting fact about hydrangea,' Joe said, ignoring Harriet. 'Looks like "Hi, stranger" to a lip-reader.' He swayed in his sitting position and blinked slowly. 'Could I possibly come in? Ask Ivy about the rooting?'

Harriet's face puckered.

'She died,' I said.

'The hydrangea?'

'My grandma.'

'Oh.' Joe blinked. 'That's terribly sad. I liked her a lot.' A tear ran down his nose.

For a moment the three of us, four if you counted Brutus, who was watching the scene with chocolate-brown, intolerant eyes, sat and stood quietly.

'So,' Joe sighed, 'I best be off.' He stood and swayed. 'It was lovely meeting you all.' He gave a pathetically fragile smile.

I gazed across at the empty common wondering if what I was about to say was stupid and would get me murdered, assaulted or vomited on. He'd been betrayed. I'd been betrayed. I felt a kinship. Plus he sort of knew my grandma.

'Look, I guess you can sleep on my sofa.'

Joe looked stunned. 'Really?' His eyes watered and his chin dimpled.

'Really, dear?' Harriet said.

'For one night only. I'll call you a cab first thing in the morning.' I took him by the elbow to guide him. 'First thing, OK?'

He nodded weakly, his subconscious already closing down for the night.

'Goodnight, Harriet,' I said.

'Yes, dear.' She watched us walk inside, a worrying hand at her chin.

'You're too kind. Most hospitable. I'll be sure to let Hamish know you need a rise.'

I sighed. 'Great.'

I assisted Joe in the removal of boots and jacket but left him to take off his own jeans. I grabbed a duvet from the spare room and as I tossed it over him on the sofa, my dressing gown fell open revealing my swollen belly straining in a t-shirt I'd outgrown two months earlier.

Joe lolled his head and peered at me. 'You're fat.' He smiled merrily. 'Got any reggae-reggae sauce?' he added, then lay back and began snoring.

CHAPTER SEVENTEEN

I sat at the kitchen table kicking my foot against the table leg. Joe's incessant snoring and the constant ping of his phone had kept me awake, and I was scowl personified. The cordless phone next to me shrilled and I answered it with a grunt.

'Oh hello, Emma dear,' Harriet said in her usual cordial manner. 'I was just ringing to make sure that young man didn't murder you in your sleep.'

'Nope,' I said, glaring at the snuffling lump on my sofa. 'Still alive.'

'He didn't try anything on, did he? He's not a sex pest? I did worry about you taking that strange man into your home. I said to Arthur, those officers really ought to have taken him away. Put him in a cell for the night.'

'I'm fine, thanks,' I said, and took a sip of herbal tea. What I needed was a strong black coffee. 'I'll get rid of him when he wakes up.'

'He's still there?'

'Uh-huh.'

'Well, if he gives you any trouble when he wakes, you just scream. I'll be listening out.'

We said our goodbyes and I waddled down the hall to the bathroom. When I returned I found Joe lying on his back, rubbing his eyes.

'Oh good morning,' I said in a passive–aggressive manner. 'Sleep well?' I trundled to the kitchen.

I was making myself a coffee, goddamn it. The baby could deal with the caffeine jitters for a day. Joe sat up and looked over the back of the sofa, confusion rippling across his crumpled face.

'Who are you?' he said, his voice gruff with sleep.

I raised my eyebrows and spooned coffee into the pot. Joe scanned the room then looked down, realised he was sitting in his boxers and arranged the duvet over himself.

'Did we . . .' He looked warily at me. 'You know?'

'Hardly.' I crossed the kitchen to the kettle.

'Whoa,' Joe said. 'You're pregnant.'

'Oh, so you can tell the difference between a pregnant person and a fat girl this morning?'

Joe considered me, wary and baffled. His hair had dried in the most ridiculous of directions.

'So we didn't . . .?'

'No, we did not.' I flicked on the kettle and turned to him, hands on my hips. 'You knocked on my door in the middle of the night offering me pie. Well, offering *Hamish* pie. My

neighbour called the police. But I told them you, well ...
you were crying about your ... You apparently knew my
grandma, but—' I stopped. I couldn't be bothered to explain
the entire logistics. I was grumpy but losing the will to maintain it. I just wanted to go back to bed. Joe sat on the sofa, the
duvet clutched to his bare chest, confused and disorientated.
The only noise was the kettle boiling.

He cleared his throat. 'Well, I guess I'd better get going.
Your boyfriend can't be too happy about me being here.' Joe
looked about the floor for his clothes.

'I don't have a boyfriend,' I said as the kettle flicked off.

'Oh. Partner,' he said, standing and wrapping the blanket round his waist. It would have taken all the strength
of Zeus not to ogle his chest. Solid and big, with just the
right amount of chest hair. I turned and busied myself with
coffee-making.

'Nope, no partner either,' I said.

'Oh. Right.' Joe sounded awkward.

'But I'm not an inseminated lesbian, if that's what you
think.' I spun round. Joe held his hands up in defence and
faltered.

'Ow. Ow. Ow.' He sat back down and put his head in his
hands.

Perched forlornly on the edge of the sofa, the duvet pooling round his middle, he took slow breaths. I felt twinges
of pity. I guess finding your fiancée straddling someone in
your bed was cause for a little drunken behaviour. And I'd
survived the night without being murdered or sex-pestered.

'Your clothes are still in the washing machine. Do you want some coffee?' Joe moved his head a fraction, displaying one grateful eye welling up.

While Joe had a shower after being sick in the toilet I flicked through my recipe book looking for a pancake recipe solid enough to sit at the bottom of Joe's tender stomach and stop him vomiting in my bathroom.

Over breakfast, I found out Joe was not a garden centre granny-stalker, but actually a green-fingered enthusiast who'd had his gardening desires stifled by his ex-fiancée's determination to live in a Shoreditch loft. He'd met my grandma by the hydrangeas (which does not at all look like 'Hi, stranger' to a lip-reader because I'd practised it in the mirror that morning) and he'd helped her choose a climbing one in the right shade of lavender, got it to the car and offered to help her plant it. She'd accepted his proposal and they'd had a lovely afternoon in the late autumn sun with tea, cake and a lavender hydrangea. It was now dormant but sturdy, Joe explained, after popping outside to check its rooting. Joe's phone pinged away during breakfast. He'd check it and put it down without replying.

The washing machine rumbled to a halt just as we finished our pancakes. I stood and began to empty it.

'I'll put your clothes on the radiator. I don't have a drier, sorry.'

'Thanks,' Joe said, rubbing his hands across his stubble. 'You've been really kind, when you don't even know me.'

'I've seen you half naked and I've wiped your vomit off the

toilet seat. I know you enough for now.' I shot him a small smile and cleared the table.

'Ned and Sophie?'

'Yep.' I sat at Sinead's breakfast table watching her sip the froth off a cappuccino. Having asked Joe the necessary questions (are you going to thieve anything, break anything or vomit on anything?) and been satisfied enough with his answer (which was '*Eh?*') I left him on the sofa with his hangover and raced round to vent to Sinead about the most recent developments in the low-budget drama that was my life. Millie was asleep upstairs and Archie was drawing pictures next to me at the kitchen table. Uncle Mike had taken Alice and Jess to a birthday party, so it was a rare quiet day at their house. I'd needed another opinion on the Ned and Sophie situation. I'd now told Alex and Helen. Alex, ever annoyingly wise, had said it was hurtful and thoughtless of Ned and Sophie to see each other behind my back, but if I did not want to be with Ned then he was free to date whoever he wanted. She'd suggested I talk to both of them and tell them how hurt I was, that I'd need time to process their relationship but I was sure we could move forward from this. 'Fuck that,' I'd said. It all sounded a bit too mature and rational for my liking. I preferred name-calling, accusations then a perpetual cold shoulder with me playing the part of The Jilted from here on in. I'd been quite surprised at Helen's reaction. 'They're perfect for each other,' she'd bellowed with a throaty laugh. I'd expected Helen's unwavering solidarity.

Me and her against The Betrayers. But Helen said she'd let Sophie know she was at the top of my Shit List (apparently it was cathartic to have one) and offered to grill her for specifics.

'Which one is Sophie? The slutty one?' Sinead wrestled the lid off the tin of baking I'd brought round and took out a large crumbly biscuit.

'No, that's Helen. And she's not a slut, she's just ... very ... open.'

'Something of hers is open,' Sinead said. 'So Sophie's the stupid one?'

'She's not stupid,' I said, surprising myself by defending her. 'She just looks at the world a little differently.'

Sinead raised her eyebrows and took a bite of the biscuit. 'Mmm. What's this called?'

'Afghan. But the point is, what should I do about it?'

'Afghan?' Sinead turned the biscuit over, inspecting its every angle.

'It's from Australia.'

'So why isn't it called an Australian? Why name it after someone from a country with known terrorist associations?'

'Maybe they named it after the dog? Afghan hound.'

Sinead took another bite out of her biscuit and looked thoughtful. 'I don't know which is weirder.'

'Yes, yes. So what should I do?'

Sinead looked me in the eye. 'Nothing.'

'Nothing?'

'Nothing.'

'Right.' I exhaled. Was no one going to stand in the bitterness corner with me?

'Do you want to be with Ned?'

'No.'

'Do you still love Ned?'

'No.'

'So get over it.'

'Fine,' I said, bristling with injustice. 'I'll do that when I get home. I just have to empty the dishwasher and change the sheets on my bed, but then I'll take a quick five minutes to "get over it" and I can start making lunch and shopping for organic cot linen, that OK?'

'Emma,' Sinead said, her voice soft. 'You're having a baby.'

'With *Ned*.'

'Yes. With Ned. And you'll want him around. Your friends too. It's hard enough being a parent without having to do it on your own.'

I mumbled imperceptibly and twisted my mug round on the table.

'Go home, take some time to feel sorry for yourself but then move on,' she said, taking out another biscuit. 'And give me this recipe, it's bloody fantastic!'

'Emma?' Archie said, putting down his crayon. 'I made this for you.' He pushed his picture towards me.

'Aw thanks, Archie.'

Stick figures in varying colours and sizes dotted the page. One had yellow hair, big round breasts and looked like it was carrying a large red carrot.

'What's this?' I said, pointing to a round circle with a cat inside it.

'That's you.' He pointed to the cat. 'And that's the zombie baby in your tummy. And that's Melody.' He pointed to the big-boobed stick figure holding the red carrot. 'She wipped off a zombie arm.'

'Excellent,' I said, looking at Sinead, who casually helped herself to a third biscuit.

CHAPTER EIGHTEEN

Back at the cottage I found Joe, bare-chested, a pink towel round his waist, watching the beginning of *Love Actually* with a cup of tea and a piece of shortbread.

'I love Richard Curtis films, don't you?' he said with a grin.

'Ah yeah, but I'm a girl. It's in my DNA to like Richard Curtis.'

Joe chuckled at the TV while I made myself a cup of tea and joined him on the sofa, wondering why I didn't have the urge to ask him to leave. Perhaps it was more I didn't have the energy. His phone pinged again.

I had no idea how long I'd been asleep but I opened my eyes to see Joe, still in my pink towel, wearing 3D glasses and giggling at the TV. It appeared he was giggling at *Ice Age 3*. It was dark again. The entire day had disappeared in a movie-watching, cookie-eating, dozing fog.

I stretched and checked my cheek. 'You're still here.'

Joe glanced sideways and smiled. His stubble was thicker.

'Yes. Still here. And I *did* see you dribble. But I figured it was fair, as you saw me vomit.' He turned back to *Ice Age* and laughed at the sloth.

'Great.' I hefted myself up to a sitting position and wiped at my cheek. 'I usually reserve cheek dribble for my nearest and dearest. You are neither. And I only *heard* you vomit. Thank god.'

'Sorry about that.' Joe patted my sock-covered feet. 'I don't usually drink that much. It's just ... at the moment ... you know.' He stared at the TV and swallowed.

'You were pretty drunk last night.'

My stomach rumbled with pregnancy starvation. An irrational 'bacon and marmalade sandwich' kind of hunger.

'Ye-es. I drink and then, unfortunately, I cry.' A flicker of sadness crossed his face and he looked at me with a wry smile.

Joe being open unnerved me.

'Me too. Give me a few gins and I'll bawl all night,' I said, trying to lighten the conversation. 'I once cried for two hours at a party because a Tracy Chapman song reminded me of a three-legged dog I saw on a poster at a Hoxton bus stop.'

'You're strange.'

'I was drunk. And you're the one sitting on a stranger's sofa in a pink towel wearing 3D glasses.'

Joe glanced down at the towel. 'You have a point.'

His phone pinged again; he looked at it then replaced it on the arm of the sofa. It bothered me that he never replied.

'What's with the constant messages? And why don't you ever reply?'

'It's my family,' he said, removing the 3D glasses. A small smile lifted one corner of his mouth. 'Well, my sisters-in-law.'

'How many do you have?'

'Three. And they all want to accommodate my "recuperation".'

'That's sweet.'

He nodded. 'Yep. I can convalesce in Malta, my eldest brother works on superyachts; in Scotland, next elder brother works in forestry, or Tahoe, my last elder brother is a snowmaker.'

'I'd convalesce in Malta. So you're the youngest?'

'I'm the baby who needs looking after.' He picked up the phone. 'Half these messages are them discussing me. I'm not required to reply.' He grinned, showing a fondness for their fuss.

'Why don't you go and stay with any of them?'

He shrugged. 'The wives, they all talk. A lot. They whatsapp, they viber, they text, they group-skype, they call. They're wonderful, really great, but . . . I'd rather do no talking at the moment. Just, you know, keep to myself for a bit.'

I nodded my understanding. I was familiar with the hide-away-with-your-misery process.

'So where've you been staying?'

'Hotels. The floor of a pub one night. Mates' couches.' He looked at me. 'A very kind stranger's couch.'

We smiled at each other. He didn't know my situation and I didn't fully know his, but we could sense a rawness in each other.

A rapid, rhythmic knock at the door propelled Joe off the sofa.

'I'll get it,' he said, tightening the towel round his waist.

'Ah . . . OK.'

'Hello. And who are you?' Helen's impertinent voice travelled from the front door.

I'd forgotten she was coming over to tell me what she'd found out about Ned and Sophie.

'I'm Joe. A friend of Emma's.'

'He's not my friend!' I called out.

'Emma's on the sofa, I've been watching her dribble and she's a little upset.'

Helen appeared in the living room unbelting her coat, a suggestive look on her face.

'He's not my friend,' I said to her raised eyebrows. 'I only met him last night.'

'Oh *really*.' Helen turned to Joe who arrived behind her, collecting his clothes from the radiator.

She looked him up and down slowly and deliberately then turned to me, eyes gleaming.

'Very nice.'

'OK,' Joe said, not at all offended. 'I'm going to get dressed because, suddenly, I feel a bit like a piece of meat. Nice to meet you . . .?'

'Helen,' I offered.

'Nice to meet you, Helen.' He looked her up and down deliberately. 'Also very nice.' He left the room grinning.

'I *like* him!' Helen dumped her bag on the kitchen

table and emptied out a stack of DVDs. 'Now, tell me everything.'

I quickly updated Helen on the appearance of Joe.

'It's not fair.' Helen shook her head.

'What do you mean?' I said, getting up and looking through the DVD collection.

'This never happens to me. You didn't have to leave the house, get your legs, lips and ladybits waxed, dance all night to crap DJ music in killer heels and a tight dress with your tits straining to get out. You're wearing trackies, it looks like Gordon Brown did your ponytail and you have dried dribble on your cheek. And yet here he is. God delivered a gorgeous man, drunk and vulnerable to your front door. It's like winning the sexual lottery.'

'Gross,' I said, rubbing my cheek.

Joe emerged from the bathroom, dressed for the first time since last night, and walked over to the pile of DVDs.

'What're we watching?' He flicked through the stack then looked up.

I thought I could read a small plea in his face. Helen was smirking and making grabbing motions at his bottom. His smile dropped. He seemed to be reading my silence as an indication to leave. His eyes went to the DVD in his hand. *About Time*. Richard Curtis.

I grabbed it. 'Let's watch this!'

Joe looked up, his expression grateful. 'And get pizza?' He turned to Helen, who immediately dropped her groping motion.

'Pizza's good.' Helen twisted her ruby mouth into a salacious smile. 'Now, come take a seat and tell me all about yourself.'

Later, after Helen had left and as I was padding down the hall turning lights off, my phone rang.

'I didn't see that young man leave,' Harriet said.

'No, he's still here.' I tucked the phone under my chin and pulled the duvet out of the hall closet.

'Are you in some kind of a hostage situation? If you are, say the code word "apple flapjack" and I'll be over with Brutus. Say it now. Use it in a sentence, like maybe—'

'Harriet, I'm fine.' I suppressed a snigger. 'He's just staying another night. He's got nowhere else to go. I'll come over tomorrow and tell you all about it.'

'But—'

'There's nothing to worry about. He's actually a nice guy.'

'If you're sure, dear.'

'I am.'

'OK, well, you know the code word now.'

'I do.'

'Apple flapjack.'

'Apple flapjack.'

'Good, good.' Harriet clicked her tongue. 'Make sure you do pop over tomorrow. Arthur's made you a key lime pie.'

'OK.'

'You're a good girl, Emma dear.'

'Thanks,' I said, touched.

I hung up and took the duvet into the living room. Joe

had fallen asleep on the sofa during *About Time* and was on his back, breathing gently, a different man to the snoring, smelly one from the night before. His hair, now clean, dried in loose curls round his head. His lashes rested on his cheeks and curled upward and his beard had grown thicker. His broad chest rose and fell with his breath. Who would cheat on a man with a chest like that? I'd been surprised when he'd told Helen he was a graphic designer. He looked more outdoorsy-lifty-lifty than indoorsy-clicky-clicky. Joe snuffled and turned, making me jump. I laid the duvet over him, turned off the light and headed to bed.

At three thirty in the morning I got up to pee for the 348th time. Then shuffled to the kitchen, got a glass of juice and two chocolate-chip cookies and snuck back past Joe. He was on his side with the duvet pulled up tight to his chin looking sweet and vulnerable. Unable to watch my predawn infomercials because of the sleeping, broken-hearted man on my sofa, I crept back to bed and flicked on my bedside lamp.

So.

Ned and Sophie were really happy together. Or so Helen had said. They'd bumped into each other on the tube after my grandma's wake and ended up going to the same bar. Sophie spent most of the night with Ned, as he'd seemed so depressed. They'd talked about the baby, about me and about life in general. But nothing physical happened that night, Helen had said patting my knee. Like that was any consolation. Oh goody for them, they managed not to get together on the night of my grandmother's funeral. Let's give them the Nobel Peace Prize and a box of kittens. A few weeks later they bumped into each other at another bar and Ned had been far less depressed and much more fun and Sophie had been very drunk. They danced and drank and kissed. And then went home together. Yuck. I'd called Sophie the next morning and it had been him I'd heard in the background, not her sick cat. I'd felt faint when Helen told me. He was there, next to her. Naked, probably. With that freshly fucked, contented, droopy-eye thing he gets after sex while I chatted on the other end of the phone. I thought back to the times after that when Sophie had been practically floating two inches above the ground, heading out on dates with a mystery man while we speculated on who it could be. She'd not said a word but had smiled and radiated that 'new love' joy girls get where your skin glows and you lose weight without even trying. And it had been Ned making her feel that way. I was beyond understanding. Apparently Sophie had had conniptions when Helen told her I'd seen them kissing. She was already quite a connip-tious soul. I can only imagine the state she'd been in. Helen had physically restrained her from jumping into her Ford Fiesta (with the ridiculous eyelashes on the headlights) and driving over to beg forgiveness. Joe had listened quietly to the conversation from the armchair, masticating methodically through a bowl of buttered popcorn.

I slunk down in bed and picked up my weekly forward-planning schedule for the movie. In a week we were heading to the Isle of Anglesey for six weeks to shoot the camping and zombie cat scenes. We'd be leaving behind Melody and meeting Scott Vander, the 'campers' and a pack of, I hoped, well-trained cats. Bradley Manor was the name of the estate we'd be filming at. It was also our accommodation for the six weeks. I tossed the schedule to the side and picked up a piece of paper with a scrawled ad for a lodger I'd made after I'd seen Ned and Sophie kissing and realised I would not be contacting him to get my money back. I was dreading the rounds of interviews and viewings I'd have to endure. But I needed the money. Having told Mum Ned was in the process of selling the ice cream van, I was forced to hand her a healthy portion of my chaperone wage each week as 'instalments'.

Joe coughed.

I glanced at the scruffy paper in my hand.

I nibbled on my cookie.

I was being rash . . .

I hardly knew Joe. He could be an identity thief who brings in a Russian girl to pose as me and then runs an international arms ring from my cottage before jumping on a cruise to the Caymans and leaving me with a global criminal record. Or I could come home to find he was trafficking Albanian teenagers into the sex industry and using my cottage as a heroin-administering centre for the girls before sending them to a brothel in Croydon.

Nah.

I shoved the rest of the cookie in my mouth and decided to present Joe with the option in the morning.

CHAPTER NINETEEN

A week later I was about to be picked up to leave for Anglesey when I got a facetime call from a breathless Alex.

'Guess what?' Her beaming face took up the whole screen.

'What?' I said, zipping up my toiletries bag with one hand and holding the phone with the other.

'Guess!'

'Ah ... the sky is blue, the sea is hot, you're going for a swim and I am not?'

'Oh, very good. But no. I'm engaged! Cal flew to Vanuatu and proposed!' She let out an excited squeal.

'Oh my god. That is so exciting!' My head said 'be happy' but my stomach dropped to the floor. I sat on my bed.

Why do you get everything? I wanted to yell. I'm pregnant by a skinny freckle farm and you get proposed to on a tropical island by a lovely investment banker with a perfect arse? They'd invest in condos and travel the world donating to charities. And they'd visit me with their pert-arsed children at Mum's house and I'd show them my new Wizard of Oz teapot I bought on eBay.

Cal's face appeared in the frame. 'Hey, Em!' he said, his straight white teeth massive on my screen.

'Congratulations!' I chirped. 'Decided to join the family, did you? Mum hasn't put you off?'

'That charmer?' he said with a laugh. 'No chance. You, on the other hand . . .'

'Oh, ha ha.'

Alex, laughing, came back into the frame, and with their two faces mushed together within the constraints of an iPhone I could see their future. Happy, tanned, philanthropic and well off. Cute babies, a well-trained beagle pup and family trips to mind-expanding destinations like Nepal, Machu Picchu and the Galapagos while the baby and I saved up for our annual week at Center Parcs.

'OK, get out now – I want to talk to my sister.' Alex gave Cal a fond shove out of the frame.

'Bye!' his disembodied voice said. 'Hope all's going well with the pregnancy!' Alex grinned in his direction then turned back towards the screen, her face shining with joy.

'So how did he propose? When did he get there? Tell me everything!' I said, forcing enthusiasm.

'I had no idea at all,' she said, grinning. 'I got this knock at my cottage door last night and it was him! I couldn't believe it! We went to the beach, where one of the locals had started a bonfire, and we sat round drinking rum out of coconuts then he pulled out this amazing ring and I said yes and the local kids all started singing and it was just . . . amazing!' She heaved a huge sigh.

I had never heard Alex so thrilled and girlish.

'That sounds . . . amazing,' I said, jealous to the point of turning solid with it. 'Show me the ring!'

'Oh, yeah!' She moved the phone and her ring came into view.

'It was my grandmother's!' Cal's voice said.

The image moved again and Alex came back into the frame, Cal's arm visible over her tanned bare shoulder.

'Em, I'm so happy,' she said.

Cal kissed her cheek, making her already wide smile wider.

'Well, you deserve it,' I said, and I really meant it.

'You'll help me plan the wedding?'

'Of course!'

'You know you're my head bridesmaid, don't you?'

'I'd better be.' I angled the phone away briefly and wiped a tear from my cheek. I was unsure whether it was a happy tear or a sad tear; I was feeling both emotions simultaneously.

'How's my baby?' Alex said, changing tack.

'Oh, good. I'm quite big now.' I moved the phone to show my large frame.

'Wow! I wish I could be there with you.'

'I do too,' I said, looking at a photo on the wall of Alex and me in our swimmers at Bournemouth beach aged five and eight.

'I'd better go, though. The Alliance Française group are

throwing us an engagement party on the beach – it's already started and we're not there!'

'OK, have fun. I miss you,' I said, feeling guilty that I was glad to be getting off the phone.

'Miss you too!'

An hour later my ride to Anglesey arrived.

'And don't forget to put the recycling out on Fridays,' I said, shuffling behind Joe as he carried my suitcase to the waiting four-by-four.

'I won't.'

'And you know how to record *Graham Norton*?'

'Yes. I have worked a television before.'

'And you'll wash the Ungaro towels separately? Mum will kill me if—'

'I won't even use the Ungaro towels. Emma, I'll be fine. I remember all the rules.' He hefted the suitcase into the boot and walked me to the car door. 'No sluts, no wet towels on the floor, no smelly socks under the sofa, no drugs, no parties, do *not* mess with your plastics drawer and . . . ummm . . . that's it!'

'And if my mother comes over with anything neon, do not let her in.'

'I'll tell her you moved.'

I looked up at him and my doubts reared again. Sure, he'd been staying at my place for the past week and had seemed perfectly normal. He did his dishes, he left the bathroom cleaner than I did and he proved to be a worthy competitor at Swear Word Scrabble. He'd taken to answering the phone in case it was Sophie, and on the one occasion it was her produced an inconsistent accent and told her she had 'zee vrong nemberz, aye mon'. He'd even graduated from the couch to the upstairs bedroom, but I didn't *really* know him. What if he brought different girls home every night and used my grandma's cottage as a sexual adventure playground, or I came home to find him wearing my knickers and hosting a PowerPoint seminar on cross-dressing?

'You're looking at me weirdly,' Joe said, a knowing smile playing at the edges of his lips. 'I'm not an amateur porn director, I will not steal all your stuff and you won't come home to find me wearing your knickers.'

'I wasn't thinking that,' I said, averting my guilty eyes.

Joe *uh-huh*ed.

'You don't need to worry about me, I'm normal.' He pulled a funny face. 'Now get in the car.'

I climbed into the back seat of the four-by-four with a degree of difficulty. At five months pregnant I could not bend in the middle without worrying about severing a foetal limb.

'It's very kind of you to let me stay,' Joe said, shutting the door and talking through the open window. 'And if I really must wear your knickers I'll make sure they're your worst pair, the ones with holes and no elastic. And I'll wash them thoroughly afterwards.'

'Just throw them out,' I said.

He grinned.

I waved goodbye as the driver pulled away and navigated

the narrow lane filled with soccer mum estates and kids on tricycles and headed round the corner to Uncle Mike and Sinead's to collect Archie. I was sure Joe was who he seemed to be. A good guy. The cottage would be fine. And all my knickers would be unworn, where I left them.

After seven long hours Archie and I drove over the Britannia Bridge to the Isle of Anglesey. Archie had been the perfect travelling companion. He'd stayed to his side of the car (mostly because he was strapped into a technical-looking safety seat that had taken the driver and I twenty minutes to get him back into after our first toilet stop) and only asked the dreaded 'how long till we get there' question once, three minutes after Sinead had buckled him in and run back into her house shouting, 'One kid down, three to go!'

A few minutes after leaving the bridge we were in country lanes. We came to the crest of a hill where the driver nosed the four-by-four off the lane and onto what looked like a farm track down a steep paddock. He shifted a few gears, then we lurched over the top and jolted roughly down the hill. I never had been one for extreme sports, preferring the safety of a couch or bar stool to that of a mountain bike or jet ski. I gripped the handle on the door with one hand and the edge of the seat with the other as the car bumped and dipped over the uneven terrain.

'This is fun,' Archie said, looking out of the window, his soft cheeks bouncing with each plunge of the tyres.

'Hmmm,' was all I could manage.

It was a few minutes later when we reached a level-ish

area at the edge of a dense forest. I decided I was going to sue the film company if my baby came out with its ears on back to front. Darkness had fallen completely by the time we broke through the trees and drove up the gravel drive to Bradley Manor. Although we were arriving from the back the building was still grand. The walls were a grey stone and multiple chimneys clustered on the peaked rooftops wafting the comforting smell of log fires. Lights glimmered in the diamond-paned windows and people bustled in and out of the manor.

The busyness made me itch with excitement. Lighting and generator trucks, camera vans, people movers and expensive four-by-fours congested the courtyard. Our driver parked up beside the camera van. Andrew stood at the back with an assistant, sorting gear. He turned as we parked and gave me a grin that sent flurries through my chest.

'Hi,' he said as I slipped as elegantly as I could from the car. 'Good trip?'

'Yeah, fine thanks,' I said, covertly dislodging my skirt from my knickers. But before I could think of anything to say that displayed my sparkling intelligence and/or wit, the assistant had recaptured his attention with an important bit of cable that should or should not have been attached to another important bit of cable.

'Can I go and say hello to Bwian?' Archie said, waving to the staunch Northern Ireland props guy in his mid-sixties who was unloading a plastic box of heads from the back of a tatty van.

'Sure,' I said warily. The last time I'd come across Brian and Archie chatting I thought I'd heard the words 'Sinn Féin' and 'active organisation'. 'But don't get in his way.'

'OK!' Archie trotted across the lively courtyard.

'And leave that bag alone!' I called out as I saw him about to reach into a bag of pre-bloodied intestinal prosthetics.

I was shown to a converted barn attached to the main house by a covered walkway, which Archie and I would share with Martha and Tilly. My heart sank. I'd be kept up all night by the crinkling and rustling of crisp packets. And I bet she snored. My visions of accidentally-on-purpose bumping into Andrew in his boxers on a trip to the bathroom in the middle of the night vaporised. But the barn house was cosy. Sliding glass doors opened on to a living room with a long velvet sofa and two armchairs set round a log burner. Fluffy sheepskins covered the wooden floor and a mini-kitchen in the corner was already stocked with Martha's snacks. It was understood that I was not welcome to help myself. I sighed a contented little sigh as I put my Kindle next to the four-poster bed. I was looking forward to the next adventure, and not least because I was away from London where Ned was searching for Sophie's clitoris.

'Paris?' I said into my mobile. '*Paris*?!'

'Sorry.' Helen had just had the unenviable job of telling me Ned had taken Sophie to Paris for her birthday. 'He's a wanker.'

'He's a cunt wanker fuck-beard,' I said, pacing outside in

the early morning sun. Archie and Tilly were playing on the grass with the manor's huge Irish wolfhound called Ivan and his sidekick, Wayne the Jack Russell, while waiting for their call to set. Martha stood nearby, eating.

'Fuck-beard? Sounds like a pirate pimp.'

'How'd you find out?'

'I called Sophie to wish her Happy Birthday—'

'What?! You called her?'

'I'm not angry with her. *You* are.'

'Yes, I am. Couldn't you join me in moral judgement? Like any good friend would?'

'I *am* a good friend. But I kind of feel sorry for Sophie. She's with *Ned.*'

I grumbled my displeasure. I was very tired. Martha had snored all night and, while we were not sharing a room, the wood-panelled walls of the barn house were not thick enough to drown out the noise she made. It sounded like someone vacuuming an octopus. I'd missed out on dinner with the film crew in the manor, and had instead eaten an early dinner of chicken nuggets and peas with Martha and the kids in the barn house, Martha making it piously clear our duties lay with the children. I felt like I'd been grounded on the night of a party. At six in the morning Martha, wanting to take the children for an awakening stroll round the lake, dragged me from slumber. I'd told her to bite me again. One day she was going to take me up on my offer. But in the end I'd trudged round the lake and had come back to the lit fire in the barn house feeling quite glad I'd made the effort. Not least because I got a glimpse of Andrew and Scott Vander going for a run in their sweats and vests, and Scott Vander was every bit as hot as he seemed in the tabloid pictures. But Martha had ruined my good mood by telling me she'd seen Amy and Andrew looking very cosy at breakfast. Not that I was entertaining the thought I had a chance with Andrew (OK, I wasn't just entertaining the thought. I'd cooked it a four-course meal and invited it to live with me permanently.) I was a very man-repellent five months pregnant with another man's baby. But I was sure there were looks he had given me. Holding my gaze for a moment too long that had made me think, maybe he can look past the swollen belly and ginormous breasts and see the single yummy mummy on the other side. Or maybe it was the ginormous breasts that so captivated his gaze . . .

'Emma, while I am in total agreement about Sophie being a senseless nut-bar with a ridiculous sense of colour, she didn't set out to hurt you. It's not like she jumped Ned the moment you broke up. It wasn't a planned thing. I think they genuinely like each other and are both genuinely surprised about it all. She's devastated about upsetting you. She really is.' Helen was being much more practical than I was used to.

'Poor Sophie,' I sneered.

'Forget about them. Pray they slip over in French dog poo and get sick from unpasteurised cheese. Now, have you seen Scott Vander's penis yet? Helmet or ant-eater?'

*

223

At the end of the day, after convincing Martha that it would be fine for me to go and have dinner with the crew, seeing as Archie and Tilly were asleep and she was sitting in the living room eating a family-size pack of Maltesers three yards from their bedroom door, I slipped out of the barn house. Much to Helen's dismay, I'd not seen Scott Vander's penis. And I was unlikely to see his penis because, despite her argument that 'I could just say I'd got lost', I was not going to accidentally find myself in his cottage in the wee hours with my camera at the ready.

Congenial chatter drifted from behind the door to the 'smoking' room. I pushed it open and was instantly enveloped in the warmth coming from a roaring fire. Three rustically battered chesterfield sofas were arranged around the hearth. Cast and crew were perched on the arms and squashed up against each other with glasses of wine and pints of ale, their cheeks ruddy and pink from a combination of alcohol and proximity to the flames. It had been a gentle first day of filming at the manor (just Archie, Tilly and Scott setting up a tent pre-zombie-cat arrival) and the moderate pace and change of scenery had everyone in good spirits.

'Hey. Martha let you out?' Caroline appeared at my side with a generous smile. 'Come and sit by the fire.' She scooted a stoned-looking Steve out of his spot. 'Drink?'

Caroline introduced me to some of the girls playing 'campers' (girls in bras) and we chatted like a group of mates out in town. Dinner was served in a dining hall with a long wooden table in the centre and ancient oriental carpets scattered across the vast stone floor. Heads of slain animals looked down on us reprovingly as we ate mouthfuls of their tender distant cousins with jus and prosciutto-wrapped runner beans.

'My mum smoked weed when she was pregnant with me and my bruvva and we're cool.' Steve, the lanky boom op, was trying to convince me to smoke a joint with him after dinner.

'I'm OK, thanks,' I said, swishing the last forkful of sticky date pudding round my bowl.

Most people had finished their meals and were leaning back in their chairs, drinking, laughing and talking with exaggerated volume.

'Suit yourself. I'll be down the lake if you wanna join. Unless you have a *Vander* invitation.' Steve made an attempt at a snooty face. He really was a very unfortunate-looking man, the snooty-face attempt only making him more so.

'A Vander invitation?'

'Oh,' he said with a smile, 'you don't have one?' He seemed happy.

'What is it?'

'Scott Vander,' Steve made his snooty face again, 'is having people up to his digs. But you have to be invited.'

'Oh,' I said, feeling like the stinky kid who doesn't get picked for a team in sports and has to sit with the teacher.

'You have to be somebody,' he continued. 'Somebody with drugs. Somebody shaggable. Or "Somebody".' He did the inverted commas thing with his smoked-stained fingers.

'I'm none of those,' I said pathetically.

Steve nodded his agreement. I glanced round the table at Claire and Caroline chatting in a group of skinny-jeans-clad minor cast members and some of the more muscular lighting guys with their tight jaws, tattooed arms and ruggedly on-trend five o'clock shadow. Even though Caroline and Claire had just finished a thirteen-hour shoot day, their hair and make-up were immaculate and they were in new outfits. Amy sat on the knee of a cameraman old enough to be her father, flicking her hair. Andrew was deep in conversation with another cameraman, the continuity lady and a wardrobe girl who looked like she should be front row at Chanel. Art department guys and girls leant against the fireplace talking about interpretive naked theatre or whatever it was arty people talked about. They would all be invited to Scott's. I turned back to Steve, who was watching me with a little smile.

'Are you invited?'

'Me?' he said, taking a battered old tin out of his pocket and starting to roll a joint in plain view of the rest of the table. 'Nah. Couldn't give a toss, neither.'

CHAPTER TWENTY

At breakfast the next morning it became apparent who did and did not have a Vander invite. Dark glasses remained on the noses of those suffering from stonking great hangovers, and only a mere handful possessed bright eyes, colour in their cheeks and the ability to eat scrambled eggs without retching. Even Steve's boom op mate with the shaved head had bleary eyes and a slight whiff of vomit about him.

'Sorry lot, aren't they?' Steve said as he piled his plate high with bread and bacon, a post-breakfast joint lodged behind his left ear.

'Yeah.' I tried to hide my resentment at being left out. 'Do you know what they did?'

Steve shrugged. 'Probably some cocaine, maybe acid. Definitely E. Claire brought a whole bag.'

'I didn't mean what drugs,' I said, although I was mildly shocked that Claire had brought a bag of E. 'I just was wondering what went on up there.'

'They partied.' Steve looked at me like I ought to up my medication. 'You have been to a party, haven't you?'

'Yes,' I said witheringly.

'EVERYBODY ON SET FOR BLOCKING!' the first AD's voice screeched through the radio clipped to Amy's waistband.

'See you soon,' Steve said, throwing a couple of rashers of bacon into a bun and sloping off to set to watch the block (a technical term for the placement and movement of actors; effectively a "you stand here, then you run this way and shove the tent pole in his eye, and *you*; you die right here, but make sure you land with your head facing that way so we can end on a close-up of your empty eye socket.").

Around mid-morning filming took a small break while Scott had zombie eyeballs fitted. These were like contact lenses but they covered the entire eyeball, were very rigid and had to be fitted by an optometrist. Normal contact lenses could be fitted by the make-up artist or the actor themselves but the full lens was difficult to get in, very uncomfortable and, being opaque, rendered the wearer almost sightless. Which is probably why Scott was using delaying tactics and had become a lot more ADHD than usual.

'OH, YEAH! OH, YEAH!' Scott, shirtless and out of the make-up chair yet again, twerked to his own tune. Admittedly, with his shredded trousers, an overtly gruesome bullet wound to the torso and zombie facial make-up, he looked hilarious. But I found it hard to laugh along with the rest of the crew knowing I'd been scorned in the invite department.

Steve caught my eye and made his Snooty Scott face again. Archie sat on my lap, transfixed by the entire eyeball process. I'd stopped checking if he was frightened because he seemed so unfazed. He was curious and wanted to be told how *everything* worked. He'd made friends with the SPFX team and now knew more than I did about blood squibs and low-grade explosives. And I'd been in the industry for six years.

'Know your lines, son?' the director said to Archie, who nodded. 'Good, good.' He pulled out a bag of seeds and nibbled anxiously.

'They've got five more minutes to get those god-awful lenses in before I call time on the children.' Martha sank heftily into a chair and directed Tilly's attention to what looked like a mathematics book.

'Chill, Martha, the kids are OK.'

Eventually the optometrist, two costume assistants, a very stern-looking First AD and Caroline managed to keep Scott in the chair long enough to fit both eyeballs and he was led by the arms towards his first position on set. As he passed Martha, Tilly, Archie and me, who must have seemed like moving orbs behind those lenses, he made a terrifying face.

'RAAAARRRRRHHHH!' he roared at the kids, who giggled, whereas Martha squealed like Nathan Lane in *The Birdcage*.

'What kind of parent exposes their child to this kind of movie? It's indecent.' Martha pressed her lips together, yet she ogled Scott's bare chest as if it were a glazed Christmas ham and she the only guest at the table.

Filming commenced and the collective hangover kicked into high gear. People yawned and burped discreetly into their fists. Caroline sipped Berocca; Claire popped pills. Cameramen leant on their tripods, the shaved-head boom op leant on his boom and the standby art director, while spurting blood from a shampoo-like bottle over a lone limb at the back of set, had paused and lingered nauseously over the rubber leg, her eyes glassy and bulging.

I ran a hand over my forehead. It was only a matter of time before Uncle Mike found out this movie was not, as Sinead had told him, a period drama/comedy like *Pride and Prejudice* mashed with *Little Miss Sunshine*.

The morning dragged. The boom op kept dipping his boom into shot, zombies forgot their lines (I mean *really*, how hard is it to say 'aarrggghhh' at a specified moment) or a key prop was missing. Stupid hung-over people. Hung over and flaunting the fact they'd been at a party when I'd sat on the sofa in the barn house watching Martha work her way through a bag of marshmallows without offering me even one. I sat behind the director's monitor, watching him nibble his way into an edgy, time-watching frenzy.

Lunch was called and the hung-over crew gratefully decamped outside grabbing coffees, dark glasses, cigarettes and Berocca. Food was devoured in a rush and the crew disappeared to various dark corners of the property to sleep for the remainder of the break. Archie and Tilly rubbed the bellies of Ivan and Wayne while Martha sat on a garden bench with Steve discussing puff pastry versus filo. I switched on my phone and was immediately rung by voicemail. Joe's upbeat voice left the first message.

'Hey Em, hope all's going well on set with the famous Scott Vander. I met him at a product launch once. Good guy, I reckon. Went home with three of the models, if I remember rightly. Anyway, I just wanted to check something. Harriet and Arthur are heading to Cornwall for a family birthday or something and can't take Brutus. Harriet's asked me to look after him because he's not so good with strangers yet. He tries to attack them. Would it be OK to have him here for the weekend? They're back on Sunday so it would only be for two nights. Apparently he has to have risotto on Friday night and casserole on Saturday night. Let me know. Oh, and don't worry, I'm not wearing any of your knickers and will only wear your bra when I host the Lady Gaga Appreciation Night next week.'

I smiled, saved the message and listened to the next one. Joe again.

'I forgot,' his voice said immediately into the phone. 'Brutus stole my house keys yesterday and buried them somewhere on the common. We looked everywhere but couldn't find them. So I had to get your locks changed. Also more flowers got delivered.' I felt my jaw clench. Ever since I'd blocked Sophie's calls she'd resorted to sending flowers with grovelling apology notes. 'They're from Sophie again. She also sent a bottle of stretch-mark cream. It's really gross – smells like rotten oranges. I think it's home-made. Oh and there's a package here from France from someone called

Diana George. Is that your mother? Shall I open it? It says "lingerie" on the packing slip. I think I should open it. OK, well ... yes, that's all ... OK, bye!'

I giggled. The next message was from the hospital confirming my scan for two weeks' time. We had a long weekend coming up. Archie and I were heading back to London and the rest of the cast and crew to their friends and family around the country before returning to set for the remainder of the shoot. I saved the message then listened to the final one. Mum.

'Hi, darling. I'm in Paris looking at wedding dresses for Alex. It's all total rubbish here. I think she should go British. McQueen, maybe. But the girl wants to wear vintage. *Vintage*? What she's saying is "second hand". Disgusting. Anyway, I was in Montmartre looking for "vintage" and I saw Ned and that friend of yours, the one with the stripy clothing, sitting in a café. I'm sorry to have to tell you this but I thought you'd want to know. In the fashion capital of the world, and that bumpkin was wearing striped tights, a moss-green corduroy skirt with brass buttons down the front and what looked to be Joseph's Technicolor Dreamcoat from a 1970s community theatre show. Unforgivable. Alex said I shouldn't tell you but I just had to, darling. You don't mind? When are you off that movie and back in London? Must go, love you.'

Ugh. Sophie and Ned again.

I dialled my home number with a quick check on Archie, who was inspecting a worm in Tilly's hand.

'Hello, Lady Emma's residence, Butler Joe speaking, how may I be of service?'

'Is that really how you answer the phone?'

'Yep. And I answer the door wearing a pinny. *Only* a pinny.'

'Ha ha.'

'You have a caller ID-reader box thingy.'

'Do I?'

'Harriet gave it to you, remember?'

'Oh, yeah. You hooked it up?' Harriet had brought round the caller ID reader a few days before I left. I had the feeling she thought the caller ID would state the name and occupation of each caller. *Paul Ellis: Residential Photographer. 5 ft 11. Salt and pepper hair. Supports Chelsea. Andrea Cammell: Organic Vegetable Box Delivery Girl. Blond, tall and bossy. Lee Rayner: thieving sex pest with a bad case of scurvy and his eyes on your electrical goods.* I'd chucked the caller ID box on the kitchen bench and forgotten about it.

'Yep, hooked it up this morning. I've also started a herb garden. You're growing rosemary, mint, parsley and basil. And I colour-coded your linen cupboard. Which wasn't too taxing, being that all your linen is white.'

'Jeez, you need to get back to work. Why *aren't* you working? Are you independently wealthy?'

'Ha! I live cheap. And I'm freelance. If I don't do any work I'm not letting anyone down but myself, and I'm OK with that these days. I've got a few contracts ticking over so there's a bit of money coming in. There's no holes in my undies yet, so I'm all good! Anyway, it's quite fun going through your stuff. I found some poems you wrote.'

'You can't go through my stuff!' I said, only somewhat annoyed.

It's not as though I had anything to hide. At school I'd be forever quelling the boredom of a droning geography teacher by scribbling limericks or poems on scraps of paper that I'd pass to friends. I still remembered one I'd given Helen during a particularly dull Latin class.

> *Helen, I am tired*
> *I feel this room is wired*
> *Wired with a bomb*
> *And soon we'll all be gone.*

Even now I found myself sitting behind the monitor during long scenes jotting on the backs of scripts. In fact, that morning I'd written one about Martha.

> *Martha, O Martha*
> *I do not see why*
> *You don't take my advice*
> *Of 'go curl up and die'*
> *You're mean and you're bossy*
> *There's no slack in your slacks*
> *You snore like a rhino*
> *And you don't share your snacks.*

'Hang on now, where is it … this is funny …' I heard paper rustling.

'Get out of my stuff!' I laughed.

'Here we go … It's called "I have a Little Secret", by Emma Patricia George.'

'Joe!'

He'd found my teenage diary. I'd been a very uncompli-cated teenager who'd had no scandal, drama or unrequited infatuation to document. Awkward kisses with boys were talked about with friends, crushes were either reciprocated or they weren't and that was the life of every teenager across the world. I didn't feel anything that happened to me was unique enough to write in a diary and hide under my mat-tress. So I wrote childlike poetry in the pink, scented pages of the lockable diary Grandma had given me.

Joe cleared his throat in mock preparation.

'"I have a little secret I don't want anyone to know".'

'Bloody hell.'

'"It's at the bottom of the garden where the daffodillys grow" … What, pray tell, is a daffodilly?' Joe said, affecting a pompous voice.

'Shut up!'

'"I go there in the night, when the moon is out, I sit and watch my secret trying desperately to sprout".'

'I'm going to kill you.'

'"It's been a few weeks since I planted my seed, but I'll just sit and wait for my little money tree". Well, Emma, I think that is literary genius.'

'And I think when I get back to London you are dead.'

Joe chuckled. It was a rumbling, heartening chuckle.

'So what do you think about Brutus? Can he have a sleepover?'

About a week into our stay at Bradley Manor, I suggested Martha eat dinner with the crew and I stay back at the barn house with the children. I'd had a broken night's sleep the night before and was exhausted. Archie had called out in the middle of the night and I'd rushed to his room knowing the scene we'd shot that day (a zombie dummy being thrown into a ceiling fan and the resulting blood shower) would have caused him nightmares. But when I reached his bedside, mentally running through a future conversation with Uncle Mike as to why his son needed sleep therapy, he'd said, 'Emma, can you do this?' then he'd done the Vulcan salute.

Martha shuffled off to the main hall early. She'd heard there were canapés, and I was left to read Archie and Tilly a bedtime story and tuck the two cuties into bed. They'd been allocated a room each as per the *Filming with Children* guidelines, but they insisted on sharing. Sinead and Uncle Mike usually read Archie his bedtime story via skype but they were at a charity event that night, so it was up to me. I loved having their small bodies snuggled against me, their wholesome faces engrossed in the story. We read *The Tiger Who Came to Tea* and disputed the feasibility of a tiger drinking all the water in a tap as it was hooked up to a mains system with a huge reservoir, most likely in Thames Ditton, but eventually agreed the author had used 'creative licence', then finished off with an A. A. Milne poem about bread and butter which was far less contentious.

'Tell Archie about Jesus,' Tilly said in a last-ditch attempt to resist the light being turned off. 'He's got it wrong.'

'No I don't!' Archie jumped into his bed. 'You do!'

'Do not!' Tilly flopped on her pillow. 'Archie thinks Jesus died eating a hot-cross bun but that's not right, is it?'

'No, that's not quite right,' I said, tucking Tilly in and smoothing her fringe out of her eyes. 'How about we talk about Jesus tomorrow? We need to turn the light off now and go to sleep.'

I kissed both kids on their little noses and switched off the light.

'See!' I heard Tilly whisper. 'I told you. Jesus died in Brent Cross.'

After putting the religiously confused kids to bed I went searching for snacks and found a suitcase filled with treats. I do not exaggerate. Martha had brought a fully loaded second suitcase of snack food. Tubes of Pringles, Twix, Bounty and Snickers bars, packets of jelly babies, Toblerones, marsh-mallows and other assorted treats lay colourful and snug in every available space. Like a completed game of Tetris. With a Yorkie bar in my fist I plonked down on the sofa, flicked the TV to yet another cooking competition and called Alex.

'I'm in a rather inclement mood. Tell me something to cheer me up.'

'Why are you in such an "inclement" mood?' she said.

The now-familiar background sound of tropical birdsong had replaced the ceaseless *tih tih tih tih tih* of Bangladeshi desk fans.

'Oh, let's see … it's probably because my ex-boyfriend took my best friend to Paris for her birthday. And not even a special birthday; she's only turning twenty-seven. He never took me anywhere, unless you count a trip to Bristol to pick up a 1950s commercial waffle maker he bought on eBay.'

'Oh.'

'Or it could be because I have no money, so have to be a chaperone for my cousin who earns double what I do.'

'He does?'

'And maybe it's because I have to work with a bunch of people who have a party every night and don't invite me. And even if I did get invited I'd have to drink water because vodka is not good for the baby that I am accidentally pregnant with. By my ex-boyfriend. Who emptied my savings account to buy an ice cream van. Who went to Paris with my best friend to eat slugs—'

'They're actually a specific breed of land snail.'

'I have stretch marks; my arse is growing like rising pizza dough; my nipples are the size of UFOs and there's a man living in my cottage, planting herb gardens and going through my knicker drawer.'

Alex was silent for a moment.

'I thought Helen was your best friend.'

'Not helping.'

'Oh, OK. Well, um, it's nearly summer?'

'It's not nearly summer, it's March.'

'Um . . . you're going to have a beautiful baby soon?'

'Which I have to get out of my vagina, a relatively painful process, I'm told.' I was not going to make this easy for Alex. 'I want hardcore good news,' I demanded. 'A pot of leprechaun gold at the end of my shit-coloured rainbow.'

'Nice image.' She laughed.

I joined in, enjoying the exaggerated grumble.

'I'm going to go now, but you think of something good in my life and you ring me back and you tell me!' I said, getting dramatic.

'Sir, yes sir!' Alex laughed.

I'd barely taken a bite of my stolen Yorkie bar when the phone rang again. Alex.

'You've got something better?' I answered.

'Yes!' she said, triumphant. 'So, I told Cal about Ned taking your money and him being with Sophie—'

'You *what*?!' I shrieked. 'Why?'

'Because . . . because that's what happened.' Alex sounded surprised that I would react the way I had. 'And he's my fiancé and I tell him everything.'

'I'd really rather you didn't talk to other people about how shit your older sister's life is.'

'That's not what we were saying,' she said with a note of exasperation. 'And he's not "other people", he's family.'

'Not yet he isn't,' I mumbled.

'Will you stop being so sensitive and let me tell you what Cal said?'

239

'OK. What did *Cal* say?'

Alex made an impatient noise, then continued. 'Well, seeing as after this movie you don't have a job,' Alex paused for dramatic effect. I clenched in anger. 'He wants to lend you enough money to buy a car, get all the things you need for the baby and cover you for a while till you get on your feet! Isn't that nice?'

'Oh my god, Alex!'

'What?'

'I don't need your fiancé bailing me out! That's so embarrassing!'

'No it's not.' She sounded offended.

'Yes it is,' I spat. 'I'm older than him.'

'So?'

'So, it's – it's *humiliating*.' I sighed. 'I wish everyone would stop trying to fix my problems and just let me get on with it. You're making me feel like I can't . . . Like you don't think I'm capable of . . . You make me feel like a complete loser.' My voice had taken on a strained note and Alex would know I was trying not to cry.

She was quiet for a minute.

'I didn't realise you'd look at it that way,' she said eventually in a subdued voice. I didn't reply.

'Em, we just want—'

'Let's talk about something else,' I said.

'OK,' I could hear her disappointment and it stung. 'We've picked a wedding date. It's going to be in February.'

'Oh yeah? But it'll be freezing.'

'I know. I'm sick of this sweaty tropical climate. We want to get married in England, in the cold.'

'Cool.'

I couldn't think of anything else to say. I didn't want to be a bitch and tell her that instead of cheering me up, her talk of winter wedding plans only reminded me how very far from the traditional 'have boyfriend, get married, have baby' agenda I'd strayed.

'We'll hold the reception at a country pub,' Alex continued. 'People can sit anywhere they want and wear Ugg boots and woolly jumpers with snowman motifs if they want. We'll have Guinness and steak pie for dinner and a log fire and everyone drinking pints.'

'Does Mum know?'

'Not yet,' she said. 'Not looking forward to that conversation.'

Alex chittered on about how they'd found a pub in Grasmere that was perfect and had a huge stone fireplace and an excellent winter menu, with my responses becoming half-hearted murmurs before we said our goodbyes and I headed off to bed.

I awoke later that night to a loud bang and a frightening groan. I shot out of bed and flew to the children's room but they were asleep, their faces soft and tranquil. Another loud crash from Martha's room had me hurtling through her door.

'Martha! Are you – ARRGH!' My hands flew over my eyes but not before I saw Martha on her knees, naked, shunting up and down with a pair of hairy, scrawny legs sticking out beneath her. Her face was as red as a tomato and contorted in pleasure. Pendulous bosoms, a fleshy stomach and pale wobbling thighs quivered with each hoist. A porcelain bust of a regal woman lay in pieces on the floor and I wondered if she'd committed suicide at the sight. I recognised Steve's droopy face behind Martha's infinite frame.

'Sorry, sorry, sorry!' I said, hustling out the door.

CHAPTER TWENTY-ONE

'I'm a very sexual being,' Martha said after seeing a depleted-looking Steve out.

She sat in an armchair and took a bite out of a Bounty, chewing languidly, her fluffy bathrobe barely concealing her modesty. Beads of sweat clung to her hairline. 'Men find my queen-size shape very erotic.' She trailed a hand across her heaving chest.

I nodded, still reeling from the thirty-five minutes of banging and grunting I'd just aurally endured.

'Men ogle my breasts; beg me to let them motorboat between my thighs.' Martha looked at me. 'You know the motorboat? Where they blow a raspberry on your clit—'

'I get the picture.'

'I actually come to orgasm very quickly. I don't need penetration.' She leant forward and grabbed another Bounty, giving me a most unwanted flash of hairy gusset. 'You know the hill we drove down to get here?'

'Yeah,' I said weakly.

'Buttered my knickers four times.'

'Oh, that's . . .' There were no words.

'Of course the driver knew exactly what was happening, the dirty bugger, and drove over the field looking for bigger holes. Had a huge hard-on when he unloaded our luggage.'

'Did you . . .? With the driver?' I asked, immediately wishing I hadn't.

'On that sofa.' Martha licked her lips.

'Oh,' I said, squirming.

'But don't worry, Tilly wasn't here, she was feeding the horses with the stable manager. Who is also quite the goer, if you know what I mean.' Martha gave me an impish wink, which propelled me off the sofa into the darkness outside, mumbling something about pregnancy cravings and going to the kitchen for a carrot and Marmite panini. I shivered under the covered walkway. Faint drum and bass floated across the estate from Scott's private cottage in the forest. I thought of Amy draped over Andrew and Claire handing round her bag of Es like they were Smarties. If I weren't pregnant I was sure I'd be up there in a skirt a little too short, a top a little too tight with a bottle of vodka a little too empty. That's where I belonged. I was young, single and fun. Well, I used to be before I had to stop having fun to grow a baby. I did not belong down here with Martha and her sickening overshare.

The next morning I lay in bed thinking about my career prospects with a newborn. I drew a long, quiet blank. I might actually have to go back to AD-ing with its

life-consuming hours. I'd have to get a nanny. A Portuguese
girl who spoke no English. The baby would end up speaking Portuguese and I'd have to learn the language just to
be able to communicate with my own child. I'd have to
take Portuguese evening classes. The nanny, of course,
wouldn't be able to stay all day and night so I'd have to get
an evening nanny. She'd probably be from Poland, so the
baby's second language would be Polish. Then I'd have to
take another night class. And get another nanny. The ringing phone stopped me reaching for my laptop and signing
up for Ukranian lessons.

'I've just read *Grazia*,' Alex said.

'You rang to tell me that?' I yawned.

'And according to *Grazia* – which, by the way, we do get
out here in Vanuatu but only if I cycle to the other side of
the island, get a fishing boat to the next island, walk up a dirt
track that is covered in snake tracks, big ones, and borrow it
from the Canadian romantic novelist who lives on the hill
(she's quite mad), then go all the way back home – *you* are
having a quarter-life crisis.'

'Bollocks.' I pulled the duvet up higher round my chin.
'That is a totally unfounded statement.'

'It says it right here in black and white next to the photos
of Russell Brand and Katy Perry. It basically describes you.
Honestly, though, what is with them, getting married on
elephants?'

'Oh, now that is *ooold* news. You spend a day of snake-
track/rickety-boat travel to get a *Grazia* that old? Look, if

you get your charity company to pay for my flights I'll bring you the latest magazines.'

Alex emitted a solitary 'ha'.

'It could be my new career. I'll get flown to remote corners of the world where you self-sacrificing types are bringing modern-day normality to the deprived loincloth-clad, and I'd bring the Western young woman's life essentials. Magazines and decent chocolate.'

'See, right there! Quarter-life crisis. You're flippant and surly.'

'I'm always flippant and surly.'

'True . . .'

'Anyway, I am twenty-seven so it's not quarter. That would mean me living to a hundred and eight.'

'That's some quick maths.' Alex said, impressed.

'I know. I have skills. Anyway, it must be more like a third-life crisis. Why don't you ring me back when you've read an ancient, out-of-date article on third-life crises and we can discuss it then? Although by the time you have gone up your writer's hill and round the island on an 1840s bicycle I will be on my midlife crisis and we will have to start the whole process again. Best just forget it.'

'Well don't come crying to me when you are two kids down the road and can't afford your psychiatrist bills.'

'I won't. Mum'll pay. Surely any therapy should be charged to her. She's probably almost *expecting* it.'

We were silent for a moment.

'So what are you doing now? Is it dinner time?' I said, glancing at my bedside clock.

'Yip. The guys caught loads of fish today. We're going to barbecue it on the beach. What about you?'

I thought of Archie's schedule for the day ahead. Four scenes outdoors, some SPFX shots and one scene involving a pack of untrained, feral chihuahuas. Cats, it had transpired, were not easily trained to act like vengeful zombies and so an inbred pack of chihuahuas had been brought in to run after the campers. VFX would digitally change them to cats in postproduction. But the chihuahuas were proving to be a disaster. One bit Caroline, one ran into the forest with a blood pouch and, as far as I could see, had not returned for a couple of days; two seemed to be mostly deaf and one (cross-eyed and with a tongue that didn't fit in its mouth) kept trying to mount his sister.

'Just more filming,' I sighed.

We said our goodbyes and I went back to fretting about Filipino nannies and where I'd fit their extended family.

After showering and breakfasting and still in a stunned, dry-retching type state from the previous night's activities, I phoned Helen while waiting for Archie in Wardrobe.

'It's kind of early for a Saturday morning, Em.' Helen answered the phone with a croaky but not unfriendly voice. 'I do hope you're phoning me with good news. The I've-just-seen-Scott-Vander's-knob-and-it's-the-size-of-an-oil-tanker-and-I-got-you-a-photo type news.'

I laughed. 'Well, I did see a knob, but not Scott Vander's.'

'Do tell,' Helen said, intrigued.

I regaled her with the previous night's events while

Helen gave satisfying gasps of disgust. Then we discussed the hotness scale of the rest of the men on set, beginning with Andrew at the top: tanned, taut and lusty, to Steve at the bottom: droopy, dreadlock-y and defiled by Martha. As we were getting to the finer points (if by some extremely unlikely chance Andrew decided a pregnant single girl was just his cup of tea), namely which sexual positions would be possible and, importantly, flattering while five months pregnant, Martha shoved her flushed face into mine.

'Archie's finished in Wardrobe and needs to go to Make-up.' She glared at my phone.

I raised my index finger in a 'one minute' gesture and got an irate nostril-flare in return. I walked behind a rack of zombie camper costumes.

'So . . .' I said, knowing I shouldn't ask but unable to stop myself, 'what's the latest with . . . you know?'

Helen let out an exasperated sigh. 'God! That *idiot*.'

I didn't know if she was referring to Ned or Sophie.

'She's given him money.'

'Oh. That's . . . quite sad really,' I said, realising the strongest feeling I had was one of pity. Poor, gullible Sophie. 'That's how it all begins. Another girlfriend-funded get-rich-quick scheme. It's ice cream now; next month it'll be an online version of *The Voice* but for parrots, or a dissolvable toothbrush.' I sighed. 'She'll never get it back. Did she lend him much?'

'A few thousand, I think.'

'A few *thousand*?!' I shrieked. 'What is she thinking?'

'Apparently she believes in him. They've ordered another

three vans. She thinks this ice cream idea could actually work if he has the money to get organic vodka and hand-churned cream, or something. I don't know, Em,' she said in a disinterested manner. 'I stopped listening after she started yapping about profit margins, decorating the vans in "flavour themes" and fair-trade cows, or whatever.'

The clothing rack I was behind swung back to reveal Martha, hands on fleshy hips.

'I have to go,' I said.

I hung up, pushed past Martha, ignoring her indignant huffs and puffs, and took Archie off to Make-up to get some zombie cat gouges on his face.

Poor Sophie. It was not going to work out well for her. I wanted to call and warn her. I even brought her number up on my phone before switching it off and shoving it deep, deep in the bottom of my bag.

CHAPTER TWENTY-TWO

A week later I was back in London, a mug of tea in my hand, with Joe proudly showing me my new herb garden and the raised beds he was preparing for the summer vegetables I'd be growing. I'd coached Archie the whole way down from Anglesey not to mention he'd recently shot a scene at night where he comes across a writhing half-torso on the forest floor, and he was most certainly not to use the words 'massacre', 'rip his head off', 'zombie motherfucker' or any other violent or death-orientated terms.

'Can I show him this?' He held up my phone, a picture of him holding a prosthetic head filling the screen.

'No.' I grabbed my phone and started the process of assigning it a new pin number.

'Can I tell him about the blood bags?'

'No.'

'What about—?'

'Just tell Daddy what we talked about. You do lots of

scenes with chihuahuas pretending to be cats, you've made a bunch of friends and you like the free doughnuts. OK?'

Archie had nodded, then asked if zombies could be killed with a nail bomb and I made a mental note to be present for all future conversations with Sinn Féin Brian.

The crew driver had dropped me off after delivering Archie to the outstretched arms of his wet-eyed mother. Despite sometimes appearing to feel otherwise, Sinead was mad about her children.

I'd gone home and had a gloriously undisturbed sleep (i.e. no porn for the plus-sized in the next room) in my own bed.

It was a beautiful crisp March morning, and while Joe primped and prettied the herbs, straightening their terracotta label stakes, I told him about life on the film set. Martha, it turned out, was a super-whore. In the last week she'd slept with Steve another two times, both loudly and dangerously (there had been another ornament death) and one of the extras who played Male Zombie Camper Number Three. That had been a much quieter affair but had gone on for a very, very long time. I'd looked at Male Zombie Camper Number Three with admiration the next day. Anyone who could stand hours of physical activity with Martha astride them was an athlete of extraordinary ability.

'Well, fat-bottomed girls do make the rockin' world go round,' Joe said, breaking off a stalk of mint and holding it out. 'Freddie Mercury said so.'

'Freddie Mercury was gay, therefore unqualified to comment on super-sized super-whores.' I took the stalk from Joe, crushed the leaves in my fingers and relished the potent scent that conjured up images of mojitos and beaches.

'It sounds like you're a little fattist.' Joe squinted at me in the morning sun. His eyes crinkled and the apples of his cheeks rose charmingly. 'Or are you jealous she's getting all the hot guys?'

'They are *not* hot, and I am *not* fattist!'

Joe had shaved his 'sad man' beard off while I'd been away, and underneath was a wide grin and an enchanting single dimple on his left cheek. He was actually quite decent-looking. In a sandy-haired, sparkly-eyed, naughty uni student kind of way. He had the kind of wicked grin that made you check to see if he'd stuck a WHISTLE IF YOU'RE HORNY sign on your back. I wondered why his fiancée had cheated on him. Maybe he had some kind of dark side I'd yet to see. Like he collected babies' skulls, or liked to go dogging but only if his girlfriend would dress as his old male physics teacher and carry a handbag full of dead bats. Or something.

'She's horrible to me all day, and at night I have to listen to her having her loud way with anything with an erect appendage and low standards.'

Joe laughed and dug a pile of dirt. I ambled down the garden wall looking at his green-fingered handiwork. Grandma's roses were trimmed and neat. Freshly turned earth lay in raised mounds with terracotta label stakes at the end of each one. Spring onions, spinach, peas and broad beans. Joe was clearly not a man accustomed to lolling idly around in a fug of self-pity. Shame; I'd quite enjoyed the weeks I'd wasted in front of the TV with my doughnuts. Men will never know the small amount of pleasure a girl gets from being shat on in the love department and the consequent 'pity party for one' they have after. Skulking around in your pyjamas and eating items that barely qualify as a food group is completely acceptable when you're heartbroken. And deep down beneath the broken heart and wounded pride, there's a tiny part of us that enjoys the self-focus. Halfway round the garden my phone rang. Alex. My stomach sank at the sight of her name on the screen. I didn't think I could have another conversation about her winter-wonderland wedding, my one-twenty-seventh life crisis or how I was such an incompetent loser her fiancé needed to pay for my mistakes. I switched it to silent and slid it in my pocket just as a clattering noise and a screech of feedback sounded from Harriet's side of the fence.

'IS THAT EMMA I HEAR?' Harriet's tinny voice came through the loud-hailer. A moment later her inquisitive face popped over the wall. 'Ah! You're back! Hello, dear.' She grinned, wrinkles furrowing in their hundreds.

'Hi Harriet,' I said. 'You're up early.'

'Yes, I am rather,' she said, her eyes flicking between Joe and me. 'Arthur wheeled out to get parsley for our coddled eggs and didn't come back for half an hour. His wheels got stuck in the lawn. I told him to take the loud-hailer, but he never listens.' She tutted and glanced over her shoulder. 'He's fine.' She turned back to us. 'Well, I haven't moved him yet. I'll have to dig him out but I've misplaced my kneepads.'

Joe and I exchanged looks.

'We manage.' She waved our concerned faces away with her knobbled hand.

'I'll come over,' Joe said, dropping his three-pronged diggy thing and brushing his hands on his jeans.

'He's a lovely young man, isn't he?' Harriet said, smiling after him as he walked back through the cottage. 'Now, Emma dear, something came for you yesterday. Joe wasn't in so I told that Chinaman courier I'd take it. He took a bit of convincing but I told him where to and what for, I did. I'll just pop inside and get it. Stay there.' Her wintry hair disappeared behind the wall. I heard her welcome Joe, give him a handful of wheelchair-digging directives, then Joe's voice boomed as he greeted the mostly deaf, mud-confined Arthur.

Moments later a ripped plastic casing with hunks of raw meat hanging from its ragged openings appeared over the wall. In two shunts it was on top of the wall in its plasticky, meaty entirety and Harriet's face popped up behind it.

'What on earth is that?!'

At my look of horror Harriet assessed the carnage.

'Yes, well, it didn't arrive like this, dear,' she patted the mess. 'Brutus and I have been watching our programmes, you know. *CSI* and the other one, the one with that lovely writer and the pretty girl with lots of emotional baggage.'

'*Castle*?'

'Yes, that's the one. Dishy, isn't he? Do you like him? I said to Arthur, if I were forty years younger and he didn't have that ginger daughter—'

'Harriet, the meat?'

'Oh yes. So Brutus has learnt a lot from our crime programmes, and I think he thought it might have been drugs,
you see. It came in one of those cooler boxes, you know, the
polystyrene ones, but ahh ...' She picked some bobbles of
polystyrene out of a drying chunk of meat and looked at me
sheepishly. 'Well, there doesn't seem to be much of that left.'
She lifted a slab and inspected its every angle. 'It seems to be,
yes, it's mostly gone, eaten, really ...'

'It could have been a human heart in there, you know,' I
said, mocking her only slightly.

'Exactly!' she said, her frame straightening like a startled
meerkat. 'Black market harvested organs! That kind of thing
is rife these days. Especially with those Chinamen.'

'Uh-huh.'

I heard Arthur giving Joe hollered instructions on the care
of green beans.

'But it was just organic meat.' Harriet looked down at me,
her cheeks flushing. 'Brutus is very sorry, dear. He made you
a card. I'll send it home with Joe.'

'That's very thoughtful of ... Brutus.'

Harriet gave a noble nod. 'It is, yes. No harm in being
cautious though, is it, hmmm?' She smiled down at me.

'I guess not. Are you sure it's for me, though? I didn't order
any meat. Did it have a delivery slip?'

'It came with a note!' She reached into her cardigan pocket,
pulled out a partially eaten wad of paper and squinted at it.
'It's from someone called Sophie, and it says she's very sorry.'

My smile dropped. Harriet continued to read.

'And "she hopes you can forgive her". Then there are, well, a few holes ...' She looked at me sheepishly. I frowned and she quickly turned her attention back to the scrunch of paper. 'Yes, anyway, here it says "something something *organic*" and ... and this bit here is blurred.' She glanced up again. 'That's on account of the drool ... then over here it says something about iron being good for the baby. Then more drool. This part of the paper is missing and, ah ... something else here, I can't quite make it out.' She looked at me again. I scowled. 'Probably not important.' She shook her head, then peered at the paper again. 'Then another blurred bit and then ... yes, then it says "love Sophie".' She made a futile attempt to fold the note with belated care, then tucked it into a ragged cavity in the meat pack. 'So there you go. Lovely thought, isn't it? To think of the baby like that? Shall I send it over with Joe?' She adjusted her glasses and smiled.

'Just give it to Brutus,' I said, feeling my shoulders edge up at the thought of Sophie reading up on pregnancy and making dietary choices for me.

'Oh no, he can't eat it. It's got polystyrene in it. Very bad for his tummy.' She pursed her lips and shook her head. 'You make a nice stew out of ...' She glanced down at the horrible mess. 'Out of what's left, yes?'

A short while later, Harriet and Arthur were inside eating their coddled eggs and Joe had come back with the ruined meat pack, a home-made card with a Brutus-sized stamped paw print on the front and a massive grin. We'd binned the meaty horror and he'd continued digging while I'd recommenced my tour of the garden.

'How about I make dinner tonight?' I said, circling back after my horticultural appraisal. 'Nothing meaty, though.' I gave a mock shudder.

Joe stood. He seemed to be assessing me, as if he thought I might be asking him out on some sort of date. Which I certainly was not. I was about to clarify this to him when he spoke.

'I'd love that. I'll do dessert.'

He spent the rest of the day attempting to teach me how to care for each and every herb and plant. I listened, nodded and promptly forgot almost everything. Some needed trimming and some needed feeding; a kind of unpleasant, violent mixture called blood and bone. For which I asked, thinking myself rather funny, if I was growing Serial Killer Spinach or Homicidal Herbs. Joe had given me a charitable little smile and continued, telling me that tomatoes needed regular fertilising and to be read excerpts from any Stephen Fry book, and asparagus crowns wanted well-rotted manure and to be told knock-knock jokes at dusk. Or the other way round. As I said, I hadn't really the mind for gardening.

At the end of a very relaxing, nanna-in-the-garden kind of day we settled on his bed under a fluffy blanket and loaded up *Thelma and Louise. Die Hard 1* and *2* sat in their cases on the bedside table.

'This is one of my favourite films.' Joe ripped open a packet of peanut M&Ms, his face a picture of glee. 'This and

The NeverEnding Story'. His expression became serious. 'If anyone from the graphics profession asks, though, you say my favourites are *The Alien Trilogy*, *Gravity* and *Requiem for a Dream*.'

'OK ...'

'You, Katy and my mother are the only ones who know that.'

'Ooh, I feel like I'm in some kind of club,' I said with faux excitement.

Joe gave me a derisory look.

I grinned. 'To be fair, it's a relatively boring club.'

Around the end of the first *Die Hard* I felt my eyes blink heavily a couple of times. I was partially aware of a packet of Maltesers being removed from my clutches and a blanket placed over me, then nothing.

CHAPTER TWENTY-THREE

'EMMA! MY KEY DOESN'T WORK!'

I opened my eyes. I was nose-to-nose with a bare-chested Joe. His dark lashes quivered on his cheeks. The digital alarm clock on the nightstand the other side of him said 6.41 a.m.

'EMMA, WAKE UP YOU LAZY TART AND HELP ME OUT OF THIS BLOODY TREE!'

Mum?

I propped myself up on my elbows. Through the triangular loft window I saw my mother dangling like a marionette from an oak tree, seemingly by the waistband of her designer jeans.

'MUM?!' I shrieked, struggling under the weight of my baby bump to sit up.

Joe woke, disorientated. 'What's going—?' He stopped as he saw the madwoman hanging from the tree and frantically beckoning me outside.

On seeing the half-naked man next to me, Mum stopped

squirming and her mouth fell open. Before I could explain that the woman in the tree in suede Valentinos was, in fact, my mother, and was as mad as a box of frogs that fell down the stairs, the phone next to the bed rang.

'Hello?' I said, holding my hand up to Mum to wait.

She dropped her arms to her sides, exasperated, then reached into the handbag dangling on her wrist and started fiddling with her BlackBerry.

'EMMA, MY GIRL,' bellowed Arthur from next door. 'I DON'T MEAN TO ALARM YOU BUT THERE'S A WOMAN IN THE TREE OUTSIDE YOUR HOUSE. HARRIET WANTS TO SET BRUTUS ON HER, BUT – OH, LOOK, HARRIET, IT'S DIANA. SHE SEEMS TO BE ON THE PHONE.'

'What a strange place to take a call,' Joe said. 'Who *is* that?'

'Arthur, I am so sorry—'

'SPEAK UP, GIRL. IT'S NO USE MUMBLING!'

Still loath to yell at an old man, and one in a wheelchair, no less, I raised my voice. 'IT'S JUST MY MUM, MR SPENCER—'

'Your mother?' Joe jumped out of bed and took off down the stairs.

'Joe, wait!'

'WHAT WAS THAT? I CAN'T HEAR YOU!'

'Nothing. Mr Spencer, I have to get my mother down—'

'HARRIET, THERE'S SOMETHING WRONG WITH THE LINE.'

'I'LL SPEAK TO YOU LATER!' I hung up, waddled

down the stairs and out the back door before Brutus bounded over the wall and got Mum's Gucci tote in his maw. Brutus would certainly come off worst in the event of a fight over a handbag. I rounded the side of the cottage, my bare feet cold on the brick path, and found my mother on the phone, her palm up to Joe in a 'wait a moment' stance. Joe grinned.

'Shut up.'

'I didn't say anything,' Joe said, noticeably appreciating the bizarre start to the day.

He waved up at the Spencers, framed in their bedroom window. Harriet, in her quilted nightgown, adjusted her camera angle; Arthur peered over the windowsill.

'Mum, get *down*.'

'Oh, no, not brocade again.' Mum covered the mouthpiece and whispered, 'Darling, I'll just be one minute, run inside and put the kettle on.'

Joe sniggered. I punched him.

'I know, darling ... Bastards ... Florence, tell them Florence ... I know, darling. I know ... I'll fly out next week.' Mum snapped her phone shut, slid it awkwardly into her jeans pocket and looked from me to Joe. 'And who is this?' She smiled, as if taking a business call at 6.45 a.m. in a tree outside your daughter's house was really just perfectly normal, thank you very much.

Joe helped Mum down, introduced himself as my friend–slash–lodger (as we'd taken to calling him) and went to put the kettle on.

'Friend-slash-lodger?' Mum said, a disbelieving look on her face.

I waited as she tucked in her shirt. 'Yes, Mum. Friend-slash-lodger. Friend-slash-lodger who sleeps in his own bed. And what the hell were you doing in the tree?'

'My key wouldn't work, and you weren't answering your phone or the door,' she said. 'It's a natural instinct to worry about your young – you'll see soon enough.'

Once inside with the blinds down to avoid having a larger role in another episode of *Harriet's Neighbourhood*, I turned up the heating and started clearing away last night's dishes.

'What are you doing here at this hour, anyway?'

'Just seeing how my daughter is. It's not been the smoothest of sailing for you recently, darling. And I have an early meeting in Kingston and wanted to beat the traffic through town.' Mum leant against the sink and watched Joe pad around half naked, making coffee. 'So you two aren't . . .?' She raised her eyebrows.

'*Mum*,' I said through gritted teeth.

'No,' Joe said with a smile.

'Oh, that's good,' Mum said. 'Because I'm not sure sex is the right thing to be doing when you're pregnant. Poor baby' – she prodded my forehead with an index finger – 'how would you like it?'

'Stop it!' I slapped her hand away.

'Although . . .' Mum lowered her voice. 'By the look of him, it might be more like *this*.' She banged her fist on my forehead with a smirk.

A collection of ethnic-looking bangles tinkled on her tanned arm. I smacked her hand away and gave her my best 'I will KILL you' look.

'Doctors say it's fine to have sex while you're pregnant.' Joe turned to face us, heaping coffee into the pot. 'It's encouraged, actually. Something about the release of "feelgood" hormones being good for the baby. But we aren't, are we, Emma.' He smiled. 'Just friends-slash-roomies.'

'Well, that's good to hear.' Mum patted me on the tummy. 'Look what happens when Emma has sex. Pregnant and single.'

'Oh. My. God.' I dumped a pot in the sink and stalked to my bedroom comprehensively mortified.

I wasted time making my bed and tying and retying my ponytail. After a few minutes my chest loosened and I followed the smell of brewed coffee.

'. . . the entire bank account. Empty! And then Emma had to get him to sell the ice cream van just to pay me back. I was going to call the police.' Mum smiled as I walked into the kitchen.

'Saying too much again, Mother?'

'Probably, darling.'

I poured myself a coffee.

'Do you think you should . . .?' Mum started, but I silenced her with a deathly look.

'Embarrass me in front of a friend—'

'Slash-lodger,' she said with an impish dip of her head.

I glared at her and continued. 'Hang from a tree in the

early hours of the morning in front of my elderly neighbours if you really must, tell the world I'm pregnant and single, but don't stop me having a coffee when I want a bloody coffee!'

Mum raised her eyebrows.

She turned to Joe with a charming grin. 'So what's for breakfast?'

Joe made bacon and eggs and we sat round the table, Mum and Joe chatting easily. Mum finished her last mouthful, put her knife and fork together in the centre of the plate and rapped her navy-painted nails on the side of her coffee cup.

'So, Joe, what tragedy brings you to my daughter's door?'

'*Mum*,' I chastised.

'What?' She feigned innocence and turned back to Joe. 'So?'

Joe grinned.

'I'm sorry about my mother, she was born without a subtlety neuron.' I shook my head. 'You learn to love her.'

'Oh, he loves me already, darling.' Mum flashed a winning grin. 'It's a woman, isn't it?'

Sadness fell across Joe's face like a sudden cloud over the sun.

'You don't have to answer her.' I frowned at Mum.

'It's OK,' Joe said. 'Yes. A woman. My fiancée.' He gazed into his coffee mug. 'My *ex*-fiancée.'

Mum nodded encouragement as I fidgeted with my mug. I'd not asked him anything for fear of him getting tearful, which would have made me feel terribly uncomfortable.

'We'd been having trouble planning the wedding.'

'Well that's not a good start—' I said before being silenced by a quick slap on the hand by Mum.

'Go on,' she said.

With a small smirk, Joe continued. 'I guess it all started when I hid a T. Rex in the "save the date" invite.'

I cracked up. 'You *didn't*? That's hilarious! What—' I dropped my wide grin at Mum's severe glower. 'Um … What happened?'

'I didn't get why we had to do a "save the date" in the first place,' Joe said, his face earnest. 'A year in advance? Seriously? Can't you just pick a date, book a venue and send out an invitation?'

'You know what a "save the date" really is?' Mum said. 'It's a note to say, "Start dieting, I don't want fatties in my wedding photos".'

Joe smiled and nodded his head in a 'guess you're right' kind of way. 'Katy chose a picture of us on a beach for the "save the date". Stylish and, you know, boring. It was all getting too serious. I wanted to have a bit of fun. Weddings should be fun, right?'

Mum and I nodded.

'So I hid a T. Rex behind the palm trees,' Joe said, his hands releasing his coffee cup and turning upward.

'Awesome,' I whispered.

Mum mouthed a noiseless tut.

'Katy didn't even notice at first,' Joe said, his eyebrows rounded and innocent. 'But then one of her friends spotted it and uploaded the invite to Instagram and Katy just lost it.'

His shoulders sank. 'We had a few heated discussions about me not taking the wedding seriously enough, nothing I thought we couldn't work our way through, then we started arguing about where we would buy a house, if we would get a dog or a cat and all this other stupid stuff that was way in the future. Then one morning,' he chewed his bottom lip, 'she said that she didn't think she wanted children.' He rubbed a hand across his forehead. 'I was floored. I always assumed we'd have kids.'

Silence descended on the table. Joe twiddled with his fork.

'You'd never discussed it?' Mum said, her voice gentle.

Joe shook his head, thoughts racing across his gloomy face. 'We organised to have a quiet dinner in that night. Have a proper discussion. No yelling. Then we went to work.' Joe sat back in his chair and gave a sad, lopsided smile.

'But I thought you . . .' I faltered, wondering whether to bring up what he'd drunkenly mentioned that first night. About her 'paddling a kayak'. 'Didn't you walk in on her . . .?'

Mum raised her eyebrows.

'Yes,' Joe said quietly. 'I felt awful. I wanted her to come home and know that . . . that none of it mattered as long as we had each other.' He paused and rubbed his chin. 'So at lunchtime I bought her favourite flowers, tulips, and went to our flat to drop them off before going back to work.'

I leant forward in my chair, as much as my pregnant belly would allow.

'But when I opened the door I saw the skirt she'd been wearing that morning on the sofa. And her shirt and bra in the hall.' He swallowed. 'I went into the bedroom and she was on top of this guy from her office. Naked except for the red high heels I'd bought her at Christmas.'

'That's horrible.' Mum shook her head. 'Which red heels? The Alaïa ones from last seas . . .' She trailed off at my look.

Joe was deep in his own thoughts. I toyed with the salt and pepper, adjusted and readjusted my cutlery. Mum watched him.

Eventually she spoke. 'Trollop. And quite clearly has terrible taste. *Tulips*? Yech.'

Joe looked up, startled. Then cracked into a surprised grin, which Mum returned tenfold.

Half an hour later Mum thanked Joe for breakfast, stood, hugged him tightly and made him promise to call her any time he felt like talking, gave me a brief hug and declared I needed some anti-frizz for my hair and headed down the hall.

'Now call your sister, Emma, she's having a terrible time with her future mother-in-law. No taste, that Lucinda. All the money in the world cannot buy taste; it's either in your blood or it's not. Did you know she wants Alex to arrive in a carriage? And I said—'

'Mum, don't you have to be going?' I didn't want to get into a discussion about how I'd started ignoring my sister's calls.

'I *am* going, darling, but not because you so rudely suggested. I have a meeting, my shipment from Argentina has arrived and I've swatches to return. Houndstooth! Honestly, when was the last time you saw curtains in houndstooth?' She looked at me expectantly. I looked at her blankly.

Mum stared back then stalked down the hall shaking her head. 'I don't know why I waste my time. Couldn't tell a plaid from a paisley. I must have a womb to a parallel universe.'

CHAPTER TWENTY-FOUR

My phone rang while I waited in a long-but-worth-it queue for a lamb burger. Alex. I flicked it to silent and adjusted a heavy bag filled with spoils from a two-hour trawl through Borough Market. I had a family dinner that evening and was supplying dessert; maple-poached, organic, Kent-grown, spray-free pears (from a family-run orchard with happy hives of pollinating bees) with hazelnut-encrusted yoghurt balls (the yoghurt from the milk of ethically raised, stress-free cows who dined on wild grasses and were allowed to come inside and watch TV with the farmer in the evenings). I was fourth person from the front of the queue and starting to salivate in an alarming fashion when a man I recognised turned away from the grill holding a freshly made burger.

'Emma? Hi!' Andrew gave a surprised smile showing impeccably straight teeth that matched his impeccably straight shoulders and impeccably straight jaw.

'Hi.' I angled my cheek to meet his kiss. 'What're you doing here?'

He held up his burger. 'Been thinking about these all week.'

Andrew stayed and chatted while I ordered.

'Do you want to get a drink at that little bar back there?' he said as the man at the grill handed over my burger.

'Oh, ah . . .'

'Oh, right.' He glanced at my belly. 'You can't drink. Care to watch me drink one then?'

We leant against a wine barrel eating our burgers and sipping on drinks, a couple of beers for Andrew and a sparkling elderflower for me. Andrew told me about the film he'd been on before this one. A spy film set in the Austrian Alps. And I chatted about Ned and the baby, hoping to provide just enough info to let him know I was available and interested but not desperate and pathetic. A fine line, which may have been crossed when I mentioned how any new suitor would need a double-jointed jaw to get their mouth round my manhole-sized nipples.

'Is that the time?' I said, catching a glance at Andrew's sporty watch. 'I've got to get home.'

I was due at Sinead and Uncle Mike's in a couple of hours with my yoghurt already balled.

'I'll see you on set,' I said with a smile I hoped was cute and void of stuff between my teeth.

'Sure will.' He picked up my groceries and handed them to me. I felt a girlish thrill as my fingers brushed his hand.

'Cute *and* a cook,' he said with a twinkle in his eye. 'You're a catch.'

Back home I peeled pears, hung yoghurt and toasted hazelnuts. Joe pottered around reading my poems aloud. I kept running *You're a catch* over and over in my head. Did that mean he thought I was a catch for him? Or just to someone who was open-minded/foolish enough to take on another man's baby and me? Was he being kind, or was he flirting? Of course he wasn't flirting. What kind of idiot are you? So many kinds – let's not go into it. I was so distracted I kept burning the hazelnuts.

'Here, what's this one about?' Joe cleared his throat while I burned my finger on a hot nut.

> *'I found a little thimble, a thimble, a thimble*
> *I found a little thimble*
> *Under mother's bed'*

I gave Joe a cautionary growl.

> *'I gave the little thimble, the thimble, the thimble*
> *I gave the little thimble,*
> *To my Uncle Ted'*

He crossed the kitchen and leant against the bench while I stirred bubbling maple syrup like a madwoman.

'Joe, could you …?' I indicated an oven mitt with

crazy-person flapping hands. He handed it to me without removing his eyes from my diary.

> *'Uncle put the little thimble, the thimble, the thimble*
> *Uncle put the little thimble*
> *In Aunty Jane's purse*
> *I've lost my little thimble, my thimble, my thimble*
> *I've lost my little thimble*
> *Where is it? said the Nurse.'*

He peered over the top of the pink floral diary.

'Now what's *that* about?' His eyes gleamed.

'It's about a fucking thimble. Now would you grab that recipe book and read out something useful.'

'OK, OK, keep your pinny on,' Joe said, swapping my diary for Grandma's recipe book. 'You know, some of those poems are actually quite good. Sort of A. A. Milne-ish. Maybe you could publish them.'

'Be quiet.' I grabbed the soggy, yoghurty muslin and jabbed at the recipe book. 'Now tell me what it says to do with these balls.'

We approached Sinead and Uncle Mike's front door, crunching across the white loose-pebbled drive, Joe holding some pink roses from the garden in one hand and the tray of yoghurt balls in the other and me carrying the tinfoil-covered pears.

'You have to have stuff ready to talk about so whenever

it looks like my uncle is going to ask about the movie, you swoop in' – I motioned the swooping-in and nearly lost my pears – 'and say something.'

Joe shot me a sceptical look.

'Keep it fast-paced.'

'But—'

'No breaks!' I said. 'No gaps in the conversation. You have to be a gap-stopper. Tell stories.'

'But I don't have any stories.' Joe looked concerned.

'Oh come *on*. All that crap you ring and tell me! Just do that all night.'

'Which ones in particular?'

'I don't know – I barely listen to you.'

We arrived at the front door and ding-donged our presence.

'Why am I doing this?' Joe asked.

I lowered my voice at the sound of approaching foot-steps. 'Because Uncle Mike will never speak to me again if he knows his son is acting in a zombie guts-and-bra romance.'

Joe shook his head. Uncle Mike swung open the leaded-light door and I plastered on a beatific grin. We exchanged hugs, handshakes, roses and tinfoiled pears and moved inside, Joe behind me muttering, 'This is never going to work.'

Joe chatted cheerfully with my inquisitive family. He sidestepped questions about why he wasn't married from Alice; Mum quizzed him about the décor in his Shoreditch loft (where his ex was still living); Sinead wanted to know at what age he was sent to boarding school and Jess wanted to know if he could armpit-fart.

Towards the end of dessert, Uncle Mike turned to me.

'So, my dear, how is the young lad doing on this movie?' He sat back in his chair and took a sip of wine. 'It's something to do with the afterlife, I gather?'

I glanced at Joe, attempting a 'you're up' eyebrow action, but was met with a look of stage fright.

'More wine, dear?' Sinead attempted a distraction.

Uncle Mike waved the offered bottle away and looked across the table with mild enquiry.

'Um . . .' I fussed with a yoghurt ball. Sinead squirmed.

Archie raised his arms, made his hands into claws and manifested the countenance of an attacking zombie. 'There are—'

Sinead kicked my shins. 'CATS!' I yelled. Uncle Mike sloshed wine out of his glass. 'Ah . . . they're ghost cats,' I muttered, rubbing my throbbing leg.

Archie frowned and opened his mouth.

'And chihuahuas,' Sinead nodded, her eyes wide.

'And—' Archie began, his claw hands up once more.

'But they're pretending to be cats,' I offered.

'I thought—' Uncle Mike started.

'There's some comedy,' Sinead faked a jolly laugh.

Archie tried again. 'And—'

'And romance,' I said.

'Not between the cats and the dogs, though,' Sinead frowned.

I shook my head. 'Noooo, that would be wrong.'

'And weird.'

'And it's definitely not a weird film.'

'No; there's *no weirdness*,' Sinead intoned.

'None,' I reiterated.

Uncle Mike frowned. 'But—'

'It's a perfectly normal film about ghost cats—'

'Played by dogs—'

'Who are definitely *not* romantic with the cats,' Sinead said.

I looked to Joe for help, but was met with blind panic. I launched a hazelnut.

'Ow!' He threw his hands over his face.

'Oh, bugger!' Sinead said, purposely knocking over her wine.

'Sinead!' Uncle Mike mopped at the wine with a linen napkin.

Mum watched the spectacle, her fingers clasped together in rapt fascination.

'Daddy, there are—' Archie began.

'Joe, don't you . . .' I said, giving Joe a warning stare of forthcoming pain.

'Has anyone seen the Russian cartoon *Masha and the Bear*?' he endeavoured, holding one hand over his eye.

I shot him a disparaging look.

Sinead flew out of her chair and clattered a few plates together. 'OK, I'm stuffed. Let's clear the table. Coffee, anyone? Tea? Whisky, I'm having a whisky. How about we retire to the music room and Jess can play the violin for you all. She's shocking at it. Up you get!'

'Thanks for dessert,' Sinead said from the front door. 'Goodnight!'

Uncle Mike gave a wave and they shut the door, leaving Mum, Joe and me in the cool darkness. We crunched across the driveway towards Mum's car.

Mum beeped her car unlocked. 'Have you spoken to your sister?'

'I tried a few days ago but couldn't get through,' I lied.

'Hmmm.' Mum frowned over the roof of her Mini, assessing whether it was worth pushing the issue. Much to my relief she decided against it and jumped in the car.

'Are you sure you don't want a lift?' she said through her open window.

'It's just round the corner, Mum.'

Joe took me by the arm. 'I'll look after your daughter.'

'I'm sure you will,' she said. She blew us kisses and roared off.

Joe and I walked arm and arm in the direction of home. I admired how well he'd handled himself for an entire evening with my boisterous family. I was thankful Joe didn't ask questions about Alex and why I wasn't taking her calls. He seemed to sense it was not a subject I wanted to discuss. I, on the other hand, had no such tact.

'Can I ask you a personal question?'

'I guess,' Joe said with a wary smile.

'What was the guy like?'

Joe's arm stiffened but he feigned ignorance. 'What guy?'

'The one . . . in bed with your fiancée.'

'*Ex*-fiancée.'

I stayed quiet, hoping I hadn't upset him.

'I don't really know,' he said eventually. 'I didn't get a good look. I left as soon as I saw them.'

'Oh.' I watched our feet move in slow unison along the chewing-gum-spotted footpath.

I imagined what it would've been like for Joe. How I would've felt if it had been Ned. But it was much, much worse for Joe. He was engaged to Katy. They were planning their future. I never intended to marry Ned. 'Did you say anything to them?'

'No.' He swallowed. 'But he said something to me.'

'What?'

'Once they realised I was there they stopped what they were doing and Katy tried to cover herself up with the duvet, which I remember thinking was kind of weird because clearly we'd both seen her naked.' He screwed his face up in an incredulous grimace at the memory. 'Anyway, I turned to walk out and the guy said, "It's nothing serious, mate, just a bit of fun".'

My mouth fell open.

Joe shook his head. 'He called me "mate". Can you believe that?'

'Why didn't you go in there and pummel his face?' I stopped walking, slipped my arm from Joe's and made energetic face-pummelling actions, throwing a fist into my upturned hand.

Joe stopped and watched. When the fictional little guy in my palm was well and truly flattened, I ceased pummelling and composed myself.

'I had to get out of there,' Joe said with a resigned shrug. 'I just kept walking.'

'Well, if you ever see him again, you point him out to me. I'll sit on his chest till he gasps his last breath,' I said, patting my pregnant belly. 'And I'll face-pummel him too.'

Joe smiled.

We arrived at the cottage gate and silently opened the door, removed coats, turned on lights and took turns in the bathroom like an old couple who'd been married for years. I stepped out of the bathroom in my pink flying-pig pyjamas just as Joe was locking the front door.

''Night,' I said.

''Night, chubby.' He stepped forward, put his hand on my shoulder and kissed me affectionately on the forehead.

When he stepped back it was clear that his action had surprised him as much as it had me. I giggled. Joe gave me a look I couldn't decipher, patted me gently on the belly and headed upstairs.

CHAPTER TWENTY-FIVE

'Miss George?' Janice, the midwife from last time, called, scanning the waiting room.

I pushed myself out of the chair and headed in her direction. Recognition quivered over her features as she saw me and glanced round.

'Just you today, Miss George?'

'Yes. Just me.' The sight of Janice brought back disagreeable memories. The kissing, the smiling, the Ford Fiesta with the ridiculous eyelashes round the headlights.

'Oh, that a shame. Your partner a lovely young man.'

'Hmmm.' I followed her into the exam room.

'And the ice cream? How he going with that? He said he bring me a pot of the Singapore Sling.' Janice chuckled and chittered while I lay on the vinyl-covered bed, impatient and excited to finally find out the sex of my baby.

I recoiled as she squirted the cold gel onto my now very protruding stomach. The image of the baby popped up on the screen. Janice took notes and measurements while I contemplated the little stranger who would soon be the most important person in my life.

'Placenta has moved.' Janice smiled. 'That good news.'

The baby looked so much bigger than the last scan, all squashed and folded in the confined space. I allowed myself a brief panic about how it was going to vacate my body leaving everything unripped and untorn, before pretending that that day was so far away it would probably never come. I was returning to Bradley Manor in two days' time and it was something I was very much looking forward to for many reasons. When I was there I was not in the same city as Sophie and Ned having sex, I didn't have to maintain the exhausting charade with Mum about how Ned's repayments were going and it was much easier to hide my guilt on the phone or over skype when I spoke to Uncle Mike about how Archie was doing on the 'lovely little chihuahua/cat movie'. Yes, Anglesey and its disconnection from my real life were far simpler.

'Can you see what sex it is?' I asked when Janice closed the folder and clicked her pen.

'No.' She looked at the monitor, then at me, her face arranged in calm defiance. 'Baby not in the right position.'

'But . . . you didn't try.' I was positive she was doing this because of Ned. 'You have to check.'

Janice stared me down.

'You have to check!' I said again.

'I been doing this a long time, young lady. Baby *not* in right position.'

Surely this was unprofessional practice. I wanted to find out what kind of baby I was having. I had rights.

'But you have to at least *try*.'

Janice gave a curt shake of the head.

'Hi, honey, I'm home!' I said, shutting the front door behind me.

Joe's favourite scuffed boots were in 'just stepped out of them' locations down the hall.

There'd been a fair amount of trouble at the hospital after an out-of-character episode in which I'd snatched the scanner from belligerent Janice's clutches and attempted to scan my own belly (a physically challenging task – akin to an upside-down tortoise trying to tie his shoelaces). A scuffle with the scanner had ensued, and some unmannerly language; I'd not achieved my goal, Janice had ended up covered in blue gel and security had been called. Once I'd explained my case, really labouring over the dead grandmother, horrible break-up/money-stealing/job-losing events, Geoffrey the security guard asked Janice to try one more time to determine the sex, to which she agreed but only if I wrote a formal apology then and there. And we were both pleased with the decision that she was to have absolutely no more to do with me after that. But the damned baby kept its uncooperative little legs so close together that Janice was proved correct. It was impossible to see bits or lack of bits. Now I'd had my final scan and would not know what kind of baby I was having until D-Day.

'Hey,' I said, dumping groceries on the table.

'Hey! How'd it go?' Joe leapt off the sofa and joined me in the kitchen. 'What're we having? Pink or blue, trains or tea sets, Jake or Maggie?'

I gave him a quizzical look.

'The Gyllenhaals ...?' he said, as if I were very, very stupid.

I regaled him with the scan events. Joe made empathising noises but called me a psycho.

'Roast chicken OK for dinner?' I said, putting the last of the groceries away and flicking the kettle on.

'That would be lovely, but I'm going out,' he said, getting out two mugs. 'My friends think it's time I got back in the saddle. My mate Tim's exact words were "time to dunk some beef".'

'He sounds nice.' I made a face to suggest the opposite.

'He's a lawyer,' Joe said with an indulgent eye roll. 'Anyway, I just need some proximity to testosterone. There's been a bit too much poetry and linen cupboards and Richard Curtis. I think I'm starting to grow breasts.' He fingered his nippular area.

'I did notice you'd ironed all the tea towels ...'

'I used lavender linen spray.'

Joe came down from his room later that evening in an outfit of snug jeans, stiff-looking brogues and a crisp blue shirt open at the chest that, I assured him, set off his eyes and in no way made him look like a member of One Direction. He left in a cloud of aftershave muttering that it had been ages since he'd gone out with the lads, and hoped they were just going to a local pub where they could actually hear each other, and really hoped they didn't go dancing.

I ditched the idea of a roast, ordered Chicken Madras, sat down with one of the pregnancy books and educated myself about what a day in the life of a six-month-old foetus was like. Apparently they could respond to light, and if you shone a torch on your stomach the baby would turn its head towards it. And, while lying on the sofa with my pyjama top hitched up and a bright orange camping torch aimed at my bare stomach, a pulsing red light across the garden wall let me know Harriet was filming again. She smiled and waved; I frowned and shut the blinds.

Sometime in the middle of the night I got up to wee and partake in a little predawn grazing. I was standing at the kitchen bench in the dark cutting thick slices of Colby cheese (I couldn't decide on savoury or sweet, so was alternating between smearing one slice with pickle and the next with jam) when I heard a rustling noise coming down the stairs. I hadn't heard Joe come home but assumed it had been quite late because I'd stayed up past midnight doing the torch thing again. But instead of Joe, an olive-limbed brunette padded into the room, naked except for a duvet, the corners of it gathered across her bust like a towel and the rest pooling behind her on the floor.

'Oh hi,' she giggled and drew the duvet tighter. Her dark hair fell in thick beachy waves down her naked back. 'Zorry, did ve vake you?'

She was tall and taut. I swear I'd seen her in a music video. One where she looked much like she did now; naked and coquettish with smudgy eyeliner and I've-just-been-shagging bed hair. Her toenails were manicured in a glossy coral that complemented her bronzed skin and she wore a delicate gold chain round her ankle. I'd bet my block of Colby she wasn't a day over nineteen.

'Ah ... no. I was just ...' I pointed to the cheese.

I became very aware of my pilling flannel pyjamas, protruding stomach and mismatched socks.

'Oh, OK,' she giggled again. 'I'm Yuliana.'

'Emma.' I pointed a jammy finger at myself.

'Yes, Joe zaid about you.' She moved towards the fridge and opened the door to the freezer. 'I vas just getting zome ice to ...' she smiled over her bare shoulder '... you know.'

I did. Blech.

'Yuliana,' Joe arrived, his whisper slurred. 'Did you get the—? Emma!' He caught sight of me and quickly threw his hands over his crotch but not before I got a glimpse of his chicken-skin bollocks and his surprisingly sizeable willy. 'Wh-what are you doing here?'

'It's my house,' I said, trying not to take in his nudity. 'You might see me around occasionally.'

'Right. Of course. So how – how are you?' He raised an arm, attempting a nonchalant lean on the doorframe, missed, stumbled, lost his grip on his bits, then gathered himself and straightened up, a pained look on his face.

I raised an eyebrow. 'I'm fine.'

'Oh, that's good, that's good.' He bobbed his head like we'd met casually outside a Pret A Manger.

The three of us stood in the dark kitchen silhouetted by the light of the open fridge. Yuliana didn't seem to have the care or the nous to spot the silent skirmish going on between Joe and me.

Who do you think you are, bringing this anklet-wearing Eastern European gypsy whore into my house?

Please go back to bed so I can get my paws on this gypsy whore with the ever-so-twinkly anklet.

Do her parents know she's out? She can't be a day over nineteen.

Her parents are Russian royalty; she speaks six languages and runs a fashion blog. And she's only nineteen!

I should not have to worry I might meet naked exchange students while I attend to my midnight snacking needs.

Is that pickle nice? Harriet made it.

She might have herpes.

She might do anal.

Eventually our unarticulated exchange became an uncomfortable stare-off.

Yuliana cocked a hip. 'Joe?' she said with a suggestive look. 'Zhall ve go upzdairz?'

Joe and I eyed each other, me trying to convey that ice sex with a teenager was not an acceptable pastime in my home and him imploring me to go away so he could bonk Little Miss Long Limbs. I crossed the kitchen to the fridge and threw the cheese on a shelf. Yuliana stepped to the side, showing off a smooth-skinned thigh that momentarily distracted Joe from his silent plead.

'Goodnight,' I said in a clipped, prudish voice.

Joe's gaze snapped guiltily back to me. I passed Yuliana, who rubbed an ice cube along her bottom lip and eyed Joe from under her lashes. Joe pressed himself against the door-frame as I walked out, protecting his modesty.

''Night,' he said.

The next morning I opened my bedroom door and was greeted by Joe and Yuliana in the open front doorway, he in just his boxers and she in a shimmery, groin-grazing dress. They were knotted in a postcoital we're-still-drunk-so-don't-yet-realise-how-inappropriate-it-is-to-grab-at-each-other's-arses-on-the-doorstep-at-9-a.m.-in-front-of-all-the-welsh-setter-walking-families-on-the-common clinch. All I could think of was how god-awful their breath must be. After much slurping they pulled apart and became aware of the schoolmarmish presence that was I.

'Oh, bye Emma,' Yuliana said in a voice husky from a night of faking orgasms. 'Look after my zexy *golubchik*.'

Joe winced as her talons dug into his buttocks. I gave a terse smile and lumbered down the hall, but not before noticing that dangling from Yuliana's manicured claws were her strappy whore heels and on her feet were a pair of fold-able ballet slippers. Had she anticipated going home with a stranger? Did all young people go out at night armed with appropriate 'walk of shame' footwear? Was this practical attitude to casual sex the norm? More slurping noises drifted down the hall, then some empty murmurs about maybe meeting up for a coffee later in the week, correct email- and number-checking. The door shut and Joe appeared in the living room looking hangdog and terribly the worse for wear.

'Oh, good morning,' I said, scooping decaf coffee into a pot. 'How are you feeling this morning? A little bit Jimmy Savile?'

'Don't start,' Joe said, plopping onto the sofa and dragging Mum's Missoni blanket over his head.

'Well I'm gonna.' I stomped out of the kitchen and stood over him, hands on hips. 'I did not care for last night's events.'

Joe uttered a dry-mouthed 'sorry' from under the blanket.

'I do not want to have to introduce myself to naked students in my own house at four a.m.'

'Not student. Intern at *Cosmo*.'

'I do not want your sex props to come from my kitchen.'

'We didn't—'

'And I do not want to spend three hours listening to your sex Olympics then watch you suck the face off a teen slut from a Pitbull music video on my front doorstep!'

Joe pulled down the blanket. He looked worse than the night he'd arrived drunk and in possession of pie. 'You thought we were Olympic-like?'

I huffed.

'I feel revolting,' he groaned.

'You *are* revolting.'

Joe rested the crook of his elbow over his eyes. I stomped

back to the kitchen and busied myself with coffee-making, getting out a second mug for the hung-over mug on my sofa.

'I've never done that before, you know,' he said from under his arm. 'Had a one-night stand.'

'Was it everything you'd dreamt it would be?'

Joe was quiet for a moment. 'It's not great, actually.'

I let out a derisive 'ha' from the back of my throat.

'She was quite . . . bossy.'

'I know.' I shuddered.

Yuliana's barked sex orders had got more Belarusian dictator-esque as the evening progressed. I wedged a box of cornflakes under my arm and carried the mugs to the sofa.

'Here,' I said, holding one out.

'Thanks.' He sat up and took the coffee.

I handed him the cereal he liked to eat directly from the box and took a seat in the armchair.

'So,' I curled my feet under me. 'I'm not the gatekeeper to the world of sex or anything, but I'd feel more comfortable if you, you know, "*dunked your beef*" elsewhere.'

Joe gave a contrite smile. 'It won't happen again. It really . . .' He shook his head. 'It just wasn't my thing.'

'You did sound a little out of your depth.'

'I was not!'

'*Put it zere, Joe. Zere! Zere! Put it. Put it zere! Joe! Put it! PUT IT! ZERE!*' I mimicked. Joe groaned.

'Where were you trying to put it?'

'Shut up!' Joe threw a pillow at me. We grinned.

'Seriously, though,' I said, reaching for the cereal box. 'I'm going back to Anglesey tomorrow. I don't want any more girls coming here using my pantry as an adult toyshop.'

Joe shook his head. 'None. I'm done. Got it out of my system.'

'Good.' I handed the cereal box back. 'We don't want Harriet to film you and end up getting arrested for accidentally making a voyeuristic porn film. I'd be questioned about harbouring a paedophile, social services would take my baby away and I'd have to move house because *Daily Mail* journalists would camp outside my door trying to get a photo of the new internet porn sensation.'

Joe beamed. 'You think I'd be a sensation?'

I threw the pillow back.

CHAPTER TWENTY-SIX

'They're *what*?!'

'Moving in together.' Douglas gulped down the phone.

'When?' I paced up and down the jetty.

Archie and I had been back at Bradley Manor for a week. We were shooting a camping scene with the feral chihuahuas-as-cats in the forest by the lake and I'd stepped off set after receiving a text from Douglas saying Sophie and Ned were moving in together.

'This weekend, I believe. They found a place in Norbiton.'

'But this means it's serious. *You* said it was just going to be a fling.'

'Ah, actually, ah, Helen said that, I believe. Yes ... ah—'

'I don't care who said it.' I reached the end of the jetty and spun round. 'I can't believe this is happening. Are they going to get married and have freckly, pixie-faced babies dressed in stripes?'

'Ah, well, I'm . . . not sure, really . . . I guess it's a possibility.'

'Douglas!' I shrieked.

I spun round again and was greeted by Martha's reprimanding face. 'What do you want?'

'Huh?' Douglas said.

'Not you, Douglas. I have to go. I'll call you later. Sorry
for yelling, really I am.' I hung up and Martha pounced.

'Archie needed to go to the bathroom and you weren't
there to take him.'

'OK, well, I'm coming back now. Keep your knickers on.'
I pushed past her in the direction of the forest. 'If you can
manage it.'

'I've taken him already. I had to leave *my* charge with
Claire, who I do not think is a particularly good role model
for small children. Her language is atrocious and she smokes
like a train.' Martha puffed along beside me as I strode back
to set.

'So it's all fine then. What's your problem?'

Martha grabbed me by the arm. '*You* are my problem!' she
said a little too close to my face for my liking.

She had large pores in her squashy nose and there was a
strong waft of ham about her person.

'You're a terrible chaperone!' Martha stabbed a stubby
finger in my direction. 'You're lazy, self-involved and always
on your phone. You don't help Archie learn his lines or
make sure he's properly hydrated. You don't support me
by adhering to the official child hours, always offering the
director another five minutes here, extra take there. You let

the children play with intestines – it's totally inappropriate – and don't think I didn't see you filming them with the torso, or detonating squibs. You think you're better than this job because you used to be a Second AD.' She walked ahead a few steps, then stopped and turned back.

'I hope you were a good AD because you're an awful chaperone, and I'll be writing to your local authority to recommend they revoke your licence immediately.' She glanced down at my baby bump with a pinched look. 'God knows what kind of dreadful mother you'll be.'

And with that, she spun on her heavy legs and stalked towards the forest. I stood at the end of the jetty, stunned. Martha was going to get me fired. I thought about what that meant for me. For Archie. If I lost my job I'd have nothing to think about except Sophie and Ned and their freckly future. And I needed the money. I'd hardly put much away for when the baby came. All of Joe's rent was going to Mum to pay off Ned's pretend instalments. And I was absolutely not contacting Ned now that he was playing house with my ex-friend. No way. I couldn't lose my job. I'd have to move in with Mum and start that teapot collection. And Martha thought I was going to be a horrible mother. Was I? I'd been quietly harbouring fears that motherhood was going to completely overwhelm me. I squared my shoulders. A new mature, responsible single mother-to-be was going to emerge, effective immediately. Well, as soon as I could convince Martha not to tell on me. I hurried along the jetty and caught up to Martha at the edge of the forest, only having the tiniest of panics that the brief jog had turned my baby into a milkshake.

'Martha! Wait!'

She turned, raising her chins. 'Yes?'

'Please don't get me fired! Please?'

'You're too late. I've already written the email. I just have to get Production's consent and press send.'

'Just hear me out. *Please*?' I decided the best approach was flattery, submission and a bit of begging. 'You're right. I'm a terrible chaperone. I'm awful.'

Martha and her glucose sweats were nonplussed.

'Let me have one more chance. I promise I'll be better. Much better. I need this job. I *want* this job.'

Martha considered me, and I had the completely unrelated thought that, with a little help from a Mac counter and heavily dimmed lighting, she could be quite pretty. Her eyes were a lovely cornflower shade of blue, and under the additional padding it looked like her cheekbones were rather well-defined. Her pores were extremely large – she could keep spare change in there – but Caroline could fix that with a flick of a brush.

'Just because you "need" this job doesn't mean you should have it.' She put her hands on her hips. 'Being a good chaperone means putting the child's needs first. Something you seem incapable of doing.'

'OK, I have a proposition for you.'

Martha narrowed her eyes.

'You don't send that email and I spend the rest of the

shoot learning from you.' The idea was just formulating in my head. Hopefully it would appeal to her superior nature. 'You become my mentor and I your . . . student, of sorts. You teach me everything you know.'

Martha chewed on her lip.

'I run everything by you and if you say jump I say when, for how long and do you want me to bake you a cake while I'm doing it?' I threw her a little smile to show I was trying.

Martha's eyes narrowed. 'You should be doing that anyway; I'm the senior chaperone.'

'I'll get your breakfast every day. And do every bedtime with the kids. And at the end of every week we sit down and you give me a performance review and tell me all the things I did wrong.'

Martha's eyes lit up. This was it. A chance to berate me at the end of each week with my full approval.

'Deal,' she said, wiping a bead of sugar-withdrawal sweat off her upper lip. 'But one more slip-up and you are gone.'

'Gone. Totally. Gotcha.'

For the next week I was degradation personified. I supported Martha when she took the children off set after their official time was up, even though with one more 45-second 'take' the scene would be in the bag. I got her pastries every morning, bathed the kids every night and reapplied sunblock on the kids every hour even though it was cloudy. And we were shooting inside. 'UV rays are extremely harmful to young skin and we are shooting near some pretty big windows,' was what I said

through gritted teeth, Martha nodding along in approval, when
Claire asked what the hell I was doing. Each night I crawled
into bed and hoped I'd survive the rest of the shoot without
smothering Martha with her empty crisp packets. I'd spend
my days trying to think of something, *anything* that could
bring Martha down a peg or nine, but it was impossible to find
something to pin on her. Martha was an excellent chaperone.

I was lying in bed about to turn off my light when I heard
Martha arrive back from dinner. By the sound of it she
had company. Within minutes, grunts and moans vibrated
through the wall. I switched off my light and pulled the duvet
over my head. I tried to recognise the male from his grunts.
It wasn't Steve because he was more of a groaner, with quite a
long *ooooh* in the middle. And it wasn't Male Zombie Camper
Number Three because his grunts were short and he blew
a quick whoosh of air out of his mouth like a long-distance
runner. The lighting guy with the tattoo of a Chinese fish
on his shoulder was generally silent, only making one loud
OH! when he came, so it wasn't him either.

This guy must be new.

And then the chatter began and it seemed I wasn't the only
amateur poet.

'Oooooh I want to tussle with your muscle,' Martha said,
her voice thick with desire. 'Come *on*,' she urged. (I really
didn't like hearing her 'urge'.) 'I want to be *under* your *thun-
der*. I want to be *humpin'* your cir*cum*ference.'

'I want you anterior to my general area,' replied Scott
Vander.

SCOTT VANDER?! Impossible!

The revelation that Scott, the movie star with a manly jaw, white teeth and year-round I–have–my–own–powerboat–in–Barbados–and–it–gets–me–all–the–chicks tan was bonking Martha the who–ate–all–the–pies–oh–it–was–me–pass–the–pudding chaperone with a chip on her squishy shoulder was just too delicious a piece of prospective gossip. I needed to find out for sure, so I grabbed my pillow, duvet and phone and headed to the sofa in the living room to lie in wait. I'd see if it really was Scott Vander when he emerged, worn out and in need of disinfecting. I'd just settled down with the duvet covering my head when a door opened and footsteps padded down the hall. I shrank into the sofa as a toned figure walked across the dark room and headed to the fridge humming the tune to 'Eye of the Tiger'. Scott-shagging-Vander. Unbelievable! By the light of the fridge I could see the outline of his willy (helmet, for those interested). I cursed myself for not having my phone ready to take photographic evidence of the extraordinary event. Scott grabbed a bunch of bananas and a pot of Nutella and strutted back down the hall. I contemplated where those poor bananas were heading. One day they're hanging off a tree in the Philippines, the next they're in chilly Wales destined for unpleasant terrain. The carnal endurance test started again but within a couple of minutes I heard a loud *OH!* followed by a dull thud and a shrill howl. An 'oh-that-hurts' howl, not a 'Jesus-I'm-coming' howl. Then, 'Are you OK? I'll get ice!'

I grabbed my phone, navigated to the camera app, turned

off the flash and waited. Helen was going to get her photo. Heavy footsteps pounded the hallway and Martha rushed into the room, naked with a smear of Nutella ... well, I don't really want to say where but it wasn't pretty. I followed Martha with the phone. She gave me an intimate view of her naked buttocks as she fished ice out of the freezer then trundled back down the hall. I lay under my duvet, finger hovering over the camera button. A few minutes later Scott appeared, fully dressed, an arm slung over Martha (thankfully clothed in a dressing gown) limping painfully down the hall. It wasn't quite what Helen had in mind but, stealth-like, through a teeny opening in my duvet, I snapped a couple of pics anyway.

'What if it's broken?' Scott whispered as he hopped along beside Martha.

Neither of them noticed the bunchy duvet on the sofa.

'It's just a sprain.'

'It feels broken.'

'It's not.'

'I told you I couldn't hold it any longer.'

'I couldn't hear you. Your face was—'

And they were through the front door. I in no way needed to know where his face was that so muffled his cries.

The next morning while everyone milled about the breakfast buffet the Second AD slunk into the room, bags under his eyes, a clipboard in his hands, and addressed the crew.

'Everyone listen up, please. Everyone. Gather round, thanks.'

People dumped sugar in their paper cups of coffee, another bagel on their paper plates and took their places in a drowsy semicircle around him. I still found it odd that zombies stood among us with their breakfast baps and their early morning yawns.

'Scott Vander has been injured,' the Second AD said bluntly.

The crowd murmured; a few girlish gasps escaped from the female cast members.

'It's OK. He'll be fine,' he said, without anything approaching feeling. 'He fell while on his run this morning and has a hairline fracture on his ankle. Or foot . . . bone.'

The cast and crew threw each other shocked glances. What did that mean for filming? Could we continue? Was Scott OK? I think it was fair to say I was the only one, besides Martha, who was next to the pastries and had paled considerably, who knew how Scott really got his hairline fracture. Naked banana athletics with a certain Nutella-coated snack monster.

'When will he be back?' someone asked.

'This afternoon, we hope. He's having a cast fitted but will be cleared to shoot from tomorrow onward.'

'But how can we shoot with a cast on his foot?' The costume designer, a woman in her fifties with smoke-harried skin said through crimped lips. 'None of his costumes will fit over a cast.'

'How will he do the forest scenes?' asked an art department guy.

'Or the cabin sequence? Chippies start tomorrow,' said another.

Different departments voiced their concerns. Equipment was hired; cast had been booked. The big zombie camper attack was due to happen in two days. The stunt department were rigging harnesses (for the flying zombies – a huge flaw in the script, according to a very perturbed Douglas because zombies can*not* fly), SPFX were rigging squibs, flame bars and all manner of retractable weaponry, and the make-up and art departments were working together to assemble severed body parts and silicone gut paraphernalia.

'Rewrites are happening as we speak,' the Second AD said over the collective panic attack.

Rewrites this late in filming were a massive undertaking. Forthcoming scenes, with their props, actors, animals, stunt coordinators and equipment already booked and paid for might get deleted from the script. Some scenes we'd already shot might not make sense and may have to be discarded. The sex-damaged ankle was going to have mammoth repercussions. I glanced at Martha, who was chewing her fingernails.

'Can't we just delay shooting till the cast comes off?' asked the silver-haired art director. 'Everything we've done is going to be compromised.'

'The manor is booked solid from the last day of shoot for the rest of the summer. Weddings every week. Overrunning is not an option,' the Second AD said. 'This is the only way. Or the film doesn't get finished.'

CHAPTER TWENTY-SEVEN

Back in the barn house, Martha was all a-fluster.

'Where've you been?' she barked. 'We should be running lines with the children.'

Tilly perched on the edge of the sofa while Martha paced the floor gripping a disorganised script in one hand and a packet of chocolate buttons in the other.

'What for?' I handed Archie a bunch of grapes, eased myself into an armchair and circled my ankles. 'The schedule's changing. We have no idea what scenes to practise.'

'Exactly! It's disastrous. We should be prepared for all of them.'

I affected a yawn and stretched my arms. 'Nah. Let's just hang.'

Martha stopped pacing. 'I *beg* your pardon?'

I picked up my phone and feigned bored texting. I found the picture of Scott and Martha. It was grainy and dark and at a jaunty angle but there was no doubt it was the two of them. And no doubt it was a clandestine encounter. Martha watched, her nostrils splaying wide and tense, wide and tense, while I exaggerated my carefree phone-twiddling.

'Here,' she said, tossing her script on the seat beside me. 'I've folded over all the scenes we've already shot. But that's not to say we won't need to relearn them. We may have to reshoot any one of them. Start running them from the beginning. I'm going to see if we can get more information. We can't work like this. Children need time to prepare.' She moved towards the door, her hoggish eyes squinting in my direction.

I picked up the script, pretending to acquiesce to her demands, then dropped it to the floor.

'No thanks.'

Tilly and Archie popped grapes into their mouths and watched. Martha stopped by the door.

'Oh, I think you've finally done it,' she said, her face spreading into a malevolent grin. She stalked back into the middle of the room. 'I was always going to send that email. I'll send it today, and with any luck you'll be removed from the position immediately.' She stopped. A flicker of agitation crossed her face. 'Why are you smiling?'

'Because I know something you don't know.'

'I doubt that.' She straightened and crossed her arms over her chest.

Her sports watch sank into the skin of her wrist like it was wrapped around a doughy loaf of bread. I pushed myself out of the armchair, took a step towards her and held my phone inches from her braying nostrils.

'I. Know. Something.'

Barely detectable stages of panic traversed her face, peaking in fury before settling on hostile realisation.

'Tilly, take the iPad and go and play in your room,' Martha said, her voice steely. 'Educational apps only.'

Tilly and Archie obediently left the room. Martha and I remained face to face, the phone held up between us.

'I sense you want something,' Martha said.

'You sense right.'

She gave a reluctant nod.

'I want you to back. The hell. Off.' I shook my index finger with each word. 'I want you to stop talking to me like I'm an imbecile. I want you to let the kids watch cartoons once in a while. I want you to give the director another ten frigging minutes if he needs it. Stop waking me up at 6 a.m. to run lines. Stop the loud goddamned orgasms – they're keeping me awake!' For this Martha had the decency to colour. 'Stop taking all the chocolate croissants, stop pretending to be so offended by the "offensive" script when you run a one-woman brothel out of your bedroom, stop taking the children's temperatures, stop bossing me around and stop being such a *fucking bitch*!' I paused to catch my breath. 'And share your snacks!'

Martha's chest heaved. She studied me, hatred pinching her face. 'OK,' she said through tiny lips.

I reached between us, slipped the chocolate buttons from her hammy clutch and popped one into my mouth.

*

New scenes arrived the next morning. People snatched them from the ADs and gasps reverberated round the room as they flicked through the scripts and noted the changes. Scott's scenes were rewritten so they could be blocked in such a way that we never saw his lower left leg. Many scenes had to be cut and most were compromised. The head of costume tossed her script to the floor and ran off in tears. Art department members said it was impossible and went outside to smoke and scuff their retro Doc Martens in the driveway shingle. The director got on the phone and yelled at LA.

For the next two days we only filmed until lunch and the afternoons were given over to the crew to implement the changes. It called an end to Scott Vander's parties as cast and crew spent their evenings prepping the amendments. Joe kept me entertained by reading my teenage poetry in funny voices to my mobile's message service. He still hadn't gone back to work, but apparently my vegetable garden was flourishing and anyway, he was too busy taking afternoon tea and scones with Harriet, Arthur and Brutus in the burgeoning warm weather. I hadn't had much news on the Ned and Sophie front, except for another delivery from Sophie – cheese this time (calcium for baby's bones) – which Joe had the good sense to get rid of (eat immediately), but that could have been because Douglas was busy with his new girlfriend Jemima and Helen was getting fit for the summer by taking home boys in their early twenties and bonking their student brains out. I still hadn't spoken to Alex. I'd realised that Cal's 'kind' offer had hurt. It meant that while they were busy planning their perfect wedding and perfect future they were also judging my life choices. Probably measuring their lives against mine and giving each other slow pitying shakes of the head.

Mum was in Buenos Aires sourcing furniture for the homes of the rich but it didn't stop her texting me drivel to the tune of:

> I had a dream last night you were having a girl.
> But it means nothing because I also dreamt I
> got a fringe and I would NEVER do that.

Then two minutes later:

> I'm still a little teary about it.

Thirty seconds later:

> I would look awful with a fringe.

A week later normal filming days resumed and everyone was bumping along as before, just a little more tired and a little more grouchy. Except me. I was having a fabulous time. And it was entirely down to that grainy incriminating photo. If I felt partial to a KitKat, I had only to tap my phone on my chin and raise my eyebrows in the direction of Martha's on-set rucksack. If the director needed another take and we were out of official 'on-set child hours', I'd waggle my phone in Martha's direction and she'd shut her protesting yap-hole and nod a begrudging assent. I helped myself to her crisps; I let the kids watch *Looney Tunes* during dinner; I chatted with Claire and Caroline during lighting set-ups instead of making Archie run his word-perfect lines over and over till they lost all meaning. And I ate dinner with the crew every night which had the additional bonus of Martha being unable to pick up alcoholically impaired crew-members so therefore had blissfully silent nights. There were no more dawn walks round the lake; no more end-of-week reviews about how terrible I was.

'Without that photo you have *nothing*,' she whispered to me one day at the end of the catering table by the sauces and dressings. 'You'd better sleep with your phone because I *will* get hold of it. And when I do—'

'You'll do nothing, right?' I said pleasantly, like we were simply discussing the recent change in season. 'Because you'll realise I would've already emailed it to my friends and myself for safekeeping.'

Martha pinched her lips into a tight circle, gripped the tomato ketchup and mumbled vicious incantations. I floated away from the sauces and settled at a lunch table next to Archie, who was attacking his steak with a knife and making zombie cat noises while Tilly giggled next to him.

'What's new with you?' Andrew sat down at our table with his carb-free lunch.

'Nothing much. I'm still researching a way of giving birth that requires no ripping or slicing and will leave my body in the exact same shape it was prior to all this . . .' I waggled my fingers over my body '. . . stretching.'

'Good luck with that.'

'And there's the dread of trans-seasonal dressing to overcome.'

'It does seem a major hurdle to happiness,' he said, laughing.

'When you have my mother it's a very serious matter.' I pulled out my phone and scrolled. 'This is from her last week.' I affected my mother's voice. "*Darling. It's officially spring. Please tell me you are not thinking about three-quarter trousers*".'

Andrew popped some undressed salad into his mouth and grinned.

'I replied: "*I'll roll my jeans up*". Then she sent: "*Footwear?*" Then again: "*And don't say Birkenstocks*". Me: "*Birkenstocks*". Her: "*You have no mother*". And it goes on and on and on – *and on*.'

I passed Andrew my phone and he scrolled down, chuckling. His thumb had a clean, wide fingernail the shape of a flat clam. It was a sexy thumb.

'Who's Joe?' he said after a few moments.

'Oh, he lives with me.'

Andrew raised an eyebrow.

'Not like that,' I said. 'He's a lodger. Just temporarily.'

'Oh *really*.' Andrew said in a dubious tone. 'Then what's with this text?'

I looked at the phone and giggled. 'It's a joke.' I took the phone back and enjoyed the split second my fingers grazed the sexy thumb. 'He pretends to wear my underwear.'

'Riiiight.'

'Really!'

'From the look of some of those texts I'd say he has a thing for you.'

'You're probably right. I sometimes forget how irresistible I am right now.'

Andrew shrugged his broad shoulders. 'Some people find the pregnant state very attractive.'

'Only the weirdos. I look like a giant butternut squash.'

Andrew let out a burst of laughter.

'But I'll take the attractive bit if you insist.'

'I do,' he said with a grin.

In our last week at Bradley Manor I got a phone call from Joe.

'What does the Tooth Witch look like?'

We'd long passed the point of 'hello', 'how are you', 'I'm fine, and you?' and went directly to the core of conversation.

'What?' I said, trying to pull my maternity jeans over my bump while cradling my phone between ear and shoulder.

'The Tooth Witch? From your poem. What does she look like? Because I had a dream about her last night and I think she has long white hair and straggly—'

'Joe?'

'Yuh?'

'You need to go back to work.'

'I can't. I'm still being sad.'

'You sound fine to me.' I stood in front of the mirror waiting to get off the phone so I could put my top on.

The stretchy fabric of my maternity jeans now hugged the bottom of my bump like a Lycra sling instead of being able to be coaxed over it. My maternity bra looked as if it had been modelled off the first bra ever invented. It was technical and unattractive and otherworldly, like an intergalactic breast-plate. Boob armour for the well-endowed Stormtrooper.

'We could go into business together,' Joe suggested.

'Doing what?'

'Children's books. You write the poems and I do the graphics. My mum thinks it's a great idea. And I've got this plan for the "Button to Lovely Land" image.'

'For god's sake.' Archie was due in Wardrobe in a couple of minutes and I still had the mammoth task of putting on my own socks. In my large state it was an increasingly difficult operation. I'd found an ingenious way of getting into my knickers: I held them with the tips of my fingers, spun them to get momentum and sort of lassoed them round my foot. But sock application was proving not as easily cracked, and I needed to devote some proper time to the activity. 'I don't even write poems any more.'

'But you could,' he said hopefully. 'Anyway, there's heaps here we could start with. Like the "Mushroom Men" one. Now, where is it? I had it a minute ago . . .'

'Joe . . .' I sighed. I heard him rustling pages.

'It's not far away . . . Yes, hang on, I left it in the bathroom.' Joe's footsteps echoed down the phone.

'Ew! You were reading my poems on the toilet?'

'No. I was in the bath.'

'Did you use the bath oils my mum sent?'

'Yes. Very relaxing.'

I sniggered. 'They're to soften my cervix.'

Joe was silent.

'Joe?'

'I feel violated.'

I laughed. 'Maybe you should stop going through my stuff and get on with some work.'

'All right.' Joe sighed. 'But will you at least think about the children's book idea?'

'No.'

'Glad to see you're open-minded.' He sniffed.

'Gotta go, Joe. To *work*. Like you should be. Bye!'

I did still write poems. Like the one I'd scrawled on the back of my script just the day before.

> *Martha oh Martha ate all of the pies*
> *Most of us hope that she fucks off and dies*
> *She stuffs her face silly*
> *Rides every willy*
> *And crushes men tightly in her cottage cheese thighs.*

Poet Laureate material it was not, but it kept me entertained.

At the end of a very frustrating day (the chihuahuas refused to run after the campers and instead took to humping each other), while I sat on the sofa, the kids in bed, tapping away on a very important, highbrow document (I was email-ing Helen about how much I hated Martha), Joe rang on skype. I clicked the answer button and Joe's grinning face appeared.

'Hey!' he said.

'Hi.'

'Whatcha doin'?'

'You're bored, aren't you?'

'Never! There's heaps to do here. Did you know your grandma had a Mills and Boon collection? What a grubby little grandma you had.'

'Those are mine, and will you stay out of my bedroom.' So accustomed was I to Joe's upfront nosiness, my body declined to blush.

'Oh really?' he said, waggling a single eyebrow.

'Is that why you called? To talk about throbbing members? Because if you want I can say the word "moist" over and over. Moist, moist, moist—'

'OK, stop!' He laughed.

'Moist, moist, moist—'

Joe threw his hands over his ears. 'LA LA LA LA – CAN'T HEAR YOU. LA LA LA—'

'Moist, moist—'

Martha walked into the room.

'Your skype sex technique is pathetic,' she said, and con-tinued her lumber down the hall.

I blushed.

'OK, I'm stopping.'

'LA LA LA LA . . .'

I waved my arms. 'Joe! I've stopped.'

He dropped his hands and listened. 'You're done being gross?'

'Done. Yes.'

'OK, good. Because I actually called to tell you a courier dropped off a freezer box for you today.'

'Another meat pack?'

He got up from the kitchen table, walked to the freezer and took out a plain white plastic tub. Like a big yoghurt container without a label.

'No.' He held it up, a knowing look on his face. 'Ice cream.' My jovial mood departed.

'And it came with a note.' He sat back down in front of the screen and reached for something out of view. 'It says,' he read from a piece of paper, 'that this flavour is Salted Whisky Caramel, inspired by the "wicked" sauce you used to make.' Joe looked up from the note. 'How come you never make me that sauce?'

I chewed on my inner cheek.

'Your mother said Ned had sold the vans,' he said after a beat of contemplation.

'I lied.'

'He's paid you back, though? And you've paid your Mum?'

'No. That's where your rent money goes.'

'You're lying to your mother.' From atop his self-constructed pedestal he gave a sanctimonious tut-tut.

'Yeah, well . . .' I did not need a lecture from Mr Nosy

Pants. I scrambled for an excellent defence. 'You're . . . scared of spiders.'

'I'm going to ignore that pitiful argument – you'll be embarrassed about it later.' He stood, moved across the kitchen, opened a drawer and returned with a spoon.

'Might I suggest,' he sat back down in front of the screen, 'that you still have feelings for Ned?'

I was most put out. 'No, you may not!'

'Then why are you protecting him? And compromising yourself?'

Why was I? I owed him nothing except maybe a very large invoice. It was just . . . Ned had such passion for these ideas. And even though none of them had worked and most were wholly implausible (starting a 'pop-up' rescue duck sanctuary in our back garden being one that sprang to mind) I was stirred by his conviction. Ned had ideas. And he acted on them. Lots of people had ideas. Lots of people spoke about them. Not very many acted. It dawned on me – and shocked me to realise – that I was sort of proud of him.

'Look,' I said, 'I know I should be demanding my money back and not lying to my mother, blah blah blah,' I flapped my hands around. 'And I know I should be worried about the future and of course I am, I mean, I've only just started saving again and I'm trained in nothing except being a Second AD, which is really not a suitable job for a parent, let alone a single one. So I should get my money back and get on with my life, but . . .' I slumped my shoulders.

Joe waited.

'I can't take it away from him now,' I said. 'He's achieving his dream. Finally.'

Joe watched me twiddle with my fingers. 'What's your dream?'

'Umm.' I frowned.

For life to be easy. For it to travel in a straight line for a while. Just so I can see what's on the horizon for once. No twists, turns or dips in the road for a few years. No surprise babies or break-ups or friends shagging exes. Just a baby, an income and regular episodes of *Miranda*. I didn't need a Happily Ever After; I needed normal. Normally Ever After.

'To not shit myself when I give birth,' I said.

Joe bobbed his head in a well-that's-that-then manner and cracked open the sealed lid on the ice cream pot.

'What do you think you're doing?'

'Trying the ice cream,' he said, plunging the spoon in.

'Throw it out. I don't want it in my house.'

Joe nodded and brought the spoon up, a caramel-coloured creamy mound resting on top.

'Get rid of it!'

'OK.' He put the spoon in his mouth.

'Traitor.'

His eyes took on that glassy, faraway look you get when your taste buds are sending multiple messages of pleasure.

'What's it like?' I asked grudgingly.

'Horrible,' he said through an ice cream-loaded mouth.

Only the dimmest of dimwits would have believed him.

'Then why are you having another spoonful?' I said as his spoon made yet another trip from tub to mouth.

'To make sure.'

'Throw it out.'

'Will do.' He ploughed the spoon into the tub again.

'I can see you!'

CHAPTER TWENTY-EIGHT

'What leaving party?' I paced the courtyard, waiting for the next shot to be lit.

Archie sat on a garden bench feeding crisps to Ivan and Wayne, waiting patiently so we could take his tugboat to the lake. In two more days we would finish shooting, and I'd phoned Helen hoping to organise a much-needed catch-up. Douglas had a girlfriend I'd never met and Helen had a new 'going out' set of friends. If I didn't want to find myself alone every night watching *Strictly Come Dine with Britain's Next Top Baker* I needed to reconnect with my friends. Especially now I was one friend down with Sophie 'The Betrayer' off playing house with my ex.

'It's Sophie's party,' Helen said and, unusually for her, she sounded a little uncomfortable. 'She quit.'

'Quit her *job*? Why?' I knew it. She'd quit because Ned had won the EuroMillions and they were off to sail round the world and spend their days eating caviar and throwing money in the ocean.

'We-ell . . .' Helen picked over her words. 'The ice cream vans have been booked for nearly every summer festival.'

'So?'

'They've had to buy another two vans and three of their flavours are being picked up by Selfridges.'

My head spun. Was Ned . . . *successful*?

'What's that got to do with Sophie quitting her job?'

'Sophie's invested in the business. She bought Gerry out. Ned was the brains behind it all, apparently. They've changed the name to Ned and Sophie's Organic Ice Creamery,' she said, making me stop pacing and lean heavily against a shiny Range Rover. 'She bought the extra vans they needed and she's quit to run the books. It's all happening very quickly.'

Ned *was* successful. Shocking. And my mother's natural home would be stocking three of his flavours. I drooped in my standing position. I'd stopped believing in Ned's schemes after the time he'd convinced me to buy five thousand left-handed scissors from China to sell at a left-handers convention in Slough. I'd had to borrow money from Mum to pay the rent and after the scissors failed to sell (Ned blaming my marketing techniques, of which I'd employed none, that apparently being the entire problem) we'd stored the unwanted scissors in the bathroom, the kitchen, beside the bed, the sterilised needles cupboard at Uncle Mike's surgery and in the car until we eventually dropped them off at a local community centre.

'But Sophie loves working in TV!' I said, my mind reeling.

'I know!' said Helen, much more animated now. 'But it turns out that cotton-brained hippy is a whiz with numbers. She's saved a third of her wages since the day she got her first job and she used to balance the books at her family's cheese farm.'

'Cheese *factory*,' I corrected absent-mindedly.

'Right.'

I thought about Ned and his ability to pick himself up after each failed idea and launch himself eagerly at the next one. He'd fail, he'd try again; he'd fail, he'd try again. And always with the wide-eyed faith that one day one of his ideas would work. I realised what an admirable quality that was. One that, after a few years of financial adversity, I'd begun to overlook. Especially after numerous instances of having the following kind of conversation:

Ned: I've got a brilliant idea.

Me: Oh, yes?

Ned: I'm going to breed chickens.

Me: Right.

Ned: (pacing and enthusing) There's a chicken
     that's delicious but super-expensive because it
     grows really slowly. Then there's a chicken that
     doesn't taste good but grows fast so it's really
     cheap. I'm going to breed them and get a fast-
     growing, delicious chicken and make millions.
     I can't believe no one's thought of it before!

Me: You know nothing about breeding chickens.
     You might get a slow-growing, gross-tasting
     one.
Ned: (looking at me as if I were dim) No, a *fast-*
     growing, *delicious* one.
Me: Or a slow, gross one.
Ned: (logging on to eBay) Fast and delicious.

I'd then had another conversation about how the money in the bank was to pay rent and bills and buy cheap, taste-less chicken breasts to put in a cheap, tasteless stir-fry, not to bid on an industrial egg incubator he had no idea how to use.

'Are you OK?' Helen said, her voice gentle.

'Yeah.' My throat tightened. 'No.'

'Sorry.'

'It's not your fault.'

'Movie night the weekend after?'

I agreed, said goodbye and hung up. The phone rang again and I answered without looking at the caller ID.

'Hello?' I sighed.

'I finally got you!' Alex's voice, while usually lifting my spirits, threw a blanket of guilt over me.

'Oh. Hi.'

'I've been trying to call.'

'Oh, have you? I've been, um, busy on the film set.' I don't know why I was bothering lying; Alex would know I'd been avoiding her.

'Of course. How's Archie doing? Got another movie after this?'

'No,' I said. 'Just this one.'

'Oh, right.'

I could hear the rush of waves from Alex's end.

She coughed uncomfortably. 'So, wedding planning is a bit crap, really.'

'Yeah?'

'Cal's mother is a control freak. We've been thinking of getting married in Singapore and forgetting the whole "big wedding" thing.'

'Sounds cool.'

Alex was quiet. The silence was weighty and I knew an uncomfortable conversation was afoot.

'I've really needed you, Emma,' she said with a faintly reprimanding tone.

'I've been busy.'

'I've left you heaps of messages.'

'My phone hasn't been working, bad reception in Anglesey.' I didn't believe in hell but I was certainly headed somewhere awful in the afterlife. Perpetual Christmas Eve in Primark, or an eternity at Camden underground station on a midsummer Saturday with a hangover.

'I've been having a bit of a tough time.'

'A tough time?' I scoffed. 'Oh *really*. What could possibly be wrong in your life?'

'What?!' Alex shot back. 'Are you so wrapped up in yourself that you can't see other people have problems too?'

'I don't see you pregnant by a guy who's sleeping with one of your friends,' I spat. 'I'm pretty sure an ex-boyfriend has never cleaned out your bank account, and your fiancé earns so much money you won't even need a career!'

'I *want* a career! And I see my fiancé for about three weeks a year!'

'At least you *have* a fiancé.'

'I've been trying to organise a wedding all by myself from the other side of the world.'

'Poor you.'

'Did you know Cal's mother had been *cancelling* my bookings? Including the one at the pub, and now they're fully booked. And she's trying to get us to have our wedding in a *castle* with about a hundred people I don't know because she says my small guest list is pathetic. No, you didn't because you—'

'Oh how *dreadful*,' I interrupted. 'A wedding in a castle. How *will* you cope?'

'Emma! Why are you being so awful?'

'Why are you being such a spoilt brat?' I shot back.

Martha strode out of the manor. 'Archie and Tilly are due on set soon and they haven't practised their lines together.'

'He's over there.' I jabbed a thumb behind me. 'I'll be one minute.'

Martha gave a look of contempt and waddled off.

'Look, Emma,' Alex's voice was softer. 'I know it's been really hard for you with the pregnancy and the whole Ned and Sophie thing, but life goes on. You've got to stop being so full of self-pity and—'

'I don't need your lecture,' I said primly.

'Well you need to hear it from someone.'

Martha prodded my shoulder. 'He's not there.' She pointed at the empty garden seat.

'Emma, you need to—' Alex continued.

'What I need is for people to just give me a break.'

'Could you stop whingeing for one second and do your job?' Martha barked.

I shoved past her and stalked round the courtyard looking for Archie between the parked cars and trucks.

'Alex, I've got to go. Why don't you ring me when you have some *real* problems?'

Alex was quiet for a moment, then burst into tears. 'What's happened to you?' she sobbed.

The Second AD stepped out of the manor. 'Archie on set, please,' he droned.

It was all getting too much. Martha was staring down at me from her high horse (how *did* it bear her bulk?); the Second AD was waiting with his hands gripping a radio, an impatient film crew on the other end; Alex was crying down the phone and Archie had disappeared. I wanted to throw the phone at Martha, start running and not stop until I reached my bedroom in Wimbledon.

'I've got to go.' I hung up on the sniffling Alex feeling a surge of disappointment in myself and headed to the barn house.

'Now they'll have to go on set without having practised their lines.' Martha fell in behind me.

'They practised them this morning.' I entered the barn house. The living room was empty. 'They'll be fine.'

'We'll see,' she sniffed.

I opened the bedroom door. No Archie. Martha huffed and puffed behind me as I checked my room, her room and the bathroom. Archie wasn't anywhere. The Second AD appeared at the door to the barn house as Martha and I arrived back in the living room.

'He in here?' he said, his dark-ringed eyes darting round the room.

I shook my head. 'Maybe he went back to set?' It was quite like Archie to discern when he was needed. He seemed to have an innate knowledge of the workings of a film set. Martha gave me a you'd-better-hope-he-is-or-you're-in-deep-shit glare as she pushed past me. We were shooting in the main entranceway of the manor so when Martha, the Second AD and I walked through the door the crew turned to face us. The expectant look on their faces told us Archie was not with them. Tilly stood in the middle of the set with a zombie camper extra, ready and waiting. I looked at the assembled crew: impatient art department, bored costume girls, a fidgety, tight-faced director and the frowny First AD.

'Where's Archie?' she squawked, giving her Bear Grylls-esque watch an agitated glance.

The first flutters of alarm tightened my chest. He was such

a responsible little man it was easy to forget he was only four and should be watched constantly. I tried to remember the exact moment I'd last seen him. It was as I'd answered the call from my sister. I remembered because he'd been playing with his tugboat ...

'The lake!' I pushed past Martha. Gripping my hands beneath my large stomach to hold the weight of the baby, I began to run across the courtyard. 'Archie!' I yelled.

'ARCHIE!' Andrew's voice boomed out from behind me.

Footsteps barraged across the courtyard. Andrew, Steve and some other crew members passed me and disappeared round the edge of the manor. I rounded the corner after them and the lake came into view. No Archie. The gathering crowd, a handful in zombie costumes, streaked across the lawns and fanned out around the lake. Andrew and Steve raced down the length of the jetty. Andrew reached the end first and with a quick scan of the water dived in. Archie! One of the lighting guys dived in from the other side. Tears blurred my eyes. I kept running. I reached the jetty and saw Archie's crisp packet caught in a clump of grass. Steve stood at the end peering into the dark water while grips and lighting guys ran round the edge calling Archie's name. Andrew came up for a breath and dived back down. I reached Steve, gasping for breath. He turned. Dread clawed at my throat as I saw what was in his hand. Archie's tugboat. The back of my neck went cold and I fought the urge to vomit. Steve grabbed my arm as my legs gave way.

'Oh my god,' I rasped.

'I can't see anything, it's too dark!' Andrew yelled as he burst up from the water again.

'Try there!' somebody shouted.

Andrew dived back under. People searched the reeds at the edges of the lake. The lighting guy rose from the water empty-handed and dived down again. My darling Archie! An anguished groan sounded, and when Steve put his arms round my shoulders I realised it was coming from me. Andrew came up again, puffing and panting.

'I . . . can't . . . see.' His chest heaved up and down under his soaking shirt. 'Can't . . . find him.'

A lighting guy burst out of the water on the other side of the lake and shook his head. Crew and cast stood in tense silence.

My little Archie.

I fought to stay conscious. Andrew ducked under the water but with less conviction. I pictured Sinead's crumpled face. How would I tell her? How do you tell anybody you've lost their 4-year-old son? And what about Alice and Jess? And Uncle Mike? It was going to break him. It was going to break the whole family. A cold sweat settled down my neck and I felt myself drifting from consciousness. Voices shouted orders, sending people to check the orchard, the vegetable gardens, the tractor shed. It sounded like I had glass jars over my ears. I caught a glimpse of Martha standing in the background, her arms round Tilly and a look of genuine fear on her face. My eyes lost focus. I was falling, slipping into a very dark place. Through the fading voices I heard a distant bark.

And then another. I tried to concentrate. Those barks … why was I focusing on the barks? I fought the irresistible pull to nothingness. Archie, Ivan, Wayne … Another bark sounded, and with my remaining strength I lifted my head and looked in the direction of the forest.

'Archie,' I croaked.

Andrew leapt out of the lake and ran, wet-bodied, towards the forest. People followed.

'Archie,' I said again, my voice stronger.

'Come on!' Steve helped me to my feet. He held my arm as we laboured along the jetty and across the field as fast as my weakened legs would allow. We reached the edge of the forest and Steve guided me through the damp undergrowth. The forest ran gently uphill. Low branches grabbed at my clothing and mud caked the undersides of my shoes. Steve's grip was firm. I heard another bark, closer now, at the top of a steep rise. I gripped shrubs and roots and pulled myself uphill, Steve behind me, his hand on my back. Finally, out of breath and covered in mud, I reached the top. And there, surrounded by the puffing and panting crew, next to Ivan who was licking himself and Wayne who was digging at the undergrowth, sat Andrew. And he was watching a big black beetle walk along a mossy log with a content and unscathed Archie at his side.

I pushed through the gathered crew, lurched over the log and fell to my knees next to Archie. The soggy soil soaked through my tights. I crushed Archie's warm, alive body to my chest and breathed in his Palmolive-clean hair.

CHAPTER TWENTY-NINE

'Knock, knock.'

'Come in.' I wiped my nose on a raggedy bit of tissue.

'How is she?' Andrew said, sliding the door of the barn house behind him with a gentle swoosh.

I was disappointed to see he'd changed out of his wet shirt. Fainting in the mud in front of everyone had most definitely been worth it when I'd come to and realised I was being carried (with a fair amount of strain I've decided to ignore) with my head pressed against his chest. But then I passed out again and had woken up on the sofa in the barn house with Des the safety officer, who had breath like the bottom of a parrot cage and a set of teeth that each appeared to come from a different species, peering into my face with a torch. The actual definition of a rude awakening.

'Blood pressure's OK now,' Des said, sucking air through his feral teeth. 'Heart rate and baby's heart rate seem stable. Blood sugar's a little low.'

'I feel fine,' I said, trying to sit up with all the grace of an upside-down hedgehog. 'Where's Archie?'

'He's with Martha in Wardrobe.' Andrew helped me to a sitting position. 'He's OK.'

I nodded. Archie would be in Wardrobe because his costume was covered in mud. Because he had wandered off unattended into the forest and played with a beetle when he should have been under the watchful eye of his loving yet self-absorbed cousin. Because Ned had his own ice cream, Sophie had her own Ned and my tropically located sister was marrying somebody in a castle.

My eyes began to water.

'Emma, it's not your fault,' Andrew said, sitting beside me and resting his palm on my back.

I shot him a you've-got-to-be-kidding grimace.

I turned to Des, who was scratching notes on a clipboard. 'Can I go back to work now?'

'Ah, I don't think so,' he said, clicking his pen and scanning his form. 'No. No, I don't think so at all. Your blood pressure has returned to normal, but it took a while. Your glucose levels are still a little low and, since you've refused a hospital check-up, I insist you have bed rest for the remainder of the day.'

'The rest of the day?'

Not only had I quite publicly shown myself to be the worst chaperone ever and cost the production two hours of filming when they were already up against it from Scott's Nutella sex injury, but I was not allowed back on set to redeem myself. I covered my face with my hands. I was flooded with embarrassment. I'd put my own cousin in danger. Martha would have every right to report me.

'Uh-huh,' Des said, still clicking his pen. 'I'll come back and check on you in an hour or so. I'm sure you'll be back to work tomorrow. But only if your glucose levels are up.' He stood. 'In the meantime, stay inside, keep warm and eat small amounts frequently.' He held out a packet of Gummy Bears sequestered from Martha's suitcase.

Des slid his pen into a technical-looking tool belt, sucked air through his teeth and took his safety kit and his bad breath out the door.

'Do you want me to see if Martha will bring Archie in here before he goes on set?' Andrew said.

Oh my god, yes. Archie. I needed to hold him. To have the solid reassurance that he was alive and well. I intended to say 'yes please', but instead burst into tears.

'I'm sorry,' I said as Andrew pulled me into a sideways hug.

'Hey, now,' he soothed. 'It turned out OK. Nothing to be upset about.'

When I pulled back and looked into his eyes, heavy with concern, I recalled a billboard I'd seen advertising some high-fructose energy drink that pictured an All Black the size of a two-bed maisonette in mid-hurl for the try line. Dreadlocks flying to the left, his knee muscles ferocious and pronounced, photoshopped sweat droplets suspended in mid-air, and, stamped down the side in bossy black capitals:

OWN
EVERY
MOMENT

I'd turned to Sophie, who was lapping at a Chupa-Chups, and said, in an affronted fashion, 'Own Every Moment. *Must* I?'

Sophie had considered the poster, her head cocked to one side.

'I mean, it sounds awfully exhausting,' I'd continued. 'Can't I just give some moments to the cast of *Friends*? Or the *Ellen DeGeneres Show*?'

'I guess it's that whole "seize the day" thing,' Sophie had suggested. 'You know, umm, Carpet diem.'

'*Carpe* diem,' I'd said.

I'd looked at the poster critically before moving away, Sophie toddling behind.

'It didn't work out so well for that fellow from *Dead Poets Society*, did it?' I'd said.

'S'pose not,' Sophie had replied. 'But I think that was more about his big eyebrows.'

With the bossy poster's 'owning the moment' message as my mantra I grabbed Andrew by the back of his neck and pulled him into a kiss. He drew back, startled, but after a blink of deliberation, bent forward and kissed me back. For a brief moment I wasn't pregnant. I was a single girl having her first kiss with a hot new guy. After a few lip-mashing seconds we pulled apart. Desire glazed his eyes and I felt that if I'd shown more encouragement, and he weren't due back on set, we would have been in the bedroom attempting 'the crab' or the 'donkey kong' or whatever other sexual positions were suitable for randy pregnant women. His balls were in my court, so to speak.

'You'd better get back to set,' I said, the rational side of my brain winning out.

'Yeah.' Andrew dragged a hand through his hair and gazed into the distance, a tad contemplative. He turned back smiling and ran a thumb down my cheek. 'I'll come and check on you later.'

'OK.'

Another gentle kiss, with only the slightest of lingering, and he stood, giving me an eyeful of extremely obvious bulge in his jeans. As soon as he slid the door shut I was on the phone to Helen.

'Guess who just kissed me!'

'Scott Vander!' Helen gasped.

'Ew, no.' I shuddered at the thought of his hands, sullied by the act of caressing Martha, touching me in any way. 'Guess again.'

'Better than Scott?'

'Way better.'

She took in a sharp breath. 'Joe! I knew I should have got to him when he was hung over and vulnerable.'

'Not Joe,' I said, frustrated. 'Why would I kiss Joe? And he's not even here. It was Andrew!'

'Who's Andrew?'

'The hot camera guy I told you about?'

'Hmmm ...' Helen said, rapid clicks from her keyboard echoing down the phone. 'Can't remember. What's he like?'

'He's hot,' I said, a little miffed.

When I'd hung up from Helen I thought about what kind of person kisses a man when they're pregnant with someone else's child. And what kind of person did that make him? Was he a lech with some kind of pregnancy fetish? Would he tell people? Would I mind? What would they think? Did being pregnant mean I wasn't allowed feelings of attraction for someone other than the father of the child? Was I only allowed to have those kinds of feelings once the child was out and my body was once again my own?

When Archie came off set at the end of the day I hugged and squeezed him till he politely asked me to stop. Then Martha strutted in holding Tilly by the hand. After setting the children up with an educational puzzle, she rounded on me.

'So.' She folded her arms across her chest, leant her weight back on one foot and tapped the other. It bothered me that she wore Crocs. 'It looks like we've come to the end of your little bribery game, don't you think?'

I nodded. 'How's this going to go, then?' I said, defeated.

'Well ...' Martha said, devoted to the upper hand once again. 'You still have your photo,' she gave a derisive leer. 'And I now have an irrefutable reason to get you fired.'

I maintained a steady gaze. I did not want her to know that I was dying of embarrassment inside.

'So?' I prompted.

'So.' Her face hardened. 'You keep to yours and I keep to mine. We don't like each other – no need to pretend otherwise any more. You stick to the rule book and I won't have to tell you what to do.'

I nodded.

'I won't send my email,' she continued. 'And you won't tell anyone ... what you know. Ever.' She kept her steely gaze on me.

'OK,' I said quietly.

She threw out a fist and snatched the gummy bears from my hands. 'And no more sharing.'

The next day was the last day of the shoot, and I couldn't muster the excited energy everyone else seemed to have. People gave me sideways glances on set. Pity glances! I would have preferred it if they were angry. Anything but feeling sorry for me. I kept to myself for most of the day, meekly complying with Martha's every whim. After Archie and Tilly's last scene everybody clapped, gave the kids hugs (Archie got given a prosthetic finger as a souvenir) and went back to set to complete the final scene. Archie, Tilly, Martha and I headed back to the barn house to pack up what had been our home for the past six weeks. Dinner and drinks were being put on in the main dining hall and it was expected to be a big night. I was dreading it. The last thing I felt like doing was hang out with a load of happy drunk and/or high people all trying to get off with each other. The next morning a car would arrive to take Archie and me back to our regular lives. I folded Archie's clothes and wondered what, if anything, was going to happen to Andrew and me. We'd only had one kiss. Yes, I was pregnant but I was still a single girl in her twenties who deserved to find happiness and love. And just because I was about to give birth (yes, I know, to another man's child) didn't make me any less attracted to people. Although I was aware that I, personally was substantially *less* attractive. Andrew was clearly man and mature enough to see past this time of my life and, I hoped, to the girl I would be on the other side.

Later, after kissing Archie and Tilly goodnight, Martha and I left the barn house and trekked through the warm early evening to the dining room in the main house. Production had provided us with a babysitter so we could both attend the last dinner with the cast and crew. Martha walked a few hurried paces in front. Now that filming was over she no longer needed to hold up the pretence that she felt anything other than contempt for me. I entered the great hall moments after Martha had let the door swing back in my face and slunk past the backs of the crew who were congregating in circles, enjoying champagne and canapés. I was helping myself to a sparkling water when Andrew approached.

'There you are,' he said, his cheeks already aglow with alcohol consumption. He bent down and gave me a kiss on the cheek. A mere peck, but it sent a tingle down my spine nonetheless.

'Hi,' I said.

Caroline came over, sipping at a glass of champagne.

'How are you holding up?' she said, rubbing my back. She'd been checking on me all day.

'I'm still really embarrassed.'

'Don't be. It could have happened to anyone,' she said with a kind smile. 'You're coming to Scott's tonight, right?'

I opened my mouth to say no but Andrew interrupted. 'Of course she is.'

Caroline shot him a look then turned back to me. 'It's the last night, everybody's going.'

I shook my head. 'I don't think so.'

'Come on. I know you haven't wanted to come any other night but it's the last night. You have to!'

I was stunned. All that time I'd thought I wasn't invited and she'd thought I hadn't wanted to come. The pregnant belly was giving out all the wrong messages.

CHAPTER THIRTY

'I never eat green apples. They are so high in sugar it basically just becomes fat in, like, a day.'

'*Seriously?*'

'Yeah, by the end of the day you'll be, like . . . *fatter.*'

'Excuse me, I've got to . . .' I realised that neither of the undernourished girls who'd played Frightened Campers cared if I stayed or went. I was rotund, unfamous and irrelevant. 'I have to go speak Dolphin to that candle and play *The Blue Danube* on those empty peanut casings.'

'Bye,' one said, looking vaguely surprised I was there at all.

I pushed through the heaving mass of bodies. Cast and crew were drunk, high and happy. Scott zoomed through the crowd in a tight white t-shirt that said 'Fuck me, I'm famous', checking people's drinks. He walked past with a tray of beer, made sure I was happy with the choice of non-alcoholic drinks with true sincerity, then boogied through the throng. Having subsisted on raspberries, green juice and undressed lettuce leaves for the past few months of scantily clad filming, Scott and Melody, who'd choppered in for the last few days of filming, had fallen upon a table of carbs like a pair of ravenous Labradors. Hot dogs, pizza and burgers served in the whitest, fluffiest, cheapest of buns with lashings of electric-red tomato sauce. The rarity of the treat had Melody in full-cheeked raptures. For me it was just a Thursday. I caught sight of Martha, who, contrary to what her size may have implied, had some serious skills in the dance department. One of the lighting guys shimmied on his knees *Dirty Dancing*-style while Martha gyrated a rap dancer's routine round him. Despite my earlier reservations, and the fact that I was the only person who had not ingested enough vodka to lend flight to a small aircraft, I had fun. Andrew flitted around the edges of my evening, catching my eye while he was at the bar, grinning while he danced with a group of costume girls, laughing at me while I attempted the same. It wasn't easy. All I was really capable of doing was rooting my feet to one spot and swinging from side to side. If I were a tad too enthusiastic I would lose the one-sided arrangement I had with gravity and lurch dangerously into someone. After Claire sang a seriously fabulous rock rendition of 'Moonlight Shadow', with a shirtless and shoeless Scott on drums, the iPod was back on and the serious partying began. Treks to the marble kitchen, where lines of coke were laid out like hors d'oeuvres, were more frequent and less covert. I'd never seen the bag of Es, but judging by the number of people who told me they 'Really,

really loved me. No, seriously. I really do', I knew they were in attendance.

Much later than I'd planned and much cheerier than I'd anticipated, I hugged Caroline goodnight and watched her head back into the party, absorbed by the heaving, lively mass. Martha was somewhere in there. I'd last seen her being loose-wristed with a bottle of tequila as she poured an already inebriated grip truck driver a shot. I headed towards the balcony stairs, sure I'd be treated to the sounds of the driver's orgasm in a matter of hours. Unless Martha was doing her tequila/erectile calculations wrong and she took him over the edge. A girl can hope.

'Do you like to "move it, move it"?' Andrew materialised before me, pulsing his hips to the current song.

I laughed. 'Occasionally. But right now I'm "moving it, moving it" to bed.'

'Noooo,' he said. 'Come dance with me!' His eyes sparkled and had that unfocused haziness men get two beers before they become drunk and useless. He ran his hand down the back of my arm and stopped at my elbow, cupping it in his hand. 'Come on. One dance.'

'I can't.'

'You can.'

'No, I physically can't.' I pointed to my stomach. 'I can only stand and sway.'

'So?'

'So,' I said, slipping my elbow out of his grip. He caught my hand in his. 'I also have to be up with Archie at 7 a.m.

Plus I'm growing the baby some fingernails at the moment and if I don't get enough sleep I'll do it wrong and the fingernails will come out on its nose. Do you want to be the reason my baby has no nails?'

Andrew glanced back inside, then swayed his attention back to me.

'I'll walk you.' His thumb stroked the back of my hand.

'You don't need to.'

'I know. But I want to. Wait here, I'll get another beer for the trip.'

He pushed his way through the crowd and, moments later, emerged with two more beers. He shunted one in his back pocket and cracked open the other, flicking the lid off the balcony, then followed me down the stairs and across the spongy forest floor. When we reached the densest part of the forest, where we could no longer see the moon, Andrew reached for my hand.

'What are you doing?' I stopped to face him.

Flutters of expectancy danced in the base of my throat. With the determined confidence that comes from being several beers past merry, Andrew slid into what my paisley-skirt-wearing social science teacher called 'my personal space bubble'. Nervy and jittery, I stepped back and hit up against a rough tree trunk.

'I can't stop thinking about how you kissed me yesterday,' he said.

'Yes.' I moved my face to get out of the stream of his beer breath. 'I wanted to apologise for that, actually. I didn't—'

'You didn't want to?' He took a step closer and rested his hand with the beer bottle on the tree above my head. His face hovered over mine.

'No . . . well, yes but . . .'

He leant down; his lips brushed the side of my cheek.

'I want to fuck you.' His breath was hot in my ear. At least he was to the point.

'I . . . I think I should probably . . .' I mumbled, my heart thudding so hard I was sure it was audible.

He pulled back.

'You are so . . .' His gaze skimmed the exposed tops of my breasts before settling on my face. 'Do you even know how sexy you are?'

I definitely wanted to kiss him. And I'd be lying if I said I hadn't thought about sleeping with him. But I wanted to do it when I wasn't pregnant. Whoever was in charge of dealing out my hand had majorly screwed up the order of the cards. I should have met Andrew before I got pregnant by Ned and shagged him then. Or, you know, *not* got pregnant, met Andrew and then done the shagging.

'You're drunk,' I said.

Andrew lowered his lids and peeled his lips back into a knowing grin. I noticed his eye teeth. Sharp and pointy. I had an inexplicably strong attraction to pointy eye teeth.

'I see the way you look at me,' he said.

'I'm just interested in how you . . . frame up.'

Andrew looked down at my breasts again. 'I'll frame you up.'

He was plastered, and traversing the very fine line between exceedingly sexy and exceedingly creepy. One part of me wanted to grab him by the waistband of his jeans and get down with the reverse cowboy on the forest floor. The other much more rational side (where had that come from?) was repelled by the thought of the reverse cowboy and was making little dry-retching noises at the thought of my naked pregnant belly hefting back and forth with the thrust of frenzied forest-floor sex. Andrew moved his face closer to me in stages, assessing my reaction with each inch. I kept my eyes on his until he got so close I lost focus. Then we were kissing. His stubble grazed my skin. He pushed closer but was impeded by my pregnant belly. My pregnant belly! What was I doing? I put my hands on his chest and prised him off. His eyes begged, his face pained with wanting. Knowing I was the cause was a powerful turn-on.

'What's the problem?' he murmured. He dipped his head and placed tiny kisses along the cool flesh of my neck.

'It just doesn't feel right . . .'

Andrew trailed his lips over my collarbone.

'. . . because of the . . .' I swallowed as he ran the tip of his tongue up the other side of my neck and kissed my earlobe '. . . baby.'

It had been years since I'd been this turned on from just kissing. Ned was more of a 'get in, get it done, get back on eBay' kind of guy.

'When was the last time you had sex?' he said. 'Don't you want it? Don't you miss it?' He ran his hand down my back and grabbed a fistful of my left butt cheek. The force of his grip had my breath running ragged. He bent down and kissed me again. I put a hand round his neck and pulled him harder against me. Encouraged, he dropped the bottle he'd been holding and clasped my breast. Beer hissed on the ground by our feet. Yes, I missed it! Back up at the party the music changed to something drum and bass-y, intensifying the atmosphere. I reasoned with myself. Andrew and I were both consenting adults. What we were doing was morally fine. I wanted this. But did my baby want this? I pushed him away again.

'I'm sorry,' I panted. 'I just don't know . . .'

He squeezed my breast, his thumb moving over the cloth of my dress making rapid circles round my nipple.

'Don't you want to?'

The strap of my dress fell off my shoulder; the bra strap went with it. Still making circles, he leant down and kissed my neck.

'Yes,' I said. 'But I . . . I'm not sure now's the right . . . time . . .'

I wasn't presenting my argument convincingly. I uttered the words but my actions, fingers dragging through his hair and my eager kisses, said otherwise.

'Just tell me to stop,' he said in my ear, his voice low and intense.

He straightened and, with his eyes locked on mine, ran a single finger down my chest, pulling at the neckline of my dress. I watched as he pulled the fabric more. More. His finger caught my bra, all the while watching me, giving me the opportunity to stop. His eyes stayed on mine as my dress and bra dropped down, fully exposing my breast. My nipple stood erect in the cool air. I gave an almost imperceptible nod. Andrew grinned, then bent down and took my nipple in his mouth, sucking and biting. I gripped the back of his head and moaned, succumbing to the zings of pleasure. I guided his face up and kissed him, now with heated purpose. I was edgy with wanting.

'God, you are so fucking sexy,' he groaned.

I reached for his belt.

'Pregnant women are so horny.'

I struggled with the buckle.

'Everything's so swollen.' He moved my hands out of the way and undid the belt himself. 'My wife used to come so easily.'

His *what*?

I pulled back. 'What?'

He'd undone his fly. He stood motionless; a single thumb tucked into the waistband of his fitted white boxers.

'You're married?'

He swayed on his feet and blinked. 'Ah . . .'

'Oh my god!'

Everything snapped into focus. I was leaning against a tree in the middle of a forest, my left breast hanging out, the strap of my maternity bra dangling off my shoulder, wide and functional like a mountaineering harness, and Andrew swaying before me, a huge erection showing through his boxers, his eyes glazed. And my pregnant stomach filled the void between us. My *pregnant* stomach.

'You're fucking *married*?!' I said, tucking my shameful nudity away.

Andrew broke out of his stupor. 'Hey,' he cajoled. 'I thought you knew.'

'No, I didn't! I would never have . . .' I shook my head and pushed him away from me.

'I'm OK if you're OK,' he slurred, stumbling on a tree root.

I hurried down the forest path, twisting my dress into position. I was even more disgusted with myself when I heard the crack and hiss of a beer opening. I looked back and saw Andrew hoisting his jeans up with one hand, beer in the other, struggling to stand straight. He wasn't even going to bother to follow me.

CHAPTER THIRTY-ONE

'I need a rest. Can we stop?' I said, spying a bench seat a few yards ahead.

'Sure.' Joe lobbed Brutus's stick miles ahead with ease. 'It's been about two minutes since your last half-hour rest; you must be exhausted.'

'I'll have you know that not only am I carrying around the equivalent of a fully stuffed piece of carry-on luggage but I'm also putting the finishing touches on a DNA helix. And growing eyelashes. It's *very* exhausting.'

'You're a creative genius.'

'I'm practically a scientist.'

We arrived at the bench seat and I oh-ed and ah-ed as I lowered myself onto it.

'It's a good thing I'm not easily embarrassed. You make extremely loud sex noises every time you sit down,' Joe said, sitting next to me.

'I do not.'

'Do too. That couple over there thought you really, *really* liked this seat.'

'Ha ha.' I closed my eyes and tipped my head back, raising my face towards the sun. Summer had landed, and every day since arriving back from Wales had been hot. Being eight months pregnant in the heat was no carnival, though. I'd taken to wearing an oversized cotton smock thing that gave maximum ventilation. I'd found it among Grandma's old 1960s clothes and immediately liberated it. Joe said I looked like my head was poking out the top of a multicoloured tepee. I cared not. It was cool and draughty and, coupled with an ice cream from the village shop, was the closest I could get to comfort in my current state.

'Crab with indigestion,' said Joe, his voice low.

I chuckled. Giving animal attributes to runners on the common was a game Joe had devised during his walks with Brutus. Joe had grown rather close to Harriet and Arthur, and because he was generally unwilling to go back to work and had already redesigned my garden, gone through all my personal things, read all my poems and was getting bored with putting my bookshelves in alphabetical order, then colour wheel order, then genre/alphabetical order with a nod to colour wheel coordination, he'd offered to take Brutus for a walk one day. One day had become every day and, now I was back, I joined them. Joe had to walk at a snail's pace and stop every few yards for me to have a rest but we occupied the time by playing the Runner Animal game. I turned my attention to the next runner, a man with his fists in tight little balls clenched near his armpits. He leant forward with his chin tucked under as if his forehead were pulling the rest of him along.

'Evil dive-bombing bat.'

'Good one!' Joe wrestled with Brutus for the stick.

My thoughts wandered to Andrew and how I used to watch him run round the lake in the mornings. The memory of Andrew brought a heat to my cheeks. The morning after the party, and the undignified forest fumbling, Bradley Manor had been a scene of quiet, hung-over activity. Heads sagged over the arduous task of packing up a film unit. The contents of the lighting truck lay strewn on the lawn while guys in dark glasses and caps pulled low made grim work of the inventory and repack. An ant-like trail of well-dressed men and women trekked in and out of the extended wardrobe trailer hauling bloodied costumes in plastic coverings. Art department guys stacked the boxes of prosthetic guts, limbs, half-cats and buckets of blood that had so captivated me at the beginning but were now mundane, in the back of the art truck. Everything had blood on it. Claire and Caroline had wheeled their boxy make-up cases to a waiting vehicle and, after exchanging email addresses with me, they'd jumped in and driven away. In the kind of silence that comes from two people who no longer need to keep up appearances for the sake of a working relationship, Martha and I had exited the barn house and stood between our waiting four-by-fours, into which Tilly and Archie were already buckled. I'd faced her, deliberating over whether I should say the obligatory but outright falsehood

'Nice working with you. Hope to do it again someday', or the more truthful 'I hate you. I hope I never have the misfortune of running into you at an all-you-can-eat buffet'. I'd opened my mouth to utter a version of the former, because deep down I'm a non-confrontational scaredy-cat, but without another glance Martha had bent down, picked up her rucksack and climbed into her car. I'd been much too ashamed of my behaviour the previous night that a final snub from Martha had barely even tickled my pride. I'd climbed into the four-by-four next to Archie and seen Andrew crossing the crowded courtyard. I knew he'd seen me by the way he'd lowered his glasses off his head, averted his gaze and was taking great interest in a technical bit of equipment in the hands of a camera assistant. Our four-by-four had swung slowly out of the courtyard and Andrew had diverted the camera assistant's attention to the rear of the camera van, enabling him to keep his back to our passing vehicle.

I looked again at the 'dive-bombing bat' guy and pondered over what animal Andrew would have been. A rat or weasel or something gross and slimy. Like an axolotl.

'An axo-*what*?' Joe said. 'I'd say more like a cockatoo with a club foot and a drink problem.'

I laughed and watched the runner in question. The left side of his body seemed to be a reluctant participant in the ordeal, and dragged a little behind the right side, giving the hobbling impression of a—

'Hey!' I said, peering closer at the runner. 'That's Douglas!'

'Who? The cockatoo?' Joe squinted at the figure.

'DOUGLAS!' I called out. 'DOUGLAS! OVER HERE!' I waved my arms. Douglas stopped and looked in our direction. Recognition spread across his face and he laboured over to us in his strange injured-bird lumber.

'Emma,' Douglas puffed as he reached us. 'You're back.' He made to give me a hug.

Brutus growled.

'I'd rather not, Douglas, you're all sweaty.'

'Oh yes. Quite,' Douglas said, sidestepping away from the grumbling Doberman. I introduced Douglas to Joe. They shook hands and immediately commented on the weather.

'What are you doing here? You live miles away,' I said, cutting through the dullness of polite small talk between two people who have just met.

'Oh, I run here with my girlfriend.'

Joe and I looked up and down the common. Not another soul was in sight.

'She prefers to run alone.' Douglas pushed his glasses up his sweaty nose. Joe and I stifled laughter.

'Have, ah . . . have you seen Sophie at all?' Douglas asked.

'No,' I said, my smile and good mood immediately dropping. 'Should I have?' Joe watched me intently. Douglas shuffled from foot to foot.

'Oh, ah . . . well, you see, she was asking, ah, when you'd be back in town.'

'Why?' I said. 'Does she want something else of mine? My house? My baby, maybe?' I was aware that I was potentially coming off as a bit of a psycho.

'Oh, ah, no, I don't think she wants any of those things.' Douglas's gaze flitted from me to Joe to Brutus, who looked up with crushing contempt. 'I think maybe she just, ah, wants to, ah . . . She's been asking about the . . .' Douglas indicated my stomach, protruding into the space between us. 'And she needed to talk about, er . . . Well, I'm not sure, entirely.'

The three of us stood quietly.

'I'm sorry, Douglas,' I said. 'I'm a bit all over the place at the moment.' I rubbed my stomach.

'Oh, quite understandable. I shouldn't have said anything.' He checked his watch. 'Golly, I must get on. If I don't keep running Jemima might catch me up on her second lap.' He looked at me with his intense bespectacled eyes for a few moments. 'You're looking truly beautiful, Emma.'

'Thanks. It's really good to see you,' I said.

Douglas arced round the vicinity of Brutus, gave me a strange, minimal-body-contact, shoulder-patting kind of hug, said goodbye to Joe and headed off down the path, the right side of his body hefting his disinclined left.

'You must meet Jemima soon,' he called out, looking behind him warily.

After another few throws of the stick for Brutus, Joe and I started our meandering stroll back to the cottage. Joe remained silent, allowing me to mull over what Douglas had said about Sophie, but as we got closer to the golf course near the cottage, he spoke.

'You know, Sophie probably doesn't want to take your baby.'

'Humph.'

'Maybe she just wants to try and make up.' Joe hooked his arm through mine. We watched Brutus allow a fluffy scrap of a dog to sniff his bottom.

'Well, what if I don't want to make up?'

'Maybe you should.'

'Why?'

'Well, if Sophie and Ned stay together' – Joe paused to allow me a grimace – 'then she'll be part of your life forever. And your baby's life.'

'So what are you saying?' I grumbled.

'I'm saying ...' Joe replied gently. 'Maybe it's time to move on?'

I stopped walking. 'You're one to talk!'

Joe took a step back.

'Your slut of an ex-fiancée is still in your flat while you live in my attic. You barely work, you have absurd ideas about making a children's book and you spend your days walking the neighbour's dog! You've made me a vegetable garden I don't even want and you watch two Richard Curtis films a day. If that's not the perfect example of someone *not* moving on, then I don't know what is!'

Instead of registering shock or outrage, Joe's face filled with pity. Guilt plunged into my sides and I stormed off knowing I'd said some cruel and unnecessary things. Joe didn't catch me up, and after a few yards of angry storming my back ached and if I didn't sit down I was in very real danger of peeing myself. Another bench seat popped into view (oh thank the sweet lord for the plentiful bench seats on Wimbledon Common). I plopped onto it and kicked the dusty ground with my flip-flopped foot. Sometime later, Joe's shadow fell across me. Brutus arrived at my feet and nuzzled my knees, leaving a shiny stripe of drool on my dress/tepee. I scuffed my feet a little longer, gathering my thoughts. The whole Andrew thing had been an undignified disaster. Douglas was busy with his new girlfriend and Helen was busy with a huge event at work. My relationship with my sister had disintegrated. She'd stopped trying to get hold of me since the day I made her cry just before I lost Archie. The hospital had recently sent me a form with a birth plan outline. I was to tick boxes about emergency caesareans, epidurals, latex allergies and so forth, and was also to indicate the names of any birth partners, which only highlighted how very few options I had. A while ago Alex and I had discussed the option of her coming home to be my birth partner, but that didn't look likely now. Helen was so queasy she pretty much had a general just to get her bikini line waxed. Sinead said she was never going into another maternity suite again. Sophie? No. Ned? Hell, no. Mum? No frigging way. Which really only left me with … well, nobody. My heart had fractured and I had no idea how or when it would ever feel whole again. I had a continual untethered sensation. And I felt very, very alone. Joe, the kind and overtly comfortable man who'd arrived uninvited into my life had been my only constant. I glanced at him standing above me, an impassive look on his face. Brutus crouched beside him with a look of doggy boredom.

'I'm sorry,' I said. 'I didn't mean any of it.'

Joe sat down and pulled me to him. He smelt of soap and dog slobber.

'Everything's just a bit crap,' I sighed. 'I didn't mean to take it out on you.'

'What exactly is so crap?' Joe asked.

I snorted a well-where-do-I-begin type snort.

'That whole thing with Andrew, for a start.' I shuddered. 'I mean, ew, how gross must I have looked?'

'Not that gross.' Joe's voice reverberated in the ear that was pressed to his chest.

'Lying to Mum is completely stressing me out. I can't make Ned sell the ice cream vans now; it sounds like he's doing really well. Uncle Mike is going to find out at some point that his son was not in a Disney-style movie about friendly cats from the afterlife and I just don't think I can take his disappointment when he finds out Archie is starring in a slasher zombie guts-and-bra film. And what if they find out I nearly lost Archie at the lake? They'd never trust me again. I'm about to have a baby and I don't know if I even trust myself!' I sucked in a big breath. 'And even though all of that is really major stuff, the thing I'm most sad about . . .' I sniffed back a tear '. . . is my sister. I miss her so much I feel nauseous.'

Joe remained quiet, stroking the top of my head.

'I'm afraid of doing this alone.'

'The baby?'

'Everything. The life ahead of me. All of it.'

'You think you're alone?' Joe said, leaning back to look me in the eye. I nodded.

Joe smiled. 'What am I, a figment of your imagination?'

'No.' I looked up at him and began to cry. 'I'd have imagined you with better hair.'

Joe pulled me into a hug and waited for my sobs to subside.

'Everything's going to be all right, you'll see,' he said, giving the top of my head a kiss.

I sat up and wiped my cheeks. 'That's it?' I said. 'That's your advice?'

Joe leant forward and scratched Brutus under his muzzle. 'Yep.' He smiled.

'Well, you're no Martha Beck, are you?'

'I have no idea who you're talking about.' He attached the lead to Brutus's collar and stood, offering me his hand. 'Let's go home.'

I stood. Joe linked his arm with mine and we crossed the lane towards the cottage in companionable silence. I headed for the front door and Joe headed for Harriet and Arthur's to drop Brutus off.

'Joe?' I said across the low wall.

'Hmm?'

'I love the vegetable garden.'

Joe grinned. 'I know.'

Later that night, after an early Thai takeaway, Joe came down from his bedroom in a nice shirt and jeans and stood in front of me as I sat on the sofa.

'How do I look?' he said, spreading his arms.

'Like a nice man about to go out for a nice night with his nice friends, have a couple of nice pints and bring home some slaggy little teen who I'll meet in the kitchen at 4 a.m.'

Joe made a face. 'It's not that kind of night.' He checked his reflection in the French doors, untucking and retucking his shirt. 'And she wasn't a teen.'

'Nine*teen*,' I said, flicking through the channels.

'It was her birthday the week after.'

'She was nine*teen* when she was rummaging about in my freezer looking for sex ice.'

Joe retucked his shirt again.

'What did happen with *Yuliana*?' I said her name in a horrible Russian accent.

'I told you,' he said, pulling out his shirt again. 'We went for coffee. And then nothing. We weren't suited.'

I smirked but decided to leave him alone. He seemed harassed enough with the challenge of shirt-in/shirt-out. He moved to the hall mirror to fuss with a perturbing curl and I moved to the freezer and found a perturbing container.

'What's this?'

'What's what?' Joe came into the kitchen pushing the curl to one side. It fell back into place immediately.

'This!' I said, pulling out with a mad flourish the unlabelled ice cream container I'd seen on skype a few weeks ago.

'Oh.'

'I thought I told you to throw it out.'

'I couldn't!' Joe appeared to be fighting a battle of

moralities. 'It's too delicious! Plus, look at this.' He pulled a notecard from behind a fridge magnet the shape of the *David*'s most interesting part. 'Each flavour from Ned and Sophie's Organic Ice Creamery is aligned with a charity. Five per cent of the proceeds of this flavour go to Bedfordshire Wildlife Rescue.' He gave me his best wounded puppy look. 'Look at the photo of the otter orphan . . . awww.'

I grabbed the card.

'God damn him,' I said, unable to tear my eyes from the baby otter's fuzzy schnozzle.

Charity ice cream? Selfridges? Orphaned otters? Ned was hitting all the right notes. He was Michael Crawford. Me and my notes? We were Prince Philip being struck with a soggy mop. There was a knock at the door and Joe trotted out of the room.

'Who's that?'

'My friends,' Joe said from halfway down the hall.

'You could have told me, I'm in my pyjamas!' I said, checking my front for gari puff.

The door opened and boisterous, deep-voiced salutations reverberated down the hall while I replaced the ice cream in the freezer and checked my PJ bottoms for butt-area holes.

'Where's the little lady?' a booming voice said, then a grinning bearded man arrived in the kitchen. 'This must be her.' He bounded over to me. 'Hi, I'm Dan. Been looking forward to meeting you!' He grabbed my shoulder with a meaty palm, planted a bushy kiss on both cheeks then thrust a cool, plastic-coated squishy lump in my hand. 'Joe says you're quite the cook. Get your dinner manglers round those and let me know what you think.'

'Right, hi, thanks,' I said, reeling from the lively greeting. 'What is it?'

'Sausages!' Dan said, grinning through his scruffy black beard. His brown eyes glowed with an inborn joy. Huge biceps strained at his checked flannel shirt like overstuffed pillows and a vast chest housed his giant voice.

'OK,' I said. 'Unusual gift, but thank you.'

Joe arrived in the kitchen with a tall man with messy blond hair and the same kind of joyful grin. 'Dan's a butcher,' he said.

'Best sausages you'll ever taste,' the blond man said. 'Hi, I'm Tim.' He crossed the room and planted two less hairy kisses on my cheeks. 'Nice to meet you, finally; we've heard a lot about you.'

'You too,' I said, remembering that Tim was a lawyer whose main counsel to Joe, upon hearing about Katy, was to get out there and shag a lot of women but to 'get a johnny round ya before you pound 'er'.

'Joe says you're the most chilled-out pregnant chick he's ever come across.' Tim placed a hand on Joe's shoulder.

'Does he?' I said, looking over at a grinning Joe.

'Remember Stephanie, that one Christmas?' Dan did a mock shudder. 'Whoa, what a psycho.'

'Who's Stephanie?' I said.

'My brother's wife,' Joe said. 'Pregnant with twins and hormonally terrifying.'

'Ran after Alistair with a carving knife,' Tim said. 'Got any beers?'

'She was carving at the time.' Joe opened the fridge. 'Not trying to kill him.'

'She was making omelettes. You don't carve whipped eggs, mate.'

Joe got out three beers, poured me a juice and we moved to the living area. For the next half an hour I laughed at Dan and Tim competing over who could tell the most embarrassing story about teenage Joe. Then, while Joe showed Dan round the herb garden, Tim divulged his plan. According to Tim, Joe had fallen for Katy far too hard and far too young. He'd never 'tested his tackle', so it was his duty to get Joe back out there and see what he'd missed since high school. I came to realise that, although a little rough around the edges (especially for a tax lawyer), Tim wasn't as bad as he first came across. His intentions were noble. He was helping his friend the best way he knew how. Getting him blind drunk and shoving him towards lots of easy women. Not an NHS-approved form of therapy, but one many still adhere to.

'Joe's been better since living here. Thanks for looking after our mate. You're a stand-up girl,' Tim said with sincerity.

'Joe's great to have around, actually. I enjoy his company.'

'He's literally the best guy.' Tim leant forward, his expression suddenly severe. 'He doesn't deserve this shit. I never liked Katy. I mean, she was the hot bird at school and we all wanted to shag her but she was out for herself, you know?

Devon wasn't good enough for her. She wanted Shoreditch. She wanted cocktails, she wanted to get black cabs everywhere and one of those Chantel handbags.' He shook his head. 'Not marriage material.' He fell back in his armchair. 'But mates gotta keep that shit to themselves sometimes.' He shrugged and looked burdened. 'He stayed with us for a couple of nights after the whole cheating thing but I think seeing the family unit was a bit too much, you know? Joe's a really sensitive guy. He hides it well but those are the ones you gotta keep your eyes on. For depression and stuff.'

'You've got kids?'

'Yeah, a daughter,' Tim's face split in a wide smile. He pulled his phone out of his pocket. 'Little Annie Lou.' He showed me a photo of a pink-faced baby in a pink Babygro lying on a pink sheet surrounded by pink soft toys. The pinkness was cloying.

'She's adorable.'

'She'll be three months next week. We're throwing her a little party. Stupid, I know, but you gotta celebrate the small things in life, right? Or the shit can cloud your view.'

I nodded. Hardly poetic, but I agreed with the sentiment.

Dan and Joe arrived back inside debating the marriage of mint and pork.

'Come on, get dressed and we'll head off.' Dan clapped his palm on Joe's shoulder.

'I am dressed,' Joe said, looking down. He'd gone for tucked in in the end.

'But your shirt's got nothing written on it . . .?' Dan said with a brief frown. 'You have to have something written on your shirt as a conversation starter.' He unbuttoned his checked shirt and held it open, displaying a snug white t-shirt with 'I can *meat* your needs' written across his chest. 'We wear these at the shop,' he said, beaming. 'The ladies really react to it.'

'Well?' I said sceptically.

Dan's smile dropped. 'Not really.' Then his grin was back. 'But it weeds out the losers. You can't handle this?' he ran his hand across the letters. 'Then you can't handle this.' He indicated himself with camp flair then commenced hammed-up flexing.

Joe laughed. 'Put it away!' He grabbed his wallet and phone then gave me a hug. 'Don't wait up.'

I got more kisses, hugs, invites to three-month-old birthday parties, invites to watch them play football on Sundays, offers to be put in touch with Tim's wife to ask any baby questions and then the noisy boys were stomping down the hall checking whose Uber account to use, what pub to start off at and bickering about who had first round. I was warmed by their obvious affection for Joe.

'Got your goo balloons?' Tim asked as the front door opened.

'You're disgusting,' Joe said, and Dan cracked up.

The door slammed behind them and it took me a further two seconds to work out what a 'goo balloon' was.

CHAPTER THIRTY-TWO

The next morning I opened my bedroom door, bladder full to bursting, and was greeted by Joe in his boxers, hair all a-squiff, kissing another long-limbed slutty-pants a day or two out of high school.

'Don't mind me,' I said in a prissy voice as I pushed past Joe's naked back. He still had his socks on, the stud muffin.

Joe de-suctioned his face. 'Emma! I was just ... this is—'

I made a shut-your-trap hand gesture and took minuscule steps to the bathroom. Any sudden movement would have the bladder gates opening and I couldn't have that happening in my hall at eight fifteen in the morning in full view of the people on the common, Joe and his teenage plaything in a body-con dress from Reiss I'd seen on the internet and lusted over, but realised I could never have because I was the size of a Peugeot 106. When I exited the bathroom Joe was still at the front door whispering to the giggling girl who really should've been at home watching Saturday-morning cartoons. I stomped down the hall to the kitchen construct-ing a suitable reprimand. Eventually Joe sloped into the room, eased himself onto the sofa and put his head in his hands.

'I think I'm going to throw up,' he groaned.

'And why's that?' I said, firmly astride my high horse. 'Because you're hung over or because you've just realised you're a borderline paedophile?'

Joe lifted his head from his hands. His face crumpled and he looked like a 4-year-old trying not to cry. His chin pitted with the effort. The lecture I'd been formulating dissolved.

'I don't know what I'm doing. I'm not this person.' He shook his head, then winced at the action. With stilted movements he rested his head in his hands again. 'I woke up this morning and she was down the end of the bed giving—'

'Ah!' I said sharply. 'Don't need to hear.'

'Sorry. Anyway, she was, you know, and I realised I didn't even remember her name. What kind of guy takes a girl home and doesn't even know her name?'

'Lots of guys, I'm afraid,' I said, squeezing my tea bag out and dropping it in the sink. 'You're clearly no different.'

Joe sighed; his broad back rose and fell with his breath. It was a hurtful thing to say. I immediately regretted it. We'd all done stupid things with the opposite sex while drunk. Hell, I'd only recently been free-boobed in the forest with a married man, and I'd been completely sober. And completely pregnant. I did an all-over body tremble to purge the image. I grabbed my mug of tea and crossed the room.

'I'm feeling a little "Groundhog Day" about this whole situation.' I placed the tea in front of him.

'I know,' he said without lifting his head. 'I'm sorry.'

I sat next to him and rested my arm across his shoulders. I felt his body lean imperceptibly into mine. It gave me comfort to know that I myself was a comfort.

'I liked her dress, though.'

Over bacon and eggs with sautéed potatoes, Joe regaled me with his evening.

'I think it was the shots,' he said gloomily.

'That'll do it.'

'I'd told the guys I wasn't that interested in women at the moment and suddenly it was all they could focus on. Like I'd laid down this great challenge.'

'Men,' I said with my mouth full.

'Tim called me a faggot and ordered a rainbow.'

'Rainbow?'

'Shots lined up on the bar in the colours of the rainbow,' he said. 'It's a gay pride thing.'

'Right,' I said, feeling out of touch with my generation.

'He said it was in honour of my faggoty behaviour.'

'Lovely.'

'I did the shots so Tim would get off my back, but then . . . I can't remember much.' He put his cutlery together, knife facing the correct way, and pushed his plate away. 'I remember being outside a club in Piccadilly. I remember Dan telling some girls I was in the market for a new girlfriend. I remember kissing someone on a light-up dance floor.' He shook his head. 'And then I woke up with her—'

'Ah!'

'Sorry.' He picked at the edge of the table.

'You going to eat that?' I pointed to his potatoes.

'I don't know what to do.' Joe pushed his plate across the table. 'Before last night, and the night with Yuliana, I'd ...' He looked self-conscious. 'I'd only ...'

I nodded, encouraging him.

'I'd only ever been with ...' He fidgeted with the syrup bottle.

'Spit it out!' I snatched the syrup from his hands. 'Only ever been with?'

'One woman.' Joe reddened.

'Yeah, I know, Tim told me.' I grinned.

Joe shook his head with fond exasperation.

'So how did that happen?' I said.

He fiddled with a napkin ring I had no recollection of buying. 'I met Katy when I was at high school. We dated on and off, and I was so smitten that whenever we were in one of our ...' he dropped the napkin ring and made quotation marks in the air '... "*time for ourselves*" periods I just waited around hoping we'd get back together. I couldn't even look at other girls. I loved her from the moment I saw her. None of that cheesy movie stuff. I really did.'

I didn't know what to say to him. I'd never felt that way. I couldn't relate. I ignored Joe's distress and contemplated my own. Was I ever going to have that feeling of all-consuming love for someone? Did I want it? It sounded terribly over-shadowing. Where would I find the time for craft? Or jetboating? Joe waited for me to say something, and when it became apparent I had nothing to add he went back to the damned napkin ring. It was bloody ugly with its orange lacquered patterns round its plastic side. I frowned at it like it would be able to take my reproach on board. Why was it here on my table, shiny and dreadful?

'How about I make that cannelloni you like tonight?' I said in a buoyant voice.

Joe shrugged.

'Extra-cheesy?' I roused.

Joe gave a weak 'Sounds great.'

'Excellent.'

I got up, snatched the vile napkin ring out of his hands and marched it directly to the bin.

'Who bought you? How did you get in here?'

Later that afternoon I returned home, supermarket bags overflowing. I kicked the front door shut and waddled down the hall.

'I'm making those brownies you like for dessert.' I dumped the bags on the kitchen table.

'Great,' Joe said in an unusually unresponsive manner, not moving from his position on the sofa. He held his phone, his face solemn.

'What's up?' I began unloading papaya, olives, custard,

manchego cheese and all manner of other things that had taken my fancy while I was waddling, hungry, up and down the aisles. 'Joe? You OK?'

It took him a moment to look up. His face was unreadable, like he'd brought down the shutters to his soul.

'Katy phoned,' he said, his voice void of emotion. 'She wants to meet after work.'

'What for?' I said with a pang of annoyance. We were going to watch *Romancing the Stone* and *The Jewel of the Nile*. Classics!

He glanced up but seemed to look right through me. 'I don't know what she wants.'

Around five o'clock, Joe came down the stairs, freshly shaved and smartly dressed, with an occupied air about him. He left saying he'd be home in time for dinner. By seven thirty I'd eaten two of the five cannelloni tubes. By 8.10 p.m. I'd eaten the rest and was watching the final scenes of *Romancing the Stone*. When the movie finished I contemplated tidying up the kitchen and going to bed but instead decided to go upstairs and, like any rational, mature young lady, look through Joe's stuff.

Joe's bed was made but strewn with clothes. It was a small comfort to know women were not alone in the dilemma of 'what to wear to meet the ex'. I tiptoed unnecessarily across the room, scanning for ... evidence? I wanted juicy stuff. Torn photos of Katy with a pin poked through her eyes; a diary with details of their sex life and how her genital warts had really got in the way of their relationship. Immature? Yes. Did you expect anything less? I'd built a picture of Katy in my head of an impossibly beautiful raven-haired witch with blood-red lipstick and a fondness for seamed stockings. I opened the bedside drawers. Nothing. And nothing under the bed. A couple of suits hung in the wardrobe. I tried to imagine him in them as I'd only seen him in jeans, faded band t-shirts and big woolly jumpers. I shut the wardrobe and spied his computer on the dressing table. I clicked a button and the screen came alive, asking for a password. Being the open person he was I knew Joe's password within the first week of meeting him. I typed 'nah-needs-garlic', his favourite line from a movie, and it opened immediately. The desktop image was Joe grinning at the camera, sunglasses on, shirt off, his toned arm flung over the shoulder of a striking blond woman in a turquoise bikini, trendy aviators and with a straight-toothed smile. A sandy beach and an aqua ocean stretched out behind them. *It could be his sister*, I thought, rather unconvincingly. Made even more unconvincing by the fact that Joe only had brothers. I was not ready to release my image of dark-haired Katy as a cold-hearted seductress looking for gentle souls to shred. In his files I found more images of the same woman and there was only one person she could be. Katy didn't seem to wear unapproachable blood-red lipstick and her hair wasn't raven but a rather lovely I-have-Swedish-heritage-so-my-hair-is-naturally-the-colour-of-organic-wheat-on-a-summer's-day-in-a-Van-Gogh-painting kind of shade. I carried the laptop across the room and made myself comfortable on Joe's bed. Scrolling through the pictures, I got a peek into his earlier life. The life before I met him. There were pictures of Joe and Katy on the tops of mountains in puffa jackets and shiny goggles. Ones at long tables with large groups of people drinking from oversized pewter mugs. Ones at temples, at the tops of iconic buildings and on boats in diving gear. I scrolled down to the most recently added pictures and stopped at a selfie-style one. Joe standing in the living room of a loft-style apartment, all exposed brick and industrial lighting, holding a 'sold' sign. Katy was at the edge of the frame, kissing his cheek. Joe grinned like the cat that got the organic Cornish cream straight off the top of the milking pail. I realised he'd been doing remarkably well for a man who'd had his life thrown upside down. Yet after receiving the call from Katy he'd let his congenial facade drop. I flicked back to some pictures of Joe and Katy at a party, dressed in togas with laurels round their heads and big glasses of red wine and zoomed into Joe's grinning face. A small part of me hoped they might try and get back together. They seemed to have had a perfect life. It would be a shame to throw it all away because of one indiscretion. But another part of me hoped Joe would tell her to go fuck herself and find himself a girl who would never hurt him in such a way, ever. I felt a huge surge of motherly protection towards him.

Around midnight I heard the gate click shut and Joe's footsteps crunch up the path. I'd been in bed for an hour but unable to sleep. I tried to deduce from his footsteps how it had gone with Swedish Wheat-Haired Witch, but his footsteps sounded like a man walking up a path at midnight trying not to wake his neighbours. He let himself in, walked upstairs and in no time at all I heard him snoring.

CHAPTER THIRTY-THREE

The next morning, walking round the sunny common, I was impatient to find out what had happened.

'Was it weird, seeing her? I mean, did you want to, you know, stab her in the face or something?'

'No,' Joe said, bemused. 'I didn't want to *stab her in the face*.'

'Chest?'

He let out an amused *pfft* but kept his gaze on his feet. 'No.'

'Chop off a toe? Rip out an earring?'

Joe shook his head. 'I had no violent urges or homicidal compulsions.'

'Oh,' I said. I was most disappointed.

We continued our meander across the common, Brutus at Joe's heels and me clutching a plastic bag full of scones Harriet insisted we feed to the ducks. She'd buttered and marmaladed them. Joe had woken up quiet and distant after his evening with Katy. I wasn't used to seeing him so preoccupied. It unsettled me. Even Brutus seemed to sense Joe's distraction and chose to trot behind rather than tussle with the stick Joe carried. A few quiet minutes later we reached the edge of the pond where Brutus commenced his usual routine, pacing six yards round the water, barking with his teeth clenched to avoid a scolding, and Joe and I tore off bits of leaden scone and tossed them to disinterested ducks.

'So what happened?' I said when we reached the end of our baked goods.

Joe appeared not to have heard. My back ached, so, in the absence of any reply, I wandered to a nearby bench seat. Joe gave a plaintive look at the scone pieces bobbing on the pond then, clicking his tongue for Brutus to heel, drifted over and sat next to me.

After a period of quiet, he spoke. 'She wants to get back together.'

'What?' I blurted. 'Is she fucking nuts?!'

The look on Joe's face made me realise the current topic required more thoughtfully edited responses.

'Sorry,' I muttered.

Another silent minute passed.

'So what did you say?'

Joe looked down and seemed to notice the stick in his hands for the first time. He threw it and Brutus, who had been sitting, statesmanlike, at Joe's feet, streaked across the dry grass. I wasn't the most patient person at the best of times, and this late in my pregnancy even less so, so the staccato nature of our conversation was driving me crazy.

'Joe?'

'Yeah?'

'What did you say when she said she wanted to get back together?'

'Oh.'

Brutus arrived and dropped the now gummy stick at Joe's feet.

'I said I'd have to think about it.'

For the sake of my sad friend I said the 'c' word in my head.

'Well, if you don't mind me saying,' I said.

Joe gave me a look.

'And even if you do . . . what's there to think about? She cheated on you.'

Further darkness crossed his face. 'I know.'

'And you weren't even married yet.'

Joe threw the stick again and nodded. I watched him follow Brutus's enthusiastic stick retrieval with dark-ringed eyes, heartache etched in newly carved lines on his face.

'OK, I'm going to try to be tactful here,' I said.

Joe gave a doubtful look that was completely deserved.

'Do you not think, and I'm only saying this because as your friend I have to play the devil's advocate, that she's, you know, a *giant* whore?'

Joe ignored me but the muscles around his jaw tightened. I wondered if I'd overstepped the mark but continued anyway.

'Does she just think you guys will get back together and carry on as normal? I mean, how would you ever be able to trust her again?'

Joe threw the stick again, then fell back against the bench seat. He looked ready to say something so I waited with all the open-mindedness I could muster. I was impatient for him to realise that Katy was scum; for him to quit ruminating over a relationship that didn't deserve even mild contemplation so we could get back to the way things were. Him and me, the scorned ones, watching *Love Actually* with a packet of M&M's.

'She thinks ...' He paused for another lengthy moment. I nearly pinched him in the neck. 'She thinks we should start couples counselling and then ...' He was like a slow-loading web page. I elbowed him. 'And then announce our re-engagement.'

I bit my tongue. I wanted to squeeze every swear and cuss word I knew into a spiky ball of vitriol and biff it at her symmetrical face.

Eventually Joe lifted his gaze from his lap. 'Well?' he said. 'Surely you have something to say about that?'

'Plenty,' I said, bulging my eyes, but smiled to show I would hold back. 'What do *you* want to do?'

He bent forward and rested his elbows on his knees, letting his hands dangle between them.

'I don't know.' He looked at the dusty ground. 'Do I really want to be doing couples counselling when I'm twenty-nine? *Before* I embark on a lifelong marriage?'

I let out a sad snort.

'Doesn't bode well, does it?'

I shook my head. I watched Brutus, who'd abandoned his

stick and was giving the place where his balls used to be a thorough washdown.

Joe sat back. 'I'm not cut out for dating. They're all so young and predatory, and everybody wants to be a C4 presenter.' He ran a hand over his stubbly chin. 'With Katy, it's ... it *was* comfortable. She was my family,' he said, his very aura burdened and battered.

The force of his wretchedness sucked and pulled like a black hole. I lay a palm on his shoulder. He drew in a lungful of air and let it out with a saddled sigh. My heart ached for my friend. I wanted to tell him that she barely warranted his contempt, let alone his love. That counselling was absolutely not the right thing to be doing. I wanted to tell him that he should tell her to go and take a nice snorkelling trip in the Atlantic with a couple of anvils strapped to her slim ankles.

'I think you should give it another go,' I said instead. Rather maturely, I thought.

'What?!' Joe turned and looked at me properly for the first time that day. I wasn't exactly convinced myself.

'What?' he said again.

'I think you should give it another go,' I repeated with more certainty.

Joe's face queried me but he seemed unable to find the words.

'It's just, you have so much history,' I said, last night's photo-snooping fresh in my mind. 'It seems a shame to throw it all away over one mistake.'

I waited for Joe's response. His eyes flitted back and forth, mirroring his racing thoughts.

'But what if it wasn't just the once?' He looked at me like the oracle I was most certainly not.

I shrugged. 'You may never know the answer to that.'

He slumped down the bench seat.

'You loved her once,' I said. 'You might be able to again. Love conquers all, doesn't it? "Love is the drug you've been thinking of". "All You Need is Love". "Love is an Open Door" – that one's from *Frozen*.' I forced a tinkle of laughter.

Joe frowned.

'Do you . . .' I found myself needing to swallow. 'Do you still love her?'

Joe turned his gaze towards me. His eyes searched mine as if I held the answer. In my opinion, if you don't have the answer to that question at the ready then you are most certainly not in love. I wanted to say as much. I wanted to tell him that I thought being in love should be easy. Black and white. Isn't being in love just a graduation from being best friends? A big graduation, granted, one with sex and commitment and so on, but still, if you're not best friends with the person you're going to spend the rest of your life with then what the hell is the point? Sex will lose its appeal when you both have hip replacements and a very small window where your bladders are strong enough to withhold any motion more vigorous than straining a tea bag. Games of backgammon, an afternoon slice of cake and conversation will be all you have left. Joe's situation was complicated.

Katy had slept with another man two months after getting engaged. Who knows what her reasons were? Maybe she was a sex addict. Or an alcoholic, and had no idea what she was doing. Or maybe she was freaking out about marrying her high school boyfriend and needed to put it out there one last time. 'It' being her vagina. Slut.

'I think you still love her,' I said.

Joe moved his head a fraction but kept his gaze on the pond.

'And I think you should go to counselling and try to work through it because, as you said yourself, she's your family. You'd been together since high school, bought a flat, got engaged, talked about children. Maybe she just freaked out.'

'But . . .' Joe said, turning to me with wide, worried eyes.

'Look, you certainly aren't cut out for the dating world. You were way out of your depth.'

Joe opened his mouth to protest.

'The last girl nearly crippled you.'

I was trying to be light-hearted but I felt a sadness creeping in. I was convincing my friend to take steps that would eventually lead to the end of our friendship. If not the end, it undoubtedly wouldn't be what it was now.

'She clearly loves you. She wants to go to counselling. You owe it to yourself to at least try.'

Joe sat motionless. He disappeared inside himself and I could almost feel the buzz of my words whirling round his mind. I was pretty sure I was doing the right thing. It was just the right thing felt so bad. Joe continued to sit in silent contemplation. I wanted to press him for a decision so I could resolve it in my own head. Where did I stand? And why did it matter where I stood?

'Joe?' I said. 'What do you think?'

He blinked out of his reverie. 'Look at that blind man.' He pointed towards the path by the pond. 'Isn't he sweet?'

Avoidance was a tactic I knew well and I wanted to call him on it, but instead I decided to give him a break. I looked to where he was pointing. An old man shuffled along the path in – despite the steamy weather – the kind of heavy formal clothing I'd expect to see on a mothball-scented headmaster in a Roald Dahl story. One gnarly hand held the reins to a golden-coated guide dog and the other swished his blind stick from left to right. A cloth bag from the organic greengrocer's hung weightily from his wrist with something kale-like sprouting from the top.

I screwed my nose up. 'I don't see what's so sweet. You only say that because he's blind.'

'Here we go again.' He stood, brushed non-existent crumbs from his lap then offered me his hand.

I accepted and hoisted myself off the bench seat, making unappealing grunting noises. Even Brutus looked ashamed.

'I bet he's a career criminal,' I said, waiting for the crick in my overburdened hip flexors to disappear.

'OK.' Joe turned in the direction of home, seemingly wishing he were already there.

'He's probably blind from an explosion in his LSD lab where he makes drugs to sell to kids who have to rob their parents and turn to prostitution and gang violence to feed their habit. There's nothing sweet about it. If anything, you should probably be calling the police.'

Joe considered me. Then he grinned for the first time that day.

'You have yourself some serious issues.'

I patted my stomach. 'Tell me something I don't know.'

CHAPTER THIRTY-FOUR

The front door swung open revealing Sinead in large black sunglasses and a formerly white apron with wet patches round the bosom and a streak of green icing from chest to waist. A whiff of stale alcohol drifted from her.

'Hi—'

'Stay away from your uncle,' she said, pulling me through the doorway.

Joe followed, a large brightly wrapped present in his arms and an amused look on his face.

'Why?'

'He's very angry.'

'With *me*?'

'You. Me. The entire British film industry.'

Oh, shit. The official wrap party, the one all the London-based office staff and execs from LA attended, had taken place the night before. I'd declined my invite for two reasons. Very sophisticated reasons. Seeing Andrew again, seeing Martha

378

again. I'd stayed at home with Joe and tried to find out where we stood on the Katy situation. He was reticent to the level of national security. It had been a week since I'd suggested he give his relationship another go and although he'd not actually gone out, except to the supermarket, the offie and one emergency trip to the plant store to resolve an aphid catastrophe, he'd taken some hushed calls in his bedroom, rather than in his usual manner of loud and cheerful at the kitchen table, which I assumed were with Katy. He was on his laptop a lot. And making a few calls that involved talk of print margins and colour saturation, so I gathered he had started working again. Which was good. But he still wasn't himself. It was the most reserved I'd seen him, and I couldn't help but think it was all a terrible idea. My terrible idea. I'd pushed him towards the she-devil with a complexion like a bar of luxury soap.

'So you went, then?' I said, handing Sinead the requested tray of cupcakes decorated with various icing bugs.

Archie had become bug mad since the beetle-on-log/ missing-near-lake incident. Of which Sinead and Uncle Mike and the rest of the family knew nothing about, so *shush*.

'I tried *everything* to not go.' With the tray in one hand she pressed the door shut and drifted down the darkened hall, placing a steadying free hand on the wall at various points. Kid's party noise wafted from the rear of the house.

'I lied about what day it was on,' she said. 'He found the invite. I pretended I had gastro; he gave me a foul-tasting suppressant pill.' She stopped in the kitchen next to a bright green monstrosity strewn across the kitchen table. I think it was Archie's birthday cake.

Joe shot me a look of horror and mouthed, *What the hell is that?*

Spider? I mimed.

'I even contemplated pushing one of the kids down the stairs,' Sinead continued. She picked up a shambolic bowl of green icing and began unskilfully spatula-ing great hunks of it onto the ... thing. 'Jess, probably.'

'So what happened?' I prompted.

Joe walked the length of the table, contemplating the cake, cocking his head to the side like an art critic.

'I came up with a plan,' she said, hitting the side of the thing with more icing. 'Get really, really drunk and talk over everyone so Mike never got to ask about the movie. Make a total arse of myself and have to be taken home early.'

'And that genius plan didn't work?'

Joe mouthed the word *Grasshopper?*

'No,' Sinead huffed. 'Because I hadn't factored in the blooper reel.'

'Oh. And?'

'Blood, gore, stuffed zombie cats, girls in bras running out of tents and tripping up, a whole horde of chihuahuas chewing what looked like a blood-covered organ (I'm assuming it wasn't real), a zombie with guts coming out of his stomach doing the running man (that was actually quite funny), Archie saying 'fuck's sake' when he got his lines wrong. More bra/running shots and a crew member pretending a severed arm was his penis.' She tossed the spatula into the bowl and stood back, assessing the insect cake. 'I thought he was going to have a heart attack.' She extracted herself from her soggy apron. 'He's been trying to call Supernanny again; he's booked a family therapist. He even phoned the producers this morning and tried to get Archie's scenes deleted. He was unsuccessful. And now he's not talking to me. And *very* disappointed in you.' She tossed the apron on the bench.

'Why me? You're the one who signed him up for the movie. I was just helping you out. Did you tell him that? Did you stand up for me?'

'No, I was too drunk.'

'Well, did you say something to him today?'

'Too hung over.'

Joe sniggered and swiped some icing with a fingertip, licked it then puckered his mouth in disgust.

'Great,' I muttered.

Outside I found Uncle Mike standing in the shade chatting to some parents and looking at Archie as if he were damaged goods. He greeted Joe pleasantly but avoided eye contact with me. Every time a parent asked about Archie's movie Uncle Mike coughed, took a swig of his soda water and said he had to check on the sausage rolls. Sinead kept out of the way in the kitchen putting the finishing touches to the terrible bug cake. Kids raced around the flat sunny lawn in fancy dress hitting each other with balloon swords. A bubble machine blew football-sized bubbles towards the cloudless sky and adults stood gripping champagne flutes while being knocked from all sides by thigh-height children with too much sugar in their systems. Helen, in a floaty, low-cut summer dress, perched on a sun lounger entrancing a couple of fathers while Mum ferried drinks and plates of canapés.

'Happy Birthday to Yooo-OOOH-oooo,' Joe warbled.

About thirty other people were gathered in the sunny garden, singing, but I could only hear Joe's deep, tuneless version. I giggled as he exhausted the last lengthy note and sucked in a lungful of air.

'You really threw yourself into that,' I said.

We shuffled backwards as keen-for-icing children surged towards the cake. Which was a praying mantis. Obviously.

'If ever there was a song to give your all to, it's "Happy Birthday" for a little kid,' he said, self-righteously.

'And "Sisters Are Doing It For Themselves" when you've been dumped,' I replied.

Joe indicated his affirmation.

'Or "Take On Me" when you're in the shower,' he offered.

'You gotta do the keyboard bit for that, so it's better if you're a passenger in a car then you can do it on the dashboard.' I mimed a 1980s synthesiser action.

'True,' Joe said with an earnest nod. 'Oh, and "The Sun Will Come Out Tomorrow", but only when you're at home alone.'

'You need to keep *that* to yourself.'

'I said *home alone*, didn't I?'

'You guys talk such crap,' Helen said, knocking back champagne.

We turned towards the knot of children and watched Sinead cut the cake and hand it out. Having made the huge cake eyesore on the kitchen table, she'd realised it was impossible to transport. So she'd flung open the French doors and five of the dads and Joe had carried the entire farmhouse table into the garden. Sinead had then conceded that kitchen duties, including birthday cakes, would remain Uncle Mike's domain and she would stick to what she did best. Which we'd struggled to define, so had lit the candles and sung 'Happy Birthday' instead.

'So, do you have a birth plan? Who's going to be your birth partner?' Sinead took a long sip of her extra-long Long Island Iced Tea. The first hangover gone, she was attempting another.

The mass of shrieky, sugared children had departed to give their parents hell at bedtime; the lawn had been cleared of chunks of uneaten cake and Sinead, Mum and myself sat round the garden furniture under the brolly relishing the afternoon serenity. Archie's birthday party was to transition into a family (plus Helen and Joe) baby shower for me. We were going to barbecue some bangers, open some gifts and discuss baby names. Uncle Mike and Joe battled to untangle a rope ladder for a new kitset tree hut while Helen perched on a chair near them gabbing away and swilling champagne.

'I dunno,' I sighed. 'And no, it can't be you,' I said as Mum opened her mouth. 'I want the nurses to *like* me. And to give me drugs.'

'Oh, you don't want drugs,' said Sinead, who was a mad-woman and had given birth four times without any pain relief. 'You don't know what it does to the baby.'

'It's Ned's,' Mum said. 'It's going to be peculiar anyway.'

'Thanks,' I said.

Mum grinned. 'Wasn't Alex going to come home for it?' She lowered her sunglasses, her perceptive blue eyes flashing. 'Is that not happening?'

I averted my gaze and shook my head.

'What happened with you two?'

'I don't know.' I rubbed my stomach, feeling the taut skin over what I thought was the baby's pointy backside. 'I don't want to talk about it, OK?'

'Fine, but I really think you—'

'*Mum.*'

She raised her hands in a gesture of surrender, exchanged a she's-reacting-just-the-way-we-said-she-would look with Sinead, and pushed her glasses back in place. We turned our attention to the men; watched them pick up a panel of wood and a glassless window frame, consult the instruction sheet then put the bits back down and take swigs of beer. Helen cackled her enjoyment and left them to it. She flung her bare limbs into a seat beside me then, spying some champagne resting in a silver ice bucket, reached across the table and topped up her glass.

'So, when are we going to open the baby shower presents?' I said, eyeing the little pile of pastel-wrapped gifts on the table.

'I guess we could do it now,' Mum said. 'Let me just get mine from inside.' She stood.

'Oh yes,' slurred Helen. 'I've put one in the freezer from Sophie and Ned. Don't let me forget.'

I stiffened.

Mum turned round. 'Why's it in the freezer?'

'Ahhh because it's ice cream.' Helen's champagne flute made a swaying journey towards her lips. 'And it would melt out here in the . . .' She trailed off at my silencing look. 'What?'

'Why are Sophie and Ned giving you *ice cream*, Emma?' Mum said, realisation hardening her voice.

Millie, in the buggy next to Sinead, began to stir. Sinead reached down to soothe her.

'I'll get some more lime soda.' I stood. 'Drink, anyone?'

Mum thrust her sunglasses on top of her head. 'Emma, you stay right here and tell me why Ned has given you *ice cream*.'

Millie's fuss became a wail.

'I think she's been bitten by something,' Sinead said, lifting her out of the buggy.

'I'll get some ointment,' I offered.

'Emma!' Mum slammed her palm on the table with a bit too much force. 'Why are Sophie and Ned giving you goddamned ice cream! Did Ned sell those vans? Emma, *look* at me!'

Helen swivelled her head from Mum to me, her expression guilty but confused.

Millie's wail intensified.

'Oh god, I really think she's been bitten by something.' Sinead stood and raised the distressed Millie to her shoulder. 'Michael!'

Uncle Mike rushed over, followed by Joe.

'Emma,' Mum said, turning her attention from Millie to me. 'Explain yourself! Did Ned sell the ice cream vans? Did he pay you back?'

I shook my head. Mum's mouth fell open. Uncle Mike glanced up from examining the now screaming and writhing Millie. Alice, Jess and Archie rushed from various corners of the garden with worried little faces.

'What's going on?' Joe asked Helen.

'I'm not sure, but it's not good and it's my fault,' she slurred.

'I think it's a bee-sting,' Uncle Mike said, concerned but calm. 'She's reacting to it. We'll have to go to St George's.'

'What?!' Sinead said, her voice catching in her throat. She tried to contain Millie's squirms and shunts. 'Is she going to be OK?'

'She'll be fine.' Uncle Mike turned to Mum. 'Diana, can you look after Archie and the girls?'

Mum nodded, her face still arranged in maternal reprimand. He pulled his keys from his pocket and took Millie from Sinead.

'Get an ice pack from the freezer. I'll meet you at the car.' He was in efficient doctor mode. 'Emma, are you in financial trouble?' he said while gathering Millie's essentials from the pushchair. He spoke without looking at me.

'Not yet,' I mumbled, burning with embarrassment.

'Good. We'll talk when I get back.' He nodded at Mum, then marched briskly towards the garage with Millie screaming in his arms.

For a moment the garden was quiet save for Millie's receding cries. Mum glared at me.

Jess tugged at Mum's shirt. 'Is Millie going to die?' Tears formed deep wet slings at the base of her blue eyes.

Alice stood alongside quietly knotting her fingers.

'No, my sweet.' Mum crouched down and pulled Jess into a hug. 'Daddy doesn't have the right medicine here so he needs to take her to the hospital to get some. She'll be back in no time at all.' Mum looked up at me and frowned. 'Emma, we need to talk.'

I said nothing.

Joe fidgeted with his watch. 'I've got to pop out to meet someone.'

'I'll be off as well, then.' Helen stood, draining the last of her glass.

Realising I had an opportunity to escape Mum's inquisition, I grabbed my bag from the ground.

'I'm going too.'

'Emma—' Mum said.

I passed Helen her handbag. 'Come on.'

Mum sighed her disappointment.

'Maybe you should stay,' Joe said.

'I can't. I have to get Helen home. She's drunk.'

'I am,' Helen said, flicking back her fringe. 'I really am.'

'Emma ...' Mum started, but at my defiant look ended up just shaking her head. I grabbed Helen by the elbow and moved away. Joe said something to Mum then jogged after us. On the footpath by the front gate Helen was fully occupied adjusting her fringe in a pocket mirror while I suffered under Joe's enquiring gaze.

'What're you going to do now?' he said.

'Take Helen home, give her a coffee and help her sober up.'

'I'd rather a wine,' she said. We ignored her.

'You coming?' I said.

'I have to meet someone.' He checked his watch again.

'Right.'

'I'll see you at home, then. I'll be about an hour. You'll be there?' The look of concern on his face prodded at the soreness of my already injured pride.

'Sure.'

He gave me one last troubled look then turned in the direction of the high street.

'Shall we go to the pub?' Helen said, looking up from under her tidied fringe. She looked perkier already.

'OK.'

My phone rang as we walked down the street. Mum. I pushed 'reject call' then turned it off, not worrying too much about Millie. Uncle Mike knew what to do.

While Helen 'sobered up' with a glass of house wine I explained why her casual comments had landed me in trouble.

'Why didn't you just tell me it was a secret?' she said, exasperated.

'Because you can't *keep* a secret.'

'That's true.' She smiled, then frowned. 'Look, why are you so worried about accepting help?' Helen leant against the faded wallpaper in a diminishing shaft of late afternoon sun. 'Your Mum would never have asked for her loan back if she knew you didn't have it.'

'I know, but—'

'Forget the *but*.' Annoyance clipped her words. 'You're just being weird about it.'

'I'm not being weird,' I said. 'I know I can ask for help and I know my family would lend me whatever I needed, but . . .' I tried to find the right words to fit how I was feeling. Helen sat across the table, petite, drunk and impatient.

'I feel like up until now I've been waiting. Waiting for my career to take off, waiting for that young feeling to finish or that mature feeling to kick in. Waiting till Ned and I fizzled out or for him to . . . I don't know. I've been waiting for my life to start. And then this happened.' I pointed both hands at the mountainous rise beneath my bosom. 'And I thought, "shit, it's already started", and I've barely been along for the ride.'

Helen's balanced features were unreadable.

'Don't you ever feel like that?' I implored. 'Like everybody else is forging through their life's itinerary and you're still at home on the sofa in the list-making stage? Like you're just a passenger, and maybe next week or next month or next *year* it'll be your turn to take the driver's seat?'

Helen frowned.

I missed my sister. She'd have an insightful one-liner that would sum it all up, offer a solution and have me laughing at myself. Everything was better with my sister.

'Do you have any idea what I'm talking about?'

'Not really. Can you say it in non-Dr-Phil-speak?'

'I just wanted to be here for the next part of my life,' I said, deflated. 'I don't want to be doing it with someone else's money. Then it's not *my life*. It's subsidised so it's not real. I'm not going to be a passenger any more.' I picked at the skin round my fingernails. Helen watched.

'It sounds kind of pathetic when I say it out loud,' I muttered.

'Yeah, it does.'

I looked up.

'Emma, I say this as your friend who loves you.' She placed a tiny paw to her partially exposed upper breast. 'Shut the hell up.'

'OK . . .'

'Get out of that head of yours and look around. You've got friends, family and a fecking three-bedroom cottage on Wimbledon Common. Life's good for you.' She rooted through her purse and checked her phone. 'Now, I have to get home to my *rented* studio flat. In *Stockwell*.' She gave me a pointed look. 'It's Saturday night, I have no date and there's a water jet in my jacuzzi bath that needs a certain seeing to.'

'OK. And *ew, gross*.' I stood, trying not to let that image enter my mind.

We made our way through the bustling pub.

'Just relax a bit,' she said with authority over the early evening hubbub. 'I wouldn't be friends with a "passenger".' She pushed open the pub doors and we emptied onto the dusk-veiled street. 'And sort out the feelings you have for Joe. It's driving me crazy.'

I stopped. 'Huh?'

She grinned. 'You're in love with him.'

'What?'

Helen just smiled.

'*What*?!' I repeated.

She winked.

'Ah . . . did you hear me? I just said "What?" in an *extremely* insistent manner!'

'If I'm an expert in one thing alone, it's matters of the heart,' she said, swaying a little.

'No,' I considered her. 'No, you're more in line with matters of the genitals.'

'Touché, my knocked-up friend, touché.' She leant forward and kissed my cheek. 'Maybe I'm wrong.' She tottered backwards towards the high street. 'What do I know? I'm having relations with a jacuzzi.' She gave a scandalous smile then turned on her wedges.

'But . . .?' I called after her.

At home, disorientated by Helen's comments, I ate a cookie.

Then another five.

I turned on my phone and saw multiple missed calls.

Texts informed me that Millie was home safe and sound and requested I come back to the house for the barbecue. Joe said he was at home and wanted to know when I'd be back. But he was nowhere to be found and when I dialled his number his phone was off. I flicked on the TV but couldn't decide on a channel.

I thought about Helen's comment.

I ate another cookie.

I tossed the remote on the sofa, grabbed my keys and went out.

CHAPTER THIRTY-FIVE

'Oh, hello dear.' Harriet smiled through the crack of her open door. 'I'll just take the latches off.' She shut the door and fumbled with chains and locks. Brutus growled and Harriet told him to go and sit in his basket with 'bunny-bunkins'. The door eventually opened and Harriet motioned with her knobbly hand to come inside.

'Come, come, dear, Arthur's just made a ginger loaf.' She raised her loud-hailer and turned down the hall. 'ARTHUR! KETTLE ON, EMMA'S HERE!'

'I won't stay long,' I said, stepping out of my flip-flops onto their carpeted hall. 'I'm looking for Joe. Have you seen him?'

'Not since he left about an hour ago.'

Harriet hobbled down the hall and I followed. She pulled out a chair at the kitchen table and patted the chintzy seat. 'Sit, sit.'

Brutus lay in his sheepskin-lined basket by the back door with his fluffy 'bunny-bunkins' wedged beside him, his dark eyes following me across the room.

'GOOD EVENING, EMMA!' Arthur bellowed from the kitchen bench where he was slicing the loaf into the kind of thickness that shows you've got to a certain time in your life where you no longer give a fig about calories.

He placed the brick-sized pieces on a patterned plate. One part of the bench had been lowered so he could reach it comfortably from his wheelchair.

'GINGER LOAF?' he yelled as he wheeled the slices from the bench to the kitchen table.

'YES, THANKS!'

Yelling at an elderly man in a wheelchair went against my entire upbringing.

'Tea?' Harriet said, getting mugs out and putting them on the normal-height bench.

I nodded and watched Harriet and Arthur move round each other without the need for 'excuse me' or 'could you move a little to your left', instinctively knowing which way the other would move from years of practice. Harriet filled the teapot then grabbed the sugar jar; Arthur passed her a teaspoon. He curled out three twists of butter like the ones you get in Devonshire tearooms; she set out three side plates. It was humbling to watch, and I found myself wishing for the security of your place in the world old age would bring.

'You said you saw Joe?'

Harriet and Arthur took their places at the table and began to pour tea.

'Yes. He left a little while ago. With a blond girl.'

'A blond girl?' The heat from the ginger hit the back of my throat and I coughed. 'Who was she?'

'I don't know, dear.' Harriet studied me through her pale-rimmed glasses. 'She was a pretty wee thing though. Sugar?'

I took the jar from her and thoughtlessly loaded my tea with four teaspoons, confused about my bubbling irritation.

'Harriet,' I said, an idea forming. 'Did you film it?'

'No.' Her tea quickly became fascinating to her.

'Harriet?' I said in a tone most commonly used with naughty children. Her eyes ceased scrutinising the contents of her teacup and flitted about the room, avoiding my demanding gaze.

'I'm not going to get mad.'

Harriet picked at a non-existent bobble of thread in the floral tablecloth. Arthur sat at the table obliviously getting the majority of his ginger loaf down the front of his shirt and blinking into the middle distance, not noticing that his young neighbour was giving his beloved elderly wife the death stare.

'*Harriet*,' I said again in a you-tell-me-right-this-minute voice.

'You promise you won't get mad?'

'I promise.'

'I was only filming your garden because Marjorie at the bookshop said you couldn't possibly have asparagus sprouting so soon after planting and I said you most certainly could and that my lovely, ah, clever' she glanced up to see how the flattery was working 'neighbour had a fine bed of asparagus. I had to film your garden to show that know-it-all-britches she was wrong.' She put both her hands flat down on the table and leant forward. 'You know, just because she works in a bookshop doesn't mean she's read every book! I know my gardening, and my Arthur,' she patted Arthur on the arm and he snapped out of his thoughts with a distracted 'eh?' 'can grow peonies in any soil, even in London. Just because I'm from the country doesn't mean I don't read. I won't have her telling me—'

'The footage?' I interrupted politely before Harriet gave herself a stroke.

'What's that, dear?'

'The footage. Did you keep it?'

'Ah . . .' She twiddled her fingers. 'Ye-es.'

Five minutes later, after much convincing that I was not going to report her to the authorities, and agreeing that yes, she really only had my best interests at heart; that the city was indeed full of rapists, robbers and serial killers, and unless you got video footage and a complete helix of their DNA these criminals would get off scot-free, I was following her upstairs to be shown the footage of Joe, a blonde and some flourishing asparagus.

'You know the neighbours at number forty-two? The Montgomerys?'

I made noncommittal noises.

'The ones with the ugly baby.'

'*Harriet*,' I scolded. 'Babies aren't ugly.'

'Oh, pish-posh!' She flapped her free hand, the other clutching the banister. 'You don't need to mind your manners with me, dear. That baby is the ugliest I've laid my eyes on. And I'm old. I've laid my eyes on a lot of babies. That Montgomery one has a face like a block of melted cheese.'

Harriet spoke the truth. The baby had a saggy, pitted little face. But still, I didn't dare agree with her. Mine wasn't out yet. Harriet continued to witter on about the Montgomerys, and how she'd filmed the husband with a suspect-looking package and was thinking about taking the footage down to Constable Smith but couldn't because he'd stopped receiving her visits.

'So I was thinking, you could take it. Hmmm?' she said, arriving at the landing.

'No.'

She grumbled.

Harriet opened the door and gave a nervous titter as my mouth dropped. Sitting on an antique desk was the largest home computer screen I had ever seen. Like a flatscreen TV at a sports bar.

'Oh my god!'

She made noises about it being not so very big and scurried over to the desk, sat down and shook the wireless mouse. The screen lit up and Harriet navigated her way through little boxes and opened new windows while I tried to fathom the level of technology she was proficient in.

'Here it is.' She clicked on a file.

A box flew open on the screen with hundreds and hundreds of files running down the page. Hundreds and hundreds of files with my name on them. I read the file names over Harriet's cardigan-draped shoulder.

'Joe and Emma dig vegetable patch – March twenty-sixth'
'Joe and Emma watch movie – March twenty-eighth'
'Joe hoes herb patch – April second'
'Joe does Zumba – April third'
'Joe and Emma watch movies – April eleventh'
'Joe and Emma . . .'
'Joe and Emma . . .'
'Joe and Emma . . .'

'Harriet!' I cried, upset that a file entitled *Emma sunbathes in the garden – June 15th* meant she'd filmed me basking in my maternity bra and pants. 'You've been filming my whole life!'

'For your security, dear,' she said matter-of-factly.

She twisted in her seat and watched me with watery eyes.

'It's . . .' I looked back at the files, unable to fully grasp that the minutiae of my home life was stored in a bunch of files on a geriatric lady's unreasonably modern computer. 'It's . . . *weird*. And I asked you to stop.' I looked away from a file labelled *Emma measures her belly* and scowled.

'I did stop. I *did*!' she said with childlike insistence. 'You can see there is quite a gap up there.' She waved her thickened, arthritic finger at the screen. 'But then there was that new postman that looked like a Nazi, and Marjorie's daughter's neighbour's gate was wide open one morning and their cat came home with one leg completely shaved, so I—'

'Harriet!' I barked, not wanting to hear why she felt that filming Joe and I *make crêpes on June 12th* or *play Jenga on June 17th* was in any way going to stop a Nazi, cat-shaving, gate-opening postal worker in his criminal tracks.

She swivelled back to the screen, chastened for now. She clicked on a file with that day's date and we waited for it to load. A black window popped up on the screen with a PLAY symbol in the centre.

'Sit, sit.' She waved her hand at a stool in the corner and pressed play.

I grabbed the stool and pulled it up to the desk as close as my belly would allow without taking my eyes from the screen. It showed a wobbly, high angle of the footpath (probably from the very office I was now in) and was focused on a postman opening a gate a few doors up from my cottage and heading out of shot, presumably to post the mail through the slot in the door. How very white supremacist of him.

'That's the postman,' Harriet divulged.

'You don't say.'

Harriet lifted her chin. The postman came out of the property, pulled the gate shut behind him and walked down the footpath.

'He shut the gate,' I said. 'I guess that means he's not a Nazi.'

Harriet grumbled and fast-forwarded. The postman broke into jumpy mail delivery pausing only to pat a cat (pat, not shave, I pointed out to a starchy Harriet) and then he headed speedily out of shot. The screen went blank for a minute and then came to life again from the same high angle but now looking in the other direction at Joe's asparagus bed in my back garden. Harriet stopped fast-forwarding.

'Look at those asparagus!' Harriet's voice from the

playback said with pride, as if the abundant spears were her accomplishment.

The wobbly footage captivated Harriet and a wrinkly smile twitched at the corners of her mouth. The frame jiggled, as if the person filming had been distracted, then panned to the left and framed up on my French doors being opened from the inside. Joe materialised in the open doorway and appeared to be talking to someone inside but I couldn't make anything out through the glass doors. A strategically placed climbing rose in a large pot obscured my view. I say strategically because it had been placed there after I'd thought I was alone one day and a flash of sunlight across a lens had alerted me to the fact that Harriet was documenting me wandering the house in my functional maternity underpants which had elastic challenges. Joe had kindly visited his much-loved garden centre and purchased a plant that didn't drop its leaf, flowered in the summer and encouraged organic bees, or whatever. For me, it was merely a sweet-scented shield from a sweet old lady I was consider-ing getting a restraining order for. On the screen Joe took a step onto the terrace and gestured to the garden. A slim form moved closer to the doorframe but remained half in shadow and half behind the organic bee rose. All I could make out was a slender arm, the side-on outline of a small bust and a flash of blond hair underneath a pale fedora with a dark ribbon. In a futile attempt to see a better image I moved my head from side to side trying to get a look round the plant.

Harriet gave me a strange look.

'Didn't you get a better angle?' I said, annoyed.

'Well I would have if *someone* hadn't placed that climbing perennial in the way.'

On the screen Joe slid his phone out of his shorts pocket, pressed the screen a few times and held it to his ear. He paced the courtyard, said something into the phone then replaced it in his pocket. He turned and looked like he was heading inside, then paused, put his arms out imitating either a fat lady or – I clenched my teeth – a large pregnant girl, and waddled back inside, grinning. He was making fun of me. To some pretty blonde answering, I assumed, to the name of Katy the Cheating Whore-bag.

Harriet's astute gaze weighed heavily.

Joe pulled the French doors shut; there was a brief shadowy movement behind the glass then nothing but the glint of the afternoon sun bouncing off the windows.

Harriet pressed pause and shifted in her chair. I stared at the frozen image of my French doors.

'They were inside for quite a while,' she said gently.

'They left together?'

She nodded, keeping her wet sparkly eyes on me.

'Where'd they go?' I asked weakly, as if Harriet's camera was some radical new model and could reach much further than the edge of the common. Maybe to Joe and Katy's apartment, able to see them tearing their clothes off each other.

'I don't know, dear.' Harriet frowned. 'I ran out of battery.' She gave the camera charging on the desk a peevish look.

I picked at my fingernails and wondered why I felt so . . . so . . . what did I feel?

Harriet studied me.

'I think you missed out on that one, dear. Shame.' She clicked a few buttons, restoring the computer to its desktop screen, a photo of Arthur and her outside the Chelsea Flower Show.

I felt as if I'd been hit in the solar plexus. And I wasn't really sure where that was, exactly, but it sounded serious and anyway, my chest felt tight and heavy.

Missed out?

CHAPTER THIRTY-SIX

The first thing I saw when I opened my front door was a pale fedora with a dark ribbon sitting on the hall table.

In the short walk, OK, waddle (Joe was correct if not offensive) from Harriet's house to mine, a seething dislike for Katy had revealed itself. And by the time I'd clicked my picket gate shut, I'd arrived at the obvious conclusion that the only reason I was filled with such hatred was because I was in love with Joe. And I would never have considered this if Helen hadn't been drunk and put those three previously ungrouped things (him; me; love) in my head in the first place.

On the walk down my front path I'd tapped out a text to Alex. Having realised my feelings for Joe at such an inopportune time (story of my life – the 'inopportune time' seemed to be the only timescale I knew) I needed to make amends with my sister. People were dropping out of my life like coconuts off a palm tree in a storm and, out of everyone, she was one person I needed back. I missed her more than I would one day miss my pelvic floor. I pressed send on the simply worded text 'I'm sorry. I miss you', took a fortifying breath and shut the front door.

'Emma?' Joe's voice carried from the other end of the house.

I tossed my keys next to the horrible hat (it wasn't horrible, it was actually very nice, very on-trend and something my mother would have wanted me to wear) and made my way towards the kitchen. Joe appeared at the other end of the hall looking terribly concerned.

'Where've you been? I've been looking all over.'

'Why?' I said, ignoring how his genuine worry ripped at the edges of my already messed-up heart. And *really*? He'd hardly looked *all* over. I'd been at our much-frequented local pub, home and the next-door neighbour's. What an appalling personal investigator he would make.

'We were worried.'

We? Him and Harlot du Fedora?

Mum appeared at his side. 'Darling, where *have* you been? You've had us all worried!'

Before I could answer, or even enquire as to why Mum was hanging out with Joe and his newly reappointed fiancée, *or* why she was holding my favourite maternity leggings and a large pair of scissors, another figure approached from behind. I arranged my face into one of polite interest so as to face this wheat-haired, fashionable-hat-wearing, careless-with-tender-hearts whore-bag with a malfunctioning moral compass and not have her see my current state of heart and mind. But I needn't have bothered. Because Mum and Joe stepped apart and the approaching figure was my sister.

My mouth fell open.

Alex gave an expectant smile.

Mum gave an expectant smile.

Joe gave an expectant smile.

I didn't. My mouth was busy making the 'O' shape.

'I miss you too,' Alex said, holding up her phone.

She glanced at my protruding stomach. Nobody said anything. They were waiting for my reaction, but unfortunately for them I had none. I'd made it halfway down the hall and it seemed like that was as far as I was going to get. If my sister wanted to engage she was going to have to make the next six steps by herself.

Which she did. At flying speed.

Before I was able to fully adjust my reality – no whorebag; sister here; must apologise for abhorrent behaviour; Joe looks nice in that shade of blue; was Alex wearing a *wedding band* (?!); get those bloody scissors away from Mum – I was in her tight embrace. I couldn't think of what to say. How could I convey that the last few months I'd barely been coping and had been trying to hide it from everyone? That I'd been living on the very stressful edge of losing control? Control of my mind, control of my life, control of my bladder at times? That the one person I wanted around, the one person I knew would make it all better, was her? That I'd never forgive myself for behaving like an ungrateful psycho when she'd only ever wanted to help me? For not being a good sister; a good friend? For not being a support on the other end of the line, skype or text like she always, *always* had been for me? How could I let her know all of that, and also that I was sorry?

'I'm sorry,' I blubbed, clasping my hands across her back.

She smelt like flowers and grass and a coconutty shampoo.

'I'm sorry too,' she said from somewhere inside my pony-tail. She squeezed me tighter. With my feet standing far enough away to allow room for my stomach, the top half of my body bent forward in the embrace and the weight of the hanging baby belly straining my lower back, I was endur-ing a fair amount of discomfort. Had I not been pregnant I would have looked like one of those unusual people who are so worried about their genitals touching when they hug that they keep their lower half as far away from the other person as gravity and physics will allow. Like hugging over the top of a wine bar without the wine bar. When the pain got too much I planted the heels of my hands on her shoulders and hefted myself to an upright position.

'How are you even here?' I asked, looking over her shoulder to where Joe was grinning and Mum was wiping away a tear.

'By the magic of Virgin Airlines,' she said, rubbing my belly. 'Oh my god, you are so *big.*'

I grabbed her left hand. 'And what exactly is this?' I said, indicating a thin band sitting alongside an engagement ring.

'Ah, that.' Alex pulled her hand back and fiddled with the rings. 'I got married.'

Over cups of tea and slices of cake, Alex told us she and Cal had snuck off to a register office in Singapore and just got it done. No enormous guest list at a castle; no amuse-bouches, personalised gift bags or textured linen invites. No ice sculptor, no duck terrine. Apparently the day I'd been blubbing to Joe on the common about missing my sister was the day she'd got married. The sting I felt at this realisation took my breath away. I cried again. Alex cried. Mum cried and handed out scented tissues. Even Joe asked for one but only because 'a bee or something had flown into his eye'. I'd made a suggestion that perhaps it was a passing red-footed falcon and was met with scorn. It was the next day, while Alex was nursing a hangover at the airport and marvelling at her sudden 'married' status, that she got a call from Joe.

'You just rang her up?' I said to Joe. 'How'd you even get the number?'

'From me,' Mum said.

'So you knew about this?'

'Everyone knew,' Joe replied.

'Everyone? Even Sinead and Uncle Mike?'

'Yep,' Alex said. 'I was supposed to turn up at Uncle Mike's for your baby shower and surprise you.'

'But darling, you ruined the plan by being financially buggered then sulking about it and storming out,' Mum said.

'I wasn't sulking,' I said, feeling a sulk coming on. 'Anyway, Millie got stung by a bee.' I turned to Joe. 'An actual bee, not a falcon.'

He furnished me with a V sign.

'And, darling, this ice cream problem? And your financial situation?' Mum tut-tutted. 'We still need to talk about that.'

I avoided her gaze.

'I'm not mad, I'm just worried.'

'Well, I don't want you to be worried. I'm going to sort it all out, OK?'

'How?'

I helped myself to another wedge of cake. 'I'll be fine, Mum. I really will, OK? I have a plan.'

'What?'

'To eat this cake.'

Mum administered herself some whisky. I turned back to Alex's iPad and flicked once again through her photos of the register office.

'Do you mind, Mum?' I asked. 'That you missed it?'

'No, I don't think so, darling,' Mum said, smoothing down Alex's hair. 'I'm relieved I won't be getting any more emails from that Lucinda woman.' Mum shuddered. 'It's a shame you didn't have a wedding, though. You've missed out on the gift registry.'

Alex screwed her face up. 'We wouldn't have done that anyway. We were going to get everyone to donate to charity.'

Mum looked at Alex like she'd said she was moving to Cambodia and was planning on getting there on a raft made of rusty kettles and almond nougat. '*Charity*?'

'Yes, Mum. The act of giving to those less fortunate? We don't need a load of pretty plates and dessert forks.'

'Yes, but when you eventually settle down you'll want nice things for your house, surely?'

I extracted myself from the ensuing argument about niceties versus necessities and made myself busy in the kitchen, stealing glances at Joe interacting comfortably with my family. He laughed frequently, the grin lighting up his face. Oh, that handsome face! When did he become so, *so* handsome?

Having missed out on the barbecue at Uncle Mike and Sinead's because of the pathetic search-and-rescue attempt (I mean, *really*. Where did they look? Under the cushions?), I cobbled together a mixed antipasto plate (one's cupboard must always be 'with olive'); which we attacked like starved cats, then sat about lounging in the living room sipping gin and tonics (Mum and Alex), a beer (Joe) and fizzy water (sigh . . . me). Alex had hovered around me as I moved about the kitchen; she'd trotted at my side when I went to the bedroom to hide my second-favourite pair of leggings. On the sofa she pretty much sat on my knee. I felt like I had my own moon.

'God, it just doesn't seem real. I'm going to be an aunty.' Alex gave my stomach another of her long, wondrous looks.

I was starting to feel like an oddity.

Joe got up from the sofa, crossed to the kitchen and opened the fridge. 'And I'm going to be Cool Uncle Joe.' He retrieved a beer, slammed the fridge door shut and popped the bottle open with a hiss. 'The go-to guy for advice on gardens, graphics and girls.' He beamed.

Catherine Bennetto

'Girls? Seriously?' I laughed.

He made an ugly face. It was still handsome.

'Right.' Mum extracted her long limbs from the arm-chair. 'I'm going home. I'm having my colours done in the morning.'

'I thought you had your colours done ages ago?' Alex said.

'Yes, but as we advance in maturity—'

'You mean, age?' I said.

Mum stood over me. '*Advance* in *maturity*—'

'Get old.'

'The skin's tone and texture changes, and it becomes essential to get your colours adjusted.'

'Mum, you might need to look up the word *essential*,' Alex said.

Mum sighed a here-we-go-again type sigh.

'Clean drinking water is essential.' Alex held up a finger for each point. 'Equality for women of all nationalities across the world is essential. Food, shelter and safe, supportive communities are essential. Making sure your blouse is the right shade of peach for your skin tone is certainly *not* essential.'

We looked at Mum. Her attention was elsewhere. Evening dress racks at Harrods, perhaps.

'Isabel Marant has a new peach range ...' Mum tapped her chin with a bordeaux nail. She snapped back into focus. 'OK, darlings, must go.'

Joe stood, ever the gentleman.

'Don't get up, Emma,' Mum said.

'I wasn't going to. Have you seen the size of me?'

Mum made an 'I most certainly have' kind of facial expression. 'And please try not to go into labour this weekend. I'm breaking in new jeans, so will be unavailable to assist.'

'I'll keep my legs crossed,' I said.

Alex giggled and rubbed my stomach playing the 'is it a bum or a head' game while Joe walked Mum to the front door and agreed with her denim 'training' schedule.

'I can't believe he just called you.' I passed Alex a pillowcase. 'Just . . . rang you up.'

'Yup,' Alex said, holding a pillow under her chin and feeding it into one of Grandma's faded floral pillowcases.

'And you got on a plane right away?'

'Pretty much.' Alex plumped the pillow, tossed it on the bed then took the corner of the matching floral sheet I held out to her.

Alex liked her bed made military-style, with proper hospital corners and not a single crease anywhere. It was an effort in anyone's world but at nearly nine months pregnant I was limited in my movements. Like a rhino doing yoga, it just wasn't physically sensible. We pulled up the thin summer duvet, each holding a top corner and lining it up so the exact same amount fell down over each side of the bed. It was nearly 11 p.m. and, even under the tropical tan, Alex was starting to look a little peaky with jet lag.

'So what did he say *exactly*?'

Alex groaned and began unpacking her backpack into an empty chest of drawers.

'He *said*,' she glared at me emphatically, letting me know she had already told me this a hundred times and now I was just being annoying. 'That he thought you were unhappy and that I could make you happy.'

'That's it?'

'That's it.'

'And that made you come home? Just because of me?'

'Yep.'

I stood at the end of the bed and watched Alex unload colourful tops and rustic-looking leather flip-flops, feeling truly humbled. I marvelled again at her presence. I hadn't seen her since Christmas a year and a half ago, yet it never seemed that long because we spoke, emailed or texted nearly every day.

'Joe really cares about you,' Alex said, shutting the drawers and pushing her backpack under the bed.

'I care about him.' I plopped despondently down on the bed but a sharp look from Alex had me hoisting myself off quick smart.

'Is there anything there?'

'With Joe?'

She nodded.

'Oh god, no.' I moved towards the door. 'No way. He's just a lodger. I mean, we're friendly, of course, and he's a great guy, obviously but no, he's . . . just a lodger,' I trailed off.

'OK then.' Alex eyed me as if she hadn't believed a word. Then she clapped her hands together and hustled me out the door. 'Right, I have to go to bed.'

'I'm really, really glad you came.'

'Yes, yes, me too.' She pushed me into the hall and shut the door. 'Night!' she called, and it sounded like she was already under the covers.

I turned and jumped at the sight of Joe.

'Well, I'm going to head to bed,' he said, yawning and stretching.

His t-shirt rode up and I caught a glimpse of the taut region below his belly button. Sparse tufts of hair peeking out from his waistband did tingly, fluttery things to my stomach. He smiled and rested against the wall opposite. With his softened, tired eyes and his end-of-day stubble he looked beautiful and familiar. I was shocked at the frisson of desire that suddenly tore through my chest and willed myself not to blush.

'Thank you for ...' I tried to find the right words. Joe had listened, *really* listened, to me. If he'd known that my sister being here would bring me such a sense of security and stillness, then was he able to read how I felt about him? I felt exposed. 'Just ... just thanks.'

'You're welcome,' he said with a weary yet generous smile.

We stood opposite each other, our backs to the walls. The gap between us felt charged. Opportunity to express our feelings hung in the air. I waited with rising tension in my chest. Joe's features became intense. His lips twitched and his brow furrowed, as if he was on the verge of saying something. But his face relaxed and he smiled again with soft, tired eyes.

'Goodnight.' His voice sounded heavy in the back of his

throat. He swallowed, his Adam's apple bobbing up and down.

I sensed a note of resolution, of a decision being made. He opened his arms for a hug.

'Night,' I said, and buried my face in his chest.

We lingered in each other's arms, and somehow it felt as if we were saying goodbye. He was letting me go. A terrible sadness tugged at my insides. He kissed the top of my head then pulled away. He scuffed his feet up the stairs and I padded slowly to my bedroom with a lump in my throat.

CHAPTER THIRTY-SEVEN

The aroma of sizzling breakfast-y foods drew me from my slumber. I wrestled into a maternity bra (nobody should be subjected to a loose boob at breakfast, especially not when trembling poached eggs were about), replaced my pyjama vest and tottered down the hall in pursuit of bacon. I found Joe in boxers and a t-shirt flipping and stirring, boiling and brewing.

'Morning!' he said in a cheerful boom. 'Tea? Pancakes? Bacon? Hash browns? Eggs? I'm in a big breakfast kind of mood!'

'Yes, thanks.'

'To what?' He shook a pan on the element.

'All of it.'

'Brilliant!' Joe got busy with tea bags and kettles and spatulas and whisks.

During one of the very wee hours of the night, one that no sensible person should be witness to, I had lain in bed informing the baby that it was an unacceptable time to thud me repeatedly in the spine and if this was an indication of its forthcoming behaviour we would be having stern words. In between the addressings, I mulled over my recently unearthed feelings for Joe. Having been expressed aloud by Helen and alluded to by Alex, the reality had slammed me in the chest and I couldn't look at him in any other way. Affection pricked the hairs on my arms as Joe dropped an egg.

'Bugger,' he said.

And then another.

'Bugger mach two.' He grinned over his shoulder then turned and concentrated on the next egg.

I had decided, in those wee small hours that reason seems to avoid, that I must tell Joe I'd given him terrible advice. That he was not to give Katy another shot. Absolutely not. He needed to stay here with me and eat brownies. Indefinitely, if possible. Having found out the hushed phone calls behind closed doors were to my sister, and not to Katy, I knew I had to act fast. I'd made firm plans to raise this topic at breakfast. To come straight to the point. Lay it all on the table with not a dilly nor a dally. I was going to be precise and forthright and do it. Immediately.

'What does erudite mean?' I said, slipping into a chair with grace. That's not true; I basically had to winch myself down. And, if I'm honest, a little fart came out. And if I'm honest, it wasn't little.

Joe shuddered his repulsion.

'I think it means "good in the wind",' he said.

'Huh?'

'You know, like those cycle racing helmets that make you look like a buzzard with its head on backwards.'

'That's *aerodynamic*.'

'Oh, right.' He poured milk, stirred, added sugar, stirred. 'What's the word you said again?'

'Erudite. I always thought it was either something to do with being Aryan and a little bit Nazi, or similar to that other word. You know, the French one. The one that means uniformly cut cucumber and carrots and such.'

Tea arrived in front of me with hasty placement, the contents swishing back and forth like a toffee-coloured tsunami. Joe shot back to the oven and checked on something. I took a sip and continued to talk while Joe made hectic little tracks from fridge to stove to pantry.

'I was talking to one of the dads at Archie's party and he said Archie was an "erudite young lad" and I agreed, thinking they were saying it because he has blond hair and blue eyes just like Hitler always wanted. And then I wondered if he was comparing him to a cut-up cucumber, saying he was neat and organised or something. Then I realised he could have been calling him *anything* and I'd just agreed. He could have been saying he was a stuck-up little arse but using a big posh word, so I went to look it up but Sinead needed help getting Jess down from the neighbour's roof and I forgot.'

'How do you spell it?' Joe said, picking up his phone, his finger poised.

'Dunno.'

'Air-rooh-dyte' Joe muttered, jabbing at his phone.

'Seriously, you guys?' Alex arrived in the doorway.

She hobbled across the room stiff-legged and baggy-eyed.

'It's E-R-U-D-I-T-E. And it means to have great knowledge or to be well educated.' She drew up a chair opposite me and sat down. 'Oh, the early morning irony.'

Joe gasped. 'I take offence.'

'It was being offered freely.' Alex rested her cheek on her propped-up hand, her whole body sagging. ''S there coffee?'

'For nice people, yes,' Joe replied.

Alex swung herself out of the chair and lumbered round Joe with lethargic limbs while he made observations about her bedhead hair, twisted pyjamas, the amount of sugar she put in her coffee, her morning breath, general attitude et cetera. I sipped my tea, listened to the two of them and gazed out at my sunny, bee-buzzing garden thinking lovely thoughts.

Joe chatted during breakfast in an overly jovial mood. I wondered what had got into him. Perhaps his coffee-to-calorie intake was a little out. Alex and he seemed to have got to know each other extremely well over the past week of furtive 'surprise Emma' negotiations and laughed like chummy siblings. Upon hearing about Joe making cloak-and-dagger calls to Vanuatu, and Alex's version of events leading up to my arrival in the hallway the day before, a mantle of happiness settled over me. I couldn't have been more content if you'd delivered me Matt Damon (pre having kids and ageing two decades) on a plate.

'More coffee?' Joe said, clearing the table.

'No thanks. I'm going to jump in the shower.' Alex delivered her plate and a few breakfast-y items to the bench. 'What're the plans for today?'

'Walk on the common, visit Sinead and the kids, late pub lunch or something?' I turned to Joe. 'You coming?'

'Actually, I'm busy.'

'Busy?' Even the notion was ludicrous.

He made brisk swipes at the tabletop with a cloth.

'I'm . . . seeing Katy today.'

A pause hung in the air.

'I've taken your advice.' He stopped wiping, stood straight and smiled. It seemed forced. Or did I just want it to?

'My advice?' I was aware that my voice sounded weird and that Alex had stopped on her way to the shower and was studying my reaction.

'Yeah; you said we should give it another go, and I thought about it for a while and realised you were right. I do need to move on. I can't be your lodger forever.' He turned away and fussed with some dishes in the sink. The word 'lodger' spiked at my chest. 'So I called her this morning and we're going to have lunch and . . .' He turned back and fixed me with a strange stare. 'And just see.'

I couldn't bear to look him in the eye, so I looked lower down then realised I'd focused on his groin and got in a bit of a flap. Heat rose up my neck. I looked out the kitchen window.

'Well, that's great,' I said, trying to muster some enthusiasm but failing dismally.

'Yeah.'

I picked at my nails.

'Great,' I repeated. 'I hope it goes well.'

Joe fiddled with a tea towel. Alex hovered in the doorway.

'You want first shower, or shall I?' I said to her.

She made an 'all yours' gesture. I glanced back at Joe, gave him a cursory smile and trundled to the bathroom.

When the door clicked shut behind Joe an hour later, Alex rounded on me.

'There is something there.'

'Where?' I looked round the room.

'Don't play dumb with me. With you and Joe.'

'Don't be ridiculous. Have you seen the baby bag Mum bought me?' I held up the offensive item. A bit too crocodile skin, a bit too gold detailing.

'Avoidance is not the way to deal with issues.'

'It's worked for me so far.'

'Oh it has, has it?'

I thought about challenging her and giving her all the ways in which denial and avoidance had worked; you know, getting my money back from Ned, talking to Joe about how I felt, pushing him towards his ex, baby due in eleven days and no real clue as to what to do with it when it got here, my financial condition, the doughnut addiction, the lies to Mum, the lies to Uncle Mike, the now-resolved sisterly quarrel over something petty.

'No, not really.'

I dropped the baby bag; Alex dropped her stern expression.

'Come on. We'll talk about it on the common. I need to walk off that breakfast.'

And talk we did. Alex began at the beginning. I was irresponsible to forget to take the pill; irresponsible not to notice my missing periods; irresponsible to quit my job and have nothing to move on to when I was going to have a baby; irresponsible to allow Ned access to my bank account. I was bloody lucky that Grandma had died (she worded it far less callously but I'm recapping quickly for your benefit) and left me half a cottage; bloody lucky I had got a job on Archie's movie; bloody lucky Joe came into my life, a fool to push him towards his ex, a fool to think I didn't have feelings for him; a fool for not getting Ned to sell the ice cream vans; a fool for not telling Mum about my financial situation and a fool for not realising my family only wanted to help. I think overall I came out predominantly as an irresponsible fool. I refuted everything and pointed out a cloud that looked like a cock and balls.

In the afternoon we popped over to Uncle Mike and Sinead's, where I endured a humiliating family discussion about my economic affairs. Complete with spreadsheets, austere expressions and solemn head-nodding. But at least me being poor, pathetic and pregnant meant Uncle Mike had put aside his anger over the Archie zombie guts-and-bra romance film deception and was instead focusing on solving my 'situation', as Mum continually referred to it. I kept trying to get the heat off me and onto the very real problem that was Jess's new haircut. That morning Sinead had dropped Jess at the hairdresser's, then taken the other three kids to a café and returned to find that, unsupervised, her 6-year-old daughter had requested a mohican. And the obliging yet dim hairdresser had given her a number two round the sides then applied electric-green hairspray to the remaining three-inch spike. But my efforts were fruitless, and everyone agreed that Jess did indeed look a bit like one of Gwen Stefani's sons but it would grow back. And money doesn't. So I should really be concentrating on more pressing issues. Impatient and wanting to get home to see how Joe's lunch with Katy had gone, I agreed to putting in a call to Ned in the next couple of days (for which Mum would be present – oh cringe, oh humiliation) and to accepting a loan from Uncle Mike and Sinead I *knew* they had no intention of asking to be paid back. It made me feel pitiable and degraded and about fifteen years old. Alex's attempt at rallying my spirits on the way home didn't help either.

'What's this poem book Joe was telling me about? He thinks you could really go somewhere with it.'

'He's an idiot. It's a bunch of silly poems I wrote when I was a teenager. I wish he would shut up about it. And you can too.'

'All righty then.'

We arrived home around five o'clock and an unashamed rummage through Joe's room and belongings told me he hadn't been home. Alex tried to engage me in conversation about baby names, breast-feeding and the environmental perils of disposable nappies, but sensing my distraction, suggested going out.

'Go out where?' I said, looking in the cupboards, uninspired.

'Into town!' she implored. 'To dinner. To a bar. Just *out!*'

I looked at her, looked pointedly at my stomach then back at her. Was she mad? I went back to cupboard-scanning.

'Oh, come on, I haven't been out anywhere that has required footwear for over a year. Every meal comes with rice and canned peas and the only drink we have contains fifty-per-cent-proof rum that can dissolve your nose hairs. Please take me out? It could be your last chance before the baby comes, you know.'

I stopped. That was true. Visions of me stuck at home for the next eighteen years flashed through my head. London as I knew it might no longer exist. Commuters would travel via rocket boots; footpaths would be conveyor belts. Cars would be replaced with hover vehicles; there'd be floating juice bars and mini-meditation booths along the traffic passages. Roads would be turned into green spaces where children played and streams filled with spawning organic salmon could be paddled in. Alex was right. I had to get out in familiar grey London while I still could.

'Oh my god, was London always so filthy?' Alex asked for about the twentieth time since we'd left Wimbledon.

'You wanted to go out,' I said, picking my way along the busy Portobello Road. Heat rose from the pavement and the smell of beer and aftershave wafted out of the open pub windows and doors. It was an exemplary British summer evening where spirits were high and dress hems were higher. Helen and Douglas were meeting us for dinner. Douglas was bringing his girlfriend, Jemima.

'I don't remember it being this filthy, though,' Alex said, stepping over what could have been a fallen kebab, chicken curry or early evening vomit.

'You don't have alcopop-laced vomit on the footpaths in Vanuatu?'

'We don't have footpaths,' Alex said, skipping out of the way of four leery young males who were kind-hearted enough to grab their crotches and shake them at her so she felt attractive and worthy.

Inside the restaurant friendly waiters and waitresses seated us with the others, asked when I was due, made sure I got an extra cushion for my back and said they could make any of the cocktails 'virgin'.

'Oooh, I'll have a virgin piña colada then, please,' I said with a grin.

'And I'll have a slutty one,' Helen said.

Alex ordered a complicated-sounding cocktail. Douglas and Jemima ordered a bottle of Cabernet Sauvignon. Contrary to my earlier reservations, being out in London on a vibrant summer evening, pregnant and unable to partake in the consumption of slutty cocktails, was rather enjoyable. Jemima was an intriguing creature. Expansive grey eyes behind outsized, non-ironic glasses rested steadily on each person as they spoke, absorbing the conversation and assessing it before pink, heart-shaped lips gave blunt, yet not untrue, observations.

'I'm a lighting designer,' she said to my 'so what do you do' question.

'Like, for concerts?' I said, trying to hide my surprise. She hardly seemed the type to chat to Steve Tyler about stadium gigs and where he'd like his shaft. Of light.

'No. Private homes. Galleries. Installations.' She sipped at her wine.

'Oh, that's cool. I didn't know there was such a thing.'

'There is,' she said.

I was interested to ask more, but she turned to Alex and asked about the corrupt nature of fund allocation within the aid sector. I quite liked her. She was so blunt she went beyond offensive and became fascinating. Douglas was smitten.

After a couple of food-, conversation- and virgin-cocktail-filled hours I was ready to go home.

'Can we just have one drink at the bar before we go?' Alex said.

I gave her a look.

'Oh please, please, *please*?' she said, her hands taking up the begging clutch under her chin again. 'The only bars I go to have no walls and broken banana pallets for furniture.'

'That sounds better than here,' Jemima said.

Alex used her begging eyes again.

'But I'll look like a desperate pregnant chav if I hang out in the bar,' I said. 'I'll be Katie Price or Kerry Katona or someone from *TOWIE*.'

'You're not orange enough to be any of them,' Douglas said.

'You will look out of place, though,' Jemima said.

'I could go another drink,' Helen said, her eyes following a group of hot hipsters moving towards the bar area.

'Please?' Alex said, expanding her eyes in an eager plead. 'Just one, then I'll come home with you.'

As soon as we hit the bar Helen disappeared into a clutch of hipsters-by-number, buttoned-up blokes. Alex wove a twisty-turny track through the crowd to the bar. I planted my feet firmly in the crowded space and took in our surroundings. It was like being in a 1980s Elton John hallucination. Heavy velvet drapes framed renaissance-style busts. Girls in short skirts perched on gilt-edged chairs upholstered in thick baroque, jewel-hued fabric. While Jemima pointed out lighting techniques to an adoring Douglas, I perused the bar taking in the young, the hip and the 'working in PR' when my gaze landed on a familiar face.

'Oh my god! It's Katy!' I said, gripping Alex's arm with clawed fingers.

'Katy Perry?' Alex accepted her pink-toned cocktail from the barman and swivelled her head. 'Where?'

'No!' I ducked behind Alex as Katy turned her head. 'It's Katy, Joe's fiancée Katy. Quick, hide me.'

'Who's Joe?' Jemima said, sipping viscous clear liquid from a thin straw.

'Emma's lodger,' Douglas offered, and at my look added, 'and friend.'

'Oh.' Jemima tracked my gaze. 'Why do you need to hide from your lodger's fiancée?'

Alex leant forward, her evening on cocktails becoming evident. 'Because Emma loves her lodger.'

'I do not!' I said.

Jemima's interest was displayed by the rising of her fawn-coloured eyebrows.

'Which one is she?' Alex said.

'The blonde. The really pretty one in the middle of that big group over there.'

Alex moved to get a better view. 'They're all really pretty.'

'Don't move, she might see me!' I dipped my head behind Alex's bare, tanned shoulder.

'I thought you hadn't actually met her,' Alex said.

'Oh,' I straightened. 'No, I haven't.'

'Then how do you know that's her?' Jemima said.

'Oh . . . I just do,' I said, taking on a shifty demeanour.

Alex fixed me with a demanding stare.

'I saw photos of her on his laptop,' I mumbled. 'But only because his computer was there, open. Right in front of me.'

'You're lying,' Alex said.

'OK, it was in his room and I was snooping but—'

Alex tutted. Douglas shook his head.

'That's an encroachment on the tenant–landlord contract,' Jemima said. 'He can sue.'

I turned back to Katy.

'Are you sure that's her, Emma?' Douglas said, pushing up his glasses and blinking at the sight of Katy getting awfully close to a bearded guy with a fringe so gelled and sloping it looked like the roof of the Guggenheim. 'Maybe, ah ... maybe that's not her?'

'Oh, that beardy man is flirting with her,' I said. 'She's touching his arm! She's taking a sip of his drink! Douglas, go and stop her!'

Douglas looked at me like I was being absurd. Jemima sipped and observed.

'You're obsessed,' Alex said. 'She's just hanging out with some friends. I think this might be your issue.'

'What are you trying to say?' I said, turning to Alex.

'I'm saying that—'

'She's kissing one of them,' Jemima said tonelessly.

Alex spun round. I peeped out from behind her. Katy had moved against a shadowy wall with the Guggenheim guy and was snogging the face off him.

'What a slut.' Alex shook her head.

'Your lodger is probably single now,' Jemima said. 'Although if she's his type I'd say you certainly aren't.'

CHAPTER THIRTY-EIGHT

'You have to tell him. You have to tell him immediately before he gets more emotionally involved with Katy,' Alex said as the cab travelled the darkened edge of Wimbledon Common. I looked through the eerie trees and thought of headless horsemen and spiders and rapists.

'She's his fiancée. I think they might already be emotionally involved.'

'You know what I mean,' she said.

I'd been vacillating between telling Joe and not telling Joe. Why would I not want to tell him? Because I didn't want to hurt him. Because I didn't want to admit I'd been through his computer. Because I didn't want him to see the hope in my eyes as I told him, the hope that he may reject her and pick me. The lights were still on inside when the taxi pulled up. Joe was on the sofa, his legs stretched out and his feet on the coffee table, tinkering on his laptop. With his jeans rolled up and a cup of tea beside him, he was a picture of calm contentment.

'How was your night?' he asked, glancing up from his computer.

'Great!' Alex replied. 'I'm going to make a herbal tea. Anyone?'

Joe shook his head.

'So how was lunch with Katy?' I said, feigning casualness while I slipped into an armchair. Joe looked up from his screen, genuinely relaxed.

'It was good.' Recollection twinkled in his eyes. He went back to his computer.

'Great.' I glanced at Alex in the kitchen and made a *what now?* face. She indicated with mime, expressive eyebrows and jabbing hands what looked to be a diminutive Greek tragedy. I made an *I don't want to* face, then added a *why don't you do it?* one, and she made some elaborate arm and face physicality I couldn't decipher. I shrugged.

She jabbed a finger from me to him and mouthed *just fucking do it!* and I poked my tongue out at her.

'Joe?' I began.

He looked up. He seemed so happy on the sofa with his toes twitching to some unheard rhythm. He looked at peace. I was going to ruin it. A blow like this could wound. I had to be tactful, sensitive and kind. I would approach it gently; make it a delicate, featherlight, wispy kind of blow.

'I saw Katy kissing a guy with a beard and a fringe that did this.' I mimed the Guggenheim course of the fringe.

Alex buried her face in her hands. I guessed I wasn't built for 'wispy'.

Joe blinked. 'Katy had a networking event with some new clients,' he replied simply.

I thought about the men she was with and wondered what kind of clients they were and if they were in some kind of Beardy Man Business. A Business of Beards.

'She was certainly "networking" when I saw her.' I did the finger quote thing and immediately regretted it. 'Sorry,' I muttered.

Joe blinked again. 'You're wrong,' he said.

'I'm not wrong,' I said, making my voice gentle. 'I saw her. We both did.' I indicated towards Alex.

Joe shifted to look at her and she nodded sadly. Joe looked back at me, his face pale and tense.

'You're wrong,' he said again.

'I'm not,' I replied. 'I'm really sorry.'

'But . . .' he shook his head in confusion. 'You don't even know what she looks like.'

'I do, actually,' I said, shame colouring my cheeks.

'How?'

I dropped my gaze to my fidgeting fingers. 'I went through the photos on your laptop.'

Joe snapped his computer shut and tossed it to the side. His face darkened.

'You did *what?*'

'It was just open; I didn't really think about what I was doing, I just looked at the photos. Nothing else, I swear,' I said in a hurried jumble.

Joe stood. 'I thought you had more respect for people's

privacy than that,' he said, his gaze and voice hard.

He stalked behind the sofa and faced the garden. His hands worked into angry little clenches.

'Respecting privacy?' I pushed myself out of the armchair and followed him, shooting a *help me* look to Alex, who made a palms-up *how?* gesture, tea bags dangling from one upturned hand.

I stood behind Joe and tried to keep my tone light and non-accusatory. 'You can't really talk about "respecting people's privacy" when you've been through all my diaries, now can you?'

'That's different,' he spat, still facing the garden.

'How, exactly?'

'They're just kids' stuff. Stupid poems.' He spun to face me. 'I'm talking about a grown-up relationship here. Something *you* don't seem to know much about.'

I faltered. Joe had never uttered an unkind word. Not even the first time he spoke of Katy and the cheating. I took a steadying breath. Joe was hurting. He didn't mean what he was saying and I needed to get the situation under control. I allowed myself a brief moment of self-congratulation. I really was being quite mature. How extraordinary.

'Look, Joe, you're getting angry at the wrong person.' I kept my voice calm. 'It's not me who—'

'I can't believe I can't trust you.' He threw his hands up in the air. 'How do I know you're not lying about seeing Katy?'

God. He was being so irrational.

'Why would I lie about *that*?'

'Oh, I don't know,' he said in a nasty voice. 'Maybe you're not happy so you don't want anyone else to be. Maybe you're jealous that I'm moving on and you're not.' He paced and threw his arms around like a madman. 'Maybe ...'

Alex took the opportunity to slip out of the room, throwing me a sympathetic look as she went.

'Joe—'

'You know, you just wobble around doing your own thing, giving out advice like you are some kind of authority on the subject of relationships.' He waddled back and forth, imitating me in an unflattering manner. If the atmosphere hadn't been so fraught I might have giggled. '"*Get back together with her*", "*Don't get back with her*". "*Katy's a whore-bag*", "*You need to move on*". You spout all this shit but you don't even know what you're talking about!'

'Joe, I don't understand why you're so angry with me.' My voice cracked.

'Because you don't even know her and you're telling me all this "Katy was kissing someone else" crap. Why're you telling me this?' He stopped pacing and stared at me, his eyes passionate and wild.

'Because ... because you're my friend and I – I don't understand ... Why do you care *why* I'm telling you?'

'WHY DO *YOU* CARE?' Joe's booming voice startled me.

I bit my lip to keep from crying.

He stormed into the kitchen and grabbed his keys and phone out of the fruit bowl where I'd constantly asked him not to keep them. Dirty keys next to nectarines? It was unhygienic. When he walked back past me his eyes looked sad and his voice was quiet.

'Why *do* you care? I'm just the "fucking lodger", aren't I?'

He stamped out of the room and up the stairs. I stayed in the same position, paralysed by shock. A minute later he clomped back down the stairs and the front door slammed. Alex arrived in the living room where I was still standing.

'Are you OK?' she said, putting a tanned arm round my shoulders.

I shook my head, tears spilling.

CHAPTER THIRTY-NINE

Joe didn't come home that night. I was sure because I hadn't slept a wink. I tossed and turned and went to the bathroom and ate crackers dipped in a tub of recently delivered Ned and Sophie's Chocolate Keep-It-Chipper (all proceeds go to anti-bullying) and tossed and turned and went back to the ice cream with a giant serving spoon. Then finally it was 5.30 a.m. (a barely acceptable time to say it was 'tomorrow') and therefore I could get up and start fretting that Joe really hadn't come home. After I'd been up for a couple of hours and had nibbled my way through half a loaf of bread, Alex emerged from the bedroom with her backpack.

'I've got to get the nine fifteen from St Pancras. How long will it take me to get there? What tubes do I get?'

Alex was travelling to Leeds to break the news to Cal's parents that they were already married and there would be no castle wedding. I gave her a brief reminder of the tube connections she'd known her whole life but had now forgotten, while making her a cup of tea. Weak, no milk.

'When will you be back?' I asked, handing over the tea in a yellow mug. Alex's favourite colour was sunshine yellow. Like her temperament. She sipped the tea, flinching at the heat.

'I'm just there for two nights. You going to be OK?'

'Oh yeah,' I said, my voice catching in my throat. 'I'm fine. I just need a little afternoon nap. I didn't sleep very well last night.'

Alex gave me a knowing look. I met her stare with an attempt at obliviousness but was unable to sustain it. I dropped the charade.

'I don't know what to do,' I said.

'You need to tell him how you feel.'

I widened my eyes and shook my head.

'Then you need to get over it and just focus on having this baby.' She looked at me with pity.

Pity? I hated pity.

'I think he knows how you feel and I think he's feeling confused.'

'So am I.' I sat forlornly on a dining chair.

'If you don't know what you want then you need to let him go.'

I picked at the edge of the table.

Alex glanced at her watch. 'Look, I have to go. I'll call you as soon as I'm up there. Let me know what happens when he comes back.'

'What if he doesn't?'

'He will. His clothes are all here. And his laptop.'

Practical as ever, Alex was. No confidence-rousing 'he can't live without you – he'll be back to declare his love'. Just 'he needs his stuff – he'll be back'.

The panic in my chest heightened. I wanted him to come back and I also didn't. I didn't want to have an awkward conversation about feelings. I just wanted everything back to the way it was. Alex left with promises to call and last-minute tube connection checks.

And then I was alone. Again.

I spent the rest of the day in a state of anxious anticipation. I tried to fool myself that I wasn't waiting for Joe's return by busying myself with acts of cleaning and sorting. While I was in Anglesey Charlie had delivered a gorgeous sleigh cot he'd had made out of sustainable wood. He and Joe had set it up in the corner of my room as a surprise. I fussed with the flannelette sheets and pastel blankets sitting folded on top of the natural fibre mattress, my mind racing over Joe's possible whereabouts. Was he with Katy? Was she convincing him I was a deluded liar? Was he breaking up with her, and would he come flying back into the house, his grin back on, dimple in full 'dimp' and make a bowl of popcorn? Did he hate me? Was he justified if he did?

Around dinnertime I heated a frozen pizza. Then at around ten o'clock, when I figured Joe would definitely need to come back home and get fresh clothes, I engaged myself with sorting the presents from the baby shower while keeping a hyper-alert ear on the front door. Not knowing the sex of the baby, I had been given white, green and lemon-yellow baby items. I objected to the lemon yellow. It made babies look like pupae. I made pointless little piles by colour. Then by age range. Then by item. Then grabbed the lot and shoved them back in an oversized Mothercare bag. I eventually conceded my front door vigil was a futile exercise and went to bed and fell asleep immediately.

At 1.34 a.m. my eyes flew open and I was so startlingly awake I thought I must have been woken by something sinister. I lay in the dark listening for the sound of a Nazi postal rapist creeping down the hall with his electric shaver but heard nothing bar the gentle hum of midnight traffic. I'd had a restless few hours' sleep with dreams involving love triangles with Joe and Katy and Alex telling me she had to go back to Vanuatu for cocktail hour while I was in labour. I got up for a wee and a snack. After squeezing out a pathetic dribble in the bathroom I waddled down the hall and felt a pang of sad longing as I passed the stairs to Joe's room. I rubbed my back – it was sore from all the cleaning and sorting – and glared, uninspired, into the fridge. Nothing looked inviting so I moved to the pantry, but again nothing took my fancy. I shut the pantry door and went through the baking tins on the bench with increasing annoyance. Cakes and biscuits – all yuck. I slid a tin of shortbread across the bench and stood in the kitchen feeling irritable. How dare there be no food in the house that I wanted to eat! I headed back to bed but couldn't get to sleep. I couldn't get comfortable. My back pain seemed to come in small waves with ever so tiny differences in the pain level. Slightly higher for a few minutes, then less so for half an hour. Was I in labour? An hour later I had counted three definite waves of a dull twinge. Not overly painful, just an awareness of previously unconsidered muscles. When the waves became more definite I phoned Sinead.

''Lo,' she grumbled in the exact kind of voice you'd expect to hear at 3.23 a.m.

'How do you know when you're in labour?'

'Hurts,' she mumbled.

'I'm not really in pain as such, but I am getting these wave things.'

'"W" kind waves?' She yawned.

I explained what had been happening over the last hour or so, including the perplexing lack of interest in any food.

'You're in labour,' Sinead said matter-of-factly. 'Call the hospital. Then watch TV. It could be ages.'

'OK,' I said, surprised by how calm I was. Somewhere in my brain, where the default setting permanently loitered on 'denial', I didn't really believe this baby would ever come. Even now, while I was quite possibly in labour, the reality of me holding an actual human for whom I was solely responsible didn't seem to be remotely correct. I felt like I'd been playing a role: Pregnant Girl; Spurned Lover; Treacherous Best Friend. At some point the credits would roll on my charade and I'd be back at my desk taking mild abuse over the radio and having a fag with Sophie by the catering skip. I hung up on Sinead and sat on the edge of the bed, the phone in my lap. I put my hands round the large bump I now had trouble remembering ever being without.

It was happening.

CHAPTER FORTY

I got out my plastic envelope containing my pregnancy notes and dialled the St George's maternity ward number highlighted in neon orange. It had been taunting me with its tangerine shade of urgency ever since I'd had my first scan. The day I was to actually use it seemed an age away. I spoke to a lady who asked for my file number – not my name. It was very strange to ring someone at three thirty in the morning and have them answer the phone in an expectant voice, like it was a perfectly conventional hour of the day to be receiving a call. The midwife on the phone told me they were experiencing a very high volume of women in labour.

'How far apart are your contractions?' she asked.

'I'm not sure. Sometimes there's a definite something and sometimes there's nothing. But then I think there might be something.'

'Is there any blood?'

'No.'

'Discharge?'

Must they *really* use that word?

'No.'

'Any unusual pain? Do you feel dizzy? Nauseous?'

'No. Actually there's no real pain at all. Just ... well, I think maybe every now and then there's a *something*.'

The midwife sighed. 'OK, love, you call back when you have a definite "something" and when those "somethings" are about two minutes apart. Or if your waters break.'

I said OK and hung up, feeling a bit naive and uncertain about what to do next. So I lay in bed and worried about Joe.

An hour later I was sure I was having real 'somethings'. I phoned Alex.

'Are you OK?' came her concerned whisper down the line.

'I'm in labour,' I whispered back, even though there was no reason for me to. But you do, don't you?

'But you're not due for another nine days!'

'Eight, actually. It's tomorrow already. Can you come home?'

'Shit! Let me look at the trains.'

I waited on the other end of the line.

'OK, the next train is in an hour.' She was still whispering. 'And it's a three-hour journey. Then down from King's Cross in a cab is another hour.' She made calculation mutterings. 'I can be with you by about nine thirty. Will you be OK till then? Why don't you ring Mum?'

'No. I can't handle her right now. Sinead said it'll probably take ages. I'll be fine. Just hurry, OK?'

'OK! I'm packing now,' she whispered. 'This wedding cancellation is causing a bit of drama. Cal's Mum—'

'Just get here and you can tell me all about it then.' I could feel the dull swell of another 'something' starting.

'You're going to do great,' Alex whispered. 'You have a lot more strength than you realise, you know. Remember that, OK?'

How could I have acted so horribly towards my sister? I thought as I hung up. She was the best person I knew. Quite literally, The Best Person. I knew no one else who worked for a pittance in poor island communities where the likelihood of death-by-spider-the-size-of-house-cat or slipping down a bank and dying alone at the bottom of a ravine that hadn't been visited in over three hundred years was quite high, when her master's degree could have got her an excessively well-paid job working at the forefront of London's urban design scene. I vowed never to hurt her again.

At 5.37 a.m. I received a text.

On the train. How you doing?

I'd had five contractions in the last hour. Not crippling in any way but most certainly the kind of pain that made you get up and walk around in a vain attempt to try and get away from it. I replied

I'm fine. See you soon

and went back to house-wandering. By seven thirty the contractions were no closer together but were much stronger. They'd surge up quickly, pinch and twist themselves through my back and pelvis causing me to grip whatever was in arm's reach with white knuckles, and then disappear, leaving me breathless but vaguely surprised I'd managed to endure it. Alex phoned just as one subsided.

'The train's stopped somewhere between Leicester and Luton. We've been sitting here for twenty minutes.'

'Right,' I said, catching my breath.

'Jesus, are you OK?'

'Just a contraction.'

'Oh, right. Well, I'm not sure how long I'll be now. They've said it's some fault on the line. Honestly, we had better rail services in Bangladesh. And at the very least if the train stopped there'd be people clambering up the sides offering chai and bhajis through the open windows. I see no bhajis here in Leicester.'

We discussed the virtues of the humble bhaji for a few minutes but had to cut it short once we'd moved on to samosas (vegetarian versus ones containing mystery meat), as another contraction bore down. Sometime later she texted again.

On the move. Get Mum over you silly cow.

I would not be calling Mum. I would not be calling Ned. I had it all planned out. Alex would arrive just as the contractions hit their two-minute St George's admittance allowance. We'd calmly arrive at the hospital, remove the baby, place the boy/girl (oh god, please don't let it be both) in my arms and pose for a photo that would end up on my mother's mantelpiece in a blocky crystal frame. In reality it went a little more like this.

A fierce wind blew and suddenly a downpour like I'd never seen in London descended.

I had a contraction.

Alex phoned to say she'd arrived at King's Cross but cabs were thin on the ground due to the rain.

I had a contraction.

Alex phoned to say she had procured a cab from a lovely businessman who was only too happy to have an excuse not to make his meeting and was now in stationary traffic outside King's Cross with steamy windows.

I had a contraction.

I'd opened the French doors as the mugginess inside was making me feel queasy. The noise from the rain thrashing at the brick patio was deafening.

A knock at the door sounded through the pelting rain and I hobbled down the hall, relief flooding my entire body. But it wasn't Alex. It was Harriet in a clear, spotted rain bonnet tied under her chin and Brutus in a matching doggy raincoat complete with hood. Brutus appeared to be mortified.

'Hello, Emma dear!' she said cheerily over the noise of the rain.

I was a tad stunned to see Harriet in her bonnet at my

front door, a summer storm thrashing at the trees on the common behind her.

'Harriet, what are you doing out in this kind of weather?'

'Oh, pish-posh, my dear. You city types are spineless, you know. Do you think we let a bit of rain stop us from going about our lives? Pish-posh. Now, I've got you a little something for the baby. May I come in?' She toddled past me dragging Brutus on his studded leash. He seemed only too keen to get inside, away from mocking eyes.

'Um, Harriet, now's not—' I began, but she was already halfway down the hall chatting to Brutus about minding his paw marks on the furniture.

I shut the front door and followed the plastic-coated pair into the living room.

'Here you are, dear,' Harriet said, rooting about in her large beige handbag and producing a gift-wrapped package in the shape of a book. She seemed not to notice or care I was in my maternity nightie.

'It's a children's book.'

'Ah, thanks,' I said, taking the package in one hand and rubbing at my back with the other. 'Look, Harriet—'

'Now, it's a little old for the baby but Marjorie said it was just flying off the shelves so I really had to get it, you see. She's already put in another order. It's by an independent publisher. A local, apparently. All the craze, this type of thing. Doing it yourself without the big companies.' She nodded to authorise her point.

'Harriet, I'm actually in—'

'That was the last one, you know!' she said, jabbing her gnarled finger at the package in my hand. 'And Marjorie was going to sell it to that ghastly Muffy who runs the Retired Greyhound Society, but I was not going to let the last book go to a lover of anorexic dogs.' Harriet's lips tightened and her wet eyes became fierce. 'You know, one of those dogs of hers sexually assaulted Brutus last week.'

'Oh, that's . . .'

'Tried to hump him.'

'Oh.'

'Brutus doesn't like being humped.'

'No.'

And I wasn't all that keen on hearing a little old lady in her eighties say 'hump'.

'The poor dear. He's terrified of them now. And anything that looks like those dreadful dogs: twigs, bike stands, that young lass who works at the juice bar with the spindly white legs. He's traumatised, aren't you, my dear boy?' She chucked him under his bonneted muzzle. Brutus glanced at me with shamed eyes. Another contraction began to work its heat across my lower back.

'Harriet,' I said, moving to the back of the sofa for support. 'I'm in a bit of . . .' The contraction tore across my back. Harriet continued, oblivious to my heavy breathing and sofa-gripping.

'And just because my son is a homosexual and my daughter has chosen the life of a "childless-by-choice" unmarried doesn't mean I don't want to buy children's books.'

I groaned. Brutus, sitting on his hind legs in his spotted bonnet, growled.

'My goodness, dear, what a horrible noise. You're frightening Brutus.' She tugged on his leash. 'Anyway, we must be off. Arthur is making scones and we're going to the corner shop to get fresh cream. Pop round and have some; Arthur does so love the company. He can't get out in this weather so well; his wheels rust. OK then,' she said, shuffling towards the hallway. 'You have a lovely morning, and I'll see you for scones a little later.' Then she disappeared.

The front door opened, sending a blast of damp air down the hall. I heard her tell Brutus that he looked lovely and all the other dogs were just jealous he had such a dashing weather protector, and the front door slammed shut and all was quiet again. Once I'd emotionally recovered from having a contraction in front of a growling Doberman, I rang Mum.

'I need you,' I said. I told her about the contractions. 'Can you take me to hospital?'

'Oh darling, you really do have consistently shocking timing. Not only is the Mini with Louis Vuitton getting new seat covers but I'm with Amanda and she's only just put the tube in.'

'Tube in?' I said, but Mum was asking Amanda how quickly she could finish whatever it was she was doing.

Then she was back on the phone. 'Darling, I think I'm going to be an hour getting to you, can you hold on till then?'

'An hour?' I said, panic in my voice.

'I'm so sorry, my sweet. I have to wait for the water to drain out. She's only just pumped it all in. About ten or fifteen minutes, and then I have to sit on the loo and let the loosened bits fall.'

'What?'

'I can't just hop off the table and come straight to you! Gravity will be working, and you can't stop gravity. Can you imagine how disgusting? The smell is awful, darling. Stuff that's been up there for weeks just falling out. I absolutely need to be on the toilet for . . .' She asked Amanda how long. 'For at least another fifteen minutes after the water has drained. She's doing it right now, darling, I can feel the withdraw.'

'Mum, what *are* you talking about?'

Pinching sensations were radiating up my lower back. Another contraction was on its way.

'Poo, darling. I'm having my monthly colonic.'

Nice.

Muscles began to spasm. I gripped the back of the sofa.

'You know you could do with a session after the baby,' Mum continued. 'Suck that doughnut diet right out of you. I can book you an appointment while I'm here . . . What's that?' Amanda's spa-treatment voice sounded in the background. 'Amanda says it can be done six to eight weeks after a vaginal birth.'

'Mum. Another contraction. Have to go.'

I hung up on Mum's flurried promises to get down from Amanda's table and off the loo as soon as gravity and aroma would allow, and groaned into the back of the sofa. Minutes later the contraction diminished and I decided to make a cup of sweet tea as the midwife on the phone had suggested when I heard the front door open and shut. Alex did not have a key yet; we'd had to change the locks back when Brutus buried the keys on the common. Mum did, but she was still at least an hour away, longer if Amanda struck something undigested. Uncle Mike always rang first (manners) and Sinead brought the kids, who knocked on the door at the same time, sounding like a small army of Victorian miners. The only person it could have been was Joe. I stood in the kitchen, my hands clasped round the French coffee tin that housed the tea bags, waiting. Hesitant footsteps trod the creaky floorboard in the hall and then he appeared, tired, wet and wearing the same clothes he'd stormed out in two days ago. He hovered in the doorway, his eyes flicking awkwardly round the room, his face displaying nothing but a sad weariness. He hadn't shaved.

'I'm just here to get my things,' he said in a stony voice.

I waited for him to say more but he didn't.

'OK,' I said eventually.

Joe looked at his feet and fiddled with the keys. I thought he was about to say something, but then he turned to go upstairs.

'Some of your clothes are in the washing machine,' I said. My voice felt thick in my throat.

He looked back over his shoulder, his body half-facing the stairs. A muscle in his set jaw twitched.

'Just some socks and a t-shirt I found in the bathroom. I forgot to hang it out, so they'll still be wet.'

He blinked, then nodded and turned away again. A ferocious contraction tore up my back, taking me by surprise. I let out a cry and dropped the tea bag tin, which clanged noisily across the terracotta tiles.

Joe spun round. 'Emma?'

I gasped and gripped onto the side of the kitchen bench, releasing low moans.

Joe was at my side. 'What's wrong?'

Tears pooled at the corners of my eyes. *Why was this happening to me?* I thought. Everything. All of it. Why me? Why was I in labour with Ned's bloody baby? Why was he so successful with his charity ice cream and happy in love with my dippy, colour-blind, cheese-farming ex-friend? Why was the only person here with me the only person I wanted to be with but was leaving? About to walk out of my house and out of my life. I moaned as the contraction reached its peak.

'What's happening?' Joe fretted. 'Are you in labour?'

I nodded, taking deep, steadying breaths.

'But it's too early! Where's Alex?'

'King's Cross,' I said through straining gasps.

The contraction dissipated. Joe waited for my breathing to return to normal, hovering behind me in a redundant manner. The pain fell back like a receding tide, leaving as quickly and completely as it arrived. I wiped my upper lip and stood facing the kitchen benches.

'Emma?' Joe said.

I arranged my face, trying to make it devoid of any sentiment, and turned towards him. Deep, dark shadows hung beneath his eyes.

A furrow of anxiety grew between his brows. 'Are you here alone?'

I drew in a shaky breath and nodded. Emotions flickered across his handsome face. I couldn't tell what he was thinking and it was breaking my heart. His eyes searched mine.

He swallowed. 'Do . . . do you want me to stay?'

I bit my lip. He'd said the one thing I wanted to hear. Except I wanted to hear it in the 'forever' sense.

'Yes, please.'

He looked at me, his face pensive and solemn.

'OK.' He dropped his keys in the fruit bowl on top of the nectarines. 'OK.'

CHAPTER FORTY-ONE

'What about your mother?'

'She's indisposed.'

Joe gave a quizzical look while fiddling with his watch.

'You don't want to know. Do not ask her. She'll give you details you can never un-hear.'

'OK, but—'

I winced and took up my favoured position behind the sofa.

'Another one?' Joe said, and glanced at his watch.

I nodded.

'They're four and a half minutes apart. I think we should—'

A knock at the door interrupted him. He looked towards the hall. It wouldn't be Alex, as she'd only just phoned to say she'd crossed Waterloo Bridge and was still inching along in traffic.

'They'll go away.' He moved to my side and kneaded my

lower back. I panted and whooshed out air. More knocks at the door. Joe ignored them and made soothing noises. The knocks got more insistent, then my mobile began playing Sir Mix-A-Lot.

'It's Helen,' I said through strained gasps.

When the contraction subsided Joe took off down the hall and opened the door.

'What took you so fecking long?' Helen said.

'Emma's in labour.'

Joe rushed back to my side. Helen appeared in heels and a claret bandage-style dress unbefitting for a Sunday morning and a bucketing one at that.

'Oh,' she said, appraising the situation from behind her glossy flank of a fringe. 'I'm not sure I can handle that.'

'What are you doing here?'

'Did you forget lunch?' she said, hesitating in the doorway, not chucking her handbag on the table and flopping on the sofa like she usually would.

I reached for my phone. 'I've been a tad preoccupied.'

I dialled the hospital while Joe updated Helen and Helen looked me up and down warily. She was squeamish in matters that involved any bodily fluid that wasn't semen. A nasally voice answered the phone and I rattled off my file number and answered all the questions about how far apart the contractions were, did I feel any pressure, was there any bleeding, had my waters broken and so on.

'Well, I'm very sorry but we just can't fit you in till you are two minutes apart or dilated at least four centimetres,' the nasal lady said. 'But I can see if we have a midwife in the area who can pop in and take a look at you, how does that sound?'

I wanted to tell the woman that I hated her. That she was the devil. That if she didn't let me come into the hospital right then I would hunt her down, pin her to the floor and shoot her repeatedly in the back with a taser for seven hours to see how she liked it. But instead I confirmed my address and hung up.

I turned back to Helen and Joe. 'Can you—'

Helen's face suddenly puckered. 'You're weeing,' she said, staring at the floor beneath my feet.

I looked down. Cloudy drips fell from my undercarriage.

'My waters are breaking.' A wave of embarrassment consumed me. This really was a humiliating process.

'I thought it was supposed to . . . gush.' Joe tried to conceal a repulsed tremor.

Helen looked sceptical. 'Are you sure you're not weeing?'

'It's amniotic fluid,' I said, but doubt was settling.

For a gross few seconds we contemplated the slow drip, drip of the undecided liquid, then we leapt into action.

'I have to get to hospital.'

'I think I'm going to be sick,' Helen said, paling.

'I'll call a cab,' said Joe.

'No!' I shouted. 'I'm not going to have my baby in a minicab that still smells of last night's beer and cigarettes. We can go in Helen's car.'

'I tubed,' she said, panicky. 'I haven't even been home yet.' She used both hands to exhibit her outfit.

'It has to be a cab then,' Joe said.

'No! I'm not—' Another contraction stopped me protesting any further. Joe rushed to my side and Helen got busy looking worried.

'Douglas!' She blurted, digging around in her handbag. 'He's hired a van to move into Jemima's flat. He's in Mitcham right now.' She pulled out her phone and dialled.

Helen bossed Douglas; Joe rubbed my back; I gasped and groaned. Then Helen packed a hospital bag and took up front-door surveillance while Joe cleaned the floor-goo and I changed out of my sodden knickers.

'He's here!' Helen shouted.

Joe grabbed my baby bag, helped me to the front door and flicked open a brolly. Helen flew out of the door first and into the back of what looked to be the smallest minivan in existence. Joe trundled me to the vehicle and flung open the tiny passenger door, revealing a bubble-wrap-covered passenger seat and a nervous-looking Douglas in cotton driving gloves.

'Do I have to sit on this?' I said, sitting down to the sounds of multiple plasticky pops.

'Oh, ah, it was Jemima's idea,' Douglas said. 'Because of the . . .' He glanced towards my groin. 'The, ahem, seepage.' He adjusted his glasses with a gloved fingertip. I conveyed my disgust with a sneer. 'Sorry,' he said.

Joe closed the door and leapt into the seatless back with Helen. He slid shut the side door confining the four of us in the minuscule, muggy van. So cramped were we that I could feel both Helen's and Joe's breath on my neck. I could have touched the back window with my hand. Rain thrashed and blotched the windscreen.

Douglas twisted in his seat. 'You can hold onto the ... ah ...' He scanned the back of the van, empty except for more bubble wrap and without anything to grip. 'The, ah, well, just hold on.' He noticed Helen's low-cut dress and turned back to the steering wheel, a matronly look on his face. 'Might I suggest that your attire is not entirely appropriate?' he said, glancing at Helen's cleavage in the rear-view mirror and quickly looking away.

He lurched the van forward; the bubble wrap beneath me erupted in a symphony of miniature explosions.

'I'm not taking advice from someone who wears driving gloves,' she said.

'It's a hired van.' Douglas flicked the windscreen wipers to hyper-swish.

'I wouldn't call this a van,' Joe said over my continuous popping.

'So?' Helen said.

'So you don't know who's been driving it.'

'Don't be ridiculous,' Helen derided. 'They clean it.'

'You can't say for sure.'

Another contraction bore down; I had nowhere to lean so I writhed from left to right, moaning and popping, while Helen ridiculed Douglas for his hypochondriac propensities and Joe patted me pointlessly but sweetly on the shoulder.

'*Some* people are a little more careful with what they

touch,' Douglas said, shuddering the van to a stop at some lights and sending Joe and Helen tumbling forward.

My contraction eased. Helen righted herself, leant over Douglas's shoulder and, giving him an almost anatomical view of her cleavage, licked the steering wheel, slow and slutty. Disgust set Douglas's lips in a hard line. A few lone pops escaped. Helen crouched back, a wicked look on her face.

'That's revolting.' Douglas used a pocket handkerchief to wipe the wheel.

'I've licked worse.' She winked at Joe.

The lights turned green and we listed forward. More frantic popping.

'Can you call Alex and tell her to go straight to the hospital?' I said to Joe, clutching onto the door handle. 'And tell her to tell Mum.'

Joe did as instructed. Helen told Douglas he was driving like Angela Lansbury and I squirmed, grunted and popped through another contraction. We bumped along Blackshaw Road, the Sunday traffic even slower due to the rain.

'She says to tell you she rang Ned,' Joe said, one hand holding the phone to his ear, the other steadying himself against the side of the van. He was so hunched over he was almost in downward dog.

'*What*?' I seethed, panting through the end of a particularly painful spasm.

Joe listened on the other line.

'She says he has a right to be there,' he listened again. 'He is the father, after all.'

'He's a cocksucking, wank-bugger cunt face,' I spat.

Joe blinked then spoke. 'Emma says "he's a cocksucking" ... right, OK ... yes, I will.' He hung up. 'She'll meet us there.'

Douglas bumped us into the hospital car park and pulled up outside the building, flinging his rear passengers to the floor again. Joe leapt out of the side door and helped me extricate myself from the bubble wrap while Helen gave bossy directives on where to park and Douglas made polite protests about needing to get back to Jemima to assist with the merging of their individual book collections.

'Just park, OK?' she said, climbing through the front in her too-tight, too-short dress. 'You're not going home to play Dewey Decimal System with your girlfriend when Emma is about to have a baby! Jemima can stick her thesaurus up ...' Helen's voice was drowned out by Douglas's gear-crunching.

Joe hoisted the hospital bag over his shoulder and guided me through the sliding doors and across the streaky lino floor.

This was it. I was arriving a single entity. When I left it would be with an additional and long-standing housemate. A dual entity we would be. I became shallow of breath at the thought.

CHAPTER FORTY-TWO

In the labour suite, atop a sturdy hospital bed with nurses coming and going, Joe patted my head with a cold cloth. It was a soothing contrast to the burning, contorting pain in the rest of my body.

'When God created woman he fucked it up,' I said.

'Yeah?' Joe gave a sympathetic smile.

'Yeah. This is barbaric. Prehistoric. We should have evolved. We should be able to grow a baby in a handbag by now.'

I remembered shooting a labour scene at my old job. It had taken twenty minutes from waters breaking to holding cute baby with reapplied lip gloss and sweaty hair miraculously dried, cascading across the actress's shoulders in loose, attractive waves. I felt resentful mine was not a scripted labour and no one was on hand to curl my hair and hand me the quietest of the four clean babies waiting off set. A lady arrived and introduced herself as Tina the

midwife. After three quick contractions and another dila-
tion check, which had me at a mere four centimetres, I
got desperate.

'Can't you just, I don't know . . . force the cervix open?' I
said, breathless. I'd moved from lying on the bed to standing
at the end, leaning forward and resting on my forearms. 'Like
with some kitchen tongs, or something?'

Tina smiled and checked my pulse. 'I promise I won't
complain to the midwife society. Look in your tool kit.' I
nodded towards a medical-looking bag Tina had placed in
the corner of the room. 'There's got to be something that can
open a cervix. We can grow an ear on the back of a mouse,
for god's sake; why hasn't anyone invented something to
open a fucking cervix?!'

Joe looked on helplessly from beside the bed. Tina continued to hold my wrist and look at her watch.

'We need a miniature thing.' I wound my free hand round
in a circular motion. 'You know!' I looked at Joe and did the
circular hand thing again.

He frowned and shook his head.

'The thing that goes like this' – I wound my hand faster –
'and lifts up a car?'

Tina dropped my wrist, put her stethoscope in her ears
and popped the chest piece under my pyjama vest, moving
it round the lower part of my abdomen.

'A jack?' Joe said, his eyes darting nervously towards the
midwife.

'Yes! That's it, a jack!' I jabbed my finger in the direction of Tina's big black bag. 'See if she's got a jack in her tool box! Or a—'

'Now, Emma, I don't want you to panic,' Tina interrupted in a calm voice.

I dropped my arm and immediately panicked.

'Your baby's heart rate has dipped, the cord could be round the neck and we need to get you to theatre.' She removed the stethoscope from her ears and pressed a red button on the wall that said EMERGENCY.

Tina got me up on the bed. Nurses arrived, fixed sticky tabs to my stomach and hooked me up to machines with blippy noises and moving lines. They checked last names, addresses and emergency next of kin, which Joe confirmed with solemnity. A doctor arrived at my bedside with a clipboard and an emergency caesarean consent form. I took the clipboard he offered and flicked through the pages. Internal bleeding, infection, necessary hysterectomy, bowel obstruction, lung collapse (Christ! How high up were they going to slice?), injury to baby, injury to other organs, heart attack, stroke, fatal blood clot, fatal scar rupture, permanent colostomy bag, infertility, risk of death of mother, risk of death of baby.

'Sounds great.' I scrawled my name illegibly and was wheeled out of the room amid a flurry of nurses and machines.

Trotting behind my quick-moving bed, Joe phoned Alex.

'She's in traffic round Clapham Common,' he said, sliding his phone into his jeans pocket. 'I don't think she's going to make it.'

'Shit.'

We arrived at some double doors with a sign that said OPERATING THEATRE 9 – NO GENERAL ADMITTANCE. My team of nurses and machines trundled through the doors. Joe stayed in the hall.

'Joe?!'

'Next of kin or birth partners only,' a nurse said from the head of the bed, a note of urgency to her voice. 'Are you the father, sir?'

Joe looked back at the waiting nurse, his face unreadable. I willed him to say he was. Alex was not going to make it. I was scared.

'Yes. Yes, I am.' He rushed through the doors to my bed-side and grabbed my hand.

'Don't go down the ugly end,' I warned.

'I have no such intention.'

The operating theatre buzzed with bodies in blue. Joe was taken aside and made to don a paper hat and smock. Masked strangers manoeuvred me, lifting me from the wheelie bed to a narrower, higher one in the middle of the room. I writhed and twisted through a contraction while nurses pressed my back or allowed me to grip their hands, then wept as the pain subsided. A kind-faced lady with square white teeth arrived, her face mask hung round her neck. She introduced herself as Lizzie the Obstetrician.

'You're going to be holding your baby very soon but right now I need you to sit up and stay as still as you possibly can while our anaesthetist puts a needle in your back.'

'How still?

Lizzie the big-toothed doctor told me that I had to stay as still as possible even if I was having a contraction or I could end up paralysed. How very frank our Lizzie was. She smiled her big-toothed smile and told me if I could do it all pain would be gone.

'Gone?' I rasped.

Another contraction started. The room waited. I gripped Joe's shoulders and sobbed into his chest. I didn't think I could take any more. If I could stay still long enough for the stranger in a smock to stick a needle in my spine I would be pain free. Stay fecking still? She may as well have asked me to swim to Australia and bring back a wombat. Or ask my mother to wear a tracksuit. The contraction subsided.

'I'm ready,' I gasped.

Somebody swabbed my lower spine with a chemical coolness. There was a tiny pinch as the needle pierced the skin. Almost instantly a chilled weightlessness drifted down my spine. As it moved it took away the pain. Like a cleansing, cooling tide.

'It's out,' the anaesthetist said.

The room soared into action. Joe stepped out of the way but kept his eyes on mine. The drugs spread swiftly and in seconds my body stopped feeling solid from the chest down. Like after my boobs I was nothing but a floating spirit. Or the bottom half of the Marchesa silk-chiffon dress Mum wore to a society wedding last year and told me would be mine if only I lost a little weight around the hips. It felt as if I'd been in pain my whole life and was experiencing comfort for the first time. It was euphoric, and without the fierce ripping sensation of labour I became very, very tired. I closed my eyes and allowed the people to fuss round me. This must be what taking heroin was like, I thought. It's loooovely. When I opened my eyes I was on my back and a sheet, much like a set of stage curtains, had been placed across my stomach, blocking my legs from view. It was like a teeny-tiny play would be taking place on my stomach. I hoped Simon Pegg was in it. A little Simon Pegg in round-framed glasses ... I fought against exhaustion, hoping the play would begin soon. A wooden bang-clatter had the entire room looking towards the open door where a young orderly stood, a look of accomplishment on his enthusiastic face.

'The father's here,' he said.

The masked strangers looked at the orderly. Then at Joe. Then at me. Ned's freckled face appeared at the small window in the other set of doors behind the orderly.

'Emma!'

Lizzie looked back at me and gave a non-judgemental shrug. 'Send him in.'

Ned shuffled in, struggling into his paper smock and tripping over his untied laces. He was as wide-eyed and jittery as a baby rabbit.

'Hello,' he said, arriving at the bedside and glancing warily up at Joe, then to Joe's hand in mine. His eyes darted round the room and he adjusted his paper shower cap.

'Ned, Joe; Joe, Ned.' I made a blasé, drug-foggy gesture with my free hand.

'Hi,' Joe said.

'Hi, yeah, hi.' Ned nodded copiously.

A nurse with magnificently sculpted eyebrows glared at the three of us like we were guests on *Trisha* who were going to erupt into a paternity scuffle and went back to her activities behind the curtain.

'OK, you ready, Emma?' Lizzie the Obstetrician said.

I nodded. The room got busy. I glanced at Joe, who was resolutely keeping his eyes on my face. Ned, on the other hand, standing next to Joe with his smock falling off his narrow shoulder, had a view of the other side of the curtain and was showing signs of alarm. I felt myself losing my purchase on consciousness. The last thing I remembered was Ned's eyes widening and a huge gulp sliding down his thin, freckly throat as Obstetrician Lizzie said, 'Making the incision.'

I don't know how much later I awoke; it could have been many minutes, it literally could have been the second after I'd shut my eyes, but I came to with the weird sensation of my lower body being pushed and pulled with vigorous bumps and jerks. As if my stomach was a washing machine and a pair of trainers was on spin cycle. A horrible sucking noise sounded, Ned went a little green around the gills and Obstetrician Lizzie announced, 'She's out.'

She?

It's a girl? I have a girl baby?

Why are they all rushing? Joe was saying something but his voice sounded like he was on the shore of a lake and I was at the bottom, floating around in my Marchesa dress. I thought I might have asked if she was OK, but I also might not have. The deep wrench of the unconscious dragged. My last sight was of Joe's evaluating stare and Ned, pale and terrified, gaping at the end of the bed, his arms hanging by his sides.

And then nothing.

CHAPTER FORTY-THREE

What felt like half a second later, I sensed myself rising from the soundless, blank place of nothingness to the unmistakable tang of public hospital. Except for the hum of the air-conditioning and medical machinery, there was so sound.

My baby!

I opened my eyes. I wasn't in theatre any more. I was in a quiet room, tucked tightly into stiff sheets in a half-upright bed. I scanned the room. Ned stood motionless against a wall like someone had taken out his batteries. He was pale. He was stunned. He was a shade prior to catatonic. On a plastic chair against the opposite wall, gazing down at a tiny bundled shape, sat Joe.

'Joe.' My mouth was dry and tacky.

His head shot up, he grinned and eased himself out of the chair. Ned looked up from whatever was so fascinating on the floor.

'Is she OK?' I said.

'She's perfect.' Joe smiled, reaching the side of my bed.

I was uneasy about being disconnected from my baby and wanted to close this airy new gap between us. I tugged my arms free, mentally scanning my body for any horrific pain and finding nothing worse than thirst. Joe lowered the petite bundle into my outstretched arms, cupping her wobbly head with his palm and I caught sight of my daughter for the first time. My stomach swirled with devotion despite the fact that she was pink and blotchy and had remnants of something that looked like it had slid off the top of a hot bagel. Some kind of jam and cream cheese mixture. She lay still, her inconceivably tiny eyelashes clumped together resting on inconceivably tiny cheeks.

'She's amazing,' I breathed. I looked over to Ned, but he'd gone back to studying the floor. My heart splintered a fraction. 'How long was I out for?'

'About twenty minutes,' Joe said.

'And you held her the whole time?'

Joe shot a discreet look to Ned, still inert but watching with guarded eyes. 'Yep.' He offered Ned a kind smile then turned back to me. 'We've discussed gardening and social economics, the importance of team sports and the meaning of life. Which we both agreed was gardening.'

I giggled and stared at my daughter's face, drinking in the absolute realness of her. She was a true and present person. A very, very small one. I pulled the blanket away and studied her froggy little legs. An ankle band labelled her 'Baby Girl George'. She was so tiny and perfect I couldn't believe I'd made her. And got to take her home and be in charge of her. And dress her in whatever I wanted.

'I promise to let you wear leggings to school,' I whispered.

Ned's phone made a vibrating sound. He looked at the screen, then up at me.

'I've just got to ... go outside. I'll be right back, I just—' He gesticulated with his hands and left the room.

I sighed. He'd been so excited at the scan I'd assumed he'd be just as excited by the actual arrival. But he seemed terrified and detached. Joe pulled over a threadbare chair and sat down. Baby Girl lay in my arms, quiet and perfect. I adored her with a passion I never expected.

'Thank you,' I said, looking up at Joe. 'I don't think I could've done it without you.' I rolled my eyes at the emptiness of the statement. 'Of course I *would* have done it without you. Obviously she couldn't have lived in there till she was twenty-one. I just mean, well, having you there made me feel ... OK, like I was going to be OK ...' I shrugged with the awkwardness of my blabbering.

Joe moved his chair closer to the bed and leant over to look at my sleeping baby. 'I'd be anywhere you wanted me to.'

I searched his face for any kind of double meaning but saw only exhaustion. 'Joe?'

A knock at the door stopped me from saying something incredibly stupid. Who the hell tries to pick up a man less than an hour after they've given birth? Clearly the same kind of person who lustily launches themselves at hot guys they work with while pregnant with another man's baby. Me. One of high hopes and low morals.

Ned poked his head round the door.

'Ah, can . . . can Sophie come in?' he said with a cautious glance at Joe. 'She's been waiting outside and . . . she really wants to see you.'

I studied him. He hadn't even viewed his daughter from a distance of less than six feet and now he wanted his girlfriend to come in. Exhausted and unable to trust my own decisions, I deferred to Joe, who nodded.

'OK, I guess.'

Ned scuttled out of the room and returned with Sophie, her eyes red-rimmed and bloodshot. My good mood weakened at the sight of my old friend. I hadn't laid eyes on her since the day I saw her kissing Ned outside the hospital. (In that fucking Fiesta.) She looked exactly the same, from her cropped pixie haircut to her slubby Rolling Stones t-shirt tucked into a brown maxi skirt with her pink Converse peeping out. Except her face was different. It was wretched. She stood at the end of the bed, Ned's hand protectively at the small of her back, twisting the suede tassels from her satchel bag round her fingers. Her eyes flitted from me to the baby, a woeful expression on her face. She wiped at her nose with a soggy tissue.

'I'll go and get you some tea.' Joe rose from his chair.

He tapped Ned on the shoulder and motioned for them to leave us to it. Ned blinked like it hadn't occurred to him. He checked that Sophie was OK and asked if she would like tea. What kind? Would she feel better with something in her stomach? A muffin, maybe? She'd had blueberry in the morning so perhaps she'd prefer something savoury? He thought the canteen had sausage rolls. Was she still thinking about doing meatless Mondays? All things I would have found incredibly sweet had they not been my ex-best friend and ex-boyfriend and they were not doing it at the end of the bed where I held my 45-minute-old baby girl who was co-created with said ex-boyfriend. Eventually, with detailed muffin and tea directives, he exited the room leaving Sophie snivelling at the end of my bed. She shuffled forward uncertainly, sniffing and hiccuping, and peeked at Baby Girl.

'So beautiful,' she said in a tiny voice. She stepped back to the safety of the end of the bed, gave me a harrowing look and burst into tears. 'I thought you were . . . going to . . . *die*,' she said between sobs.

I watched, my natural instincts wanting to quell the gushing tears but my heart unwilling to forget the past few months of Parisian crêpe-eating and ice-cream-manufacturing she'd had with the father of my child.

'I'm fine.'

'But the cord . . . and the heart rate?'

'All fine,' I said, looking away.

A baby cried in the next room. I felt Sophie's teary gaze on my face.

'It wasn't meant to happen like this, Emma, I swear,' she appealed. 'Ned and me. It was an accident.'

I looked back, wanting and not wanting to hear more.

How did she 'accidentally' start a relationship with Ned? Trip and land on his face, then decide to stay there for the next few months? Sophie rubbed at her nose with the disintegrating tissue.

'It wasn't meant to happen at all, really.' A tear ran down her face. 'I didn't plan it. I mean, I wasn't waiting for you guys to break up, like some double-crossing hussy or anything. I just, well, I was sad after your nan's funeral and went to that party. It was a dumb party, you'd have hated it, they had a rumba. And I saw Ned, and he was so funny.' She paused to blow her nose. 'And he was so sweet and then we realised that we both liked ice cream, I mean, who doesn't like ice cream? But we both *really* liked it. But we didn't have genital sex. Not then. Just, like, a kiss and other stuff but no genital sex.'

My skin crawled.

'But there was you . . .' She indicated me with her fist of mucus and tissue. 'And you were gonna have the . . .' She moved her snotty fist towards the baby. 'And I thought it was just the one-night thing and, well, also the fact I'd been doing shots of chartreuse (which I thought was actually good for you because it's made by monks but it turns your vomit green). We didn't have genital sex then, either.'

'Please stop saying *genital*.'

'What? Oh, right. Sorry. Anyway, and then there was the fondue barbecue and Mum did the thing with the lobster salad and Aunt Patty taught him to crochet and, well, you can see how it happened.'

I couldn't, actually, what with that utterly ridiculous explanation. Crochet? Lobster salad? Rumba? And (ew!) *genital* sex? I tried hard to keep my expression detached and unemotional but her misery was threatening my fortitude. She sniffed back a sob and pressed her lips together.

'And now,' her voice got high and squeaky, 'you hate me.'

I watched Sophie, the pathetically wretched, colour-blind, punk fairy quivering miserably at the foot of the bed.

We'd survived and supported each other through the hell that is dealing with Y-list celebrities. I'd spent fourteen hours a day with her every week for almost the past five years. She'd played many a Stab Victim and Injured Protestor when I'd forgotten extras, and I in turn had been there when she needed Mangled Cyclist or a Drug Addled Whore. And on the odd occasion we got a full weekend off, we'd book a cottage in the country but be so exhausted we'd sleep the whole time while Helen said 'fuck ya, then' and went to the pub on her own. We'd sat together through midwinter night shoots, being the only two people in a deserted, freezing office, talking boys and life plans and ordering midnight pizza on the Production account. We'd partied, we'd worked, we'd stressed, we'd drunk and we'd laughed till we'd nearly wet ourselves. Sophie had seen me at my best and at my worst. My happiest and my most vulnerable.

And I her.

'I don't hate you,' I said, mildly annoyed at my lack of resolve.

I was planning on giving Ned and Sophie the 'freeze-out'

for at least the next decade but somehow that seemed less important now that I had a baby. And Sophie was just plain miserable. I looked down at my daughter. If Sophie was going to be a part of Ned's life, then she was going to be a part of my baby's life as well. And I didn't want my daughter to think of me as some bitter old lady. God knows, it was going to be fun at 'Dad and Sophie's' what with all that free ice cream. *And* it was organic. I fiddled with the stiffly starched bedsheets. Sophie blew her nose.

'Do you love him?' I said, my voice quiet.

Sophie paused, trying to deduce whether it was a trick question, then nodded, her eyes filling with tears again. I watched her trying to suppress her sobs. Her entire existence seemed sodden.

'Then God help you.' I held out a hand.

She rushed forward and grasped it with, thankfully, the hand without the tissue. Her nails were bitten down to the skin and bore the last few chips of a sparkly blue polish.

'It will take a bit of time . . .'

Sophie nodded vehemently.

'But,' I hesitated, 'we will be friends again.'

Sophie's petite shoulders heaved in time with her sobs.

CHAPTER FORTY-FOUR

Joe and Ned, an unlikely pair, returned with cups of tea and muffins so stale I could have biffed them through the wall and knocked out a new mother three rooms down. Joe had evidently asked about the ice cream and Ned was animated once more, regaling him with the thrill of flavour-balancing with a real spark in his eye.

Soon after, a chaotic dialogue reverberating down the ward let me know my family and friends had been let in.

'I had to rush out. I don't think Amanda got all the Vaseline off. My cheeks are slippery when I walk.' (Mum.)

'Diana, *must* you?' (Uncle Mike – long-suffering.)

'It's a natural thing.' (Mum.)

'A tube up your arse is natural?' (Sinead – grossed out.)

'Up your arse?' (Helen.)

An uncomfortable cough. (Douglas.)

'Mum, can you please not talk about your colonic in public?' (Alex.)

And then she appeared in the doorway.

'Oh my god!' She rushed over to us. 'I can't believe I missed it!'

My tangle of visitors traipsed in and cheered, making Baby Girl do a weird four-limbed jolt.

'Tell me everything,' Alex said from prime position by my shoulder. 'I want a no-holds-barred account.'

'A what?' Alice said, standing at the foot of the bed holding a grotesque Bratz doll.

'No holds barred,' Joe said. 'It's a wrestling term.'

'I thought it was no *holes* barred,' Helen said.

'You would,' Douglas said with a sniff.

For the next hour my family and friends demanded extra chairs, visited the vending machine, fought over who got to hold the baby, competitively compared stories about labour (Mum and Sinead) and generally pissed off all the nurses that came in and asked for quiet. Baby Girl got introduced to Charlie, who was speaking at a biodegradable plastics convention in Frankfurt, via a facetime call. It was so thrilling for her she slept through the entire thing. Douglas had an in-depth debate with Archie about the incongruities within the zombie storyline. Jess was sporting her mohican and practising her latest fixation, Capoeira. It wasn't best suited to a small and crowded hospital room, especially when she was about as coordinated as a duck on skis. Alice sat cross-legged on the end of my bed dressing a tiny-waisted doll and Archie perched on a stool against the wall perusing another storyboard. Apparently he'd been asked to audition for a regular part in a kids' show for the BBC. Uncle Mike had agreed but only after quizzing the producer about the level of bloodshed and how much nudity was involved. Considering it was a CBeebies production I can only imagine how confused the producer would have been. Sinead sat with Millie on her lap, who was ejecting a glutinous mess of rusk and saliva down her front, and Uncle Mike stood wherever it was safe from Jess's inadequately executed leg and arm flails. Ned and Sophie huddled together amid the fray, seemingly nervous about how my family might receive them, but no one appeared to care. Although it was more likely Alex had given them a strict code of conduct.

My baby had been passed from person to person, all except Ned, who glued his arms to his sides if she ever came near him, and everyone stood, sat or leant around the room sipping mediocre NHS tea from disintegrating paper cups. Joe drooped low in his chair in the corner, face unshaven, surveying my animated family and friends with drowsy interest.

'Aren't you just the cutest little lapse in judgement I ever did see,' Mum cooed, cradling my daughter in her arms.

'You can't call her that.' Alex stood so close to Mum's shoulder she was practically in her handbag. 'And are you going to let anyone else have a hold *ever*?'

'That's true,' Mum said, ignoring Alex's plea. She fixed me with a look. 'What *are* you going to call her?'

'Oh.' I glanced at Ned. 'I'm not sure.'

Again, the fact that I had no inkling of what to name her reinforced the notion that I'd not fully believed nine months of pregnancy would end in a newly created person. One that would be linked to me for the rest of my days. I would never again make a decision that did not involve this individual. We were two, where there used to be one. And I had found one rather challenging.

'Any ideas?'

A cacophony of high-volume opinions erupted.

'How about Ophelia, from *Hamlet*?' Douglas said.

'Or Ivy, after your grandmother?' Uncle Mike said, redirecting a roundhouse kick from the testicular region.

'Or Elsa from *Frozen*?' said Alice.

'Or Alex? After me!' Alex grinned persuasively. She held out her arms, vying for another hold. 'Now *give*!'

'She looks like a Mabel,' Mum said, handing her to Alex.

Helen peered at the pink-faced baby. 'She looks like an internal organ.'

'*Helen*,' Douglas chided.

More names came forth in multiple broadcasts. I looked at the baby in Alex's arms and wondered how she could be right next to me, made of me and from me, but be nobody. I considered how strange it was that you were no one till you were labelled.

'How . . . how about Dixie?' Ned spoke over the competing babble.

'Why should she have your last name?' I said. 'Did a stranger with rubber gloves stick his hand up your vagina and measure your cervix?'

Ned, Uncle Mike and Douglas gave a synchronised wince. Archie glanced up briefly from his storyboard.

'Did you spend fifteen hours in pain so unspeakable you wanted to climb out of your own body and shred the curtains with your teeth? Did someone rearrange your insides like a jigsaw puzzle? I don't think so.'

'I meant,' Ned said, paling, 'what about both of our last names? We could—'

'No double-barrelled names,' I said. 'We do not live in a horse-orientated novel.' I motioned for Alex to return my daughter.

'No, what I mean—' He gulped under Mum's impatient glower. 'What – what I mean is—'

Mum sighed audibly. 'What *do* you mean?'

'I mean, Dixie as her first name. And . . . and George as her last name?' He gave a dejected shrug. 'That's both our names . . .' He trailed off in the growing silence.

I considered Ned, then looked down. Our baby lay in my arms, divine and placid. Calm as a summer lake. One that didn't have any kite surfers. Or old men fishing. Before the summertime revellers arrived with their picnic baskets and their slippery sunscreen-ed children. A very early-in-the-morning summer lake. Back to the baby.

Dixie . . .

I looked up. 'I love it,' I said.

Ned blinked his surprise.

'Lovely idea, Ned,' Mum said, bestowing upon him a magnanimous nod.

Ned's lower jaw dropped. 'Ah, thanks Mrs George.'

'Well you *were* due,' she said, haughtiness restored.

'Dixie.' I tested the sound.

Peace settled across the room as we ran the name through our respective minds and Dixie established herself as the newest person in our lives.

'We got you a gift,' Sophie said, breaking the quiet. She nudged Ned with an elbow.

'Oh yes.' Ned dug in his back pocket, retrieved his phone and padded his finger over the screen for what felt like an age and two thirds.

Just as the kids started to fidget and Joe nodded his final exhausted nod and crumpled to sleep in the shape of the letter G in his chair in the corner, Ned located what he was looking for.

'Look.' He stepped forward, offering his phone.

He'd done that to me a few years ago. I'd looked at the screen and seen a close-up of his ball sacs. This time it was a Lloyds account.

'What's going on?' I said, my heart beating a little faster.

'That's what I owe you,' Ned said with a shy grin.

Sophie beamed like a caffeine-wired sprite. Mum and Alex exchanged glances. Jess fell over.

'But . . .' I shook my head, looking back at the amount on the screen. There was more money in the account than he had taken. Quite a bit more.

'It's all the money I borrowed, and,' he glanced to Sophie, 'your share of the business. We're partners!' he exclaimed, raising his arms in a self-conscious 'hooray' motion, still wary of Mum's scrutiny.

'What?' I said.

'I told you ice cream was a good idea.' His face broke into a wide smile. 'You, me and Sophie.' He took hold of Sophie's hand. She was nodding so fast I was briefly concerned it might actually be some kind of fit. 'Equal thirds partners.'

'Let me see.' Mum took the phone from my hand, studied the screen then raised her eyebrows.

Alex snatched it off her, said a bad word and showed it to the rest of the room.

'Holy shite,' Helen said, shoving a pirouetting Jess out of the way.

'Well done, young man.' Uncle Mike gripped Ned's narrow shoulder.

Ned, shy but chuffed, acknowledged the praise with a smile. Alex passed me back the phone. I checked the balance again then turned to Ned. He waited for my response, his face expectant and unconcerned. He'd been the one that looked to the future with an innocent faith that all would be well while I'd worried about bills, the housing market, my career, getting enough sleep and bowel cancer.

'But . . . why partners?' I said. 'You didn't have to.'

'You've always believed in me,' he said.

Shame sunk in my stomach like a block of granite. No, I hadn't.

'I know you were under pressure to get the money back,' he shot a quick look at Mum. 'But you gave me a chance. You gave me lots of chances. I'd failed before. Loads of times. The scissors? The disposable ladder? The Jesus boots?'

I nodded.

'Everything you did was for us.' He blinked, his eyes sincere. 'And while I may not always have shown it, I knew it. I'd never have come this far without you.' He shrugged, like giving away a third of your business was no big deal.

I chewed the inside of my cheek to keep from crying.

'We're small now,' he continued, 'but we're getting bigger.'

'Every flavour will be stocked in Selfridges by Christmas and the vans are all booked for this festival season and next!' Sophie interjected, a near-hysterical squeal threatening the edges of her voice.

'And we have this meeting set up in a month, but next year we're going to . . .' Ned turned to Sophie.

'We're, um, taking it to . . .' Sophie started, and then became interested in her fingernails.

'We're going to . . .' Ned tried again.

'To New York?' I said.

Ned bit his lower lip. 'Yeah.' He reddened and dropped his gaze to the floor again. I felt an overwhelming and unexpected sense of loss. Ned was moving on.

But so was I.

I blinked away a threatening tear. 'That's . . . that's really great, Ned,' I said.

A smile spread across his open, harmless face.

'Thank you,' I said. 'I'm really proud of you.' I held out my free hand. Ned stepped forward and took it in both of his. Sophie sniffed and searched for a tissue in her bag, dropping various items including a box of coloured pencils, tampons, a whistle, craggy balls of paper and a mitten, even though it was July and mid-heatwave.

'God give me strength,' Helen groaned. She plucked a crisp handkerchief from Douglas's shirt pocket and thrust it at Sophie. 'You're leaking from every-fecking-where.'

At that moment Jess decided to try a twisting flying kick that went horribly sideways and booted the doll from Alice's hand. It flew across the room and got Millie right in the mush. Alice's squeal was piercing. Dixie gave a start in my arms. Millie sucked in the amount of air that meant a spectacular scream was imminent. Jess tried to make it all better by trying again.

'Jess! Enough!' Sinead stood and jiggled the bucking, inhaling Millie.

'But *Muuuum*, Mr Fantasma said I needed to practise if I wanted to go pro.'

'Mr Fantasma is a fleecing bastard.'

'Sinead!' Uncle Mike glanced shamefaced at Douglas. Jess burst into tears.

A large-bosomed nurse poked her head round the door. 'Visiting hours finish in fifteen minutes.' She glowered at the three bawling children.

'Jesus.' Mum adjusted her handbag and spoke over the din. 'Shall we give Ned and Emma a moment?'

She bustled everyone from the room. Everyone except Joe, who slept through the demonstration of bedlam my family was exceptionally proficient in.

'What the hell?' Sinead muttered while stepping into

the corridor. 'Ned has a successful business? I can't fucking process that.'

'Sinead, *language*,' Uncle Mike implored.

'*I* always thought he was destined for something,' Sophie declared.

'I always thought he was destined for low-level drain maintenance,' Mum replied.

The door shut and in the subsequent silence I gave Ned a sheepish smile. 'Sorry about them.'

'It's OK,' he smiled his warm, everything's-just-fine-and-dandy-shall-we-order-pizza-you-can-choose-the-toppings smile. The sparkly-eyed, safe one I'd fallen in love with five years earlier.

'I was in love with *you*, not your family.' He gave a wry grin. 'Although they do get under your skin somehow.'

I looked down at Dixie. The two-hour-old innocent product of an already broken home. I hoped she'd grow up normal and not psycho killer-y.

'What happened to us?' I asked. 'We used to be so . . . in love.'

'I did love you. *So* much.' He smiled. 'I still do.' He looked across the room to Joe. 'And, I think, so does someone else.'

'What?' I turned towards the sleeping figure in the corner then back to Ned, my expression demanding clarification.

He nodded. My mind raced. I still held his hand, as if letting go would be the final indication that life was turning out very, very different to what I had prearranged when I was twenty-two and knew absolutely everything. How very *dare* it. The quiet, hand-gripping moment became uncomfortable. I remembered Sophie outside the room and let go. Ned smiled and looked at Dixie, the space between his ginger eyebrows pleating with apprehension. I angled her towards him. His hands twitched and I sensed his breath quicken.

'Why don't you hold her?' I said.

Ned's face dropped. 'Oh, I—' He took a quick step back, fastening his arms to his sides. 'I probably shouldn't. I've . . . I've . . .' He inched back towards the door. 'I haven't washed my hands and—'

'That doesn't matter,' I said. 'Here, just take her.'

'She needs her rest, she looks whacked. *You* look whacked. Although not bad, not ugly or anything, you look lovely. A bit sweaty, but—' He backed into the wall and stumbled.

'Jesus, Ned. She's your daughter! You have to hold her at some point.'

'I will, I will. It's just, I – I've been sneezing a lot lately and . . .' His face set in a serious expression and he commenced authoritative nodding. 'And I think I might have been near some Ebola the other day.' He opened the door. 'But you . . . I'll be . . . I'll get checked out at the clinic and if the Ebola comes back . . .' He did the thumbs up. 'Then I'm – I'll definitely – *that's* when I'll . . .' He stopped in the open doorway and dropped the act, his arms flopping heavily at his sides like one of Grandma's crocheted and politically insulting Golliwogs.

'Ned, please?'

He searched my face with troubled eyes, then hung his head. 'I have to go and check on Sophie.' He mumbled and left, shutting the door behind him.

Dixie snuffled. 'That's Daddy,' I said to her serene face. 'I'm ever so sorry.' Her tiny lips pursed. The sweetness of her was unbearable. I watched, captivated by the simple and unbelievably boring-for-anyone-else action of my baby modifying her lip position. She snuffled again then settled into her slumber, exhausted from the arduous trip from womb to embrace she'd undertaken. I leant over as far as the C-section would allow and laid her down in the plastic cot. She made not another peep, nor lip pucker.

'It bodes well you sleep through chaos,' I said. 'I don't think I know of any other life setting.'

My gaze turned to Joe. His arms folded across his ribcage, his head resting on the back of the chair, his chest rising and falling, slow and relaxed. I loved him. I loved him from his curled sandy hair to his toes that so often waggled to an unheard tune. Happy toes. How could you not love a man with happy toes? But was Ned right? Did Joe feel the same? How could Ned know for sure? Ned often didn't know for sure if he'd remembered to wear underwear. And what about Katy?

No. Joe would wake and he would leave. He would promise to stay in touch but, as he got increasingly busy with work and a normal person's social life and I got increasingly busy with shitty nappies and coffee mornings, he'd slip slowly out of my life. He'd be that person who once lived with me and left behind only memories and a herb garden. The thought pained me.

Joe shifted in the chair and I quickly looked away in case he caught me staring like some desperate single mother yearning to hitch her wagon of woe to him. My eyes fell on the baby bag on the side table. A corner of the gift Harriet had dropped off while I was mid-labour stuck out of the top. I picked it up and tore at the wrapping, carefully so as not to wake the two sleepers, which, I decided, was entirely unfair as neither of them had just provided the world with another human being. If anybody should be flat-out exhausted it should be me. Yet I felt strangely alert. I pulled the present free and let the wrapping float to the floor. It was a book, as Harriet had stated, the cover an intricate digital collage of what looked like a child's fantasy world. I ran my hand across the enchanting images and suddenly got that parallel universe feeling where you're not quite sure if you're dreaming or awake or on a very unsuccessful concoction of drugs.

CHAPTER FORTY-FIVE

Across the top of the cover it said *Button to Lovely Land*.

It couldn't be . . .

I opened the book to a random page.

'I have a little secret I don't want anyone to know.'

What?!

I flicked back to the cover. Curved round the petals of a pansy, little swirly letters said: *Poems by Emma George. Artwork by Joe Fisher.*

I snapped my head in Joe's direction. He snored softly, now resembling a wiggly letter 'R'. He'd published my poems! I turned my attention back to the page and read the words I knew so well but which, now printed on thick, glossy paper and bound in a hardback book, seemed fresh and strange. On the opposite page to the text was an exquisite collaged garden. A tree stood in the foreground. Its branches were made from close-up images of bark, chocolate, brick and all manner of other textured brown articles. Each leaf was an image of a different banknote. Clusters of shiny coins took the place where berries would have been.

I flicked over the next page.

> *I've got a button; it's to a land*
> *I don't think Mummy will understand*

I closed the book and looked at the front cover again. Giant daffodils and poppies grew up the side, their petals collaged from images of yellow rubber ducks and bright red feathers. Petite fairy children with pansies for backpacks ran along the bottom amid tall grass made out of images of a green glass, palm leaves and watermelon rind. In the blue sky an ice queen perched on top of a carriage made of clouds blowing glossy bubbles through a ring of icicles. Her silvery white gown, made of tiny pearls, silver cars, platinum rings, teardrops and icebergs, hung down and turned into rain that bounced off the leaf brollies held aloft by the mushroom people in their mushroom village. Stunned, I went through the book from front to back, savouring each page. The 'Tooth Witch' collage had a castle with walls made entirely from teeth. Chandeliers had flames of rubies and orange segments. The witch, swathed in a black cloak made out of images of liquorice straps, sat beneath them at a polished molar table reading a newspaper called the *Toothy Times*. 'Mushroom Men' had a busy little village with a mushroomy-soft town square and market stalls. The mushroom people rode lady-birds, walked fluffy-bottomed caterpillars and talked on their acorn mobiles. 'Button to Lovely Land' had a waterfall made from various tiny images of crystals or waves cascading down with the 'singing salmon' careering up the stream, their lyrics written in swirly letters beside them. The more pages I turned the more astounded I was with Joe's artwork. I had a random thought about what kind of image he would have to create for the poem I'd constructed a few months earlier.

> *No orgasms for you*
> *Sophie, the hater*
> *'Cause Ned can't find it*
> *So get a vibrator*

I pushed the image of a collaged dildo world with a blindfold Ned lost in a cave of clitorises out of my mind and flipped the book closed, looking at the back cover. It was nearly the same picture as the front except everything was night and all the little mushroom people were asleep in their mushroom houses and the Tooth Witch was flying across the moon. I ran my hand over the cover and felt the mysterious sensation of being watched. I turned. Joe sat awake in the chair. His slumber-creased eyes flicked to the book, then back to me. His features were soft with exhaustion and serious, like he was trying to figure out if E really did equal MC squared.

'Joe, I . . .' I ran my hand across the pages of the book again. 'I can't believe . . .' I stopped.

I'd practised denial for a fair amount of time now. I'd go

so far as to say I was proficient in the art. And through my dedicated study I could conclude that it didn't fucking work. It really didn't. If you wanted anything in life, well, you just had to go for it. Ned did. And he'd failed plenty of times, but look where he was now. I was going to tell Joe how I felt. Even if it meant he said 'gee, thanks', got a cab home and carried on with his life. Or went back to Katy. Oh *god*! Katy . . . Ahhh! She could go jump.

'Joe? I think . . .'

Joe concentrated on me, his face impassive.

'I didn't really notice until the other day but . . . I think that while I was busy doing other things . . .' I took a breath and eased it out. 'I think I fell in love with you.' With the release of the words came a release of emotions. A tear ran a tickly course from the edge of my eye down the side of my face. Joe's expression remained unreadable although his chest rose and fell faster than before. I worked harder at my cuticles. Why wasn't he saying anything? I'd freaked him out.

'God! I don't know what I'm saying! I'm coming off some pretty strong drugs. Have you ever taken heroin? Is it—'

Joe stood, crossed the three paces from chair to bed and, with a dance of emotions across his face, bent down and kissed me. And what was weird was that it wasn't weird.

He pulled back a fraction. 'While I was busy doing nothing,' he said, 'I think I fell in love with you too.'

I laughed and pulled him into another kiss. His hand found mine on the bed and we interlaced our fingers. We'd touched before; we'd shoved one another in the kitchen and fought over the cosiest dent in the sofa from where to watch movies. We'd hugged as friends, bumped into each other as roommates and played endless hours of thumb war of a boring evening. I'd laid my pregnancy-weary feet in his lap and he'd even subconsciously massaged them before realising what he was doing and dropping them in disgust. But now, this new touching, this new access to one another's bodies . . . It was wonderful. We pulled apart, studied each other's reactions and grinned like goofs. Joe sat on the edge of the bed and held my hand, working his thumb over the ridges of my knuckles. I had to ask.

'What about Katy?'

Joe gave a smile that said he knew that question was coming. 'I went and saw her.'

'Oh.' I looked down at the sheets. 'And?'

'I told her I didn't want to get back together,' he said. 'I'd fallen for you.'

I looked up at him, his face so tired, so beautiful. So sincere.

'She got pretty mad,' he said with a grimace. 'She threw my iPad at the wall. But it turned out to be her iPad and she got even madder.'

I giggled. 'Are you sure about this?' I said, extracting my hand from his and flicking a finger back and forth between us. I turned towards Dixie, silent and sweet in her plastic cot. 'I mean, I've got a baby. And a Ned. And a Sophie!'

Joe shook his head, a laughing look on his face. I knew every crease of his smile. 'Emma.'

'But I'm not worldly, like you!' I said, warming to my panic theme. 'I've never eaten bugs in Vietnam or had a piña colada or been caught in the rain.' I sang the last few words and Joe gave an amused shake of his head. 'I've never been to the ballet; I've never seen *Spartacus*. I know the line everybody does: "*I am Spartacus!*" but I don't know what happens next. Or before. I'm still not entirely sure what a concept store is, and I do not get the hashtag thing. #MyHappyPlace, #OCDmyCannedGoods, #MoreCrumbleThanFruit. Then what? What do I *do* with that?' Joe tried to say something but I spoke over him. I needed to make sure he knew what he was signing up for. I pointed to my boobs. 'These aren't usually this size, you know. After breast-feeding they're going to be down to here.' I pointed to my hip area. 'You'll have to lift one off my stomach and stroke it like a Daschund.'

Joe laughed.

'Are you sure you wouldn't rather—'

'Emma,' he said, the laugh still in his eyes.

'Yuh?'

'Shhhhh.' He leant forward.

A knock at the door stopped us mid-kiss. Alex popped her head round. 'The nurses are kicking everyone out.' Her sharp eyes darted to my hand in Joe's. She frowned. Then beamed.

'Come in.' I beckoned her in.

Alex swung open the door and everyone filed in. I got kisses on the cheeks, goodbyes and final congratulations. Helen spied the poem book and it was passed round with increasing excitement.

'So ... does that mean you're a published author?' Douglas asked, flicking gently through the pages.

I looked to Joe.

'I guess it does,' he said. 'I self-published it and asked Marjorie if she could put a few on the shelves in her bookshop to see what happens. It's sold pretty well, I hear. There could be a future in it, I guess. If Emma wants to write more.'

Everyone turned to me, expectant looks on their faces.

'Ah, excuse me, I've just had a baby and become a third equal partner in a very successful ice creamery, thank you very much.' If Ned had had feathers they'd have quivered with pride. 'I'll consider conquering publishing tomorrow, if you don't mind.' I grinned.

Dixie began to stir. The little pink baby making a muffled mewing noise employed everyone's attention. Joe picked her up, cooing softly.

'Can I have one last hold?' Alex sidled up to Joe and put her arms out.

Dixie got handed round the room receiving declarations of love and appreciation for her various 'cute widdle nose' or 'insey-winsey pinkies'. After Mum made a one-sided agreement that Dixie would never *ever* set foot in a Primark, she passed her back to Joe. The only person who had not held her, aside from Sinead with Millie on her shoulder who stated, 'Do I look like I need to hold another baby?' was her father. Joe crossed the room and offered Dixie to Ned, who did not shake his head and back into the wall but instead, with panicky eyes and an encouraging nod from Sophie, took the baby tentatively into his arms. Mum stepped forward as he struggled with her head.

'Diana,' Uncle Mike said, holding her back. 'Leave him.'

Helen narrowed her eyes. We watched with nervous interest as Ned discovered his daughter for the very first time.

'Hello,' he whispered. 'I'm . . .' He took a steadying breath. 'I'm your dad.' He looked up in wonder. 'She's so tiny.'

'I know,' I said through happy tears.

Ned bent his head down and planted a kiss on Dixie's forehead. Even Mum looked tempered by his reverence.

But then she broke it. 'Darling, I'm so sorry but I really need to get home.' She pulled at the seat of her jeans. 'I've got Vaseline bum and it's making my cheeks sweat.'

'Diana!' Uncle Mike said.

Alex laughed and dug her phone out of her bag. 'Come on, everyone. Smoosh in.' She stood in front of the bed holding up the phone. Everyone gathered round and grinned at the camera.

'Say cheese!' Alex said.

'Say sweaty cheeks!' Helen countered.

'SWEATY CHEEKS!'

Alex checked the photo, passed it to me and went back to fawning over her niece. I gazed at the grinning faces in the photo while the assembly of people I loved gathered their bags, dolls, flip-flops and singular mittens, bobbles, iPhones and lipsticks and talked about dinner and hospital parking fees, and Helen told Sophie her skirt didn't match her top, and Ned passed Dixie back to Joe, and Sinead asked Mum about babysitting, and Mum said she was going to East Africa, nowhere specific, just far away for a long time, and Jess snored on Uncle Mike's shoulder, and Alice told Archie not to say 'penis' near a baby, and Douglas choked on a chocolate, and a male nurse poked his head round the corner and asked for Helen's number, and Sophie told Alex about the new ice cream for lactose-intolerant people called 'Ice Bean' made entirely from Chinese red beans and Joe, still holding my beautiful daughter, moved through the fracas and kissed me on the lips.

And Ned noticed and smiled.

And my heart fused back together.

ACKNOWLEDGEMENTS

Huge thanks to my brilliant editor, Clare Hey, for her all round fabulousness.

Also at Simon & Schuster I'd like to thank Emma Capron for taking the reins, Richard Vlietstra for his tech teachings (which I'm still a bit rubbish at) and Pip Watkins for a fabulous cover.

Massive thanks to my agent, Alice Lutyens, for her dedication and spot-on advice. My children think she is a spy because we call her Agent Alice and she can lip read. Books are her cover. Get it? Books? Cover? Ok . . .

Thank you also to the team at Curtis Brown Creative: Anna Davis, Rufus Purdy, and to my tutor Chris Wakling. And to my classmates whose feedback was invaluable. In particular I'd like to thank Alice Clark-Platts, Heidi Perks, Alex Tyler, Grace Coleman, Dawn Goodwin, Elin Daniels, Julietta Henderson and Moyette Gibbons for the ongoing emails and support.

My family has given me many demands for this page. If I complied with them all I'd need another 400 pages and a big lie down.

My first younger sister wants a whole paragraph. I'm to use her full name, Andrea Lillian Cammell, and to tell everyone she is 'my inspiration and without her the book would not have been possible'. I said 'This isn't about you, it's about me!' and she replied 'What, are you going to acknowledge *yourself*? Loser.' And I said 'Quite right. But you're not getting a full paragraph!' And then I wrote this. And she did.

But she does deserve a big thank you for all the scanning, reading, couriering, texting and listening. And that goes for my other sister too, Stephanie Brown, who is very funny and has brilliant ideas.

Thank you also to my mother, Tricia Brown (Mum, are you Trish or Tricia? I just know you as Mum . . .) for allowing the dog vomit story to go in. It was her folks!!

Thanks to my father, John Williams, for his constant encouragement and for being just the right amount of nuts. And to my cousins, uncles and aunts for allowing me to borrow pieces of their lives.

A big thank you to my darling sons, Jonnie and Wolfie, who are an endless source of inspiration. You are just so goddamned cute.

I've had a lot of other help along the way in the form of feedback, childcare, quiet places to work, caesarian accounts etc. – you know who you are so thank you!

And lastly I would like to thank my husband, Edd Bennetto. You're wonderful and I love you very much. Even though you haven't read the book yet. And you tell people you came up with most of the ideas. Thank you for everything.

WIN A HOLIDAY OF A LIFETIME AT
BANYAN TREE VABBINFARU IN THE MALDIVES!

Included in the prize:

- A seven night stay at Banyan Tree Vabbinfaru in a Beachfront Pool villa for two people
- Full board basis, incl. soft drinks, excl. alcohol
- Return transfers from Male to Banyan Tree Vabbinfaru
- Two x return economy flights from London to Male up to a value of £700 per person
- Trip to be taken between 1 November 2017 and 30 April 2018. Blackout dates include 27th December 2017 – 05th January 2018

To enter the competition visit the website
www.simonandschuster.co.uk